Praise for *Katana:*

"An action-packed page-turner."

—Booklist

"Starts with a bang and never lets up. Prepare yourself for a smart, sassy heroine, and seriously swoony romance … with a little butt-kicking thrown in for good measure. A cracking debut."

—Antony John, author of
the 2011 Schneider Family Book
award-winning *Five Flavors of Dumb*

To Bub, no matter how many books I write,
you will always be my greatest accomplishment.

SENSHI

COLE GIBSEN

Woodbury, Minnesota

First Edition
First Printing, 2013

Book design by Bob Gaul
Cover design by Adrienne Zimiga
Cover illustration © Eric Williams/The July Group
Editing by Rhiannon Nelson

Flux, an imprint of Llewellyn Worldwide Ltd.

Library of Congress Cataloging-in-Publication Data
Gibsen, Cole.
   Senshi/Cole Gibsen.—1st ed.
      p. cm.—(Katana; #2)
   Summary: "After learning she is a reincarnated samurai, nearly getting killed (several times), and reuniting with a past-life soul mate, Rileigh Martin decides to put her warrior life on hold to focus on her senior year of high school"—Provided by publisher.
   ISBN 978-0-7387-3261-9
   [1. Samurai—Fiction. 2. Martial arts—Fiction. 3. Supernatural—Fiction. 4. Reincarnation—Fiction. 5. Love—Fiction. 6. High schools—Fiction. 7. Schools—Fiction.] I. Title.
   PZ7.G339266Sen 2013
   [Fic]—dc23
                                                                    2012040393

Flux
Llewellyn Worldwide Ltd.
2143 Wooddale Drive
Woodbury, MN 55125-2989
www.fluxnow.com

Acknowledgements

You know how they say it takes a village to raise a child? Well, it takes an entire Death Star filled with Storm Troopers to make a book. So I want to give a quick shout out to my fellow dark-side compatriots.

First of all, a huge thank you to Brian Farrey-Latz, Rhiannon Nelson, Kathy Schneider, Marissa Pederson, Steven Pomije, Mallory Hayes, and all the amazing people at Flux.

A big thank you goes to Chris Richman for his eternal optimism and his never-surrender attitude.

To my crit partners Brad Cook, T.W. Fendley, Sarah Bromley, and Michelle McLean, thank you for never being afraid to dice my work with shuriken. And to my therapists, Sarah Bromley, Amanda Bonilla, Windy Aphayrath, Shawntelle Madison, Shaun Hutchinson, and Butch Wilson, you are all worth your weight in Xanax.

As always, a special thank you goes out to Pat and the rest of the SUCers over at Query Tracker. I never would have made it this far if not for you guys.

To my Southern Illinois Bookends, thank you for all the cheerleading. A girl can never have enough pom-poms in her life.

To the wonderfully supportive and awesome group that is the Apocalypsies, I am so very blessed to count myself as a member of such an amazingly supportive group.

A huge thank you goes to St. Louis writing superstars Heather Brewer and Antony John. Thank you for taking me under your wings and teaching me how to navigate the sometimes choppy waters of the publishing world.

Heartfelt thanks go out to Alison Donelly, librarian extraordinaire, who single-handedly planned the world's greatest book launch party for me. Thanks also to the indies Afterwords, Main Street Books, and 6th North for your support of local authors. It means so much to have you behind me.

And to the beautiful, gracious, and always delightful Hasume-san and Umeka-san. One does not come across many kindred spirits in their lifetime, but I knew we were the second I met you.

Last but not least, thank you to my husband, daughter, and family for understanding why the dog hair is rolling across the floor and we're eating takeout again. You're the best family a girl could hope to have and I'm so lucky to have you all in my life.

1

A grime-covered alley was not exactly the romantic date atmosphere I had in mind.

My boyfriend Kim pulled his silver Trans Am next to a graffiti-covered Dumpster and cut the engine.

The smell of rotten food wafted through the car. Covering my nose with my hand, I turned to Kim. "Um, when you promised me a night out, just the two of us, I was thinking along the lines of a nice dinner and maybe a movie. But this... is really something. What's the occasion? Did I forget our anniversary?" Something scurried in the shadows. A rat? I shuddered. "Where are we, anyway?"

"An art gallery." He didn't look at me but continued to stare down the alley.

I twisted in my seat so I could study the street behind us. A single streetlight illuminated two beer bottles and an empty potato chip bag floating on a puddle in an otherwise deserted road. "Yeah, I think they're closed."

"They are."

I dropped my hand from my nose. Something stank worse than the Dumpster. "What aren't you telling me?"

He turned to me, his eyes pleading. "Please don't be mad. The Network called right before I picked you up. I promise this will not take long." Each word held the slightest pause, the only giveaway that English was not his first language.

"Are you *serious?*" I flopped back against the seat with a sigh. The Network was a government agency that kept an eye out for reincarnated souls. They had us running missions practically every night—which was kind of annoying when you were trying to have a relationship. Kim and I shared a past life where we lived together, fought together, and slept tangled in each other's arms. But in this life, we'd only been reunited for several months, and it wasn't easy finding a starting place—especially when we hardly had a minute to ourselves. "But you said tonight was going to be about *us.*"

His shoulders slumped. "You're mad."

"No, Kim, not at all. Prowling around an alley that stinks like ass, breaking and entering, and looking for bad guys is every girl's dream date." I narrowed my eyes but knew my glare didn't hold any heat. It was impossible for me to stay mad at Kim—he'd saved my life too many times. Still, I could pretend. "I just thought that, after spending 500 years apart, we deserved, at the very least, a movie. And maybe some popcorn. Heck, I'd settle for just the popcorn—provided there's extra butter. But there's not going to be any extra butter, is there, Kim?"

He sighed and ran a hand through his black hair. As soon as his fingers left his scalp, his layered locks fell back into jagged strips around his face. "You think I don't feel the same way? I want to take you on a normal date. But the problem is we're not a normal couple. We're samurai. We have obligations."

I rolled my eyes. It wasn't like I asked to be a samurai. In fact, only a couple of months ago I'd been a normal teenage girl who only worried about perfecting my ollie for skateboarding tournaments and keeping my grades high enough to get into a decent college. (This was before I'd transcended—a fancy way of saying I smooshed my past life with my present life, threw the whole mess in a blender, and put it on frappé until smooth. The end result was an ex-samurai skateboarding Rileigh-Senshi smoothie with just a hint of raspberries.) Now I had so much more on my plate. Enemy attacks, past-life memories, and my growing ki powers were only the tip of the iceberg. And, while I felt a sense of rightness about joining up with my samurai brethren, part of me longed for the normalcy I had before. Was one interruption-free date night with my boyfriend really too much to ask for?

"Rileigh." Kim reached for my hand, his voice soft. "The rest of the team should be here any minute. We just have to do a quick sweep of the building." He leaned into me and whispered the last part against my neck. "Afterwards, we can pick up exactly where we left off."

It was as if a thousand hummingbirds fluttered inside my body. I shivered happily. "Promise?"

He sat back and smiled. "Promise. This shouldn't take long at all. The gallery was broken into last night, but it doesn't look like anything was stolen. The cops have come and gone, but just in case, the Network wants us to check it out. You know when it comes to artifacts, it's better to be safe than sorry."

I nodded. Especially because antiques and artifacts were the key to transcending. They stored the energy of every person to come in contact with them. It was this energy that had power to awaken the past-life memories.

Kim shrugged. "It was probably a bunch of wannabe-thugs screwing around. If that's the case, with all the attention they've drawn, I highly doubt they'll come back."

Someone rapped a hand against Kim's window, and we turned to find Braden waving at us, a crooked grin on his face. Michelle and Drew stood behind him. "Hi, guys! Are you ready to get down to business?" He paused. "Why are you two dressed so nice?"

I opened the car door and stepped out into the alley. The stink from the Dumpster was stronger here, a tangible wall of sickly sweet smells that almost forced me back to the car. "Oh, you know. I always like to look my best when I go traipsing through alley sludge."

"Huh." The smile fell from Braden's face. "That's not really a good idea. You could ruin your clothes doing that."

Michelle sighed. "*Anyway,* we should get this over with. My mom thinks I'm studying at the library. I have to be back before my curfew at eleven."

"And I've got Sunday brunch with my grandma in the morning," Braden added.

Drew leaned over, his long blond braid falling over his shoulder. "Yeah, and there's a Star Trek marathon on tonight—the good series—with Captain Picard."

Kim shook his head. "What a scary bunch of warriors we've become. Our enemies are sure to tremble with fear." He gestured to the door. "Shall we?"

I was about to answer him when my phone rang. I pulled it from my pocket and glanced at the screen. My mother. I shook my head. "It's Debbie. Looks like you're going to have to start without me."

He frowned.

"Go on." I shooed him with my hand. "I'll just be a minute."

He nodded and turned to Michelle, who was already at work picking the lock on the art gallery's rusty side door. I climbed back inside the car to muffle the sounds of the breaking and entering taking place a few feet away. "Hello?"

"Rileigh." My mother's voice was breathless and tinged with a hint of excitement. I'd heard it enough to know it was her money-making voice. She didn't wait for me to respond. "Look. I need your help. Remember that blonde boy you went on a date with a couple of months ago? The one with the really great cheekbones?"

She was talking about Whitley. Of course I remembered him. When a boy drugs your food, sets your house on fire, and tries to ritually sacrifice you to claim your soul, it kind of leaves an impression.

5

"Yeah?" I braced myself for whatever came next.

"I need his phone number," she said. "Abercrombie needs a male model for their next shoot, and this guy would be perfect. We're talking huge numbers here."

I should have known that my mother, the talent agent, would only call if there was a major deal at stake. Too bad for her I'd left Whitley pinned to the wall in my bedroom while the house burned down. I sincerely doubted that a fistful of ashes would sell clothes as well as a set of greased-up abs. "I wish I could help you, Mom. But he moved."

"I don't care," she answered. "This could be a seven-figure deal. Get his number. I'll track him down."

"You can't." My mind raced for a answer that didn't involve his burning to death in our old house. "He moved to … Lithuania. He joined a monastery."

"What?" There was no disguising her irritation. "Rileigh, if you're—"

I cut her off. "And there are no phones there. Not that it would matter. He's devoted to God now. Not underwear. Sorry." I clicked off the phone before she could argue with me further—a move I was sure to pay for later.

I shoved the phone in my pocket and glanced around the empty alley. Time to get down to business. But as I reached for the car door, the metal clink of a soda can skittered across the alley behind the car. I froze and peered into the rearview mirror just in time to see a guy with shoulder-length blond hair run past the building. It was too dark for me to be sure, but from where I sat, it kinda looked like Whitley.

Awesome. Now, thanks to my mother, I was seeing ghosts. I continued to stare into the mirror waiting for, I wasn't really sure. Did I expect the guy to come back and tell me he wasn't the ghost of the boy burned alive? Yeah, because that was going to happen. But still I remained frozen in the passenger seat, my eyes glued to the mirror.

The alley remained quiet.

Get a grip, Rileigh. I chuckled under my breath. I survived a couple murder attempts and now every shadow was out to get me? Embarrassing. The more likely explanation was the guy I'd seen had been a night jogger. It was dark and, because of my mom's phone call, Whitley was at the front of my thoughts. That's the only reason the jogger had resembled him. It made perfect sense.

Again I reached for the door handle, but again I stopped when invisible ice-crusted fingers curled around my throat, forcing me to gasp.

"Son of hibachi." I ducked down. My heart beat so frantically it felt like it might burst through my rib cage. Not a fun feeling. It'd been 500 years since I had it last, but I knew exactly what it meant.

Climbing onto my knees, I twisted on the seat so I could have a better view of the alley. Nothing moved. But that didn't mean they weren't there. Watching me.

I wanted to laugh at the craziness of it all. How did they find us? In this century? In this alley? But I knew better than to doubt myself. When it came to danger premonitions, I'd never been wrong in this life. Or the last. And this particular feeling only meant one thing.

Ninja.

2

Nothing moved in the alley. Not that I thought it would. *Think, Rileigh. Think!* If the ninja weren't already here, they would be soon. Somehow I had to get inside the art gallery and warn the others. My first thought was to honk the horn, but that would alert the ninja to my position.

"Crap," I whispered. The pressure in my chest expanded and pushed against my ribs. The ninja were closing in.

Plan time. The first thing I needed to do was get out of the car. A small space could quickly become a cage in a fight. I popped open Kim's glove compartment and fumbled around in the hopes of finding a weapon. Unfortunately, besides an owner's manual, the only thing inside was a tire pressure gauge.

Making a mental note to pay for the repair, I took the thin piece of metal and slammed it into the dome light, cracking the plastic and shattering the bulb underneath. Without the light to give away my presence, I opened the door, slid out of the car, and pressed myself against the jagged edges of the brick wall behind me.

So far, so good.

Keeping my back to the wall, I used my fingers to guide me to the side door Kim had disappeared through. The sharp concrete chipped away at my freshly painted nails. Somebody owed me a manicure.

Several heartbeats later, the brick gave way to cool metal, and I knew I'd made it to the door. Without taking my eyes off the street, I patted the area behind me until I found the door handle. With a relieved sigh, I gave the door a tug.

It didn't budge.

Double crap.

It wasn't like I could bang on it and hope Kim would hear me. Nothing says, "Hey, if you want to come kill me, I'm right over here!" like a buttload of noise.

I took a deep breath and slowly exhaled through my mouth. *Okay, no biggie. Ninja are coming, and you're alone in a dark alley with no weapon, and no way to alert your friends. Do you: (A) Call the cops and hope there will be pieces of you left to identify when they arrive? (B) Jump inside the Dumpster and hope they mistake you for a rat? (C) Fight?*

I snorted at my own options. Option A sounded bloody and option B sounded dirty. This was a no-brainer. I cracked my knuckles.

Something stirred in the darkness barely beyond the edge of my vision. Like a hand moving under a black sheet. I couldn't see the object itself, but its movement distorted the shadows. I straightened my stance, balancing my weight on my back foot. My insides screamed from the pressure consuming every inch of my body, from my tingling toes to my eyeballs that felt ready to pop from their sockets.

I balled my hands into fists. "I know you're out there!" My voice echoed off the walls and spilled onto the street. "You may as well save us both some time and show yourself."

A chuckling answered me. "You can sense us. Impressive." The male voice echoed around me. Before I could wonder where it came from, a shadow peeled off the wall several feet away and, like a cookie fattening in an oven, became whole.

I rolled my eyes. "Seriously? Materializing from a shadow? After 500 years, you couldn't come up with anything new? No theme music? No dance number? As it stands, I'm kinda disappointed."

Two more shadows pulled free from the wall, materializing into figures that flanked the first. They were dressed head-to-toe in black from their boots to their face masks.

I folded my arms across my chest. "And what's with the black suits? That's so 16th century."

The figure on the right, the smallest of the three, cocked its head. "Do you always talk so much when facing death?" Her voice was low, just above a growl.

"Actually, I talk when I'm *bored*."

The wink of metal glinting under the streetlight answered me. The girl removed a small, sickle-like blade from her belt. The short handle was attached to a chain that she swung menacingly in front of her.

A kusarigama—designed not only to cut but to ensnare. Triple crap.

My alarm must have showed on my face because the middle figure laughed. "So you're the great *Senshi*. I'm afraid I don't understand the hype." His eyes traveled the length of my body. "I was expecting... *more*."

The buzzing within me electrified my blood, skipping my pulse into an erratic rhythm. So they knew who I was— or at least who I'd been—which meant they'd been searching for me. Now the only question was *why?* "What do you want?"

The middle ninja cocked his head. "Your head on my blade."

I sighed. Ninja always wanted me dead. How come they never wanted to take me for pancakes? That would be a nice change.

The middle ninja dropped his arms to his side, exposing the hooked blades protruding from his knuckles.

This was getting better by the minute. I cast a quick glance at the side door. *Dang it, Kim! Where are you?*

"Let's do this." The remaining ninja—definitely male given his linebacker build—pulled two short curved blades from his belt. He ran at me, the blades arched above his head. In the space of two heartbeats, his blades dove for my skull. I had just enough time to duck the first slash when the kusagirama wedged itself into the brick wall inches away from my nose.

My own wide eyes stared at me from the blade. *Sloppy,*

Rileigh. I pushed off the brick just as the ninja with the blades lashed out with a spinning kick.

Diving to the ground to avoid the blow, I only had a millisecond to mourn my ruined shirt, now soaked with muddy rainwater and whatever else was in the murky puddle I rolled in. I planted my palms onto the asphalt, wincing as jagged pieces of gravel dug into my skin. A second later, I was back on my feet. Just in time to face the ninja with the blades on his knuckles.

His first strike was high, giving me plenty of time to duck. But his second came fast and low. I jumped back—not an easy feat in my skinny jeans—and, even then, two of his blades snagged the fabric of my shirt, slashing through the hem.

My breath came in rapid bursts. Two close calls within the space of seconds. I was going to have to do better than that if I hoped to leave with my head.

Knife ninja was in front of me.

Darting to the left and ducking to the right, I dodged the knives that struck at me like a pair of silver cobras. Behind me, the sound of a chain unraveling echoed through the alley, alerting me it was time to dive and roll before the kusagirama invaded my personal space—and by personal space I meant spleen.

Thanks to my quick movement, the kusagirama missed me, and instead grazed the shoulder of knife ninja. He cried out, dropping the blades in order to clutch his bleeding shoulder. "Watch where you're aiming!"

Kusagirama girl's eyes narrowed behind her mask. "Then stay out of my way!"

I used their standoff to make a dive for the discarded blades. Clawed ninja seemed to guess what I was about to do and lashed out with a kick. He missed my head (point for me) but caught my shin with his heel (point for him). Pain blossomed under my skin as I staggered to my feet with the knives in my hands.

Kusarigama girl pulled back her blade and wound the chain around her arm. She left two feet dangling from her hand and began spinning it over her head.

My body, bruised from the kick and scraped from the asphalt, tensed. Every muscle inside of me strained, ready to leap in the opposite direction of wherever the kusarigama struck.

She released the chain viper fast, the blade aimed for my chest. I had just enough time to bend over backward as the kusarigama sailed past my body, close enough to ruffle the tattered edge of my shirt. It sank into the wall, crumbling bits of brick onto the ground.

Gritting my teeth through the burn of my aching muscles, I jabbed a knife into the chain above me and twisted until it was locked in. Using my new grip on the chain, I pulled myself back up into a standing position and ripped the blade from the wall. I raised the chain above my head, spun, and pulled down, wrenching the kusarigama from the ninja's grip. She stumbled to her knees.

Sensing the clawed ninja, I swung the end of the chain behind me. The ninja grunted as it wrapped around his calves. He fell forward. Using his momentum, I dropped to my knees and propelled him over my shoulder, where he landed on top of the girl. She cried out as one of his clawed hands pierced her thigh.

I made a face and whistled through my teeth. "Ouch. That looks like it hurts."

The third ninja glanced nervously between me and his fallen friends from where he stood clutching his bleeding shoulder. A steady trickle of blood seeped from between his fingers. His entire left arm looked useless. Bad news for him but great news for me.

A rustling noise caught my attention, and I turned back to see clawed ninja pushing himself off the ground. His eyes crinkled behind his mask, indicating a smile. "You think you're good, don't you?"

I shrugged. "You're the one coming back for seconds."

He laughed. "It's a shame it has to go down like this. I'll admit, I kinda like you."

I held the knives in front of me, forming an X. "Aw, you're sweet. Too bad for you I don't date ninja. I *kill* them."

He opened his arms wide, beckoning me forward. "You can *try.*"

I spun the knives in my hand, casting a quick glance at my surroundings. The other two ninja were licking their wounds exactly where I left them. Kim was still nowhere to been seen. I was tired, dirty, and my clothes were ruined. The last thing I wanted to do was to keep fighting. But it didn't look like I had much choice.

Clawed ninja ran toward me and I met him in the middle

of the alley in a frenzy of clashing metal. He swung a clawed hand at my face, which I dodged, and then I quickly darted to the side of his other reaching fist. Just as easily, he blocked my blows. My punches were sidestepped, and my kicks deflected by his blocks.

He aimed a high kick for my head, which I ducked under. When he brought his foot down, he balanced his weight on his back leg and leaned back, bringing his arms up in a defensive pose. We stared at each other a moment, both of us using the pause as a chance to catch our breath. The skin on my arms burned, and my muscles pulsed from blocking strikes that were meant to break bone. If I survived, I was going to look like a Dalmatian with bruises for spots.

The clawed ninja, as if sensing my exhaustion, charged. His fists were a blur of metal and death, an angry cyclone trying to suck me inside its razor-edged core. But just as fast as he could swing a fist, I could duck. Rolling and dodging. Weaving and sidestepping. I bounced his claws off my knives, leaving the clang of metal ringing in my ears.

A thin line of sweat trickled along my temples. I wasn't sure how much more I could take. My body was already trembling from exertion. With his claws pressed against my knives, I stepped closer and stood on my toes so I could meet his eyes. When I spoke my voice was strained. "Who sent you?"

"That's a secret." He rotated his arms up and under, wrenching the knives from my hands and sending them skittering across the asphalt into the shadows.

Son of hibachi. I cast a quick glance at the door to the

gallery. How long did it take to search a building? Surely not as long as Kim and the others had been gone. Why hadn't they come looking for me yet? I took a step backward. "If you can't tell me who sent you, maybe you can tell me why?"

He stepped closer and shrugged. "Why does any ninja do what they do? Money? Power?" He chuckled, his laugh husky from exertion. "Or maybe we do it just because we *can*."

Kusarigama girl giggled from where she sat tearing fabric from her pants and wrapping it around her leg.

I took another step back, only to bump into the brick wall of the building. There was nowhere to run. I needed a plan and I needed it fast.

Clawed ninja closed the distance between us in two long strides. He lifted his arm and struck before I could move. His claws sank into the brick next to my right ear, dusting my shoulder with crumbled rock. I choked on a scream before it exploded up my throat as a gasp. I pressed myself against the wall, as if by sheer force I could sink into it.

"Not so sure of yourself now, are you?" He slowly raised his right hand in the air. "That first strike was just so I could see the fear in your eyes before you die. This time I won't miss."

3

A wind stirred inside of me, burning an icy trail just beneath my skin. It looked like Senshi was finally coming out to play. At least now that I had transcended and we were more or less the same person, I knew how to fight and control my ki—or spirit energy—without the voice of my past self whispering inside my head. I closed my eyes and, when I opened them again, my lips curled into a smirk. "You better hope you don't miss. Because I *never* do."

He hesitated, his arm hovering in the air.

I wondered if he could sense the change in me—if he could feel the power buzzing around me as much as I felt it pulsing within.

His eyes flicked nervously from me to his fallen friends. "I hardly think you're in a position to make threats." But his voice held a waiver of uncertainty.

"Oh yeah? Here's where I get to see the fear in *your* eyes." I released a small amount of ki. The wind brushed through my skin and, once outside my body, became something hard and stiff. It struck clawed ninja in the chest, snapping his head back. He grunted and doubled over.

That should have been the end of it.

But it wasn't.

I tried to reel my ki back inside me, but the more I pulled at the energy flowing from my body, the faster it spilled out. In fact, I seemed to be creating power faster than I could expel it. It pushed against my bones and stretched under my skin. I felt like a balloon stuck to a helium tank. Gritting my teeth, I staggered backward, my arms wrapped around my stomach. Something was really, *really* wrong.

Clawed ninja screamed and tried to tug his bladed fist from the brick. And when that didn't work, he released his grip on the metal handle, leaving the claws behind as he felt his way along the wall, shielding his head with his arms. "What are you doing?"

I opened my mouth to explain that it wasn't me—that I'd lost control—but my words were replaced by a cry of pain. Doubling over, I gripped my sides. Something snapped. A rib? This was followed by a ripping sensation so intense it brought tears to my eyes. I cast one last longing glance at the door. *Kim, where are you?*

"Please!" kusarigama girl cried out, shielding herself from the cyclone of wind that filled the alley. "Stop it!"

I tried. But it felt like trying to pour the entire ocean into a coffee mug. My body shook as my ki continued to flood from every pore. A person only had so much spirit energy. I remembered enough from my past-life ki lessons to know that if I didn't find a way to stop the flood from within, I'd lose all of my ki. And then I'd be in a permanent state of dead.

Already the effects of my ki loss were taking a toll on my body. My knees buckled and I dropped to the ground, each of my limbs too heavy to move. The energy I needed to stand, to lift my head and even beat my heart, drained from my body with each passing second.

And I wasn't the only one in trouble. The three ninja cried out in pain—or fear—I couldn't be sure. Their screams echoed off the brick walls before the wind picked up and tore the voices from their throats. Aluminum cans, discarded lottery tickets, and other trash swirled around us, hitting our bodies only to fly away and strike again.

I mustered enough energy to cover my head with my arm, protecting it against the onslaught of debris. Again, I tried to retract my ki, and again I failed. I couldn't explain it, but something inside of me felt … off. Unfortunately, I didn't have time to figure it out. I didn't have time for anything.

I was out of options.

The clawed ninja sank to the ground beside me, tearing at his throat, gasping for the air being sucked out of him. The other two ninja lay huddled against the wall, their heads tucked under their hands like they were protecting themselves from a tornado—and in a way, they were.

The ground trembled beneath my body. A shriek of metal pierced my eardrums, and I looked up to find the Dumpster sliding across the asphalt. Where were the other samurai? There was no way Kim and the others couldn't hear what was happening outside, no way they couldn't feel the building shake around them.

Was Kim in trouble too?

A beer bottle skipped across the asphalt before wind picked it up and smashed it against the edge of the Dumpster. Dozens of jagged pieces swirled in the air like a swarm of glittering wasps. The first shard to come my way only grazed my arm. But the second bit into my cheek with enough force that warm lines of blood streaked across my face. If something didn't happen soon, I'd be cut to pieces before my spirit bled out of me.

Beside me, the clawed ninja howled in pain. I looked over to find him pulling a jagged piece of glass out of the side of his neck. Another shard brushed across my back, leaving a burning trail in its wake. Hissing in pain, I tried, one last time, to focus, to harness the energy back inside of me like I had so many times in battle. But each time I tried to mentally tug it, it tugged right back, drawing even more energy from within me.

Dying sucked.

I'd killed myself in my first life. Of course, it was to keep from being taken prisoner (and whatever torture-filled plans my enemies had for me). So I could attest to how much suck was involved in dying (hint: it didn't tickle). Not to mention that, if I did die, it meant losing Kim all over again. I wouldn't, *couldn't,* let that happen—at least not without a fight.

I grunted as a sliver of glass sank into the back of my arm. First things first—I needed a shield. I held my hand up to protect my eyes and did a quick scan of the alley. The Dumpster, while sturdy, was sliding around, making it way too hazardous to hide behind. Kim's car, on the other hand, would provide the perfect shelter from the glass storm. Using the last of my strength, and with one arm shielded over my head, I half shimmied, half crawled toward the Trans Am. My leg bumped something along the way and a glance showed me it was the clawed ninja, motionless, on the ground. I kicked him in the stomach as I crawled by. It may or may not have been an accident.

Inch by inch, I pushed myself through the beating wind and pelting glass. It wasn't until the Trans Am's back bumper was several feet away that I thought I might actually make it. But the first squeal of rubber against asphalt told me just how wrong I was.

I didn't believe it at first when the car shuddered. I thought my flying hair and the wind had distorted my vision. I mean, sure, it was windy enough to move the Dumpster, but a car weighs a lot more, right? There was no way my ki had gathered enough power to move a car. But no sooner had the thought passed through my mind than the Trans Am's brakes released a toe-curling shriek and the car began rolling toward me.

Son of hibachi! I tried to stand, but my knees buckled. Not only was I immediately blown over but more glass pelted my body. As I fell onto my back, the glass protruding from my arms dug farther into my skin. My head hit the ground, and I heard a crack. Could have been more breaking glass. Could have been my skull. Either way, it hurt like a mother. If I didn't move—like *now*—I was going to be Rileigh Martin, human speed bump—not exactly an ideal obituary article. I pushed up onto my hands and feet and attempted crab-crawling backward.

The Trans Am picked up speed.

I tried moving faster, but my body refused to respond. Another foot and my back met with something hard. Twisting my head, I looked to see what was blocking my path. The Dumpster. My heart fell into my stomach. I didn't have enough time to move around it. The Trans Am was only seconds away.

Okay, Rileigh, you have one shot at this. Make it count. I flattened myself to the ground, ignoring the sting of asphalt and glass that bit into my back and legs. Maybe I'd get lucky and the car would pass over with me safely between the tires. Maybe I'd miscalculated and would be crushed.

Either way, I closed my eyes.

4

Japan, 1491

Akiko pressed her hands against her hot, swollen eyes. But still, tears worked their way through the crevices of her fingers, trailing down her wrists where they soaked into the sleeves bunched at her elbows.

"Stop rubbing your face!" Akiko's mentor Etsu scolded her as she jerked and combed fistfuls of Akiko's hair into a topknot. "You are ruining all of my hard work. What a mess!"

"I do not care," Akiko muttered.

The older woman tsked. With stiff, hooked fingers, she removed a bundle of silk from within her robe. "Such an attitude! You should be excited! This is a great honor, after all." She picked at the cord knotted around the bundle until it loosened. Carefully, she peeled back the layers of silk and revealed the dagger within.

Akiko flinched, causing Etsu to laugh softly. "Silly girl.

You cannot keep acting like a child, Akiko. You are fifteen today."

"Which means I am a woman now. *I know*." She didn't bother to hide the bitterness in her voice.

"Well." Etsu's gaze wandered to the white cloth draped across the sleeping mat waiting for Akiko's virginal blood. "Not yet, you are not."

Despite her best attempt not to, Akiko shuddered. The cloth would be not only a souvenir, but also insurance to the winning bidder. Proof that he was getting exactly what he paid for.

A ball of fury burned in the pit of Akiko's stomach. She hated that cloth more than she hated anything in her life. She wanted to rip it apart with her fingers, tear into it with her teeth, and set fire to whatever pieces remained.

As if sensing Akiko's thoughts, Etsu patted her shoulder—the first tender touch Akiko could remember receiving from the gray-haired woman. "This is a great honor, Akiko." When Akiko didn't answer, Etsu added, "It will be over before you know it."

Akiko said nothing, only bit her trembling lip.

The old woman sighed and shook her head. "Such a stubborn girl." She lifted the dagger from its bed of silk and inspected the edge with her thumb. "Perfectly sharp," she muttered.

Akiko's heart skipped as Etsu brought the dagger closer to her head. Again, Akiko's gaze was drawn to the white cloth. "Make it fast," she whispered.

Etsu nodded and wove her gnarled fingers into Akiko's hair. "Do not move."

Akiko couldn't if she wanted to. The old woman had her fingers so firmly entwined into her scalp that she would have her hair ripped clean from her head if she ran—a possibility she considered.

But Etsu's blade was faster than Akiko's plans for escape. The younger girl felt a tug on her scalp followed by a release, as her newly shorn hair fell to her shoulders.

"It is done," Etsu told her.

Akiko cracked open her eyes, startled to find she'd closed them.

"See?" Etsu put down the dagger and held what remained of Akiko's topknot in the air. The hair spasmed in her arthritic grasp like a dying creature taking its last breaths.

Akiko's stomach clenched, and she fought the urge to snatch her hair back from the older woman. But it wasn't her hair to begin with—not really. Akiko had no right to anything, as her mentor was so found of reminding her—not her hair, not her body. Akiko's eyes were drawn back to the white cloth. She didn't even have claim to her own blood.

Tears, hot and stinging, sprang to her eyes.

Etsu sighed impatiently. "If you are going to cry about it, I will let you keep it."

If she wasn't between sobs, Akiko would have laughed at that. Why would she want to keep her cut hair? It would only serve to remind her of this day and everything that was taken from her. She shook her head and waved the old woman's offering away. That's when a glint of silver caught her eye.

Etsu's dagger, forgotten on the floor.

Akiko sucked in a breath. Surely, the old woman wouldn't leave it.

"Suit yourself." Etsu shrugged and pocketed Akiko's discarded hair. She made no move to reclaim her blade as she struggled to her feet, joints popping, and hobbled to the door where she paused. "Akiko?"

"Yes?" The girl's gaze darted away from the dagger. Her pulse quickened.

Etsu sighed. "Sometimes there are things in life we must do. Things that are not always pleasant." She paused. "A courtesan's life is a good one. You will have wealth. Honor. Respect."

Akiko struggled to keep her eyes locked on Etsu's face. So badly she wanted to stare at the dagger, as if it would disappear if she did not keep watch. "But what about freedom?"

"Freedom?" The woman waved a gnarled hand. "You think you could survive on your own? That you could make a better life for yourself?" She laughed. "Here you will be taken care of. Protected. Out there on your own?" She shook her head. "You would not last a day." Etsu slid the door open and disappeared.

Akiko didn't move for several heartbeats. When she was sure that the older woman wasn't returning, she scrambled to the dagger and slid it into the folds of her robe.

We shall see who survives.

5

The first time I died, it had been a relief. Though I remembered very little about it, I did remember passing beyond the barrier of a broken and bleeding body, away from the smell of blood and burnt skin, and into the comfort of darkness. It was inside that darkness that a hand waited to envelop my own.

This was nothing like that.

This darkness was cold. It spun around me, or maybe I was the one spinning? Either way, I was about to throw up.

"Rileigh!" Even Kim's voice sounded different. Last time it had been a calm beacon that urged me from my body. This time he sounded scared, frantic even. "Rileigh, don't you go anywhere. Stay with me."

Like I could leave if I tried. The black room had no doors, no windows, only strange distorted lights that blinked at me from the edge of my vision. Lights that, upon staring at them, grew larger and fuzzier until the world opened up around them and I realized I was staring at the streetlight in the alley next to the gallery.

"Oh, thank God." Kim's body, which had been so tall and rigid in front of me, seemed to deflate under the weight of what could have been. "Rileigh, I thought you were—" His voice caught in his throat. "You weren't moving...I..." He placed a fist against his forehead and bowed his head as if he really was thanking God.

"It's okay. I'm okay." But even as I said it, my vision swam in a kaleidoscope of color. I placed a hand against my head as if that could stop the world from moving under my body. It was then that I felt the baseball-sized lump on my forehead. "I think I have a concussion."

Michelle, who I'd just now noticed crouched by my side, said, "You're lucky you're not dead! We found you under Kim's car." She looked around the alley before meeting my gaze. "It looks like there was a tornado out here. What happened?"

I tried to sit up but immediately stopped when my vision teetered. "Let's just say that even after 500 years, ninja still suck."

"What?" Kim's head snapped up at the same time Braden and Drew raised their arms in fight stance and scanned the alley. "What do you mean by *ninja*?"

"I mean"—I took Michelle's offered hand and let her pull me up into a sitting position—"the three bloodied and bruised guys in the black pajamas just over," But when I looked past my shoulder to where the three ninja had been before Kim's car ran over me, no one remained. "Huh."

Kim jumped to his feet, the muscles in his jaw flexing as he studied the shadows in the corners of the buildings. "I knew it! I knew I recognized ninja black magic."

Slowly, and with Michelle's help, I stood. My head throbbed, and I swayed lightly on my feet. "What magic?"

Drew glanced at me. "We were trapped inside the art gallery. The doors wouldn't budge, and the windows wouldn't open."

"Kim even threw a chair against one window, trying to break the glass," Braden added. "It just bounced off like it was made of rubber."

"That's when we knew we'd fallen into a trap," Michelle said.

"No." Kim walked up to me, his eyes locked on mine. "The trap wasn't *inside* the building…" He placed his hands on either side of my face and drew me closer to him. "Was it?"

The words caught in my throat. I didn't want to tell him that I was in danger again. I knew by speaking the words I'd break the delusion I'd allowed myself to fall into—that being a samurai again didn't have to change my life. I should have known better. I was a protector. It was who I was born to be—I felt sure of it. And with that came responsibility. Even if it meant forgoing a trip to the movies to tango with ninja in a dirty alley. It sucked, sure. But I could handle it because I had Kim and my friends. And they made my life better no matter what I was doing. "I don't know if it was a trap. But they definitely expressed a strong desire to kill me."

Kim made a strangled noise and released me.

"I don't understand." Drew approached us. "Why was the trap for Rileigh only? Why were they sent to kill her and not the rest of us?"

Kim shook his head. "I don't know." He looked at me, his lips pressed into a thin line. "Did they say anything else?"

"You mean after they started throwing sharp things at me?" I examined the tattered edges of my shirt. "No."

Braden poked his head out from behind the Dumpster. Something about the trash bin didn't look right, and it took me a moment to realize that it was on its side. He kicked his way through the garbage bags and cardboard boxes that spilled from it. "You know what else is weird?" He paused to pull a candy bar wrapper off his shoe. "Why send so many ninja after just one person? Kinda overkill. I mean, look at this place." He gestured to the torn-apart alley. "How many were there? Twenty?"

I lowered my gaze and studied my grease-stained jeans. "Yeah … um … would you believe three?" Even without looking I could feel the wide-eyed stares of my friends boring into my head.

"Wait. What?" Michelle let go of me. "Rileigh, look at this place! The Dumpster was overturned. Kim's car was pushed backward—with you under it! You're telling us that three ninja did all that?" She hugged herself and shivered.

"I didn't say that." I ran my fingers through my hair, gently pulling apart the tangles.

Kim frowned and folded his arms across his chest while the rest of them waited for me to continue.

I dropped my hands from my hair and sighed. "It was me, okay?"

Braden and Drew exchanged incredulous looks while Michelle made a choking sound.

"How is that possible?" Drew asked.

"My ki." I shrugged. "I kinda lost control."

"I'll say." Braden's eyes swept the alley.

Kim took a step forward. "You did this? The Dumpster? My car?"

I nodded.

He muttered something under his breath that was distinctly not English.

Michelle spun a slow circle, her eyes scanning everything from the trash on the ground to the tops of the buildings. "Well, this is going from bad to worse."

I leaned against the building, which steadied the Tilt-A-Whirl I seemed to be riding. "It's not a big deal."

Kim gave me a look that clearly told me he didn't agree. "Really? What's under your nose?"

I touched my upper lip and felt something flake against my hand. I raised my finger up to the streetlight. Flecks of dried blood dotted my fingertips. Huh. "Probably hit my face when your car ran over me. It doesn't matter." I dusted my hands on my jeans. "That's not the big issue. Why are you freaking out about my ki when we should be freaking out about the bigger issue?" When no one said anything, I groaned. "Hello? *Ninja*?"

"Good point." Braden stood from where he'd crouched to study the front of Kim's car. "Ninja do suck."

I gestured at Braden as if to say, *See?* But Kim didn't look convinced. "We can't ignore this, Rileigh. Ninja, we can handle. But this?" He gestured to the alley. "You could have killed yourself."

I rolled my eyes even though I knew he was right. Never before had my power refused to listen to me. If I hadn't knocked myself out with Kim's car, would I have continued to bleed my spirit out? A chill crept along the length of my spine.

Kim stepped forward and put an arm around me. "While I am glad you were able to defend yourself, this— I'm just worried."

I softened. "I know." I was worried too.

He sighed and kissed the top of my head. "I don't know who we're going to find to help us with this. It's not like there is an abundance of ki masters running around these days. I can check with the Network. Maybe Dr. Wendell—"

"No!" I cut him off. Dr. Wendell was the obnoxious and annoying doctor/government agent who wouldn't stop dating my mother despite my constant threats. I didn't need him more involved in my life than he already was. Besides, I wasn't dumb enough to work with someone until I knew the motivations under their shiny exterior. Call me paranoid, but when you die at seventeen, you aren't so trusting in the next life. "It's just that, while I agree the whole ki situation is serious, I don't think it takes priority over the ninja who want us dead. Do you?"

"Another good point," Braden said. "What if we dealt

with the ninja first, and in the meantime, Rileigh could just ... *not* manipulate ki."

Kim frowned at him. "That's supposed to be a plan? We try not to die and in the meantime Rileigh doesn't manipulate ki?"

Drew raised his hand. "Actually, I'm in favor of any plan that involves *trying not to die.*"

I had to agree. It was the trying not to manipulate ki part that had me worried. Manipulating ki was part of who I was, and I didn't always have a choice when it decided to rise inside of me. "Kim, if you have a better plan, now would be the time to share."

His silence was my answer.

6

As if chemistry class wasn't bad enough.

I flexed my tingling fingers and let out a quivering breath. It had been a month since the ninja attack, and so far Kim had no leads on who they were or where to find them. And while the thought of a bunch of ninja on the loose who wanted me dead didn't give me the warm fuzzies, I had bigger problems to deal with.

Much bigger.

The tingling under my skin turned into pinpricks, like a thousand tiny needles digging beneath my flesh. I wasn't sure what caused it, only that it started happening to me after the ninja attack. I shifted in my seat, hoping to distract myself from the pain.

My best friend Quentin pushed his metal stool away from the lab table. He eyed me nervously while addressing the doe-eyed brunette sitting between us. "Seriously, Carly, you need to give it a rest."

"What?" His twin sister snapped her gum. "If people

were talking smack about me behind my back, I'd want to know." She patted my hand, a touch I could barely feel through the buzzing beneath my skin. "Rileigh, you should know that people are ... worried about you. You're super jumpy all the time, you have horrendous bags under your eyes, and, sweetie, when's the last time you exfoliated?" She wrinkled her nose. "Are you having a breakdown or something?"

I snatched my hand away from hers and clenched and unclenched my fingers. All the relaxation techniques I'd remembered from my past as a samurai had failed. But still, I tried. Sucking in a deep breath of lab air (a sickly sweet combination of formaldehyde and ammonia), I counted to ten and exhaled slowly. Some of the tightness inside me unwound but the pressure remained—like unzipping a pair of too-tight jeans but not being able to take them off. "I am *not* having a breakdown."

She shrugged and snapped her gum again, a sound that made my teeth grind. "Are you sure? Because you're totally on edge. And the last time I saw you this stressed, you flipped out on some poor homeless guy."

If by "flipped out on some poor homeless guy," she meant "saved everyone's life from a nunchaku-wielding assassin," then I guess I did. "That guy was dangerous, Carly."

She rolled her eyes. "Please. He was just some doped-out homeless guy. Stop being so dramatic."

The electric hum pulsed beneath my fingertips and a heaviness filled my lungs. I tried to expel it with a slow steady breath, but the weight didn't budge. "I'm sorry, you're calling

35

me dramatic?" Did she somehow forget the fact he threw a shuriken at her? She either had the long-term memory of a gnat, or she was in denial. My money was on gnat brain.

Quentin shot me a pleading look and snatched the box of matches sitting in front of me. "I think I'll light the Bunsen burner, if you don't mind."

Carly shrugged. "The truth can be painful."

So can an axe-kick. I gripped the countertop. *Must. Resist. Kicking. Carly's. Stupid. Face.*

"Listen." She leaned across the table to meet my eyes. "Honey, it's not that I don't understand. You and my brother were attacked."

I laughed through clenched teeth. If only I could make it through my classes without losing control, then I'd get to see Kim at training tonight and I'd feel better. Kim always made me feel better. "Oh, I'm so sure you *understand*."

"Ri-Ri," Quentin warned.

Carly flipped her hair over her shoulder. "Of course I do. It makes sense that both of you are going to be traumatized or whatever. Just … maybe tone down the drama while you're at school? You don't want anyone thinking you guys are bigger freaks than they already do."

My body shook as every muscle tightened in anticipation of the explosion to come. Beads of sweat prickled along my forehead as I fought to gain control. If I lost control here, how many people would I hurt? I couldn't let that happen.

"Wow." Quentin shook his head. "It's hard to believe I'm the one who wants to be a psychologist. Your ability to empathize is astounding, you know that?"

"Right?" She nodded. "See, Rileigh? Quentin gets that I'm just trying to help."

He snorted. "Even so, I think your services are best provided elsewhere. Don't you have minions to text or something?"

I shot Q a thankful look before I pulled my water bottle from my backpack. I unscrewed the lid and took a long drink, hoping it would cool the anger burning inside of me.

"*Ms. Martin.*"

I paused mid-sip to glance at the chemistry teacher, Mr. Fritz, leaning across a lab table at the front of the room. "I thought I made it clear on the syllabus that there is no food or drink in this class. There are dangerous chemicals in this lab and I'd hate to see anyone get hurt."

I set the bottle on the table. "If you're worried about someone getting hurt, you might want to reconsider the seating chart—" Q shoved an elbow into my side before I could finish.

Mr. Fritz crossed his arms and frowned. "I'm sorry. What was that?"

I glanced back and forth between Mr. Fritz and Q. The identicalness of their scowls was uncanny. Finally, I sighed. "Not important. I'm sorry about the water bottle, Mr. Fritz."

He nodded, the movement sliding his glasses to the edge of his nose. "One strike, Ms. Martin. Don't let it happen again."

"I won't," I replied glumly and stuffed the bottle back into my bag.

Seemingly satisfied, Mr. Fritz nodded and moved on to another table.

"*Anyway.*" Carly smacked her gum, each pop like a hammer pounding the base of my spine. She poured the contents of a test tube into a beaker. "I didn't want to do it—I know you guys are best friends and all—but I had to tell Mom that I didn't feel safe with Rileigh coming over to our house anymore." She looked up at me and smiled. "At least not until you work out your *issues.*"

Quentin made a choked sound as I whirled around to face her.

"What?" My pulse jumped from a jog to a sprint as the pressure built inside of me, pushing against my ribs until I thought they would crack. It was no secret that Carly and I couldn't stand each other, but she'd never tried to come between Quentin and me before. He'd been my best friend since first grade. Not to mention he was the one person who kept me firmly grounded in this life. Without him, I'd be more lost than ever.

Invisible hands ripped into my chest, trying to claw their way out. What little control I had was slipping away—and fast.

Quentin, as if sensing my distress, snatched the empty test tube from Carly's hand. "Carly, oh my God, you got something on your face."

Wide-eyed, she patted her face. "Where? What is it?"

Quentin pointed to his nostril.

"Oh, God." The color drained from her cheeks. "Mr. Fritz!" She leapt from her stool, ran to the front of the classroom, and snatched the wooden hall pass from a hook on the wall. "I have to go to the bathroom!"

He looked up from assisting a table of students and waved her away with a sigh. "Hurry back. Your table is behind the rest of the class. You should have your Bunsen burner turned on by now."

She nodded and ran for the door.

Quentin gave a nervous glance to the matches in front of him. "Don't listen to her. My mom loves you and she knows Carly's a drama queen. She'd never ban you from the house." He looked at me. "Are you—are you okay?"

Not even close. But maybe if I lied to him I could fool myself. "I'm good." I tried to sound convincing, but my voice came out strained.

He took a match from the box but didn't strike it. "Besides, I love you and isn't my opinion the only one that counts?"

"I just thought she'd be more understanding, you know? I'd assumed since I saved her life, lost my house, and almost died, she'd get off my back." I shook my head and closed my eyes, trying to harness the energy swirling inside me. It felt like I was being torn in half.

"Yeah, well..." Quentin turned on the valve that released the gas. "Welcome to high school." He struck the match and raised the lit tip to the nozzle.

At that moment, the hum of ki burst through my skin. To make it worse, I'd spent so much of my energy trying to keep it from escaping that I had none left to control it when it did. It happened so fast, I was helpless to warn Quentin about the attack coming his way.

The Bunsen burner exploded in an angry fireball that ricocheted him off his stool, and he collapsed onto the floor. He buried his face in his hands while uttering a stream of obscenities under his breath.

"Q!" I leapt from my chair and joined him on the floor. The acrid stench of singed hair stung my nostrils. "Oh my God! Are you alright?"

He didn't move but continued to mutter every curse word I knew, in addition to some awfully creative ones.

"Mr. Fritz!" Fear strangled my voice into a garbled mess.

My chem teacher was next to us in an instant. He placed his hand on Quentin's back, his eyes wide with alarm. "What happened?"

"I—I—" *Oh, you know, I lost control of my ki and set my best friend on fire.* "I don't know. Quentin was lighting the Bunsen burner, and then—" I sucked in a ragged breath. "And then—"

"It exploded," Quentin mumbled miserably against his hands.

Mr. Fritz held his arms up and glanced at the students who'd left their seats and were climbing over each other to get a closer look. "Okay, I need everyone to calm down."

I stared at him in disbelief. Calm down? I'd nearly roasted Quentin's face off, and he wanted me to be calm about it? My stomach twisted until I thought I'd double over from the pain. What if it'd been worse? What if—

Before I could finish my thought, the Bunsen burner

flared to life again, issuing a beach ball-sized fireball that dissipated with a whoosh into black smoke before reaching the ceiling.

"What the—" Mr. Fritz stumbled backward, knocking over Carly's abandoned stool. I jumped in front of Quentin and grabbed onto a metal leg, righting the chair before it could fall on him. At least my reflexes hadn't failed me.

Mr. Fritz's skin paled to the color of the plastic skeleton mounted on the wall. He grasped the counter and pulled himself to his feet. "Gas leak. It has to be a gas leak." He looked at us, his eyes impossibly wide. "I want all of you"— he scanned the entire classroom—"outside and in front of the gymnasium. NOW."

The stunned silence erupted into squeals and shrieks as my classmates scrambled to grab their belongings before stampeding from the room.

"Ms. Martin." Mr. Fritz grabbed Quentin's elbow and motioned for me to do the same. Together, we lifted him to his feet. "Get Mr. Farmer to the nurse. I'm going to the office to alert them about the gas leak. The school needs to be evacuated." Mr. Fritz placed a hand between my shoulders and gave me an urgent push forward.

I nodded even though I knew there was no gas leak. Wrapping my arm around Quentin's waist, I guided him out the door and down the hall. I whispered how sorry I was more than a hundred times, but still he refused to look at me and kept his face buried beneath his hands. How badly had I burned him? Would he scar? Guilt twisted my insides.

Carly had been right about me.

I was dangerous.

7

The good news is, you'll live." The nurse, a tired-looking woman with a sloppy gray bun at the base of her skull, patted Quentin on the cheek. His eyes stayed locked on the mirror in his hands.

I stood by his side, my chest tight with worry. "So he's going to be okay?"

The nurse smiled and tugged on the ends of the stethoscope wrapped around her neck. "They're just eyebrows, dear. They'll grow back." She glanced at Quentin. "It is interesting, though. If you were as close to the Bunsen burner as you say, I'm surprised you weren't burned. You're a lucky young man. I'm going to get some salve for your face. I'll be back in a minute."

When she was out of the room, Quentin set the mirror aside, closed his eyes, and groaned.

"It's not that bad." I stared at the bare skin where his eyebrows used to be. The nurse was right. While the flames had burned away his eyebrows, his skin wasn't even inflamed.

"Not that bad?" He turned angry eyes on me. "Give me a robe and an ugly pedicure, and I could play the bad guy in those wizard movies!"

I flinched. In all the years we'd been friends, he'd never once yelled at me. "Q, I'm so . . . I just . . . I'm sorry."

He closed his eyes and exhaled loudly through his nose. He stayed that way for a moment, like a deflated balloon, as the silence between us pressed against me so thick and heavy I thought I might suffocate. Finally, he opened his eyes. "I know." He patted his hand against the vinyl table where he sat. I jumped up next to him and leaned my head against his shoulder. Maybe Quentin wouldn't stay mad at me. Hope picked at the knot inside my chest.

"I know you didn't *mean* to hurt me," he said. "But you need help, Ri-Ri. You've been struggling to control this ki thing of yours for what—a month? And this?" He wiggled the skin where his eyebrows had been. "This should tell you that you can't keep doing what you've been doing."

"But I haven't been *doing* anything."

He gave me a pointed look.

"Oh. Right." But that was going to change. Before today, I'd assumed the real threat was the ninja; that's why finding them had been my top priority. Turns out I was wrong. The real threat was me.

I met Q's eyes. "I'm sorry I let things get so out of control and put you at risk. From this day forward, getting control of my ki is my number-one priority."

"Good." He smiled, but his eyes remained serious.

"Because next time, someone could lose *more* than their eyebrows. You understand that, don't you?"

I sucked on my bottom lip and nodded. I understood. Until I got my ki under control, I was a ticking time bomb.

No one was safe.

8

A daimyo was the ruling lord of a village. In my previous life in Japan, Lord Toyotomi had been that man. But to call him *just* a ruler was like calling Tony Hawk *just* a skater. Lord Toyotomi had been my teacher, my counselor, and the closest thing to a father I ever had. Like me, he'd been gifted with the ability to manipulate ki. And he was the one who taught me to understand and use that power to my advantage.

If I had any hope of doing so again, it seemed only logical that I should start with his teachings. And rule number one for controlling ki? Meditation. Easy to do when you're in a silent courtyard surrounded by cherry trees and koi ponds. Not so easy in the middle of a city full of sirens and flashing lights.

Don't get me wrong, our new downtown St. Louis loft was nice, but it didn't feel like home. Despite the fact they were tinted on the outside, the floor-to-ceiling windows that made up an entire wall of my room left me feeling exposed. Debbie said the new location was only temporary, until we could find a house. The problem was her job as a talent agent and Dr. Wendell's constant (and annoying) presence kept her too busy to look.

After tossing my backpack next to the bed, I placed several incense cones on a ceramic plate on my desk and lit them, hoping the citrus smell of satsuma would calm me. But city life made that nearly impossible. As a trained warrior, I couldn't unwind—as much as I tried—surrounded by steel towers and mechanical noise. In other words, a place of dead energy.

So, yeah, the meditation wasn't going so well.

But I still had to try.

The entire school had been evacuated thanks to my handiwork in the chem lab. That meant I had four hours of uninterrupted meditation before I had to leave for training with Kim and the other samurai.

I unrolled my yoga mat and plopped down with my legs crossed. After putting my earbuds in, I picked up my iPhone and a pang of guilt washed over me as I scrolled through my playlists.

I knew I should call Kim and tell him about my incident, but I couldn't bring myself to pull up his number. It wasn't that I wanted to hide what happened. I just wasn't in the mood for a repeat of the conversation we'd had every day for the last three weeks. The *CliffsNotes* looked like this: I'd tell Kim about my latest ki-related accident and he'd get all broody and frowny-faced. Then I'd ask if he had any leads on the ninja. He'd say no and get even broodier and more frowny-faced. Then he'd launch into his Power-Point presentation on all the various ways I should be careful because there were ninja after me. Meanwhile, I'd smile and nod, but would actually be wondering if October was too late to keep highlighting my hair platinum or if it was time to darken it with the changing leaves to a honey color.

Yeah, I'd tell him later.

I found my meditation playlist and hit play. Instantly the sound of crashing waves filled my head and unraveled the coils of tension in my shoulders. I brought my palms together in prayer pose.

After several minutes of sucking in deep, even breaths, I closed my eyes and fell into the darkness behind them. Two lifetime's worth of memories waited for me. I don't know how long I pushed through the flashes of images, searching for the one I wanted, but it only felt like seconds until I found it.

And just like that, I was there. Seeing, through closed eyes, a memory so vivid I could almost smell the blossom-scented oil Etsu drizzled across my skin and feel the pointed blade nestled into the folds of my robe.

9

Japan, 1491

After Etsu had left her alone in her room, Akiko threw up twice and tried to mask the smell by burning incense. A cup of lukewarm tea bobbled in her shaking hands. A cup she promptly dumped in her lap when the sliding doors shoved open.

The samurai looked only a few years older than Akiko. This was good, she thought. Some girls had to service old men, a possibility that made her stomach lurch. But when the boy smiled, Akiko's relief vanished. His eyes held a predator's hunger that had nothing to do with desire.

The crack of the door sliding shut vibrated through Akiko's bones. With shaking hands, she tried to bury the tea-soaked silk of her robe beneath dry folds, lest the samurai find her clumsy and demand his money back. But as Akiko reached for the fallen teacup, a hand snatched her wrist and pulled her roughly to her feet.

"Forget the tea." The boy's voice held the edge of a threat. "Now is my time. You will concern yourself only with me." He encircled her body with his arms, leaving no room for escape, and ran his lips along her neck. Akiko gasped and instinctively pressed a hand against the samurai's chest, trying to wedge free from his grip. This only made him laugh and hold her tighter.

The other courtesans had told her that the first time, while painful, was usually fast. They told her not to be afraid because the men paid more for the privilege than the pleasure. But each passing second in the boy's arms felt like an eternity. Taking a breath, she closed her eyes and swallowed the acid burning the back of her tongue. Maybe if she could imagine herself somewhere, anywhere else, she could get through this. Akiko tried to conjure the fields where she gathered flowers with her younger sister and the market square she ran through with her best friend, Haruki. But the samurai's breath, hot and sour on her neck, broke her concentration. The faces of the people she loved vanished, leaving her alone in the dark.

This is an honor, Akiko reminded herself. *This is all part of being a highly respected and well-paid woman of pleasure. The benefits are worth the sacrifice.* But when a hand pulled at the corner of her robe, Akiko could no longer believe her own lie. It was then she realized she'd rather be a beggar on the streets than the recipient of this particular *honor.* She opened her eyes and twisted out of his arms. "Please," she whispered. "There has been a mistake. I-I cannot do this."

The boy smiled. "Oh, yes, you can." He reached for her

shoulder and pushed her to the ground. "And for the price I paid, more than once."

His words unwound something inside of her. Despite the fresh bruise from her fall and the pain coursing through her leg, Akiko could only feel the slow rise of anger as it burned through her veins. "You cannot do this if I do not allow it."

His laugh was quick and harsh. "I am a samurai. I can do anything I want." He leaned on top of her, pinning her to the floor, and slid his calloused fingers down the front of her robe.

Akiko shuddered, bile fresh on her tongue. "I will scream."

His breath came out faster. "It is your first time. I think they expect you to." His hand moved lower.

The sour smell of the sweat that beaded along his skin made Akiko dizzy. She sucked in air through her mouth as she fumbled a hand inside of her robe. She knew if she fought him she'd be cast out of her home, arrested, maybe even worse. But none of that mattered. She'd choose death a thousand times over rather than let the smelly, sweaty, foul-mouthed samurai have his way with her.

As his hand moved lower, almost to the curve of her breast, she found what she'd been searching for. There was no going back.

Before his fingers could grope her further, Akiko slid the curved dagger from its hiding place and pressed it against his cheek. He froze.

In a voice barely louder than a whisper, she said, "You *will* get off me."

He didn't move. "You cannot be serious." His eyes widened in disbelief. "If you go through with this, I will have your head for a trophy."

To prove how serious she was, Akiko dug the knife into his skin until he gasped and a thin line of blood trickled along the blade. "You will get off me," she repeated. "That was not a request."

Slowly, he removed his hands from her robe and backed away. His eyes burned with rage.

Akiko stood, keeping the knife in front of her. To her surprise, her grip on the weapon remained sure and unwavering. "You will leave me. Now."

His hands balled into fists that trembled at his sides. "You have no idea what you have just done." With blood trailing down his cheek in a steady stream, he spun on his heels, whipping his robes behind him, and left.

But he wasn't gone long.

An hour later he returned with two of the daimyo's guards to place Akiko under arrest for assaulting a samurai. There was only one punishment for such a crime.

Death.

10

I slid my sunglasses on so Quentin couldn't see my clenched-shut eyes. We were about to cross the Jefferson Barracks Bridge that would take us into Illinois, and I couldn't bear to watch. Being a samurai, the list of things that scared me was short, but Quentin's driving made the top.

A semi truck's engine grumbled, shaking the Mini Cooper as Quentin weaved into the next lane. A car honked to the right of me and I tightened my already white-knuckled grip on the seatbelt.

"Learn to drive!" Quentin yelled before swerving the car to the left.

I opened my eyes to find us narrowly missing the car in front of us. "Q!" My throat was so tight with fear I practically had to spit out his name. "I didn't live through a ninja attack only to have you kill me in a car accident."

He rolled his eyes and waved his hand dismissively. The Mini veered toward a tow truck until he brought his hand back to the wheel and steadied the car in its lane. "Please. I'm the only one on the road who knows *how* to drive. You should thank me for keeping you alive."

"You better hope you do, because if you kill me, I'm totally haunting your ass."

He laughed. "You know what your problem is, Ri-Ri?"

"My best friend is a reincarnated stunt-car driver?"

"No. You're too stressed out."

I settled back against my seat. "Understatement of the year."

"You should try meditating." Quentin flipped on his blinker a nanosecond before turning onto the off ramp. "It's been proven that people who meditate can actually move brain waves from the stress-housing right frontal cortex to the calmer left frontal cortex."

"Uh-huh." I was glad Quentin couldn't see me roll my eyes under the dark shades. "For your information, I tried meditating after school today. It just … didn't go so well." I thought about the memories I'd resurfaced and how they left me anything but relaxed. "Anyway, I can see you're enjoying your birthday present."

He nodded. "Yes, thank you."

For Quentin's birthday I'd renewed his subscription to *Psychology Today*. I supported his dream of becoming the world's next great psychologist. That was, when he wasn't trying to psychoanalyze me.

Quentin whipped the car around a corner at breakneck speed, forcing me to close my eyes. I didn't open them again until I heard gravel crunching under the tires, signaling our arrival at the Waterloo Community Park.

In the Midwest, we only have four months out of the year when the outdoors isn't covered in ice or hot enough to melt the mascara off my lashes. October is one of those months, so Kim decided we should take advantage of the cooler temperatures and train outside.

Quentin parked his Mini next to Kim's silver Trans Am and my pulse jumped into my throat, like it did every time he was near. It'd been that way between us since the moment we first laid eyes on each other in Lord Toyotomi's courtyard. Five hundred years later and my skin still tingled from the familiar pull that drew me to him like a wave to the shore.

I hesitated before unbuckling my seatbelt, noticing that Quentin had turned off the ignition but made no move to leave. Instead, his fingers thrummed nervously against his legs. "Um, are you okay?"

He nodded but didn't say anything. I followed his gaze to where Kim and the others were stretching under the shade of a large oak tree.

I placed my hand over his drumming fingers, which froze under my touch. "You don't have to be nervous, you know. It's not like this is your first time training with us. You're a total natural, and you're getting better all the time."

"Who said I was nervous about training?" he snapped. His head swiveled and his eyes met mine. "Maybe I was just scouting the scene for fire hazards." He pointed to his eyebrows. "Can't be too careful, after all."

I recoiled against the seat like I'd been slapped. It wasn't like I didn't deserve what he'd said to me—it was just that Quentin had never spoken to me like that before. His eyes remained fixed on me, with something so much more than anger burning through them. "Q, I..." But I couldn't think of the words that would make things better.

But just as quickly as he turned on me, his face softened. "Rileigh, oh my God, I didn't mean it." He pressed a hand to his temple. "I have this killer headache, and it's making me a little crazy. I swear, I don't know what got into me. Can you forgive me?"

My lungs tightened, refusing to move air. I thought I'd choke on my words before I forced them off my tongue. "Forgive *you*? After what I did?" I twisted toward the window so he wouldn't see how much trouble I had trying to breathe. If Q was angry with me, I could handle that—I could make it right. But if it was something worse? What if he was afraid of me? "Q, I promise you that I'm going to do whatever it takes to get this ki thing under control." And then, after a pause, I added, "We're cool, aren't we?"

"Totally." He gave me a strained smile and shrugged. "Why would you even ask?"

Oh, I don't know, I thought. *Because some invisible wedge has been driven between us. Because, even though we're sitting in the same car, I feel like you're miles away.* But with the words unwilling to fall from my tongue, all I could do was shrug.

"Dork." He reached over and ruffled my hair, a familiar gesture that made me feel a smidge better. He opened his mouth but before the words came out, someone tapped against my window.

Startled, I looked over my shoulder to find Kim smiling at me. Instantly a slow flame burned through me, starting at my toes and ending at my fingertips. You'd think that some of the intensity would wear off after time, but it never did. My breath still caught in my throat, my fingers still curled into fists to resist the urge to reach for him, and I had trouble blinking for fear of having him out of my sight for even a millisecond.

A seatbelt unclicked beside me. "See you on the field," Quentin said. "It looks like we're holding things up."

Way to go, Rileigh. I scrambled to release my own seatbelt. I couldn't afford to go all starry-eyed at the same moment I was trying to repair my friendship with Quentin. Besides, I knew Kim wouldn't mind if I spent less time with him and more time with Q. Kim and I were soul mates, after all.

Now that we were together, there was nothing that could come between us.

11

Quentin got out of the car without so much as a glance in my direction and made his way over to Drew, the oldest member of our group at twenty-one. Drew stood up from his runner's stretch and shrugged his braid over his shoulder. Even from the car I could see the frown form on his face. He said something to Quentin, who nodded and pointed to his missing eyebrows. Both guys turned and looked in my direction, their expressions unreadable from where they stood.

I sank deeper into the seat. Just when I thought I couldn't feel any worse.

Kim opened the door and the scent of sandalwood enveloped me like a familiar blanket. His mouth twitched, as if he were fighting off a frown. "What is this face you are wearing? I do not like it."

I stuck my tongue out at him. "Is this one better?"

The corners of his lips folded under into my favorite

upside-down smile. "Some would speculate that death would break a strong spirit."

I smiled back at him. "They obviously haven't met *me*."

"Obviously." He reached for my hand and pulled me out of the car into his arms. He leaned down and pressed his lips against mine, igniting a fire inside of me that threatened to burn me out of my body. When he pulled away, it took me several moments before I could remember how to be human—how to open my eyes, how to swallow, how to breathe. "How was school?" he asked.

If blood could simultaneously turn to ice and catch on fire, that's exactly what his breath, warm against my neck, did to me. "Oh, you know ... school's school."

"*Uh-huh.* Want to tell me what's wrong?"

I huffed and fell limp against him, pressing my lips against his T-shirt so that my words muffled into cotton. "Not really." The sooner I could start punching things the sooner I could ignore what felt like acid eating a hole in my stomach. "Can we just get on with training?"

"*Senshi.*"

Ribbons of silk unraveled beneath my skin. I leaned back and gave him my best *nice try—using my past-life name in a super sexy voice will not get me to swoon* look. At the same time I fought off the shivers licking the length of my spine. "*Yoshido,*" I answered in what I hoped was an equally sexy, breathy voice.

His lip twitched, as if he was having trouble keeping a straight face. "You had another episode today, didn't you?"

I turned away from him and pretended to study a hang-nail.

"*Rileigh.*" Kim sighed. "I just want to help. Why does everything with you have to be a fight?"

Did it? I hugged my arms to my chest. Even if he was right, what could he expect? I was a samurai. Fighting was what I was trained to do—it was all I knew *how* to do.

In the distance, Michelle and Braden competed at sit-ups. As Michelle lifted her torso from the ground, Braden leaned over and surprised her with a kiss. She laughed before shoving him away. A pang of jealously dug into my side. It boiled down to this: Michelle loved Braden, Braden loved Michelle, and she hadn't burned anybody's eyebrows off recently. Her life seemed uncomplicated, while mine had always been anything but.

A tingling along the back of my arm pulled me from my thoughts. I spun away from Kim's outstretched hand in time to see his fingers close on air. "Seriously?" I tsked. "That was just sad."

Despite shaking his head, he couldn't hide the humor in his eyes. "I wasn't trying to surprise you. I just wanted to get your attention."

"Well, you got it." I placed my hands on my hips and smirked. "Sure you can handle it?"

Something flashed through his eyes and I fought the urge to squirm underneath his gaze. I knew this look. It meant things were about to get interesting. I tossed back my shoulders, dipped my chin, and narrowed my eyes…right before I punched his face. Or at least I tried to, but he dropped into a crouch seconds before my swinging fist would have connected with his chin.

He laughed as he stood. "You'd really rather fight than talk about what happened?" Before I could answer, he settled his weight on his back foot and lashed out a front kick with his other.

The hair that stood out from my ponytail tickled my scalp as his foot brushed past. "Talking is overrated." I ducked low and swept my leg behind Kim's legs, knocking his feet out from under him.

Rather than land on his back, he lifted his arms over his shoulders, touched down on his hands, and used the momentum to swing back to his feet.

"Hey!" Michelle called from across the field. She ran toward us, stuffing her red curls inside a rubber band. "No fair starting without us!"

"Who's starting?" I asked. "Kim and I were just having a friendly discussion."

"*Riiiight,*" Braden said, jogging to Michelle's side. "Nothing says *How have you been?* like a punch in the face." He pushed a stray lock of auburn hair beneath a bandana.

"Which reminds me." I held my hands up in a fight stance and motioned him closer with my fingers. "I haven't had a chance to say hello to you yet, Braden."

"Funny." He rolled his eyes but didn't move.

"So how are we going to do this?" Michelle bounced from foot to foot. "Teams?"

"Great idea," Braden told her. "I'll be on a team with you and Rileigh. We should do shirts versus skins, and as an official representative for our team, I call dibs on skins." He whipped his shirt off and tossed it to the ground and flashed us an innocent look. "What are you waiting for?"

Both Michelle and I groaned.

"Wait for us!" Drew yelled from his spot in the shade. He and Quentin trotted over and took their positions on either side of Kim.

At Kim's signal we met in the middle in a whirlwind of fists and kicks. To an onlooker it might have looked like we were actually trying to kick each others' teeth in. In reality, each calculated move was softened in the event of impact. Each punch carried with it an opportunity to learn, each kick a chance to reinforce what was already known.

And that was why, despite refusing the past for so long, sparring with the other samurai was one of the few occasions my skin seemed to fit my body. Most of the time I felt trapped inside myself—buried beneath layers of blood, bone, and tissue. Suffocated. But when I fought, I could hear the thrum of my heartbeat, taste the sweetness of adrenaline, and feel the pulse of my blood as it buzzed through my muscles like a jolt of electricity. As someone who could remember the tight, hollow feeling of her dying breath, I craved my living moments like a starving girl sinking her teeth into an apple.

"I'm out!" Braden stumbled away from the group to a nearby tree, which he used to lower himself to the ground. He draped an arm over his face, his chest heaving sporadically. "Holy hell, I'm gonna be sore tomorrow."

Quentin flopped on the ground beside him. "I'm so with you."

Drew propped an arm against the tree and used the edge of his T-shirt to wipe the streams of sweat along his temples. "Me too."

Michelle hunched over with her hands braced on her knees. "Me three." There was a hint of a wheeze between her words. "How long have we been going at it? Twenty minutes? It feels like twenty hours."

I had no idea. I only knew that my body hummed in excited waves, a feeling I wanted to cling to for as long as I could before the exhaustion set in. "Go ahead, you guys. I'm not done with Kim yet."

Braden made annoying kissing noises while Michelle giggled.

"Fine with me," Kim said. He pulled his shirt over his head and threw it to the ground. Sweat glistened on the tight muscles of his chest. Standing under the orange glow of the setting sun, he looked like a golden statue brought to life.

"That's not fair." I struggled to swallow past the sudden dryness of my tongue. "That's distracting."

He flashed me a grin that ignited a fire low inside me. "That would be the point. Call it a tactical move."

Braden used the tree to pull himself up. "Well, boys and girls, I think it's time we moved along. This fight is about to lose its PG-13 rating."

Michelle nudged him in the side. "I think it's cute."

Something prickled on the back of my neck and I turned to find Quentin staring at me with a look somewhere between confusion and pain. As I tried to decipher its mean-ing, Kim used that moment to snatch my wrist and twist it behind my back. He pulled me in, pinning me against his chest, and lowered his head to place a kiss just below my ear.

"I may need to take notes." Braden pretended to open an invisible notebook. "So, what do you call this martial arts style, Kim? Kung fu-ling around? How about jujits-you-some?"

Michelle shook her head and tugged on his arm. "Leave them alone, Braden. You guys up for Sonic?"

"Sounds good." Quentin's face looked relaxed and normal. He pulled his bandana lower on his head to keep the bare skin that used to be his eyebrows from showing. "Wanna ride with me, Drew?"

"Sure," Drew answered.

Quentin smiled and waited for Drew to catch up. Had I just imagined his strange, angry look? I detected no trace of weirdness about him now as he and Drew walked to his car.

"Go on ahead," Kim said. "Rileigh and I will meet you there in a few."

Michelle waved. "See you there."

We stretched and shook our muscles as they climbed into their cars. After they pulled away, Kim turned to me. "You want to save yourself the trouble and just admit defeat now?"

I snorted and lashed out at him with a hook he ducked and an uppercut he dodged.

Kim spun back and kicked. I grabbed his foot, absorb-ing the shock by taking a step back. Before I could act further, he pushed off the ground and twisted his foot free from my grasp. After he landed, he brought his hands up into a defensive stance. "At the rate we're going, we could be here all night."

I lifted my arm and used the crook of my elbow to wipe the sweat off of my eyes. "I could think of a worse fate than spending all night alone with you."

He dropped his hands. His mouth opened but something froze the words on his tongue. It took him several tries before the word escaped his mouth. "Ninja!"

I choked on my heart, which sat thick and heavy on the back of my tongue. Spinning on my heels, I scanned the edges of the park. How could the ninja be here *now*? And more importantly, how could I not have sensed the danger? I studied the shadowed curtain that lay beyond the trees, waiting for something to move. "I don't see anything," I whispered.

Kim didn't answer. I glanced over my shoulder just in time to watch him sweep my legs out from underneath me. My arms swung wildly and I braced myself for impact with the hard earth. It never came. Instead, his arms wrapped around my waist and lowered me onto the grass.

Kim grinned as he climbed on top of me. "I can't believe you fell for the oldest trick in the book." Before I could react, he pinned my wrists to the ground. "Looks like I win."

Already the parts of my body he touched had begun to tingle like a hand held too close to a fire. How much closer until it burned? My voice, when it decided to work, came out a pitch too high. "You totally cheated! Are you really comfortable with that kind of victory?"

He shrugged. "I think I'll find a way to live with myself." He lowered his face, the touch of his lips like a brush of satin against my own. My heart sped up, struggling to cool the boiling blood that burned my fingers and pounded in my head. I closed my eyes. Even though I was drowning in fire, I wove my arms behind his back and pressed him closer. Sometimes I would wake in the middle of the night convinced this was all a dream. That my Yoshido was nothing more than dust in a 500-year-old grave. I pulled him tighter, pressing my fingers into his skin to assure myself that the arms I clung to wouldn't dissolve when I opened my eyes.

Kim pulled away and stared at me. The sinking sun reflected golden flecks within his brown eyes. He sucked in a breath and turned away.

"Kim?"

He didn't immediately look at me but when he did, a thousand emotions passed through his eyes at a speed too fast for me to grab on to a single one. "I just wish I had a lead on the ninja. Every day I think about that night in the alley. I thought . . . " He swallowed and tried again. "I thought I'd lost you . . . again. It was the closest I'd ever stood to hell."

"Kim, I'm so sorry, I—"

"No," he said, cutting me off. The breeze blew a stray lock of hair into my eyes and Kim brushed it away. "I just want you to know that I haven't given up. I believe the ones who attacked you are hiding. But I will find them and I will make them pay. I won't . . . I won't lose you."

"You won't," I promised. "I'm not going anywhere."

He kissed me again, rolling us over so that I was on top of him with his arms locked tightly around my waist. His fingers lifted the edge of my T-shirt, searing my skin as they drew circles on my back, traced ribbons along my ribs, inching higher and higher until...

The theme music from the movie *Psycho* blared from his pocket.

Kim cursed under his breath as he gently lifted me off of him and dug for his phone. He didn't have to say who was calling him; I'd set her personal ringtone myself—Sumi.

Kim answered and before he could even say hello, Sumi's shrill voice blared through the speaker.

How did she do it? How did she always call at the perfect moment to spoil our time together? A dull ache throbbed in my jaw, alerting me that I'd been clenching my teeth. My fingers curled into fists. Sumi was a student of Kim's that he allowed to manage the front desk of the dojo in exchange for martial arts training. But I knew it wasn't martial arts she was interested in. She'd made it clear to me that she wanted Kim for herself and wasn't about to let me get in her way.

Kim's lips stretched into a tight line. "Sumi, calm down. I don't understand. What's the emergency?"

Of course. I rolled onto my back with a groan. It was always an emergency with Sumi. I wondered what it would be this time. Were they out of stamps? Maybe there was a spider on the ceiling? Perhaps the faucet was leaking? She would use any excuse to get Kim back to the dojo and away from me.

Kim nodded to a question I couldn't hear and sighed.

"Alright. Try to stay calm. I'll be there in a minute." He hung up and flashed me an apologetic look. Before he opened his mouth, I held my hand up to stop him.

"Save it. It's not your fault. Just go and make sure everything is okay."

"Thank you." He kissed my cheek. "I'll drop you off at Sonic so you can get a ride home." He stood and, after brushing the grass from his pants, offered me a hand up. "I was wondering ... can I swing by your place later? I know you have school tomorrow and I won't keep you up late. But between Network missions, training, and now the ninja hunt, we haven't spent much time alone and ... I hate being apart from you."

A hundred dragonflies somersaulted inside of me. I smiled. "Sure. Just don't make me wait too long."

He shook his head and tilted my chin up for another kiss. "I waited a lifetime to be with you. I don't plan to waste a second."

12

Quentin, Michelle, Braden, and Drew sat around a picnic table outside the restaurant. Kim didn't bother parking, only waved to the others as I climbed out of his car and drove off seconds after I'd shut the door.

"Where's he going?" Quentin asked, handing me a half-melted Hey Batter Batter Blast.

"Sumi called." I shoveled a spoonful of ice cream into my mouth and chewed angrily. "Another *dojo emergency*."

Michelle rolled her eyes. "That girl doesn't give up, does she?"

"Nope." No longer hungry, I stirred my shake into a soupy mess.

"Relax, Rileigh." Braden dug his fingers into my neck in what I guessed was supposed to be a massage but felt more like pressure-point combat. "Nothing will ever break you and Kim up. You guys are soul mates."

"I know." My eyelids fluttered as I fought the urge to

wince as his fingers continued to pinch the tendons along my neck. "I just wish that Kim and I could have a normal relationship—without all these obstacles in the way."

"It'll be fine," Michelle said. "You'll see."

But it wouldn't be fine. Nothing would ever be fine again until Braden let go of my shoulders. Mercifully, his talonlike fingers released me before he separated my head from my neck. "Wow. You were tense. But you should be good now. I give the best massages. Michelle doesn't need her neck worked on for a month after I give her one."

"Is that so?" I rubbed my screaming muscles and eyed Michelle. She refused to meet my gaze and, instead, studied a black patch of flattened gum on the concrete. I stood and threw my cup away. "Well, you better keep those magic fingers warmed up, Braden. Michelle told me earlier that her neck was bothering her."

Braden cracked in his knuckles. "Will do."

Michelle shot me a fiery look and mouthed the words, *Why do you hate me?*

I stifled a laugh and turned to face Quentin. "Q, it looks like I'm going to need a ride home after all."

"Oh." His eyes widened and darted to Drew and back to me. "Um, I already told Drew I'd give him a ride home because I thought you'd be with Kim. I'd take you but the backseat of my car is loaded with crap and—"

Braden spoke up. "We'll give you a ride."

"Sure," Michelle said. "Downtown isn't that far from South County."

Quentin looked relieved. "Problem solved." He slung

an arm around my neck and squeezed me against him. "I'll see you tomorrow, then?"

Since when was I a problem? "Yeah, okay…"

He started to walk away.

But it wasn't okay. The growing number of knots in my stomach pulled tighter with each step he took toward his car. "Wait! Q!"

He stopped and looked at me.

I couldn't just sit by and let our friendship disintegrate. If I had to apologize to him every minute of every day to make things right between us, then that was exactly what I was going to do. "I know I've already told you, like, a hundred times, but I'm so, *so* sorry about what happened today." I pointed to my eyebrows. "I'm working on it. I swear I'll get it under control."

"I know." He opened his mouth to say more but winced and pinched the bridge of his nose. "God, this headache is something." He offered a weak smile. "I'll see you at school tomorrow."

I nodded and watched him go with one less knot in my stomach. His headache—of course! That's what the weird look and attitude was all about. It made perfect sense. But still, I couldn't ignore the feeling that there was something else going on, festering unseen, like a botfly burrowed into flesh.

Michelle tugged on my elbow. "You okay?"

I turned around and saw Braden already sitting in her car. "Oh, sorry. It's just been a stressful day, you know?"

Michelle gave me a sympathetic smile. "I know I'm not

as close to you as Quentin and Kim, but I just wanted you to know that I'm your friend, too, Rileigh. So if you need anything … " She shrugged and stared at her feet. "I just want you to know I'm here for you."

That was unexpected. For a moment all I could do was blink at her. It hadn't occurred to me that she'd been trying so hard to be my friend. The shame of not noticing washed over me in a hot wave. "Cut it out, Michelle." I gave her a playful bump with my hip. "If you make me cry they'll revoke my samurai club membership."

She grinned and bumped me back. "If they do, we'll kick their ass."

"Or worse—have Braden give them a neck massage."

Laughing, we climbed into her car and, for the first time in months, I actually felt like a normal teenager. We sang along with Michelle's iPod, took pictures of each other with our phones, and laughed until we approached my building.

Then the laughter died on my tongue.

He was standing across the street, half-bathed in the shadows cast by the streetlights. Waiting.

"Stop!" I screamed.

Michelle slammed on the brakes as I fumbled with my seatbelt. She called out to me as I pushed out the door but I ignored her. I had to get to him. Had to prove that he wasn't a figment of my imagination.

But no sooner had I stepped out onto the street than a horn blared, freezing me in place. I had only an instant to come to my senses and throw myself back on the sidewalk before a Metrobus would have mowed me down. I turned my head away from the bus and braced against the back-draft that whipped my hair into my face. When it passed, I scrambled to my feet and readied myself to weave across the busy intersection. But as I looked for a gap in the coming traffic, my eyes went back to the place where the guy had stood doing who-knows-what. Watching? Waiting? I guessed it didn't matter.

Because he was no longer there.

I leaned against a street sign for support and a chance to steady my breathing.

Whitley was gone—if he'd even been there at all.

13

The doorman, a kindly looking man with fluffy white hair, pushed open the heavy glass door and ushered me inside with a smile. He said something. I watched his lips move, but I couldn't hear the words over the pounding of my heart.

I smiled and nodded, hoping that was an appropriate response, and kept walking. What was wrong with me? Was I going crazy? It was the second time I'd seen Whitley —or a guy that looked a lot like him—within a month. I didn't know what to make of that. I didn't believe in coincidences, but I didn't believe in ghosts, either.

The frigid temperature in the lobby—or the mausoleum, as I liked to call it—was cold enough to sting. I hugged my arms across my body to ward off chills as I raced across the polished granite floor to the elevators. My temples throbbed as a stress headache built behind my eyes. *Awesome.* The perfect ending for the day from hell.

One of the elevators opened with a ding and I darted

inside. After the doors closed, I pushed the twelfth-floor button and waited. As the elevator ascended, I stared at the reflection of myself distorted by the steel doors. The girl that stared back was thinner than me, pale, with black eyes and bones that twisted in inhuman waves. As I studied the ghostly version of myself, I couldn't help but think about how close I'd come to actual death. It had only been four months since Whitley—the reincarnated version of my samurai nemesis Zeami—had nearly succeeded in killing me. In turn, I'd left him pinned to my wall with his own shuriken as the house burned down around him. If he wasn't dead—and that was a long shot—I could only imagine how pissed off he would be.

This time my shivers were not from the cold.

I folded my arms across my chest and watched the floor numbers change on the digital screen. As soon as an eleven appeared on the digital screen above the buttons, the elevator shuddered and I reached out to grasp the handrail to keep from falling to the floor.

"Of course," I muttered. The stupid elevators were always breaking down. And today I was lucky enough to be inside of one when it happened. At least I was only a floor away from home.

The elevator continued to rise, jerking its way up at half its normal speed. When the digital twelve flashed on the screen, I thought my trip was over. The door chime dinged my arrival, but, after waiting several moments, I realized the door wasn't opening.

"Seriously?" I hit the door with my hand and immediately regretted the action when something squealed over-head. I crouched down just as the lights flickered once and then left me alone in the dark.

"What the—?" But I didn't have time to finish. The elevator shrieked—a horrible sound that pierced my eardrums like a knife. It dropped a foot before jerking to a stop. My hands fumbled in the dark until they found the metal hand-rail. Something above me—either the cable or the brakes—groaned and I tightened my grip on the rail right before the elevator shuddered and fell several feet.

"Son of hibachi!" Alone in the dark, I could almost hear the rush of blood pounding beneath my temples. What the hell was going on?

As if reading my mind, the digital twelve disappeared from the screen, followed by the scrolling words, *Hello Rileigh. How does it feel to know you're about to die?*

I sucked in a breath as a chill descended my spine on spindly insect legs. No matter how hard I tried or how many times I blinked, my brain refused to decipher the words on the screen. It was too crazy to make sense. Obviously elevators didn't try to kill people all on their own. Someone had to be controlling it, someone who wanted me dead.

The answer slammed into me with enough force to sway my body. Whitley! He had to be the one behind this. Somehow he had escaped the fire and now he was back for revenge. It made sense. Why else did the ninja only attack me? He had a score to settle. I whirled around in the dark, as if he might appear next to me. But of course he didn't.

Which—*duh, Rileigh*—made sense because I was about to plummet to my death.

The floor lurched under my feet and the elevator began to ascend much faster than normal. I struggled to swallow past the lump wedged inside my throat. I *so* did not have a good feeling about this.

The screen flashed as more words scrolled across. *They don't make elevators like they used to,* the scrolled words told me. *You can't just cut a few cables and expect them to fall to the ground. They have built-in brakes that prevent that from happening. But many modern elevators have computers. Like this one. And computers can be hacked.*

Fan-freaking-tastic. The cables whirled as the elevator rose faster than should have been possible. I couldn't even be sure what floors I'd passed, only that I'd heard more than a dozen dings. I had to do something quick—but what? I could barely operate the cable remote let alone figure out how to deprogram a hacked elevator.

My heart thrummed inside my head, the sound spilling out of my ears and echoing off the walls. My eyes gradually adjusted to the red glow projected from the digital numbers. But it wasn't an improvement. All it did was make me aware of how tight a space I was trapped in, and the last thing I wanted was to die inside this metal coffin.

The elevator squealed and began to slow. I had a feeling I was nearing the twenty-fifth floor and after that—well, I didn't know but it couldn't be good.

I felt my way to the corner of the elevator and used the two walls as leverage to get a leg up on the handrail. Carefully,

I stood on the rail, one foot balanced against either corner and felt my way along the ceiling like I'd seen done in so many movies. There had to be a trap door of some sort.

Fingering the smooth metal ceiling, my fingers grazed the lip of a door. Success! I pushed against the trap door. It didn't budge. "Perfect," I muttered.

The elevator dinged and came to a halt. I pounded against the door. That's when the edge of my palm came in contact with something sharp.

Hissing in pain, I jerked my hand back for just a second before reaching out and brushing the edge of the door with my fingertips. What I found was a jagged piece of metal at the corner of the door. Balancing on my toes, I stretched my arm farther and discovered a similar piece of metal in the other corner. My stomach fell into my knees. Bolts. The door was bolted shut.

The digital screen flashed with new words. *Going down?* Oh. Crap.

I froze, still balanced on my toes with my fingers on the ceiling. There was no way out. A wave of nausea rolled over me. Now what?

The elevator screeched as its brakes released their hold on the cable. The sudden descent sent me crashing to the floor. A shock of pain bolted up my leg from where I'd landed on my knee. But that didn't matter. Nothing did except for the fact that I was free-falling to the ground and, judging from my speed, nothing would be left of me when I crashed to the bottom.

My heart leapt inside my throat, threatening to choke

me with each pulsing beat. But breathing was the last of my worries. I needed to focus. I tried to stand but found I couldn't balance at the breakneck speed I was traveling. Instead, I crawled my way along the floor.

Finally, I reached the handrail.

Ding after ding sounded as I dropped down the shaft. Only seconds remained before I reached the bottom.

The weight of gravity pulled at me like invisible chains as I hoisted myself to my feet. More dinging. More floors. Time was running out.

"Son of hibachi!" I spit the words from my mouth. What do I do? What *could* I do? The trap door was bolted shut and I had no idea how to rewire an elevator. Hell, I barely knew how to reboot my laptop after it froze. I chewed on my lip as I stared at the elevator buttons. And that's when the first whisper of an idea drifted into my mind. There was *one* thing I knew how to do.

The elevator picked up more speed, whining and shaking so much that I wondered if it might fall apart before we even hit the bottom. I gripped the handrail so hard that the metal edge bit into my palm. I didn't care. I had one shot at this and I couldn't screw it up.

A scream that had been building in the back of my throat spilled from my lips. I lifted one leg in the air and brought my foot down as hard as I could into the control panel.

The plastic buttons cracked under my heel, spilling their multi-colored wired guts. I reared back and struck again, this time ripping into the wires as I brought my heel back down.

The elevator shuddered, the lights flickering on once before going back out.

My plan had failed. I was going to die.

And so I closed my eyes and waited for the crash that would be the end of me.

Seconds passed.

But the crash never came.

Instead, the floor jerked, bringing me to my knees. The shriek of the brakes grinding against the cables squealed so loudly I wondered if the sound might pierce right through my skull. But it wasn't until the elevator came to a grinding halt and the scream continued on that I realized it was coming from me.

My knees lost their ability to support my weight and I slid to the floor, panting. The digital screen above the buttons flashed a red *ERROR*.

"I'm not dead," I whispered to myself. My voice trembled but I didn't care. I just needed to hear the words out loud, to confirm I was still alive.

I heard a commotion outside the doors and jumped to my feet, bringing my shaking fists in front of me. Whatever was going on, it wasn't over yet.

A sliver of light appeared before me in the dark, widening with a groan. I was forced to squint until my blurred vision regained focus.

"Young lady? Are you okay?"

I blinked several times to make sense of what I saw. The

white-haired doorman stood wide-eyed in front of me. He offered me a hand but kept his feet planted in the hall. "I could hear the screaming clear outside."

I wasn't sure if he was talking about me or the cables. With shaky steps, I moved forward and took his offered hand. He pulled me from the elevator. Once I set foot on solid ground, my knees wobbled so violently that I collapsed against his chest. His cologne was spicy and warm, something only a grandpa would wear.

He patted my back awkwardly. "Do you want me to call an ambulance?"

"No. I'm okay." I pushed off of him to see if I could support my weight. I teetered to the side before righting myself. "Just … maybe call someone about that elevator? It's a death-trap waiting to happen."

He nodded and let his hand slide from my shoulder. "I'll call right now." He hesitated. "Are you sure you're okay?"

Before I could answer, the shrieking cry of metal against metal pierced my ears. We both turned back to the elevator in time to see it drop from view, leaving only a dark empty shaft. The crash that followed shook the ground beneath our feet.

"Sweet Jesus!" the doorman yelled. He grabbed my arm and scrambled backward, dragging me with him. "I don't understand. How—"

"Bad cables?" I offered, even though I knew it was anything but.

He shook his head. "That's impossible. The elevators were just inspected today. They all passed."

I jerked my head away from the empty shaft. "Today?" I thought about the Whitley look-alike I'd seen only ten minutes ago. "Was the inspector young? Did he have long blond hair?"

The doorman scratched his chin. "No. There were three of them. Here before lunchtime. Two guys and a gal—all of them with dark hair. They were fairly young. But thorough—spent a lot of time poking around."

"Uh-huh." So, not Whitley. But they possibly fit the description of the ninja from the alley attack. Which got me thinking, if the ninja kept popping up every time I had a Whitley sighting, that couldn't be a coincidence, right? But was I ready to believe that Whitley was alive and working with the ninja? I just wasn't convinced ... I'd left Whitley pinned and burning. How could he have gotten away? "Just to play it safe, I think you should call the inspectors back. *Different* inspectors. And it's probably best to keep everyone off the elevators until they get the all clear."

"Yes. That's probably for the best." He paused, his brow wrinkled into lines of confusion. "Do you think the inspectors had something to do with this?"

I answered him as truthfully as I could. "I'm sure they were just doing their job."

14

od, I hate ninja.

GI opened the stairwell door and stumbled into the hall-way. There was nothing like climbing twelve flights of steps after a near-death experience to put a little wobble in your step. I crossed the hall and leaned against my condo door for a moment to catch my breath. Between the fireball at school, Kim ditching me, and the elevator attack, this day had to be a top contender for worst day *ever*. At least I was alive. That, coupled with the fact I would never ride another elevator for as long as I lived, thus giving myself great thighs, was all that mattered.

See? I could find the silver lining.

But as soon as I opened my condo door and caught sight of who waited for me, I wondered if this really was an improvement from the hijacked elevator.

"Rileigh!" Dr. Wendell smiled at me from the couch with his arm around Debbie. A reality cooking show played on the flat screen across from them. "Just the girl I wanted to see."

"That's funny." I marched past him without a glance. "You're just the guy I wanted to avoid."

Debbie made a choking noise behind me. "Rileigh Hope Martin! That is no way to speak to an adult."

I wanted to argue whether someone who looked and dressed like the lead singer of a boy band could *actually* be considered an adult—but I decided not to press my luck.

"It's all right, Deb," Dr. Wendell said. "It's normal for teens to act out when their parent brings someone new into their lives." He raised his voice so that it followed me as I trudged down the hall to my room. "Children thrive on consistency. Everything will work out, especially when Rileigh realizes I'm here to *stay*."

I caught myself before I could say something snarky back. I didn't have time for this—I had ninja to find. Not to mention I needed to search my room for signs of a ninja break-in. But even as I rooted through my drawers, I started counting under my breath, "One … Two … Three … Four … Five … "

There was a knock at my door.

Groaning, I shoved a wad of mismatched socks back into my drawer and slammed my dresser shut. "You're off your game tonight," I said as Dr. Wendell stepped inside my room and closed the door behind him. "I counted all the way to five before you knocked."

He shrugged. "Everyone has an off day."

A cold, slippery feeling rolled beneath my skin, a

warning of the ki growing inside of me. I tilted the hinged mirror on my dresser and grasped along the underside until I located the sheath duct-taped to the back. I grabbed the hilt and withdrew my katana, not because I felt I was in danger or even because I liked the way Dr. Wendell's eyes bulged when I held it. But whenever my fingers curled around the hilt, I could hear the beginning measures of a song that could only be played on instruments of steel and blood. A dark melody that, so far, was the only thing that could keep my ki in line. Unfortunately, at a school that banned students from taking nail files to class, katanas weren't exactly considered a fashion accessory.

The second the sword was in my grip, the prickly feeling recoiled, like a waterfall in reverse. I took a moment to polish the sapphire embedded in the hilt with the edge of my T-shirt before I opened my closet and sorted through the clothes hanging inside with my free hand. "How long is the recruitment pitch going to last this time? I have work to do."

His gaze never left the sword grasped in my hand. "Who says I'm here to recruit? Maybe I just want to talk about our relationship. Specifically your dislike of me." His voice was a pitch higher than normal. "I'm dating your mother. I hope you'll eventually understand I'm going to be a constant presence in your life."

"But are you *really* dating my mother?" I closed my closet door and turned to him, swinging the katana in front of me in slow arcs. "Do you honestly have feelings for her? Or is dating her just some lame attempt to keep harassing me until I give in?"

"Why?" He swallowed, his Adam's apple trembling in his throat. "Is it working?"

I laughed and took a step forward, noting with pleasure that Dr. Wendell retreated from my path until his back pressed against the door. "Let me tell you something, *Jason*. For reasons I don't understand, my mom really likes you. Trust me when I say you do not want to hurt her." A bead of sweat trickled down his temple as I continued swinging the sword between us with enough force to sway the dark, curly hair framing his face. "I have had a bad day. *A really bad day*. But still, it'll be bunnies and rainbows compared to what would happen if you hurt my mom. You don't want that to happen, do you?"

"No." His hand searched the door until he found the knob. "I heard about today. When you got upset and set off a fireball in your chemistry class."

It was my turn to take a step back. "Wait. How did you hear about that?"

Looking a little more confident, Dr. Wendell's hand fell from the knob. "Look, Rileigh, contrary to what you think, I really do care about you. I want to help you … before someone gets hurt."

I folded my arms, the blade of my katana resting against my side. "You didn't answer my question."

Dr. Wendell sighed and pinched the bridge of his nose. "I know what goes on with you because it's my business to know."

Anger warmed the pit of my stomach and fueled the rise of ki within me. My skin tingled as a buzzing sensation stretched and pulled beneath the surface. I gripped the sword tight enough that each ridge of the eel-skin-wrapped handle dug an impression into my palm. The buzzing died down but it still took me a moment before I could answer him, spitting the words through clenched teeth. "You mean it's your business to spy on me!"

His hand fell to his side. "You're not even giving me a chance! The Network only wants to help."

"Yeah? Well, you guys are doing a great job. Did you know that I just went on a death ride in a hijacked elevator?"

His jaw fell and it took him several tries before he was able to speak. "What?" His fingers fumbled inside his shirt pocket for his phone. "This needs to be reported!"

"Forget it." I held a hand up to stop him. "Kim and I will take care of it. You can help by leaving me alone."

"Rileigh, I..." he looked back and forth between me and his phone. "I have to make this call. We need to make sure the building is secure and"—he looked around the room—"that the condo hasn't been compromised."

I rolled my eyes. "I'm already on it. Besides, my spider-sense hasn't gone off so that's a pretty good sign there's no ninja hiding under my bed. And Kim will be over in a couple of hours." I patted his arm condescendingly. "Why don't you just sit back and let the professionals handle it. Mmm'kay?"

Dr. Wendell's face puckered. "I'm not the bad guy here."

"Whatever." I waved him away with the flick of my wrist. He left shaking his head. I kicked the door closed behind him. It was almost funny that he thought I needed his help (which I obviously didn't). I had Kim. Not to mention a life-time of samurai experience. I knew his offer of help was just another sad attempt to lure me into joining the Network.

Please.

I dropped my sword on the mattress and kicked my skateboard into my hand. Clutching the battered wooden board against my chest, I inhaled its scent of dirt and asphalt. Just like my sword, the skateboard was a part of who I was—a part I would have to give up if I joined the Net-work. Oh sure, Dr. Wendell had tried to sugarcoat the facts by telling me that the Network would only require a moder-ate amount of my time. *Yeah, right.* I saw what they did to Kim—between running the dojo and the various "missions" he was assigned, he barely had enough time to spend with me. I didn't want that. I had school, training, friends, a *life.*

It wasn't fair. I didn't ask to be a samurai (*at least not in this life)* and I definitely didn't ask for the ability to manipu-late ki. All I wanted to worry about was passing trig, not setting my friends on fire and staying alive until graduation.

I couldn't, *wouldn't,* pledge away a life I'd barely begun to live.

15

The acrid stench of burning hair stung my nostrils. I wanted to run but a wall of flames surrounded me, trapping me inside a cage of fire. The heat pressed against my skin like a thousand angry needles. I whimpered. The tears burned from my eyes before they could fall.

"You're pathetic."

I looked up to find Whitley staring at me from where he stood, pinned against a wall of black by the razor points of his own shuriken. Gone was the wide-eyed crazed expression he wore the night he tried to kill me. This time he looked... disappointed.

And then I knew, despite the heat that pressed closer to me still, blistering my skin. "I'm dreaming."

"Are you?" The shuriken dissolved into the wall and Whitley stepped forward until he stood just beyond the flames.

For a dream, the pain was amazingly real. The smoke twisted inside my lungs, choking me. I coughed and crouched low to the floor. "Yes. Because you're dead ... aren't you?"

Whitley folded his arms. "If I am dead, I sure look a helluva lot better than you." He ran his fingers through his shoulder-length blond hair, as if to illustrate his point.

And he was right. The flames did nothing to him as he stood just outside their grasp. Meanwhile, the blisters on my arms blackened and slowly ate their way along my skin. I screamed. "Help me!"

He gave me a *you should really know better* expression. "Can't."

"Can't?" I coughed. "*Won't* is more like it." My heart beat against my ribs so hard I thought they would crack. The fire cooked the skin on my arms, turning them black. The skin crumbled away to reveal the bone underneath. I bit down on my tongue to stop another scream. Blood, hot enough to burn, trickled down my throat.

"Can't," he repeated. The amusement fell from his face. "But you are going to need help. You won't be able to put this fire out alone."

"But who?" The charred skin of my chest collapsed, exposing a blackened heart beating underneath. "I'm ... dying ... " It was the last word I was able to mutter before my shriveled tongue fell from my mouth.

Whitley rolled his eyes. "Come on, now. You're not going to play the stereotypical dumb-blonde card, are you? Think, Rileigh. The answer is pretty obvious."

If it was so obvious, why didn't he just tell me? But I didn't have a chance to ask. The flames were on top of me now. Pulling me apart piece by piece and leaving only black ash behind. I wanted to scream but my shriveled lungs only rattled around inside the hollow cave of my chest.

Whitley's laugh was the last thing I heard before the world went dark.

———

I shot up off the couch with a gasp. It took me a few seconds of running my hands along my body to determine I'd been dreaming. But that didn't explain the white fuzz raining down around me. I picked up a clump of the soft white cotton off my lap and ran it through my fingers—stuffing. I looked around and discovered the tattered remains of a throw pillow scattered around the room like confetti. Great. As if losing control of my ki when I was awake wasn't bad enough, now I was losing control in my sleep.

"That was … um … quite impressive." Dr. Wendell stared at me wide-eyed from his perch at the kitchen bar. He clutched a cup of coffee between his hands. "Do you always greet the new day by exploding something?"

I buried my surprise at seeing him behind a mask of indifference. "Why? Wanna volunteer?"

He shook his head and went back to reading the news on his iPad. I bent over and began picking up the cotton when his words, echoing through my mind, hit home. *Greet the new day.* I let go of the stuffing and whirled around. Sure enough, the first edge of sunlight peeked around the building across the street, its rays purpling the darkness in the condo. "Wait a minute. If it's morning, why are you here?"

I looked at him and that's when I noticed his flannel pants and slippers. "Oh, gross!" I shouted before he could answer. "You know what? I don't want to know. Where's my mom?"

He hid a grin behind his coffee mug. "Debbie had an early meeting. You wouldn't have even known I was here if you hadn't slept on the couch. Besides, it wasn't like I could leave you unguarded—especially after learning you'd been attacked in the building."

"Are you trying to make me puke?" My stomach convulsed and I was glad it was empty. I picked up the remaining stuffing. "And I don't need guarding. I can fight my own battles, thank you."

"If you're so confident, then why sleep on the couch?"

A strangled sound escaped my throat. "I'm not afraid of sleeping in my room if that's what you're implying."

He shrugged.

"*Please.* The only reason I was on the couch is because I fell asleep waiting for Kim who, thanks to the ever-annoying *Network,* had to stand me up for some dumb mission when there's an actual crisis going on right here."

"A mission?" Dr. Wendell put down his coffee, all traces of amusement gone from his face. "Kim told you he had an assignment?"

"Well, he didn't get a chance to. I fell asleep, remember? Jeez, I thought doctors were supposed to be smart." I dumped the batting in the trash can and brushed my hands along my sweatpants. Kim standing me up was nothing new; the Network often ruined our date nights with their last-minute missions. I couldn't be mad at him. It wasn't like they gave him a choice. Besides, he always left a message when he had to cancel. I probably had one waiting for me now.

"Um, Rileigh ... "

I reached into the cabinet and pulled down a coffee mug. "Yeah?"

"Kim wasn't assigned a mission last night."

"Of course he was. Otherwise he would have been here." After filling my mug, I searched the refrigerator for my vanilla-caramel creamer. "Apparently, Dr. Wendell, you're not as important as you think you are. You're obviously out of the information loop."

His sigh was impatient. "I can assure you that's not the case. Need I remind you that I'm your *assigned* handler?"

My teeth pressed together so hard my jaw ached. I hated the word "handler." It made me feel like a show poodle. "So?"

"Well, since you and Kim are so close, part of my job involves staying abreast of his missions."

"Ew. Can you please stop saying skeezy things this early in the morning?"

"*Abreast* is not a *skeezy* word—whatever *that* means. Abreast translates to 'well-informed.'"

"Don't care. It sounds gross."

He sighed and pressed a finger against the bridge of his nose. "I need a raise."

"Or better yet, a new job." I took a sip of coffee. "The stress isn't good for you. You should quit. Immediately."

He glared at me and I fought the urge to smile. "Rileigh, you're missing the point entirely. I know for a fact that Kim was not on assignment last night because it's my job to keep track of him so I can better keep track of you."

I slammed my mug down on the counter, ignoring the burning liquid as it sloshed over the side and onto my hand. "Okay, first of all, stop stalking me because it's not sexy when an old guy does it—it's creepy and gross. Second, I think I know Kim better than you. The only thing that would keep him from me is a mission assigned by your dumb Network. I bet if I go get my cell phone, there'll be a message from him telling me just that."

He folded his arms. "I guess there's only one way to find out."

"I guess so." Stupid Dr. Wendell. How could he think for even a second that he knew Kim better than I did? I left my half-empty mug on the counter and went to my room where my phone sat on my desk. I pulled it free from the charger, pressed the green button, and stared at the surprise waiting for me on the screen:

Voice Message Inbox: 0

Okaaaay. There had to be an explanation. Maybe he emailed? I clicked another button and connected to my email account. Two messages waited, one announcing a sale at my favorite skate shop and another telling me I'd won the Bazillion lottery and could collect my earnings as soon as I sent them my checking account number. *Sure.* Because I really needed to add identity theft to my growing list of problems.

I sank onto the bed as knots of worry wove across my chest and bound my lungs in a too-tight embrace. Had something happened to him? I hit the first number on my speed dial. Kim's voicemail clicked on without a ring.

Why wasn't his phone turned on? I sighed right as the

automated message ended. "Kim, it's me. You didn't show up last night and you didn't leave a message. Something happened to me when I got to the condo and … well, I'll tell you about it when you call. I'm starting to get a little worried. Obviously, I have school, but could you just shoot me a text so I know you're okay?" I hung up feeling like my stomach had fallen from my body through all twelve floors of the building, then proceeded to be run over by the cars below. Something was wrong. I felt it with every nerve in my body.

"Rileigh?" Dr. Wendell stood outside my open door.

I slumped deeper into the bed. "I don't want to hear your *I told you so* speech right now. Okay?"

"I wasn't going to." He took a tentative step inside my room. To my surprise, his usual *I know everything* expression was gone, replaced with a look of genuine concern. "I just wanted to make sure everything is all right." When I didn't answer, he prodded, "Is it?"

"I … I don't know." This was a first for me. When it came to Kim I knew everything … or at least I thought I did. He wouldn't just stand me up. I felt the wrongness of it creeping over my body. "He didn't leave a message and his phone's not turned on. Something doesn't feel … right. I was attacked last night. Maybe he was too."

Dr. Wendell moved closer. "Are you having a danger premonition?"

"No." The tightening of my muscles and tingling inside my head that alerted me to danger weren't there. This was something else, something sour that flowed through my blood like a spreading infection. "I don't think he's in danger … but … I have a bad feeling."

He nodded. "That's good enough for me. Will you let me help?"

Another surprise. I had to admit, as much as I detested the man, the fact that he trusted me without question earned him extra points. "Maybe you … could check on Kim for me?" If he wasn't wearing pajama bottoms—reminding me of where he slept last night—I might have felt the teensiest bit bad for my behavior toward him.

"Absolutely." He placed a hand on my shoulder and, for once, I didn't shrug it off. "Even though I know you don't believe it, I'm here to help you, Rileigh. I'm on your side. If you're worried about Kim I'll check into it. Even if I have to drive to Waterloo to do it."

I stood there, staring at him. Maybe, just maybe, Dr. Wendell wasn't as bad as I thought he was. "Thanks."

He smiled and released my shoulder. "Like I said, I'm on your side. Now, I don't want you to worry about it anymore. Get to school and I'll handle everything."

It sounded like a good plan, but I couldn't shake the nagging feeling in my gut. The certainty that something wasn't right. "What if you find Kim and he's in trouble? Will you call me?"

"I promise." He held his hand up like he was swearing in before a judge. "But you don't need to worry. Kim is a skilled fighter. I can't think of single situation that he can't handle himself in."

I nodded. "You're right." Only he wasn't. I could remember all too well one particular situation Kim hadn't been able to fight his way out of—and his failure had cost him his life.

16

Japan, 1491

The samurai wrenched Akiko's arm behind her neck. While his grip hurt, it was nothing compared to the look Akiko's mother had given her before the guards apprehended her for assault. The look told Akiko she no longer had a mother.

I do not have anyone, she thought as she was pushed into the daimyo's mansion and shoved to her knees. A hand at her neck kept her face against the floor. *But at least, if I have to die for my actions, it is because I defended myself when no one else would.*

"Zeami?" A man's voice crackled like a crumpled piece of parchment. "What is the meaning of this?"

Akiko tried to lift her head, but the hand smashed her forehead back down to the bamboo floor.

"Lord Toyotomi." Zeami panted slightly. "I bring before you a prostitute charged with the crime of attacking a samurai. I would be honored to save you the trouble and behead her myself."

"This small girl?" Lord Toyotomi laughed softly. "She assaulted you?"

"My Lord?" Zeami released his hold on Akiko's neck. "You find this amusing?"

Free from his grip, Akiko stole a glance of the daimyo. Even though he ruled their small village, she'd never seen the man and hadn't expected him to look so … frail.

Lord Toyotomi rose from his chair and walked toward them, his back hunched as if the weight of his robes were too much to carry. His beard ended at his waist and hid his clasped hands. Akiko wondered how he could possibly see out of the crescent slits that were his eyes. He beckoned her with shaking fingers, ignoring Zeami completely. "Come child. Tell me what happened."

Akiko reached out a hand and Zeami pushed it aside as he stepped in front of her. "I will tell you what happened! An enemy sent her to lure me to my death. She is a traitor to you, my Lord, and must die!"

Akiko leapt to her feet. "That is not true!" The words burst out before she could stop them. Anger buzzed in her chest like a nest of hornets. Her eyes widened and she staggered back. *Oh, no! Not now!* Akiko turned her back to the men and tried to suppress the energy inside her with deep slow breaths. But it was too late. The pressure was too large, too sharp, like an animal clawing its way through her ribs. The power surged from her body, ripping a scream from her throat. She didn't have long to worry about where it would hit. A teapot on a nearby table exploded, splattering the floor with steaming amber liquid.

Akiko sank to her knees, saying a quick prayer of thanks to the ancestors that she hadn't hit Lord Toyotomi. Regardless, her secret was out. They would surely put her to death now. She turned to Lord Toyotomi. "I am so sorry." She closed her eyes to hold back the tears. "It is just that … I do not know how … I cannot … "

"Control it?" Lord Toyotomi asked.

Akiko was surprised that his voice was gentle and not at all angry. She opened her eyes, daring a look, and found him smiling down at her.

"My child." He shook his head as he helped her up. "Ki manipulation is a very rare and powerful gift. I can teach you how to use it."

Zeami jerked upright, as if struck by an invisible bolt of lightning. "You cannot be serious! She is a traitor. You must understand—"

But Lord Toyotomi cut him off with a look. "Zeami, you speak as if I have asked your opinion."

Zeami quieted but his glare was sharp enough to make Akiko's skin itch. She ignored him and instead addressed Lord Toyotomi with the question that had plagued her since the energy first began to burn within her body. "My Lord, can you teach me to … make it not hurt."

Lord Toyotomi smiled. With a snap of his fingers, the three porcelain teacups surrounding the shattered remains of the teapot shattered. "Does that answer your question?"

Akiko stared at the broken porcelain, frozen. Lord

Toyotomi was cursed, like her, only he seemed to think it was a gift. She was afraid to speak. Afraid the words would wake her from the dream she found herself in, a dream where she no longer had to be a woman of pleasure and where the explosive pain that built inside of her could be cured.

Zeami made a sound of disgust and marched from the room.

Lord Toyotomi waved a dismissive hand. "Do not worry about Zeami, child. He will learn to accept you. When you become a samurai, you will be part of the family. You will see."

His words echoed through her head, but no matter how many times she turned them over, she couldn't decipher their meaning. Surely the excitement of the day had affected her hearing. "I am sorry, my Lord, but I thought you said I was to become a samurai." She laughed a little, hoping he would find her mistake as funny as she did.

Lord Toyotomi laughed as well. "I did."

Akiko made a choking noise, her laughter dying on her tongue. "A samurai? Me? That is impossible. I am a girl! And I was not born to the samurai class."

He snorted. "I have always believed that nothing outside of you can dictate who you will become. Only in your heart does your destiny lie. You have the gift of ki manipulation. You have been chosen for this." He raised a single bushy eyebrow. "Unless you prefer to return to the pleasure district? That can be arranged ... "

"No!" Akiko yelled before smothering her mouth with her hands. She bowed her head. "Forgive me, my Lord. I forget myself."

He nodded, his long mustache lifting to hide the grin underneath. "Good. That is what I want you to do. A long path has been laid before you. If you walk it with the weight of your past, you will tire and fail. Do you understand me?"

Akiko nodded. Try as she might, she couldn't keep the room in focus. How had she gone from Akiko, failed woman of pleasure, to Akiko, samurai? She dug her fingernails into her palm to prove to herself she wasn't dreaming. One thing was clear; Lord Toyotomi had spared her life and given her a second chance. She lifted her chin and dared to stare him in the eyes. "I will not let you down."

17

When I arrived at Quentin's house, his mom greeted me at the door in a faded purple bathrobe and holding onto a spoon still dripping with pancake batter.

"Rileigh, dear, what are you doing here?" Mrs. Farmer tilted her head, oblivious to the batter dripping on what was probably a very expensive rug. That was one of the things I liked best about Quentin's family. Their house, a 3,000-square-foot mansion, was pristine on the outside, thanks to the landscapers that came by weekly. But, once you walked inside and took in the sink full of sippy cups and the always-sticky television remotes, you realized this family cared more about living their lives than making an impression.

I took a step back as a glob of blueberry batter narrowly missed my sneakers. "It's my day for carpool. Is he ready to go?"

A toddler squealed upstairs, the youngest of Quentin's

five brothers and sisters, and Mrs. Farmer looked over her shoulder distractedly. "I'm sorry, honey, but Quentin rode with Carly today." She cocked her head and gave me a sympathetic look. "Carly told me you've been under a lot of stress lately. Are you sure you didn't get your days confused?"

Yeah, I'm sure that wasn't all Carly told you. I plastered a fake smile on my face. "Thanks for your concern, Mrs. F. I'm sure that's what happened." But I knew it was so much more than that. Quentin would never willingly subject himself to riding with his twin. He was obviously avoiding me. I opened my mouth to excuse myself, but something crashed in the kitchen followed by the sound of a child crying. Mrs. F sighed and shot me an apologetic look. "Sorry, dear. I have to go." She slammed the door, but not before I heard her yelling something about no Irish step-dancing on the table.

Sometimes I was reminded that being an only child wasn't a bad thing.

I drove straight to school, skipping my morning stop at the Starbucks drive-thru. The last thing I needed was to add caffeine to my already-jumbled emotions. I marched straight to Q's locker, where I found him wearing workout clothes and shuffling through a duffel bag.

"Q!" I weaved around the kids who were starting to filter through the hallway.

His shoulders straightened, but he didn't look at me.

I stopped in front of him so he'd have no choice but to acknowledge me when he stood. "Where were you this morning? Tuesdays are my day to drive."

He rose slowly, juggling a stick of deodorant between his hands. "Yeah, I'm really sorry about that. I forgot to tell you that I needed to be at school early. Since Carly had pom practice, I caught a ride with her. And, figuring you stayed up late with Kim, I didn't want you to get up any earlier than you had to. I thought I texted you."

"You didn't." I folded my arms across my chest. "And for your information, I wasn't up late with Kim." Because he never showed up, but that was beside the point. "And why did you have to be at school so early, anyway?"

He shrugged and hoisted the duffel bag over his shoulder. "I wanted to work out in the school's weight room."

"But why? We get plenty of exercise with martial arts. Why would you want to sit in a room that smells like mold and stinky feet and touch equipment that at least a hundred other guys have sweated all over?" I shuddered. "I hope you used sanitizer."

He pulled a bottle of Purell from his bag and held it up. "Of course I did. I don't have a death wish." He dropped the bottle back into the bag.

I nodded. "Okay, but why the need to bulk up? And why not tell me about it?"

He shrugged and made his way down the hall, forcing me to follow. "I didn't realize I had to run everything I do by you."

His words hit me like an invisible wall and I jerked to a halt. "What?"

He stopped walking and looked at me, only he wasn't really *looking* at me. There was something about his eyes, a glazed-over quality, like he couldn't quite focus on any one thing.

What the hell was going on with him? The mood swings, the dazed expression ... was he on drugs? My skin began to buzz with invisible electricity—a warning that I had to get my emotions under control and quick. I placed my hand on my hip and took a deep breath.

Quentin blinked rapidly and shook his head. When he looked at me again his eyes were focused. "I'm sorry. It's these damn stress migraines. I thought if I exercised a bit more, my brain would release enough serotonin to counteract the migraine-causing norepinephrine produced from stress."

That sounded a little more like the Q I knew and loved. When the prickling sensation receded, I looked at him. "But what stress is causing the nor-uh-whatever? Is it me? Because I can't control my ki?"

His eyes widened. "You think this has to do with your ki?"

My hand fell from my hip. "Doesn't it?"

"No, Ri-Ri." His face hardened. "It's not always all about you, you know."

I flinched like I'd been hit. "Q ... I didn't mean ... I didn't—"

"I have no idea why I said that." His eyes widened and he looked horrified. He shook his head and pinched the bridge of his nose. "I swear I didn't mean it. This migraine is killer and I've had it for a couple of days now. It's ... I ... I don't know. It's making me act crazy." He dropped his hand from his head and took my hands within his. "I'm sorry I snapped at you like that. You forgive me, right?"

I nodded dumbly. I could understand a migraine making someone cranky. Lord knew, I turned into a snarling she-beast every time I got PMS. But this felt more extreme than just a headache. "Of course I forgive you. We're best friends, right?"

He smiled and squeezed my hands once before releasing them. "Totally. And we'll talk. I promise." He glanced at the clock on the wall.

"You have somewhere to be?" I guessed.

"I'm sorry." He gave me a pleading look. "But I only have forty minutes to shower and get dressed. You know I need at least twenty minutes to make my hair look like I didn't do it."

I sighed. "I know."

He gave me a quick hug. "We're going to talk. Soon. I promise."

"Ew. Go shower." I pushed him away and ushered him toward the locker room door. "Before your man stink rubs off on me."

He gave me one last squeeze before hoisting the duffel bag over his shoulder and taking off down the hall.

I folded my arms across my chest as I watched him walk away. Despite his assurances that he had a migraine, I couldn't ignore the nagging feeling that something was wrong. It was like an itch on the wrong side of my skin. If there was something else going on with him, I had to get to the bottom of it.

"Hey, Rileigh."

Startled, I spun around and almost planted my nose in the center of Carson Ashcroft's chest.

"Oops, sorry." He laughed as he took a step back, exposing his straight, white teeth. He was tall and lean with jagged brown hair that fell to his cheeks. A dozen multi-colored bracelets adorned one wrist while a two-inch thick wrist cuff covered the other. I'd seen him around the park enough to know he was good skater. Almost as good as me.

Carson was definitely swoon-worthy. Or, at least he would have been, before Kim. Now he didn't even blip my radar. "Oh, hey, Carson. How's it going?"

He ran a hand through his hair, his biceps straining against the rolled cuff of his flannel shirt. "What are you doing at school so early?"

I shrugged and walked across the hall to my locker. "Just call me Rileigh Martin, overachiever." I turned the combination on the dial.

His laugh was too loud to be natural, which made me halt in putting my books away. I glanced at him over my shoulder and his eyes were everywhere—on the ceiling, on the floor, down the hall—why was he so nervous? I shut my locker. "Is something up?"

He rubbed the back of his neck. "Kinda."

I folded my arms and waited as Carson continued to rub his neck until the skin under his fingers turned tomato orange. I cringed. It had to hurt.

"It's just that, I heard you were seeing that Whitley guy over the summer," he said.

"Ugh." I rolled my eyes. "Please don't remind me."

For some reason that seemed to perk him up. His hand fell to his side. "Really? Does that mean that you guys are on the outs?"

I shrugged. If only it were that simple. Between the look-alikes on the street and now the dreams, it really did feel like Whitley was haunting me.

"Sorry," he said, but he looked anything but. "Breaking up sucks."

"Meh. I'm over it."

His smile was immediate. "Cool. You think you'd want to do something sometime?"

Do something? It took my brain a moment to process his request. *Rileigh, you idiot, he's asking you out.* Suddenly I became aware how crowded the hall had become, not only with students gathering their books for first period but also with a cluster of guys from the skate park shouldered against the nearby lockers with their ears perked in our direction. Crap. If I didn't play this just right I could embarrass him—and Carson was a nice guy.

"Oh. You see ... " I swallowed and shoved a lock of hair behind my ear. "I would, Carson. It's just that ... uh ... my grades haven't been great and I'm kinda grounded until they get better."

His face fell. "That sucks."

"Yeah. It does. I'm really sorry." I began pulling books that I didn't need from my locker just to give my hands something to do.

He looked over his shoulder and exchanged glances with the skate park guys. "Right. Maybe some other time."

I smiled weakly. "I'll let you know." The history book slipped from my grasp and tumbled to the floor.

Carson bent over at the same moment I kicked my

locker door back so I could reach for it. The metal door clanged against his skull.

"Oh my God!" I reached for him even as he shuffled away from me with his hands cupped over his nose. A thin trickle of blood escaped through the gaps between his fingers. "Carson! I'm so sorry."

His friends howled with laughter.

"It's cool," Carson said, his voice muffled. I stepped forward and he stepped back, his hands still locked on his face. "Just a nosebleed. No big deal." His watering eyes told me otherwise.

Stupid, stupid Rileigh! As if turning him down wasn't bad enough I had to go and break his nose! So much for letting him down easy. I looked around the hall for something or someone that might be of help. "Do you want me to get the nurse?"

One of his friends, a tall boy with several tattoos despite the fact he wasn't yet eighteen, took him by the arm. "Love hurts, doesn't it, Carson?" He laughed.

Carson shrugged him off without taking his eyes off of me. "No. Don't worry about it. It's cool. I'm cool." He let go of his nose and shook his bloody hand once, spattering the linoleum with a sprinkle of crimson—like party confetti gone horribly wrong. "I'm just going to ... go. Now. I'm going now."

"Okay. Sorry." As I watched him amble down the hall and dart inside the bathroom I couldn't help but feel a growing sense of unease.

Was I destined to hurt everyone who crossed my path?

18

As soon as the bell rang signaling the end of seventh period, I took my phone out of my pocket and stared at the blank screen. The troubled feeling I'd felt from the moment I awoke this morning had grown at a steady pace. All I could do was watch the clock above the whiteboard and count down the seconds until class was over. *Why haven't you called me, Kim?* I dialed his number for the hundredth time and, like every time before, the call went straight to voicemail.

I shoved my books inside my bag, trying my best to ignore the way my stomach was folding in on itself like an origami crane. *Deep breaths, Rileigh.* I sucked in air, held it for the count of ten, and exhaled. Some of the pressure in my chest loosened. *Dr. Wendell promised to check on Kim*, I reminded myself. If something was really wrong and Kim was in trouble, Jason would have called me. No news was good news, right?

I whipped my backpack over my shoulder and darted from my seat. I hurried through the crowd of students milling about the hall, weaving and dodging until a body appeared in front of me. I stopped short to avoid colliding into it.

Carson, wide-eyed, took a step back. His T-shirt was a mess of dried blood. His nose was red and swollen. Purple circles rimmed both of his eyes.

My hands flew to my mouth to smother the gasp. "Oh, Carson. I'm so sorry."

"No worries." He attempted to smile, but it looked more like a grimace. "It looks worse than it really is."

Somehow, I didn't think so.

"Anyway . . . " He jammed his hands into his pockets and shrugged awkwardly. "I gotta go." He jutted his chin toward the doors at the end of the hall.

"Yeah. Me too."

"Maybe I'll see you at the skate park sometime?"

Before I could answer my phone rang from inside my backpack. "Sorry." I dropped my bag to the ground and fished my phone out. "I have to take this."

Carson nodded. "Sure. Catch you later."

I didn't answer, glancing instead at the number on the phone screen. I didn't recognize it. "Hello?"

"Rileigh? It's Jason."

My throat tightened. This was not good. Why was Dr. Wendell calling and not Kim? I took a step back and leaned against the lockers before my knees gave out. "What's wrong?"

He hesitated and I could feel the seriousness of his silence like a weight bearing down on me. He cleared his throat. "I need you to meet me at the dojo ASAP."

No longer able to stand, I slid to the ground. My stomach convulsed in tight ripples. "Why? What's happened?"

"Listen to me, Rileigh. I need you to remain calm. Do *not* panic."

I laughed and the pitch was too high, too crazy-sounding. Several nearby students cast me curious glances. I turned away from them, pressing one cheek against the cool metal of the locker and shielding the other side of my face with my free hand. "How can I be calm," I hissed, "when you won't tell me what's going on?"

He paused and cleared his throat before answering. "We have a problem." His breath hitched, betraying the fear underneath. "A big one."

19

The blood in my veins turned to ice. *We have a problem?* Could he have been any more cryptic? "What does that mean, exactly? Is this an, 'Oh no, we ordered the wrong color uniforms' problem? Or is this a 'Help! We're under a ninja attack!' problem?"

"Now is not really a good time to discuss this," he answered. "Just get to the dojo." He hung up before I could ask another question.

"Rude!" I huffed and swept my fingers through the blonde tendrils that had fallen in front of my eyes. Dr. Wendell was dangerously close to losing all the brownie points he'd earned this morning. Climbing to my feet, I slammed my palm against a locker, startling a huddle of freshman girls. The shock of pain to my hand did little to distract from the anxiety burning through me. This was exactly what I didn't need. I had enough problems without adding to the list.

Ninja attacks, Whitley sightings, and runaway elevators—none of that mattered. Because the latest problem had to do with Kim. That trumped everything else.

Across the hall, Quentin skidded to a halt, his hand pressed against the side of his head. "It's the craziest thing, I've taken two Tylenol and I swear this migraine only got worse—" He looked at me and stopped short, his hand falling away from his face. "What's wrong?"

I marched past him, hiking my backpack higher on my shoulder. "I've got to go to the dojo. Kim's in trouble."

He was at my side in an instant, matching my swift stride. "I'm coming with you." It wasn't a question. And with that one sentence, I was able to forget for a moment about all of the tension between us. Whatever was going on with him, at least it didn't stop him from being there when I needed him.

Quentin followed me to my Fiesta and climbed inside as soon as I unlocked the doors. After clicking my seatbelt, I started the car and peeled out of the parking lot. If I hadn't been crushed under a wall of worry, I might have smiled. "Thanks, Q."

He looked confused. "For what?"

"For being my best friend."

He touched my hand that gripped the gear shift but didn't say anything. We drove for several miles in silence until we crossed the Mississippi River. After I turned onto the Illinois exit ramp, Quentin spoke again. "Do you know what's going on?"

I shook my head, trying to blink back the tears blurring my vision. "Kim never came over last night. I tried to call and got no answer. Dr. Wendell said he'd check on him and later called me to meet him at the dojo because there was a problem."

"A problem," Quentin muttered. He shrugged. "Maybe it's a small problem? Maybe Kim caught the flu or something?"

I nodded, but the sour waves rolling through my stomach told me it was unlikely to be something that simple.

The dojo was located on a lone stretch of highway between two small towns. Surrounded by cornfields, the building—a converted pole barn—sat between a small brick apartment building and a lumberyard.

I pulled into the gravel parking lot and parked the car. Both Quentin and I had our doors open the second I pulled the key from the ignition. Michelle's Cavalier, Drew's Vespa, and Dr. Wendell's Audi were already in the lot. Kim's silver Trans Am was nowhere to be seen. The sick feeling in my stomach spread.

I pulled open the glass doors and ran inside the building where Michelle, Braden, and Drew paced in the lobby.

"Rileigh!" Michelle ran up to me. "What's going on? Where's Kim?"

"I have no idea." I hoped I didn't look as helpless as I felt. I turned to Braden and Drew. "I guess that means you guys don't know, either?"

Drew shook his head. "We hoped you did."

Braden leaned against the viewing window that divided the dojo from the lobby. "All of us received a text message from Wendell to meet here because there was some sort of problem."

I bit my lip before replying. "I think Kim is in some kind of trouble. He never showed up at my house last night and he hasn't answered my calls."

"Kim?" Drew frowned, the surprise evident in his voice. "He seemed fine this morning."

"What?" The muscles in my body tightened but refused to budge. It was as if I was trapped in one of those nightmares where I was stuck moving in slow motion. "You saw him this morning?" That didn't make sense. If Kim really was okay, why couldn't he have at least called to tell me?

Drew nodded, swishing his long braid behind his back. "Sure. We live in the same apartment building, after all. I knocked on his door this morning to see if he wanted to go for a jog—he said he couldn't because he had something else to do." Drew shrugged. "He didn't look like he was in trouble. He did look really tired, though."

Okay, but that still didn't explain why he didn't show up last night when he said he would. And what was his excuse for not returning my phone calls? Something didn't add up.

The door separating the dojo from the lobby creaked open and Dr. Wendell poked his head out. "Oh, good. You're all here."

I folded my arms across my chest. "Care to tell us what this is all about?"

He shook his head, looking more worn out than I'd ever seen him before. "I think it would be best if I let Kim explain." He moved to the side and motioned us through the door.

Kim was here? I followed the others into the dojo, each

step heavier than the one before—as if my body already knew the news waiting for me was not good.

The actual dojo was a large room with blue and black rubber mats covering the floor. The wall opposite the door was covered in floor-to-ceiling mirrors. The mirrors were great for watching your form and for marveling at how pissed off you looked, like I did at this very moment. Mounted on a side wall was every bladed weapon you could imagine— and some you'd wished you hadn't. Despite the assortment of pointy objects of death coupled with the aroma of sweat and rubber, this was my second home. A place I'd always felt comforted by.

But now, it felt dangerous.

"Where's Kim?" I asked.

Dr. Wendell glanced at his watch. "He should be here any minute now."

"Why can't you just tell us what's going on while we wait?"

Michelle, Braden, and Drew muttered words of agreement.

Dr. Wendell sighed. "Look, guys, I want to tell you. But Kim was quite insistent about telling you himself."

Drew folded his arms across his chest. "I don't like the way this sounds."

"No," Dr. Wendell agreed, "I don't imagine you do. And I wish it wasn't about to get so much worse."

Fingers of worry tore into my heart, which set off an electric buzz that prickled the tips of my actual fingers. I quickly balled my hands into fists, in the hopes of keeping the energy from building. "Get it together, Rileigh," I whispered.

As if sensing my distress, Quentin moved closer to my side and slid an arm around my shoulder. "You're okay," he whispered. "Everything is going to be okay."

I nodded, willing myself to believe it even as my insides screamed under the pressure building within my body.

Dr. Wendell approached me, his expression worried. "Are you feeling okay? Do you need some air?"

No. I was far from okay. But I wasn't about to go anywhere until I saw Kim. "I got it under control."

"You sure?" Braden took a step back and covered his eyebrows with his hands.

I gave him a dirty look and exhaled loudly through my nose. The buzzing subsided just enough that I thought I might be able to suppress it. "I'm fine," I said through clenched teeth.

But the others didn't look convinced. Everyone, except for Quentin, began inching away from me.

Drew motioned to the clock. "This is messed up. If Kim doesn't show in the next five minutes, I'm going to go look for him. We deserve an explanation."

"And you'll get one."

At the sound of Kim's voice, a gasp tore from my throat.

He stepped through the door and I pulled away from Quentin and started toward him. But something about his expression, a silent pleading in his eyes, stopped me after one step. For the first time I could remember, in this life and the last, he looked nervous.

I held my hand out to him. If he would just come closer, if he would only slip his fingers through mine, everything would be okay. Whatever had him so upset, I was sure we would be able to handle it. Together.

But Kim didn't move. He only stared at my fingers. The weight of his rejection piled onto my hand, heavier and heavier with each second it remained empty, waiting. Finally, I had no choice but to drop it to my side. "Kim?" His rejection didn't make sense. Was he mad at me? I wracked my brain for any instance where I might have pissed him off and couldn't come up with anything. Even so, if he was mad, I wished he had just punched me. The pain would have been less.

After a moment of tense silence, Kim shook his head, his eyes locked on the floor. "Sumi called me yesterday."

Sumi. I should have known this had something to do with her. Whatever she'd done, I'd make her pay. When I got my hands on her—

The buzzing in my chest grew stronger, forcing me to abandon my plans for revenge. "Puppies, Rileigh," I muttered. "Little yellow Labrador puppies prancing in a meadow singing songs about rainbows and moonbeams."

Quentin gave me a curious look but said nothing.

Michelle folded her arms across her chest. "What does Sumi have to do with this?"

Kim looked up from the ground, his gaze sweeping over all of us before settling directly on me. "She's awakened."

The weight of his words hit me like a bus, staggering me on my feet.

"How is that possible?" Drew asked. "Who does she say she is?"

Kim's eyes burned into mine. "Chiyo Sasaki."

20

Japan, 1491

Lord Toyotomi patted Akiko's cheek. "Before you get settled, there is someone you should meet. Come." He turned and shuffled down a wide hallway.

Akiko picked up the hem of her robe and hurried after him. She still couldn't believe he had chosen to make her a samurai instead of sentencing her to death. She followed him down several halls. Their paths twisted and turned so often Akiko lost all sense of direction. Finally, they emerged on a balcony overlooking a garden.

"Right where I thought he would be," Lord Toyotomi murmured.

"He?" Akiko didn't know who he was talking about. At first glance, the garden appeared empty.

Lord Totyotomi nodded to the cherry tree just beside a stream bubbling with fat orange koi.

That's when Akiko first saw *him*.

He knelt under the tree with his head bowed. His waist-length hair spilled over his shoulders, hiding his face behind a curtain of black. Every so often his chest heaved in a silent sob, unsettling the pink blossoms in his hair that had fallen from the branches above.

A hundred paper cranes took flight inside of Akiko's stomach. Such a strange sensation and not one she understood. She watched from the balcony as his shoulders shook, his body hunched under the weight of grief. She felt embarrassed, as if she had intruded into someone else's nightmare. She did not belong.

Lord Toyotomi placed a hand on her shoulder, startling her. "That is Yoshido, the captain of my samurai."

Akiko couldn't look away. There were always men in the pleasure house. Laughing, hungry men. Men drunk off of saki and opium. But Akiko had never seen a man so open, so raw, bleeding his misery for anyone to see. "Why does he cry?"

Lord Toyotomi leaned his hands against the balcony rail. He sighed. "Yoshido is in mourning. His betrothed, Chiyo Sasaki, was murdered by bandits." He shook his head. "So tragic. Even though he was not there, Yoshido blames himself for her death."

"But why?"

"Because he could not stop it from happening."

Akiko moved to stand beside him at the rail. "He must have really loved her."

Lord Toyotomi remained silent for a moment before

answering. "Love does not weigh a person down. There are heavier emotions."

"Like what?"

"Guilt."

Akiko studied Yoshido, still hunched over with more than a dozen pink petals in his hair. "But if he was not there . . . how can he blame himself?"

Lord Toyotomi shook his head as if he, too, wanted the answer. "Because that is his way, child. If the world ended tomorrow, he would blame himself for that, as well. But"— he squeezed her hand—"that is where you come in."

"Me?" Akiko took a step back. She couldn't understand how she would be of any help to the lost warrior.

Lord Toyotomi nodded in Yoshido's direction and coughed loudly. The samurai looked up and, upon seeing them, ran the palms of his hands down his face in attempt to erase the trail of tears. "Yoshido," Lord Toyotomi called out, "I would like you to meet our newest samurai." He gestured at Akiko, who couldn't help but duck her head to hide her flaming cheeks.

Yoshido's face remained impassive.

Akiko bit her lip. She waited for him to storm away, angry, as Zeami had done.

Lord Toyotomi continued, "I sense something in her, Yoshido."

Yoshido nodded and walked toward the balcony. "You are never wrong about your inclinations, my Lord."

With the warrior standing under her, Akiko guessed his age at around eighteen. He had wide shoulders, a defined jawline, and dark, piercing eyes that loosened something in her knees and made standing a challenge. She tightened her grip on the railing.

Lord Toyotomi smiled. "That is why I am entrusting *you* to train her to fight."

"And so I will." Yoshido bowed slightly at the waist. "What will be her weapon?"

"Hmm." Lord Toyotomi frowned and stroked his beard. "The selection of a samurai's weapon is a serious matter." While he studied her, Akiko fought the urge to squirm under his unblinking gaze. Finally, he turned his attention back to Yoshido. "As it were, she already has some skill with a blade. Our own Zeami bears proof of that."

Yoshido's eyebrows shot up, his laugh muffled behind a fisted cough. "Very well, may I suggest the katana?"

Lord Toyotomi leaned in so closely that Akiko could smell the citrus oil in his hair. "That is the first time he has laughed since his betrothed died."

Akiko wasn't sure why, but this information renewed the fire in her cheeks.

Lord Toyotomi straightened and addressed Yoshido. "That will do nicely. Begin the training immediately."

Yoshido bowed. "Yes, my Lord. What is her, uh"—he met Akiko's eyes, stirring a whirlwind of flower petals inside her—"*your* name?"

She opened her mouth to answer, but Lord Toyotomi stopped her with a raised hand. "Senshi," the daimyo replied. "Because she has a warrior's heart. And because," he said, his voice dropping so that only she could hear, "we cannot be weighed down by our past."

Before she could react, Yoshido said her name—her new name—and just like that, it was as if Akiko had never existed.

21

Kim's words hit me like a shuriken to the chest. If it wasn't for Q's arms around my shoulders, I would have staggered to the floor.

The others remained motionless. Dr. Wendell only shook his head.

Chiyo Sasaki. Yoshido's betrothed killed by bandits. The girl he mourned until the day I met him in Lord Toyotomi's gardens. "She has to be lying," I said.

"But I'm not." Sumi entered the dojo from the adjoining lobby. She walked straight to Kim and looped her arm through his. He stiffened but said nothing.

Bile burned the back of my tongue. What the hell was going on? "Kim?" I needed to hear him say it again. To prove I wasn't trapped inside another nightmare. The buzzing within me grew stronger until goose bumps appeared on my flesh.

Quentin must have sensed the change. He released my shoulders and slowly sidestepped away from me.

"Please, Rileigh." Kim looked at me, his eyes pained. "So much has happened. I can't—it's just—"

"He's pledged to me," Sumi answered, smiling.

My hands reflexively curled into fists. Pledged to Sumi? "What are you talking about?"

Kim opened his mouth, but Sumi answered for him. "Because of the pledge he made to me in our past life—the pledge he left unfulfilled—Kim is honor bound to me."

Michelle's eyes narrowed. "What pledge?"

Sumi tossed her head, rippling her glossy black hair down her back. "He was my betrothed and failed to protect me. I died and he moved on to love another. Because he is a samurai, he is honor bound to keep the promise that was broken."

Kim's brow furrowed and he looked like he might say something. But Sumi pressed herself against his side, a sight that rolled waves of nausea through my stomach, and he remained silent.

The energy humming along my skin began to scratch and push for a way out. *Focus, Rileigh. Relax.* I inhaled deeply through my nose and exhaled through my mouth. I repeated this several times until I felt able to speak without screaming. "This is ridiculous." I glared at Kim, who immediately averted his eyes. "You don't seriously think you have to honor a 500-year-old betrothal, do you? That's insane."

But he wouldn't look at me, let alone answer me. Why wouldn't he answer me?

Sumi's eyes narrowed into slits. "You think promises and honor are something that can be disregarded? What kind of samurai are you?"

"The kind that's about to kick your ass." I stepped forward, but a hand gripped my shoulder and pulled me back.

"Rileigh," Dr. Wendell whispered in my ear, "I need to you to be calm. This is a delicate situation."

Calm? How could he expect me to be calm when my entire world had turned upside down? I jerked out of Dr. Wendell's grasp. My ki pushed against my barriers with enough force that I had to clench my teeth together to keep from crying out in pain. Yoshido once told me Chiyo had been a gentle soul. Well, there was nothing gentle about Sumi. Somehow she'd managed to find out information about Kim's past and was using it against us. That was the only explanation that made sense. "Kim, come on. How can you let this psycho manipulate you? Can't you see she's lying?"

"No." He shook his head, which elicited a smug look from Sumi. "She's not lying. She knows things that only Chiyo would know."

"So what?" The power inside me surged forward, but I managed to rein it in before it escaped. "Who cares if she is Chiyo? How does that change anything?"

"It changes everything," he answered.

I could feel the power jumping from my fingertips like a Taser on charge. "It doesn't have to."

"You're wrong." Sumi slid in front of Kim, all the while keeping her hold on his arm. "He was my betrothed. A lifetime doesn't change that."

"Of course it does!" I stepped forward and Quentin made a warning sound in his throat. I knew only seconds remained before I lost control—but I couldn't seem to work up the ability to care. The only thing that mattered to me was yanking Sumi's hand off of Kim's arm.

Kim opened his mouth, but the words wouldn't come. Lines of confusion pinched his brow and he appeared lost inside his own thoughts.

It terrified me. Gone was my confident warrior. In both of my lifetimes I couldn't remember a time when Kim looked so lost—so unsure of himself.

After a few seconds, Sumi gave an impatient sigh. "What Kim's *trying* to say is he can no longer be with you."

Her words slammed against me like a fist to the spine. "What?" My hold slipped and a burst of ki pushed through my skin. The weapons rattled against the wall.

Sumi's eyes widened. "What was that?" Her head whipped around as she studied each sword shaking on its mounts.

Q, Dr. Wendell, and the other samurai eyed the walls nervously. Kim, however, seemed oblivious to the trembling weapons. "I'm so sorry, Rileigh. I never wanted to hurt you."

Isn't that what everyone said after the fact? But I knew it was a load of crap. If he hadn't wanted to hurt me, then he wouldn't have hurt me. I flexed my fingers out to expel the power prickling my fingertips. Several swords shook so violently they fell off the wall and bounced against the rubber floor. I couldn't hold on much longer.

Dr. Wendell reached for me, but I shot him a look so venomous he dropped his hand back to his side. "Listen to me, Rileigh. I need you to calm down." His voice was tight with fear. "Take a few deep breaths and count to ten."

Through the open windows of the dojo came the sound of tires crunching over gravel.

Dr. Wendell's eye followed the sound to the front entrance. "Of all the times ... Who could that be?"

Drew shrugged. "Probably just a parent wanting to sign their kid up for karate."

"I'll get rid of them." Dr. Wendell marched to the door. Before he stepped into the lobby, he gave me a long look. "Stay calm, Rileigh."

I ignored him. It was easy to deal out advice if you weren't the one having your heart filleted. As my emotions ricocheted inside of me, my ki did the same thing outside of me. The glass observation window separating the lobby from the dojo crunched as a spiderweb of cracks zigzagged across it. A second later, it shattered to the floor.

Sumi screamed. Her honey-hued skin had paled to the color of cream. "What the hell was that?"

Kim ignored her. "I have a debt to pay, Rileigh. I failed Chiyo and now I owe her my life for the loss of hers. You know that a man—let alone a samurai—is only as good as his honor."

I shook my head as the wooden shelf on the back wall splintered, which sent the trophies on top of it hurtling to the ground. The door separating the lobby from the dojo flew open and banged shut on its own. Sumi screamed again. I could feel the energy pulling at me, begging to be released, but by some miracle I was able to hold on. "I have no idea what that means, Kim. How do you owe her your life?"

His shoulders slumped. "Sumi and I are getting married."

His words cut me deeper than any blade could have. I staggered from the pain left in their wake.

At that moment Dr. Wendell walked back into the dojo, his eyes lingering on the broken glass littering the mats as he made his way toward us. "It was just a meter reader."

The tiniest shiver of a warning broke through my pain and tickled the back of my neck. I pulled my eyes off of Kim and looked at Dr. Wendell. "Why would you say that?"

He shrugged. "A couple of power company workers—young guys." He nodded to a window. "They walked around back to check the meter. They said they'd only be here for a second or two."

Oh no. Not here. Not now. My blood went cold as an icy wind fluttered through me. "Were they driving a power-company truck?"

"No. But that doesn't mean anything. They're probably contractors."

I glanced at the window and saw two figures sprint by, which could only mean one of two things. One: they were engaging in a friendly game of *Who can read the meter the fastest?* (Which I'd totally play if I was a meter reader.) Or, two: they were ninja. And I knew from experience that when ninja ran, it was because they'd left something unpleasant behind. I looked at Kim and, even though he'd broken my heart, given his grim expression, it appeared he could still read my mind.

He whirled toward the front doors. "Everyone, out of the building!"

"Why?" Sumi glanced between Kim and the doors. "What's going on?"

I couldn't help but smile a little. If she wanted to be with Kim so bad, here was her chance to see what she was getting into. "We're under a ninja attack."

Q looked at me and after I nodded, he jogged toward the front entrance.

But Dr. Wendell and the other samurai didn't move. They glanced around the room as if they expected the ninja to jump out of the shadows. I knew we wouldn't be that lucky. Ninja were cowards and preferred to avoid hand-to-hand combat.

"Are you sure we're in danger?" Drew asked.

"Has she ever been wrong?" Kim motioned to the doors. "Let's move. NOW!"

Whether it was his words, or the tone of his voice, something snapped the other samurai into movement. As a group, we ran for the front door. I hung back, letting the others get in front of me—something I remember doing even in the past. But we'd only reached the door dividing the dojo from the lobby when the warning bell in my head turned into a scream. That noise meant only one thing—time had just run out.

22

et down!" I screamed.

Kim had managed to reach the door in time to push Sumi outside along with Q. I heard her scream of protest even as the explosion ripped through the back of the building.

But the others hadn't reached the door yet and it was only a matter of seconds before we were engulfed by the wall of flames at my back.

I dropped to my knees and flung my arms behind me, releasing the ki already pulsating at my fingers. I hoped it wasn't too late.

The power inside me ripped from my body—like a scab pulled too soon—and left me hurt and raw. Sparing a glance over my shoulder, I could see it spread behind me in a shimmering blue wall. The flames and debris beat against the wall, each strike I felt as a push against my own skin, but I gritted my teeth and held on.

Someone yelled as a beam fell from the ceiling and landed a couple feet away from where I crouched. Sunlight filtered in through the hole in the roof left in its wake.

"Rileigh!"

The urgency in Kim's voice let me know it wasn't the first time he'd called my name. He held the door open as Michelle and Braden ducked under his arm to safety. Dr. Wendell stood behind him looking helpless.

Kim held the door back with his foot and reached a hand out to me. "Get up! Get out of there!"

The explosion continued to rock the shield at my back. I wavered, trying to keep it from falling. If I dropped the wall now, the others could still get hurt. I couldn't risk it. I shook my head. "I'm not leaving. Not yet." A chunk of flaming wood fell from the ceiling and landed by my feet. A spark bounced off and singed through my jeans into my flesh. My shield flickered.

Something large and silver—possibly one of Kim's swords—flew past me. Kim ducked out of the way before it shattered through the glass door.

Concentrate, Rileigh!

With a scream, I focused all my ki into the shield. It glowed a more solid shade of blue in response. I couldn't let go until the explosion was over and my friends were safe.

Chunks of ceiling and bits of flaming rubber rained down around me. Through it all, I held on. My muscles burned and my arms trembled from exhaustion. I closed my eyes. The ceiling groaned and bits of drywall pelted my body. An electric charge—a warning—coursed down the length of my spine, alerting me I had only seconds before the ceiling gave in.

Arms slipped around me and hoisted me up. With my concentration broken, the shield evaporated. I opened my eyes to find myself in Kim's arms, being carried through the lobby as it collapsed around us. Too weak to fight, I held onto his neck to keep from being jostled as he ducked and dodged over burning debris.

How could he do it? How could he tell me he was marrying another girl one minute, and run into a flaming building to save me the next? Did he actually love her? Had he really ever loved me? Was I nothing more than a rebound girl for his murdered betrothed?

Something whined and I looked up in time to watch another beam fall—seemingly in slow motion—directly above us.

"Kim!" I shouted.

He ran faster.

But I knew it wouldn't be fast enough. Gathering the last of my strength, I held up a hand and released what little ki I had remaining and prayed it would be enough.

The beam shuddered in the air, as if caught by an invisible net. The force of holding back so much weight cut into my body like razor blades. I screamed.

"We're almost there," Kim shouted back.

The beam dropped a few feet and stopped. I couldn't hold it much longer. Darkness seeped into the edges of my vision. I'd lost too much ki and was going to pass out. *Son of hibachi.* I could feel the cottony thickness of unconsciousness press inside my head, making my thoughts thick and slow. When I spoke my voice sounded far away. "Kim...I can't..."

But I didn't get to finish. Even in my semiconscious state, I could hear the crash of the beam and feel myself being thrown from Kim's arms.

But instead of hitting the ground, I fell into darkness.

23

Japan, 1492

Senshi looked at the dead man on the floor and pressed her palm to her nose. The smell of decay made her stomach clench and she struggled not to vomit. How long had he been dead? From the smell of him, she guessed at least a week.

"Are you all right?" Yoshido's lips twitched as he fought to keep from laughing.

Senshi drew her shoulders back and dropped her hand from her nose. She could do this. She had to do this. Tilting her chin up, she stared Yoshido in the eyes. "I can do this. The corpse smells no worse than Zeami."

Yoshido chuckled. "Right." He turned to leave but hesitated in the doorway. His eyes darted between her and the corpse. "I could stay if you like. I would not tell the others."

Senshi knew he'd only said it to be kind, but his words cut into her skin like needles. "How many of the other samurai have you offered to stay with when it was their turn to sleep with the dead?"

His eyes dropped to the floor. "None."

"So why offer to stay with me? Do you think I will not be able to handle it? That I will be reduced to tears moments after you leave me?

"No!" His eyes widened. "It is just—"

"That I am a girl?" Senshi offered. "That I am smaller and weaker than the rest of my samurai brethren and therefore need to be coddled?"

Yoshido opened his mouth, closed it, and then laughed. "Of course I don't think that. You are one of the fiercest fighters I know. Have you considered that maybe it was I who longed for company?"

She made a face. He could say whatever he wanted to spare her feelings, but she knew better. As the only girl in a clan full of boys and men, she had to fight double to earn their respect—which wasn't much. Tonight she faced another test in her path to become a samurai. Tonight she would prove she did not fear death or the dead by spending the night with a corpse. She didn't need Yoshido messing it up by treating her like a baby. She would prove to them she was worthy of becoming a samurai. "If you are so lonely, go to the pleasure district. I am sure you would find suitable company there."

Yoshido blinked before a smile crept onto his face. "Perhaps I will."

"Good." But as soon as she said it, Senshi had the awful mental image of Yoshido in the arms of a courtesan, which caused something to shift uncomfortably in her chest. When she spoke, her words caught in her throat. "Now go."

Yoshido raised his hands in surrender. "As you please." He bowed, his long black hair sliding across his shoulders like the folds of a silk kimono. When he straightened, he smiled at her, sending an odd mixture of sparks and chills down her spine. Strange.

Senshi watched him back out of the room. After he slid the rice paper door shut, she released the breath she hadn't realized she'd been holding. Ancestors help her, he was infuriating.

She sank to the floor and crossed her legs. The sooner she fell asleep, the sooner she'd wake up and this night would be over. She cast a look over at her companion, a lifeless middle-aged man with a long black beard that reached the middle of his bare chest. Death had turned his skin the same gray color as the skin of an onion. Aside from his smell, Senshi was pleased the corpse didn't bother her. This was going to be an easy test. She eased herself to the ground, closed her eyes, and waited for sleep.

"*Senshi.*"

Senshi pushed off the floor and glanced around the room, searching for the source of the whisper. Her heart beat the pounding rhythm of a taiko war drum.

"*Seeeeeeenshi.*"

There it was again—her name—uttered in the faintest of whispers. Was the corpse speaking to her? She shook her head as if to dislodge the idea from her brain. That was impossible. But still, she eyed the dead body in front of her and took a cautious step back. "Who is there?" She was proud of herself for sounding more fearless than she felt.

"It is I," the voice whispered back. "The ghost of the dead farmer Hotaka."

She continued to stare at the unmoving corpse. Something strange was going on. The voice that spoke to her sounded muffled and far away, almost as if it came from outside the room. Senshi pivoted on her heel and that's when she saw the shadow of a figure crouched outside of the door. The silhouette of a curtain of long hair gave away his identity.

Senshi pressed her hand to her lips to smother the laugh. She knew she should be furious with him for not leaving when she'd told him to. But as much as she tried to muster any anger, it simply wouldn't come. "Why have you come for me, oh spirit of the farmer Hotaka?"

"To warn you," the voice whispered through the walls.

"Why?" She grinned and settled back onto the ground. "Am I in danger?"

"No." There was a pause. "You are the danger."

Her? Dangerous? Senshi didn't know what game Yoshido was playing, but she decided to play along to prolong his presence. "That does not sound good. Who am I a danger to?"

"There is a samurai. His name is Yoshido."

"Ah yes." Senshi inched closer to the silhouette on the other side of the wall. "The irksome one. I have heard of him."

The voice sputtered a couple of times before continuing, making her laugh. "Yes, well, be cautious with him."

"I thought you said I was the dangerous one?"

"You are," he answered. "Be cautious of his heart. You hold it."

Senshi's breath quickened and, for reasons she didn't understand, she trembled. Suddenly, this wasn't the game she'd thought it was. "I-I-do not understand."

The black outline of a hand appeared on the wall next to her face. When Yoshido spoke, he spoke clearly, no longer hiding his identity. "I love you, Senshi."

The room tilted on its side. "Is this part of the test?" It had to be. There was no way someone as handsome, as kind, and as good as Yoshido could love a girl from the pleasure district.

He laughed. "That was not the reaction I was hoping for."

She shook her head. "You know where I come from, Yoshido. You know what I was."

"No." Even from the other side of the rice paper wall, Senshi could see his muscles tense. "I know only what you are—a samurai."

Her breath hitched in her throat as she slowly raised her hand. Yoshido truly loved her? How had she not noticed? It was true that during the last year she'd been consumed by her samurai training, desperate to prove herself as a capable warrior, lest Lord Toyotomi change his mind about her. And if she'd been naive enough to ignore Yoshido's feelings, had she also been burying her own? "Why are you telling me this now?"

He shrugged. "I leave for a battle tomorrow. I might die. I thought you should know how I felt about you."

She placed her hand on top of his. The heat from his skin seemed to melt through the paper into hers. So this was what love felt like? She smiled. Yoshido would go off to battle, but he would return. She had no doubt. He was the greatest warrior she'd ever met. But he also carried the weight of the world on his shoulders.

She traced the outline of his shoulders with her free hand. "Lord Toyotomi told me I have great ki power."

"I know," Yoshido said.

"I am going to be a great samurai."

"I know."

She stopped tracing his shadow and placed her hand flat on the wall. Yoshido copied her movement so that his heat melted into both of her hands. She shivered. "Soon, I am going to fight in great battles."

"I know."

Senshi thought back to the first time she'd seen Yoshido, the grief-stricken warrior under the cherry trees. She knew Yoshido had been betrothed to another woman. And that his guilt over her death nearly killed him. She wouldn't give her heart to a man haunted by another woman's ghost. She lifted her chin and steeled herself for the words she was about to say.

"So if I am going to love you, Yoshido, I am going to love you greater than any woman has ever loved a man. And you, in turn, will love me just as much."

There was nothing but silence from the other side of

the wall. Senshi had a brief paralyzing moment where she wondered if she'd demanded too much of him. But even as the thought crossed her mind, the silhouette of Yoshido's face darkened as he brought it so close to the wall Senshi wondered if she might feel his breath through the paper.

"I know."

24

When I opened my eyes, I was surprised to find myself in my own room. Even more surprising was finding Kim seated at the foot of my bed looking grim. For one fleeting moment I wondered if Kim breaking up with me followed by the ninja attack had only been a nightmare. But, after I glanced down at my bruised body and charred clothing, I'd realized the real nightmare had been waiting for me to wake.

I pushed myself to a sitting position and immediately regretted it when my vision wavered. "Whoa." I placed a hand against my head. Another concussion was the last thing I needed. I was struggling enough in school to add actual brain damage to my problems.

Kim frowned but made no move to help me up. "You need to take it easy. You almost killed yourself trying to save everyone."

I dropped my hand. "And did I?"

He nodded, a quick jut of the chin. "Yes. Everyone is fine."

The knot in my chest loosened and I sagged against my pillow. "Good." At least something positive had come out of today. But through my relief, a new sensation had taken root inside me—a raw ache in my chest. I had ninja to worry about, I didn't need the distraction of a broken heart.

As if reading my thoughts, Kim shifted his gaze to my window. "I never meant to hurt you. I never meant for … any of this."

I almost laughed. Was that his idea of an explanation? Five hundred years and that was all I got? The first spark of anger warmed my stomach. I swung my legs to the floor and stood. I couldn't just lay there like an invalid while my world fell apart. But, without a course of action, I could only pace the floor. "So what are you doing here? You knew I was going to be all right when you got me out of the building, so why wait for me to wake? Did you want me to gain consciousness just so you could break up with me all over again? Because you could have saved yourself the trip—I heard you the first time."

"No. That's not—it's just—" He swept a hand through his hair. "It's not an easy thing to explain." He met my eyes, his expression asking if I understood.

I didn't.

"We spent a lifetime together, Kim. I loved you. I *love* you. I just can't believe you would throw all of that away."

"I know." He stood and walked toward me but stopped when I retreated to the back of my room. "It doesn't make a lot of sense to me, either. The last thing I ever wanted to do was hurt you. But something inside of me is telling me this is what I have to do. I have a debt to Chiyo."

I made a disgusted sound. "Chiyo is dead."

"Because of me!" He sucked in a breath and stared at my ceiling. After a moment, he lowered his face and looked at me. The expression he wore mirrored the grieving warrior I'd seen under the cherry trees so many years ago. When he answered, his voice was quiet. "She died because of me."

I thought about my sword taped to the back of my mirror and how much I'd like to grab it and smack the broadside of the blade against Kim's thick skull. "Can you even hear yourself? Do you know how insane that is? You didn't kill Chiyo. She was kidnapped by bandits. You had nothing to do with her death."

His jaw flexed. "As her betrothed, she was my responsibility. It was my duty to keep her safe. And I failed."

God, he was stubborn. Why couldn't he see that we lived in the 21st century and didn't have to abide by the old ways? But even before I asked the question, I knew the answer: Kim was, and always would be, a samurai before all else. And, as much as it broke my heart, the samurai in me was proud of him.

"So that's it? We're over?" The pain of saying the words out loud ripped through my heart like the prongs of a sai. It hurt to breathe.

Kim didn't look so great either. His shoulders fell and every tendon in his jaw stretched taut. He took another step toward me and I took another step back.

I couldn't let him get close to me. Because if I did, I

wasn't sure I could stop myself from running into his arms and begging him not to leave me.

And Rileigh Martin did not beg.

"I don't have a choice, Rileigh." He took another step and this time the wall at my back ended my retreat. Son of hibachi. Kim stepped in front of me so I had to tilt my chin up to look at him unless I wanted my face crushed by his chest.

My pulse beat frantically against my temples and my fingers itched to cling to the fabric of his T-shirt and fold myself against his body. I quickly balled them into fists at my side. "What do you want from me, Kim?" As much as I wanted to, I would not look away. This was one staring contest I would not lose.

He brought his head down so I could feel his breath, hot against my skin.

"I want you to be safe. The ninja have made it very clear they are not going to stop until you're dead. And I know you are struggling with your ki."

A bitter-sounding laugh escaped my throat. "Please. I'm a big girl. You don't have to pretend to care about me, anymore."

He slammed his hand against the wall, startling me. "I will always care." His eyes bore into mine. "Please." He leaned his head down and I had to press my face against the wall before the urge to kiss him overpowered me. Little bits of textured plaster bit into my cheek.

"Sumi may have my vow, but you have my heart, Rileigh Martin. I will never stop loving you."

I shook my head as much as the wall allowed it. "You don't treat someone you love like this, Kim. You don't leave them for someone else." I felt the first of many hot tears trail down my cheek. Damn. So much for holding it together.

He placed a finger under my chin and tilted my face to his. His own eyes shimmered dangerously with tears. "I can't stop being a samurai. It's who I am." He closed his eyes and brought his lips to mine.

It was my undoing. Every word, every thought in my head vanished until all that existed was the kiss. Our last kiss. Before I'd realized what I was doing, my arms reached around his neck, pulling him closer to me. It was as if by sheer force I might somehow change his mind.

But Kim pulled away with a gasp before I could. He backed away from me and looked around my room, his eyes wide, as if he were unsure of where he was. "I don't—I wasn't—" He pressed his palm to his temple and shook his head. "Everything is wrong."

"What is?" Sumi? Our kiss? I closer to him, aware of how cold and empty I felt without the heat of his body against mine.

He looked at me. "Rileigh, I am so sorry." He backed toward the door. "I've got to go."

"Where?"

He blinked, as if he wasn't quite sure. "Sumi," he finally answered. "She needs me."

And just like that, all the anger and hurt lying dormant inside of me swelled, pushing against my skin and electrifying my fingertips. The hair on the back of my neck rose in response. The pictures I'd taken over the summer of Kim and me rattled off my dresser onto the floor. "Fine. Go." I flexed my fingers, hoping to contain the power growing inside.

"Rileigh?" Kim looked around my room from the tubes of lip gloss and mascara bouncing on the vanity to the stuffed animals performing flips off of my bed. "Are you okay?"

Why did people always ask that when it was so obvious you weren't? "Get out, Kim." A tendril of ki burst from my body and rattled my door on its hinges.

Kim stared at me for a moment longer. Finally, he nodded and turned to leave but paused at my door. "I can't see you anymore."

"What?" The shock of his words intensified the buzzing inside of me. I pressed my teeth together to keep the stream of insults from tumbling out. I was better than that. "You're a dick, Gimhae Kim," I said using his real name. Okay, so maybe I wasn't better than that. Sue me.

Kim's shoulders tightened, but he didn't turn around. "When you're around me, I get confused. And I can't have that—especially when I have ninja to hunt."

"That will be kind of hard, considering I'll be hunting the ninja with you. I'm their target, remember?"

"I know." He nodded. "And your safety is the most important thing in the world to me. But I have to hunt the ninja without you, Rileigh. I'm not leaving you alone—I'll make sure the other samurai are watching—but I have to put distance between us. If you have an update, report it to the others. I can't…"

"What, Kim?" I spit between clenched teeth. "You can't *what?*"

He was quiet for several heartbeats before answering, "You're off the team—it's for the best." Before I could respond, he left my room and shut the door behind him.

25

Quentin pulled into his assigned parking spot in the school lot. He turned off the ignition but made no move to get out of the car. I could feel his eyes staring at me even though I hadn't looked up from the latte in my hands. The post-breakup haze left me numb and empty. The heat the caramel macchiato lent to my fingers was the only sensation I'd felt in more than a week—since the night Kim had stolen into my room, kissed me, and told me he never wanted to see me again.

"How are you holding up?" Q asked, his eyes full of concern. At the very least, Quentin's migraines had become fewer, which meant he was acting like my friend again—and for that I was grateful.

I lifted my sunglasses so he could see how red and puffy my eyes were from my crying marathons. It was embarrassing, really. I didn't want to be *that* girl. The one who moped for months on end and stopped eating and sleeping all because a boy broke up with her. But wanting to get over someone and actually getting over someone were two different things.

"All right." Q nodded. "I'm sorry. Stupid question, I know."

"I thought I was stronger than this," I told him. "I hate feeling like my heart is this shriveled apple core inside my chest. I should be moving on. I shouldn't be thinking about him as much as I do. And missing him—God, do I miss him." I looked at Q. "You love psychology, right? Please, tell me how I'm supposed to do this."

"What do you mean?"

I pointed to the school. "Just... *this*. How do I go back to my old life? Am I supposed to pretend I was never a samurai? I don't know how to do that. How am I supposed to give a damn about homecoming dances and composition papers when half of my heart is missing and the other half is falling apart? Hell, my whole life is falling apart."

Quentin reached over and squeezed my arm. "You have to start with now—the moment you're in. The first thing you do is open the car door. The second is to walk into school. You have to tackle each step as it comes. Remember, your friends are here to help. C'mon." Q opened his car door. "I'll walk you to class."

I nodded, hoisted my backpack on my shoulder, and opened the car door. Even with Q by my side, I couldn't help but feel alone. When your heart breaks, you can't help but look at the people around you who breathed without difficulty, the people who knew how to smile, and wonder how you forgot to do all of that—and if you'd be able to do it again.

I got out of the car and spotted Michelle and Braden walking through the parking lot two rows down. My heart warmed at the sight of them. Q was right. If I was going to survive this breakup, I needed to be with my friends. "Guys!" I waved my hand in the air.

Michelle frowned. Braden whispered something in her ear and she nodded. Together, they ducked their heads and hurried to the school doors.

An invisible cord pulled tight around my stomach. What the hell was that about? I knew they saw me—they looked right at me. So what was the reason for the blow off?

As I watched them disappear into the building, the ki buzzing beneath my skin amplified. It was bad enough I woke each morning with energy already humming in my veins—not a good thing for any pillows or Bunsen burners in my vicinity. The constant worry I would slip and lose control put me on edge. And to make it worse, now I had the feeling there was something going on with my friends.

On a scale of one through ten, my stress meter officially hit eleven. So when a hand clamped down on my shoulder, it was all I could do to hold on to the whirlwind swirling inside of me. But that didn't stop me from throwing my coffee in my attacker's face.

I rocked back on my heels and raised my arms in front of me. I was ready for a fight.

The only problem was my attacker wasn't an attacker after all.

In front of me, Carson stumbled back blindly, his hands covering his face.

"Son of hibachi." I dropped my fight stance and rushed to his side. Guilt stabbed through my gut. Of all the people, why Carson? Why *again*? "Are you okay?" I touched his shoulder as he frantically wiped coffee from his face. Red blotches decorated his skin where the hot liquid scalded him.

Quentin darted around his car with a look of horror on his face. "What happened?"

I shrugged helplessly. "I threw coffee at him."

Quentin gave me a look suggesting he was considering having me committed.

"I didn't do it on purpose! He surprised me."

Carson groaned in response.

"We have to get him to the nurse." Q frowned at me and wrapped Carson's free arm around his neck. "Carson, I'm going to lead you inside the building. Do you think you can make it?"

"Yeah. I don't think the coffee did anything to my eyes. I can see okay." He blinked several times. "I'm not hurt. Just startled."

"Hot coffee to the face startling?" Q said in a clipped voice. "Imagine that."

Something told me angry, moody Q was about to make an appearance—so not what I needed at the moment. So I ignored him and focused my attention on Carson. "I'm so sorry. I swear I didn't mean to hurt you."

"I'm fine." Carson looked down at his button-up flannel

and the massive coffee stain soaked into the fabric. "But I think my shirt is ruined."

"I'll buy you another one," I offered.

To my surprise, he grinned. "It's fine, really. I just know better than to sneak up on you again."

"C'mon." Quentin gave Carson's arm a gentle tug. "I'll take you to the nurse just to be safe. I need to go there anyway and get some ibuprofen—I'm feeling one of my migraines coming on. Then we can stop at my locker. I keep a few extra shirts in there."

"Yeah, okay." Carson pulled at his shirt. "This stuff stinks."

My cheeks burned. "I'm so sorry."

He waved my words away. "Forget about it. I thought if I snuck up on you I might make you laugh. You looked so sad this week I wanted to make you smile." He shrugged.

Wow. Just a second ago I'd thought I couldn't feel any worse. There's nothing like dumping a caramel macchiato on a boy who's just trying to make you feel better. That plan backfired.

"Please don't feel bad, Rileigh," Carson said. "It was an accident. And it was my fault for sneaking up on you. Besides"—he gestured to Q—"if I borrow one of Quentin's shirts, then I won't smell like a coffeehouse all day."

I offered him a weak smile.

Quentin shrugged. "You're forgetting the most important point. You *get* to wear one of my shirts. This is a privilege. I have incredible taste."

"I'll say." Carson's eyes lingered on my face long enough

that heat burned up my neck into my cheeks. I didn't think he was talking about clothes anymore.

I walked behind Quentin as he led Carson to the school entrance. Once they'd passed through the doors, I stopped. The tingling in my fingertips remained. Today was the first day the buzz under my skin showed no signs of relenting. Definitely not good. I'd hoped I'd gradually be able to regain control of my raging ki. But the reality was what little control I had was slipping away each day.

I turned and walked away from the building to the bus stop down the block. I heard the metal door squeak open behind me as I made my retreat.

"Where are you going?" Q called behind me.

"Mental health day," I answered without stopping. I had to figure out how to get my ki in check before something really bad happened. Everything had a breaking point and I was dangerously close to mine.

26

The wheels of my skateboard coasted along the city sidewalk creating a gentle vibration that thrummed through my body. I tipped my head back and let the wind glide through my hair, which hung loose under my pink helmet. This was exactly what I needed.

I coasted along, tipping my weight back and forth so my board serpentined past cracks in the concrete, people leaving work, and street musicians until I lost momentum and had to kick off the ground with my foot.

I'd spent the entire day skating along the sidewalks of downtown St. Louis. And it was well worth the detention I was sure to receive for skipping class. I'd forgotten how much pleasure I could get from my board and how much skating had been a part of my life before my awakening— before Kim.

My heart clenched inside of my chest and I wobbled dangerously on my board. I slid to a grinding halt, kicked my board into my hand, and took a moment to gather myself.

I leaned against a building until, after a couple of minutes of sucking in breaths that ripped through my lungs, I felt confident enough to stand. I used the metal bars covering a broken shop window to hoist myself up. That's when I realized that during my skate-induced bliss, I'd accidentally rolled into a bad neighborhood. To further prove this, a breeze kicked up the smell of rotting garbage and—uh, gross—urine from the nearby alley. As long as I left before it got any darker, I should be fine. I dusted my hands on my jeans and dropped my board to the ground. But before I sped away, a reflection on the broken glass of a guy walking up the stairs of the building across the street caught my attention.

I turned away from the window with a gasp. My eyes had to be playing tricks on me.

But no. The guy was really there. In fact, as if sensing my presence, he paused with his hand stretched for the door handle, and glanced at me over his shoulder. Even though his chin-length blond hair covered half his face, there was no mistaking who it was—Whitley. He winked at me and disappeared inside the building.

The world slipped out from under my feet and I fell back against the bars. No. It was impossible. I had to be seeing things. Whitley was dead. I'd left him pinned to the wall in my burning house. There was no way he could have escaped. I curled my fingers around the flaking bars for support. The first stirring of a cold breeze rustled beneath my skin and turned my blood to ice.

If Whitley wasn't real, why was I having a danger premonition? It didn't make sense.

A shadow spilled across my feet as someone stepped out of the alley next to me. "My, don't you look pale. Almost like you've seen a ghost." The figure shrouded in black stopped a couple of feet away from me and crossed his arms. I'd recognized his voice as one of the ninja who'd attacked me in the alley more than a month ago. I was willing to bet it was the same ninja who'd also hijacked my elevator and bombed the dojo.

Awesome.

Despite my heart doing backflips off my spine, I pressed a fist into my palm, cracking my knuckles. Rule number one with ninja: Never let them see fear. "Wow. All this attention? I gotta tell you, though, despite current pop culture references, girls do not like being stalked. A simple spa gift card would suffice."

He laughed and shook his head. "Don't flatter yourself. Even though the boss is pretty pissed you're not dead yet, we actually have another mission for tonight. Finding you here is an added bonus."

Wrong place, wrong time was fast becoming the theme of my life. And what did he mean by another mission? This was a run-down, nearly deserted neighborhood. What could they possibly want ... But then it hit me. Whitley. This was the third time I'd thought I'd seen him only moments before a ninja attack. He was the link. They must be following his orders. And, after I'd ruined his plans to steal my ki and left him to die, it only made sense he'd want me dead.

Son of hibachi.

I rocked back on my feet and sank my weight into my heels to prepare for the fight that was sure to come. "Why don't go you go tell Whitley to come out here and fight me himself?"

The ninja laughed. "He's got more *important* things to worry about."

Just then, another shadow spilled out of the alley, bleeding onto the concrete until it rose up and became solid. This ninja was shorter and curvier. It had to be the girl. She took a step forward and I noticed she moved with a slight limp—most likely the result of her thigh getting pierced in our first battle.

I lifted my hands and assumed a fighting stance. I wondered if the third ninja was waiting for a surprise attack or if he'd join them. "Where's your buddy?"

The girl snorted. "He can't fight. His arm is practically useless thanks to you."

There was my silver lining. "Two against one? I like my odds."

The girl darted forward. "Let's see if you like this." She reached into her pocket, withdrew two pointed shuriken, and hurled them at me.

I didn't have enough time to get out of the way, so I kicked my board into my hand and held it in front of my face. The stars sank into the wood with a soft thwack. I turned the board over and examined the damage. The shuriken had created a crack wide enough that my board was no longer usable.

I dropped it on the ground. "Oh, come on! Can't you destroy something I don't care about? Like my history paper?" I unclipped my helmet and threw it to the side. It was *so* on.

The clanging sound of a chain unraveling caught my attention and I twisted in time to see the guy ninja had unraveled a manrikigusari. It looked to be about twenty feet of chain capped off with two lead spikes. The point of this weapon was to bludgeon someone to death. And I was that someone.

A typical manrikigusari was only a couple of feet long. I had no idea how the guy planned on handling such a long weapon. Or, at least I hadn't until he tossed one end of the chain to the girl.

Awesome. It was apparent I was about to become an unwilling participant in the world's deadliest game of Double Dutch. The girl hurled her end of the chain at my head at the same time the guy threw his at my chest. I ducked down, managing to miss both spiked ends as they sailed above me, but the ninja recovered each other's end of the weapon and yanked forward, sweeping the chain behind my feet.

My head smacked against the concrete with enough force that fireworks exploded in the dark pockets behind my clenched eyes. I rolled over with an "Oof," just as a metal spike kissed the sidewalk next to my neck, leaving a divot.

As the girl reined in her discarded chain, the other ninja threw his end at my chest. Still on the ground, I reached above my head until my fingers found my board. I quickly grabbed it and smacked the metal spike, sending it spiraling backward. The guy had just enough time to dive to the ground to avoid getting hit.

I jumped to my feet with my board held in front of me. Who knew skateboards made such good weapons?

The girl swung her end of the chain and ran at me. To avoid the whirlwind of lead, I ducked to the left and then again to the right to avoid her blows. Before she could strike again, I thrust my board into her chain. The momentum of the swinging chain ripped the board from my hands, hurtling it onto the street where it broke into two pieces. It gave me enough time to dart beside her and deliver a hook kick to her back.

She cried out as she stumbled onto her knees.

But I didn't have time to celebrate. The guy had recovered his end of the chain. As he launched it at me, the first pinpricks of ki needled beneath my skin. I ducked just as the girl threw her end at my knees. I jumped over the hurtled spike and barely recovered my breath before the ninja exchanged ends and struck again.

The buzzing intensified. My throat constricted and I swallowed. I had to fight it—the last thing I needed was to lose control right now—especially when I'd almost killed myself last time.

I dodged another strike. My lungs burned and my legs began to tremble. I couldn't fight them forever. How long had I been fighting them, anyway? Ten minutes? Twenty? It felt like forever. Something had to give.

I evaded another spike and ran down the length of the chain. Before he'd had the chance to recover his end of the chain, I landed a blow to his gut. He doubled over with a grunt.

"Enough." The girl dropped her end of the chain, reached into her belt, and withdrew two kunai, a diamond-shaped tool with a sharpened point that could be used as a blade. She flipped the kunai in her hands so the blade end pointed down, and crossed her arms over her chest. With a scream of rage, she attacked.

She swiped high and I ducked. Her second swipe was aimed at my gut and I had enough time to pop back on my toes with my stomach sucked in before the world got to see what I'd eaten for lunch. If I didn't know better, I would say her attacks had become even more intense. How was that even possible? Wasn't fatigue rippling through her muscles like it ripped through mine?

She stabbed again, only this time I didn't pull back in time. Fire burned across the newly made gash in my arm. A warm line of blood ran its way down my arm and dripped from my fingertips. I cursed under my breath and shook my arm, sprinkling the sidewalk with crimson rain.

The buzzing beneath my skin intensified and moved into my arm where it welled under the cut. I bit my lip and shuffled backward until my back hit the concrete wall of the building behind me.

The ninja smiled, as if she had me where she wanted me. She had no idea what she'd done.

The other ninja righted himself and moved beside her. "Any last words?" he asked.

I rolled my eyes. Why did people always ask you that

before they killed you? It wasn't like you were going to say something that would make them change their minds.

"Yes," I answered. The first tendril of power pushed through my wound and wisped the hair around my head. If I was going down, at least I would take them down with me. "Why did the chicken cross the road?"

She hesitated and glanced at the guy. Her eyes were scrunched in a way that I knew she was frowning under her mask. The other ninja looked at her and shrugged.

I licked my dry lips. "To escape the onslaught of exploding ki headed his way." Before they could move, I closed my eyes, focused on the energy raging inside of me, and let go.

27

The ki ripped from my body so viciously, it felt as if it were pulling bits of flesh along with it. It didn't make sense. After I'd transcended and regained my past-life memories, I had been in complete control of my power. So why now was everything falling apart?

I fell to my knees, my hands pressed to my chest as I gasped in pain. God. *The pain.* My vision burned white hot from the agony of it. Was I dying? Why else would it hurt so bad?

Another burst of energy pushed through me hard enough to slam my back against the wall. I cried out and crumpled into a heap in the shadow cast by the building.

The same burst hit the two ninja and sent them flying into the middle of the street. I slowly pulled myself into a sitting position and tried to blink away the spots in my vision. My muscles ached and refused to respond as fast as I wanted them to. I knew the ninja wouldn't stay down long and I had to get to my feet before their next attack. But after having the wind knocked out of me, my stiff body screamed to stay down.

The girl rolled onto her side and let out a low groan as the guy slowly climbed to his feet. I had the satisfaction of seeing him brace a hand against the small of his back as he glanced in my direction. Hopefully, whatever injury I'd inflicted would slow him down enough for me to get away. As banged up as I was, retreat was my only option.

He held out his hand to the other ninja who waved it away before staggering to her feet.

I pressed my palms against the building and used them to guide myself up.

The girl took a step toward me and stopped. "I don't understand it." Her eyes darted up and down the sidewalk. "Where did she go?"

I frowned. Pretending not to see me was a ninja tactic I was not familiar with. What did they want me to do? Wave my arms and call them over?

The other ninja scanned the edges of the building, his gaze falling over my body with each pass. "I don't know. She was right there."

Seriously? Were we in junior high? What was the point of this game? Even though the sun was moments from disappearing into the horizon and I was draped in the shadow of the building I leaned against, there was no way they couldn't see me.

The guy cursed under his breath. "The boss is going to be pissed she got away again."

The girl cried out with frustration. "We *had* her!" She punched the air before pointing to the side of the building. "She couldn't have gotten very far. I'll check this side and you check the other."

The guy nodded and they both trotted around their assigned corners.

"What the what?" I whispered. Why were they messing with me? I glanced around, waiting for them to jump out at me with a "Aha! Tricked you!" But they never did.

Something warm trickled down my neck followed by the sharp metallic smell of copper. Blood. I must have hit the wall harder than I thought. I used my hand to feel for the wound at the back of my head. When I found it, hot and burning beneath my fingertips, I brought my hand in front of my face to see how much blood stained my fingers. The only problem was, I didn't see any blood.

I didn't see anything at all.

A strangled sound escaped from my mouth as I choked on my own breath. It didn't make sense. I was holding my hand in front of my face, therefore, I should see my hand in front of my face, but all I really saw was the empty street in front of me. I spun a circle, trying to catch a glimpse of my arms, my legs, my feet, my *anything*. But all I saw was the building next to me, the street in front of me, and the sidewalk beneath me.

I, on the other hand, wasn't there.

28

My knees shook so hard they banged together. A wave of goose bumps spilled down my body and I fell back against the building.

What the hell?

The female ninja darted around the building and stopped in front of me. I pulled myself up straighter and clamped a hand over my mouth to stifle my gasp.

She froze and tilted her head to the side, listening.

I held my breath.

"Mike?" Her eyes scanned the shadows where I stood. "Did you hear something?"

The guy ninja, who I assumed was Mike, appeared seconds later from the opposite alley. "Did I hear what?"

"I don't know, exactly. I just thought ... " She shook her head. "Never mind. Do you think she went inside?" She nodded to the building Whitley had disappeared inside.

Still holding my breath, I pressed myself harder against

the wall, as if by pure force I could melt into the concrete, and took a giant step to my left. I had no idea how I had turned invisible, or how long I could keep it up. I wasn't about to take any chances.

"Maybe," Mike answered. "Let's check it out." He started for the street.

The girl followed him.

At that moment, my foot hit a chunk of concrete and sent it skittering across the sidewalk.

The girl froze with her foot hovered over the curb. "Wait." She turned and walked a direct line straight for me.

Crap! A trickle of sweat slid down the length of my spine.

The ninja stopped inches from where I stood.

I turned my head so she wouldn't feel the exhale of my breath.

"What are you doing?" Mike asked from across the street.

She didn't answer him but continued to study the ground where I stood, her eyes sweeping over my toes.

My heart thundered inside my chest loud enough I was sure she heard it. My thighs burned from the exertion of holding still. *Please,* I silently willed my body, *just a little bit longer.*

She crouched down. "Blood." She reached out and swiped the sidewalk with her finger. She brought her finger to her face and rubbed the crimson droplet between her thumb and forefinger. "Still warm."

I wrinkled my nose in disgust. Even though it was my

blood, it was still nasty. The drops must have come from the kunai wound on my arm. My only guess was that my blood became visible after it fell from my body.

I glanced at my arm to make sure, but of course I didn't see anything. But I could feel the warmth of something trickle down my forearm and fill the creases of my wrist.

Son of hibachi!

I pressed my arm against my shirt before any more of my blood appeared on the ground in front of them.

The girl stood. "She's nearby. I can feel it. She has to be in the building."

"Let's go." Mike motioned for her to follow with the wave of his arm, and the two disappeared inside the building across the street.

I counted to ten before I dared to exhale the breath knotted inside my lungs. Now what? I had maybe ten minutes for the ninja to search the building and realize I wasn't inside. I needed to get the hell out of there.

Slowly, I stretched my arm in front of me. Just like before, I didn't see anything but the street and sidewalk. An icy tremor nipped the back of my arms. What if I was stuck this way?

I kept my hand out and took another step forward, this time reaching beyond the edge of shadow cast by the building. And that's when I saw them. Purple painted fingernails hovering above the ground on floating fingers. Gasping, I withdrew my hand back into the shadows where it disappeared.

"What the what?" I whispered. After taking a moment to calm my racing heart, I decided to try again. This time, I reached my entire hand past the shadows and, just like before, a hand appeared under the streetlight, floating as if by magic.

"Gross," I muttered. This was a really sick special effect. If only I could figure out how it worked or why. Obviously, the shadows had something to do with it, but beyond that, I had no idea how I'd done it or if I'd be able to do it again.

I stretched my arm farther, marveling at the way my skin appeared to grow out of the darkness itself when I heard the sound of the door opening across the street. With a gasp, I jerked my arm back into the shadows and flattened myself against the building as the two ninja emerged from the building. They glanced in both directions before hopping over the stair rail and jogging down the street.

I watched them until they disappeared from view. Only then did I take off running in the opposite direction.

29

Samurai training tip #152: Jeans were not made for jogging.

If only the ninja could schedule their attacks with me ahead of time, I could dress appropriately.

I huffed and picked up speed as I ran to my condo. A few people lounged on the concrete steps of crumbling buildings. They eyed me curiously as I passed and, aside from a couple of catcalls and lewd gestures, left me alone—which was good because I'd met my quota for altercations that evening.

My mind still reeled over the invisibility incident. But I couldn't really mull it over as I darted through side streets and alleyways. I focused soley on getting home alive.

I jumped over a broken chunk of asphalt and paused to catch my breath. So far, no ninja. But that didn't mean anything. After the elevator incident, it was pretty obvious they knew where I lived—not the most comforting thought in the world. At least I had my danger premonitions … well, when they worked.

I jogged the rest of the way to my building and climbed the twelve flights of stairs to my condo. Once inside, I shut the door and leaned against it to catch my breath.

Debbie looked up from the take-out menus she and Jason studied at the kitchen bar. She frowned, pinching a line above the bridge of her nose. "Why is it, Rileigh, that every time you come home lately, you look like you've been involved in a street fight?"

"Not a street fight—that implies gang members or thugs." I strode past her to the refrigerator where I snagged a bottle of water and took a long drink. After swallowing nearly half the bottle in one gulp, I screwed the cap back on and looked at her. "I was jumped by ninja."

Jason stiffened, his hand crumpling the pizza menu he held.

Debbie snorted. "Very funny."

I shrugged. "Well, if the whole ninja-fighting thing doesn't work out for me, at least I have a career in comedy to pursue."

Debbie rolled her eyes and handed me a Charlie Gitto's Italian menu. "But seriously, how did you get so banged up? That cut on your arm looks serious."

"It's not. I fell off my skateboard—I'll live." I handed the menu back. "Order me the toasted ravioli, please. I need to shower."

Debbie reached for the cordless phone. "Okay. But let Jason take a look at those cuts. He *is* a doctor."

If only she knew the half of it. I sighed and motioned Dr. Wendell to follow me. "Come on, *Doctor.*"

He frowned but followed me into my room. After he'd shut the door, he whirled on me. "What happened to you? Were you really attacked by ninja? Again?"

"Yup." I opened my dresser and began rooting through the folded clothes until they were nice and rumpled. Only then did I find the sweatpants I'd been looking for.

He groaned and bit onto the edge of his thumbnail. "This is no good. After the attack on Kim's dojo, the Network doubled their efforts to track down them down, but the ninja stay one step ahead."

I folded my arms. "I'm fine. Thanks for asking."

His eyes widened and he dropped his hand. "I'm sorry. You're right. Are you okay?" He held out his hand, and when I didn't move he added, "Come on, Rileigh. Be a sport. I just need to examine your wounds to make sure you're okay."

I made a face. "Yeah, like that's going to happen. I'm fine."

"But your arm—"

"I know how to open a bottle of peroxide."

He sighed and held his hands up in defeat. "Okay, fine. But we need to figure out what to do about the ninja."

"We?" I dropped my hands to my side. "Haven't you heard? I'm no longer a samurai. There is no *we.*"

Dr. Wendell shifted uncomfortable. "Yes, well. Kim did mention he thought that was for the best."

Anger churned inside of me. My hands tightened into fists. "Then don't pretend I'm still on the team or that I give a crap about your efforts and what *things* you need to figure out. Call Kim. Isn't that his job?"

His gaze dropped to his feet. "Yes, well, he's been a little preoccupied."

I barked out an angry laugh. I could only imagine all the ways Sumi was keeping him distracted. "Oh, really? Because I hadn't noticed. I mean, he promised to take care of the ninja and—spoiler alert—they're still trying to kill me. Make sure you tell him I really appreciate the absolutely nothing he's done." I smiled and gave a double thumbs-up.

He frowned. "It's not like that. I promise you, Rileigh, the other samurai and I are doing the best we can to deal with Kim's current situation *and* the ninja. I know it may not seem like it to you, but we're all in this together."

"Oh, totally." I waved a hand dismissively. "I got kicked off the team and the other samurai are giving me the cold shoulder, leaving me to fight the ninja by myself. If that's not teamwork, I don't know what is."

Dr. Wendell looked confused. "Wait, the other samurai aren't speaking to you?"

"As if you didn't know." I flopped onto my bed.

"That doesn't sound right—"

"It's because of Kim," I interrupted. "He said he had to cut ties with me. I'm pretty sure that meant the other samurai had to do the same." Why else would Braden and Michelle have completely ignored me this morning?

He chewed on his bottom lip.

"Don't believe me?" I pulled out my cell phone, put it on speaker, and dialed Michelle's number. After it went to voicemail, I hung up and dialed Braden's number. When the same thing happened, I dialed Drew's. When his voicemail picked up, I hung up and tossed my phone on the bed. "I rest my case."

Dr. Wendell opened his mouth, but I cut him off.

"It's okay. I can't really blame them for not wanting to get involved in the breakup." Okay. That was a lie. I thought we were friends and couldn't help but feel hurt they wouldn't even *talk* to me. Breakup or not, friends just didn't abandon friends—unless we hadn't been as close as I'd thought. "Anyway, I'm doing just fine on my own. I found out who's behind the ninja attacks."

His head jerked upright, his eyes wide. "And you're just telling me this now?"

I shrugged. "I just found out. I mean, I had my suspicions, but I wasn't for sure until I saw him for myself."

"Who?"

"Whitley."

Dr. Wendell's face relaxed and he scoffed. "But that's impossible. Whitley's dead."

"That's what I thought too. But I can promise you he's alive and probably pretty pissed I left him to die in the fire."

He crossed his arms. "You're telling me you actually *saw* Whitley. In the flesh?"

"Yup. I saw him go into a vacant building on Page right before the ninja showed up and attacked me."

Dr. Wendell blinked several times, looking like he might have trouble processing this latest information. Finally, he looked up at me. "Grab your jacket. You're taking me there."

"*Seriously*?" I whined. "I've already been in one fight today. I really just want to take a shower, eat dinner, and pass out. Can't this wait until tomorrow?"

"Would a samurai really let something like this wait until tomorrow?"

I scowled at him. "You're forgetting—I'm not a samurai anymore."

He marched over to my closet, snagged a fleece jacket from a hanger, and threw it at me. "That's a load of bullshit and you know it. You can no more stop being a samurai than you can stop your heart from beating. So stop whining, man up, and let's go take care of this."

I stared at him, open-mouthed, until the shock of his words wore off. If it was a different situation, I would have told him exactly where he could shove his orders. But as much as I hated to admit it, he had a point. A samurai wouldn't sit back and relax while an enemy lurked nearby. But that didn't mean I had to like it. "Fine. Geez." I pulled my jacket on and stood. "Let's go. I hope you enjoy getting your ass kicked."

He looked at me one long moment before speaking. "I'll be fine."

I laughed. "Oh really? Think your black belt has prepared you for a ninja fight?"

"No." He shook his head. "But I'm with you. I don't need any more protection than that."

Dammit. Why did he have to say something like that? I could feel the scowl melt off my face. "C'mon." I marched out the door with him in tow before he got the idea that his proclamation of trust actually meant something to me.

I only hoped he was right.

30

You're positive you saw him come here?" Dr. Wendell asked me for what had to be the hundredth time. Using a flashlight to guide us, he led the way through the vacant building where the only sign of life was an empty room littered with fast-food wrappers and a smelly old sleeping bag.

"Yes." I wrinkled my nose and pushed aside a McDonald's hamburger wrapper with my foot. After I'd cleaned the cuts on my head and arm, we'd told my mom that Dr. Wendell was taking me to the hospital for a couple of stitches.

"It looks like the only one who's been staying here is a homeless person."

I looked up from the pyramid of Quarter Pounder boxes stacked by the sleeping bag. "So you're saying you don't believe Whitley was here?"

"No, no." Dr. Wendell swept the flashlight in the corner just in time for me to see something small and furry skitter away.

I shuddered. "Well, he was."

"I'm not arguing with you, Rileigh. I'm just wondering *why* Whitley would have been in a place such as this."

He had a point. When I dated Whitley, he drove a BMW and wore designer-label clothing. This wasn't the kind of place he'd want to hang around. "The ninja said something about meeting him here. Maybe this was his secret meeting place?"

"Maybe." Dr. Wendell shrugged. "It just doesn't make a lot of sense to me why he'd go through so much trouble."

"He's Whitley." I shook my head. "He's a reincarnated super villain who's into rituals and sacrifice. In case you didn't get the memo, he's psycho."

"You're right, of course." He nodded and waved his flashlight at the door. "Ready to go? I think we've given this place a thorough sweep and found all we're going to."

"Yeah, I guess." I kicked another bag across the room just for good measure, and the empty spot left behind revealed a business card. "Huh." I bent down and picked up the card. The moonlight filtering in through the shattered windows didn't allow enough light to make out the words.

Dr. Wendell stopped just outside of the door, aiming his flashlight at me so I had to squint into the light. "What did you find?"

"Probably nothing. It's just a business card for..." With his added light I angled the card so I could read it. "Ace Elevator Services."

The flashlight beam fell as his hand dropped to his side. "Rileigh—"

I fished my cell phone out of my pocket and held it up. "I'm already on it."

I waited until we were safely inside Dr. Wendell's car and on our way back to the condo before I dialed the number.

"Ace Elevator Services," a gruff voice answered.

"Yeah, hi. I'm calling about the elevator work you guys did at the building on Washington.

The guy snorted. "Is that supposed to be some kind of joke?"

"Um…"

The guy continued, "Are you with the building management?"

"Uh, sure?"

"Good," he said. "Just so you know, our invoice is in the mail. It doesn't matter that we didn't do any work. You called us out, and we showed up. There's a fee for that."

"Wait, why didn't you do any work?"

The guy sighed impatiently. "Well, I can see how this mistake happened in the first place. You guys are really disorganized."

"What mistake?" I prodded.

"Didn't your door guy tell you?" There was an edge to his voice and I knew I had to get my answers fast before he lost his cool and hung up. "You called us about an elevator repair, but when my guy showed up, we found the elevator had already been serviced by another company that same day."

That didn't make sense. Why would Whitley call a legit elevator-repair service *after* the ninja had reprogrammed the elevators?

"Were you scheduled to show up in advance?"

"No! That's what I've been trying to tell you. You called us an hour before we showed up, probably when the other guys were already working on your elevators." He sucked in a breath. "Look, before you waste another company's time, I suggest you guys get organized. Our invoice is in the mail." With that, he hung up.

I put the phone down and looked at Dr. Wendell. "That didn't make an ounce of sense."

"What did he say?"

"Basically, someone called them around the time when the ninja hijacked the elevators. It's almost as if whoever called wanted the ninja to be caught."

Dr. Wendell frowned and adjusted his grip on the wheel. "You're right. That doesn't make sense."

"Right? If Whitley called, why would he want to thwart his own assassination attempt?"

"Well..." He shrugged. "You said that the ninja were there to meet him. Maybe one of them dropped the card."

That didn't make a lot of sense, either. "I don't know. That would imply one of them wanted me to live. And my past experience with them has proven that's not the case."

"You're right." He sighed. "Just add it to the list of things we don't understand."

"That's getting to be a pretty long list." I leaned my head against the headrest. "We might have better luck making a list of things we *do* understand."

He stopped at a light and gave me a sidelong look. "Oh, really? Name one thing you understand."

Huh. He had me there. I stared at the people walking along the sidewalk as I thought about it. Between Q's mood swings, Kim breaking up with me for Sumi, the samurai not speaking to me, and my archenemy returning from the dead, I had nothing. But there was one thing...

"You," I said.

"What?" Dr. Wendell looked at me long enough that the car behind him blared its horn to alert him of the light change.

"Yeah." Even though Dr. Wendell was a major pain in my ass, it seemed like he really wanted to help. And I needed all the help I could get. "You're not as bad as I thought."

He laughed. "It's not a glowing endorsement, but I'll take it."

I shrugged. "Oh, and before I forget, if we're making a list of things we don't understand, I have something else to add."

"Yes?"

"I can turn invisible now."

"You what?" He jerked the wheel to the side, squealing the tires and sending the cars behind us into a chorus of horn beeps and shouted curses.

I smiled and settled back into my seat. Sometimes, I just couldn't help myself.

31

sank into the movie theater seat and tried to avoid touching the sticky armrests. It had been a week since my last run-in with the ninja and, given that I was no closer to stopping their attacks, a movie felt like the last place I should be. "I don't know why we're here," I told Quentin, who happily slurped a cherry ICEE. "I hate this theater. I hate this actress. I hate this movie." I folded my arms across my chest. "I hate my life."

Quentin spit out his straw and looked at me. "I gotta say, this new emo thing you're doing? Not working for you." He grabbed a bag of licorice and held it out to me. "Twizzler?"

I wrinkled my nose. "I hate Twizzlers."

He dropped the bag into my lap. "No you don't."

I sighed, pulled out a Twizzler, and bit into it. "No, I don't." I knew I should appreciate what Q was trying to do. But between breaking up with my boyfriend and the ninja assassination attempts, going to the movies just seemed stupid. And, because I was a glutton for punishment, I called Michelle to invite her to go with us. But she never picked up and never returned my calls. Apparently, the freeze-out of Rileigh Martin was in full force. I could only guess Michelle and the other samurai didn't want to get caught in the middle of the breakup. I understood that reasoning, but it didn't make it sting any less.

At least Q had let me pick the seats—a dark corner in the very back row. I'd received several dirty looks from couples coming in late—they'd wanted their make-out corner and I'd wanted a vantage point where I didn't have to worry about any sneak attacks. My life sucked.

I twirled a piece of licorice in my hand. At the very least, I should be happy that Q was acting like himself. The only weird part of his behavior was how insistent he was to see this particular romantic comedy—which was *so* not our thing. Especially not with the latest bloody action flick playing one theater over. "Are you sure you don't want to sneak into *The Face Punch of Death*?"

Q shook his head and put a finger to his lips. "Shh. I think the movie is about to start."

I faked a gag and settled back into my seat. If the onscreen kiss-fest made me barf, I was so aiming for Q's lap.

He stirred his ICEE with his straw. "Being here is good for you. You've been surrounded by enough pain and violence, you don't need to watch a movie about it. I'm putting an end to your pity party."

I narrowed my eyes at him. "Please. I'm not having a pity party."

"Oh really?" He held out his hand. "Hand over your phone. I want to see if you've added any new music stations to Pandora."

"Um." I fidgeted in my seat, hoping he couldn't read the guilt on my face. He totally had me there. But wasn't crying along to angsty music one of the steps for recovering from a bad breakup? Surely Q couldn't fault me for that. Although, maybe I shouldn't have named my newly created emo station—

"Kim," Q said.

The licorice I'd been chewing on dangled from my mouth. "How did you—" But I stopped when I realized Q hadn't been reading my mind. He wasn't even looking at me, but instead staring at something at the front of the theater. I followed his line of sight and realized it wasn't a *something* but a *someone*.

Kim.

Son of hibachi. My stomach dropped from my body and landed somewhere between the center of the Earth and China.

He stood at the base of the stairs holding a bottle of water in one hand and a soda in the other. He hadn't looked in our direction yet, so as far as I knew, he didn't know I was here.

Quentin reached for my hand and squeezed my fingers a little too tightly to be comforting.

The licorice fell from my mouth onto my lap. "Oh God,"

I whispered. This was the last thing I needed. I could pretend as much as I wanted that I was doing better, that Kim pushing me out of his life hadn't ripped my heart into ribbons of flesh. But not when he was in the same room as me, breathing in my air until I felt suffocated. I stood on wobbly knees. "I think I should go. I need to go."

"Are you crazy?" Q put a hand on my shoulder and pushed me down. "If you get up now, he'll see you."

"So?"

"If you leave then he'll know you're leaving because of him . . . and so will *she*." He inclined his head and that's when I saw her. Sumi. She bound up the stairs to where Kim stood waiting to usher her to their seats. She sat and, if I didn't know better, glanced over her shoulder directly at me before planting a kiss on his cheek. But that was impossible, right? It was too dark in the theater for her to see into our corner.

Kim didn't react to the kiss. He kept his eyes trained on the previews flashing onscreen and handed her the soda.

"Wow," Q whispered into my ear. "He's about as passionate with her as I am with my sister."

I had to agree. Even so, the contents of my stomach raged, a sea of bile and licorice. My fingers curled around the armrests, a flimsy anchor, to keep my body, tense with the desire to run, in place. But I wouldn't run—despite how badly I wanted to. Being with Kim had been easy, natural, thanks to a lifetime of loving him. Now it was up to me to figure out how to be without him. Despite Q's good intentions, it wasn't something someone else could help me figure out. I had to do it on my own.

Easier said than done considering I hadn't done such a great job existing in the same world as Kim, much less in the same movie theater.

I took several deep breaths. *You can do this, Rileigh.* Kim was made of flesh, blood, and bone just like every other guy in the theater. There was absolutely nothing special about him—nothing I couldn't live without.

Yeah … and since I was living in a fantasy world, I may as well add that I'd love a pony.

Q shook his head. "I just don't understand why he's doing this."

"You and me both," I said through clenched teeth.

"I mean, just look at them." He thrust his hand in their direction.

"I'd rather not." But even as I said the words, my eye refused to look anywhere else. Kim sat rigid in his chair, perfectly still while Sumi leaned her head against his shoulder. She might as well have been cuddling a brick wall for all the affection she received.

"It's so obvious he doesn't like her," Q continued.

"He says he's obligated by *honor.*" The word tasted bitter on my tongue.

"Yeah …" Q shook his head and took a long draw on his Icee. "I'm just not buying it."

Me either. But that was the sucky thing about breakups—they didn't come with answers, or sometimes even a warning. One minute, you're together, kissing in the middle of a field as he tells you how much he loves you and the next minute, you're alone, picking up the pieces of your heart that he scraped off the bottom of his shoe.

My eyes burned with unshed tears. No. I closed my eyes before they had the chance to fall. But that didn't stop the prickling sensation just beneath the surface from growing until it pushed against my skin. I tightened my fingers on the chair hard enough to make my fingers ache. A wind— either from me or the overhead air conditioning vent— tickled the hair framing my face.

Q turned to me with wide eyes. "Ri-Ri, are you okay?"

I shook my head. "I'll be fine. I'm fine." Lies. I clenched my teeth together so hard my jaw ached. I couldn't lose control now, not in a theater full of people ... and *them.* My muscles tightened as my entire body braced for the power about to rip through me.

Q put his hand on top of mine.

And just like someone had flipped a switch, the buzzing sensation died, my muscles relaxed, and my ki fell silent, retreating inside of me. For the first time in more than a month, I felt like I wasn't a bomb moments away from exploding. I felt ... normal.

We exchanged sidelong glances.

"What the hell was that?" I whispered.

"Beats me." He slowly withdrew his hand.

It didn't make sense. I was on the verge of losing control, Q touched me, and then I wasn't. "Did you—did you do something?"

He laughed out loud, which made several people turn

to us with scowls. "Uh, no. I am neither a samurai nor am I able to manipulate ki. That was all you, babe. Maybe you're just getting some control back?"

I frowned. Was I? And if I was gaining control over my ki manipulation, how was I doing it?

Q's smile disappeared behind a grimace of pain. He hissed and pressed his palm against his head.

"Q!" More dirty looks from the people in front of us. "Seriously?" I asked them. "It's just the previews!" Before any of them had a chance to say something back, I turned to Q. "What's wrong?"

He shook his head and winced. "Nothing. Just another one of my damned migraines. I've had quite a few of them lately."

I bit my lip. That wasn't good news. "Have you been to a doctor?"

"Yeah." His hand slid from his face and he blinked several times. "I had blood drawn, a CT scan, an MRI, the works, and they still couldn't find anything wrong with me. At the very least, they gave me something for the pain." He reached into his pocket and pulled out a small metal box. He flicked it open and dumped two pills onto his palm. He tossed them into his mouth and chased them with his Icee. "They don't work that great, though."

"Then why don't we go?" I stood.

"No." He waved me back down. "It's cool." He gave me a weak attempt at a smile. "Besides, the movie is about to start."

The last preview ended, leaving the theater in darkness.

The people around us became faceless shadows. It occurred to me what a potentially dangerous place the theater really was. The dim lighting made it hard to make out the things around you and the exits were a good distance away. At least, from our vantage point in the back, I had a clear view of anyone entering and leaving.

Unfortunately, I also had a clear view of Kim's unmistakable outline. Sumi leaned over and whispered something to him, her lips practically brushing his ear. My stomach convulsed and I tasted something sour on my tongue.

Just watch the movie, Rileigh. I pried my eyes off the real-life drama a couple rows ahead of me and focused on the screen, though I hardly took in anything I watched. It wasn't that long ago Kim told me even though a person's soul remained the same, rebirth made everyone a new person capable of making new choices. Kim wasn't Yoshido anymore, so I guessed it was possible we weren't the soul mates I thought we were. Since I couldn't go back in time and have Yoshido back, I had to accept the fact he was gone forever.

And who knew? Maybe in time I could learn to live my life without Kim just as easily as he lived his without me. Maybe I'd even find someone to care about again ... but first, I'd have to get rid of the ache inside of me Kim left behind. The hurt wasn't so much that he'd left me for Sumi. No, the real pain, the tearing, crushing feeling that kept me awake at night was from the doubt he ever loved me in the first place.

I must have made a sound because instantly Q's hand was around mine. The throbbing ache in my chest faded.

I took a deep breath and leaned my head on his shoulder. I was a trained warrior. I'd survived countless battles and defeated thousands of enemies. I would survive this. I might hurt every second of every day for the rest of my life.

But I would survive.

32

It wasn't until the lights in the theater turned on that I realized the movie was over. And I hadn't watched a moment of it. I couldn't stop thinking about not thinking about Kim. I kept waiting for him to stand up and tell me that he'd made a horrible mistake, beg for my forgiveness, and promise me he'd never leave me again.

Of course, that remained the fantasy it was.

Instead, I watched Kim and Sumi stand, gather their trash, and walk down the aisle together, hand in hand.

"I'm really proud of you," Q whispered in my ear.

"Yeah?" I kept my eyes locked on Kim until he'd disappeared around the corner. "You might not say that if you knew all the things I'm thinking about doing to Sumi as we speak."

He laughed. "Yes, but you didn't do those things even though we all know how capable you are of doing them. I'd call that progress."

"The night is young."

He grinned and offered me his hand when I stood. I took it and we exited the theater together. I'd made sure to take my time so we wouldn't have any accidental run-ins with the lovebirds. But when we stepped into the lobby, I heard someone call my name.

"Rileigh! Hold up!"

I recognized the voice and knew it wasn't Kim's. A wave of both disappointment and relief washed over me. I turned and forced a smile to my face. "Hey Carson."

He smiled back and shoved his hands in his jeans pockets. His nose was only a little red and nearly all the black was gone from his eyes.

Q leaned into me and whispered, "Try to have a civil conversation with the boy without bruises, blood, or blisters, okay?" Before I could shoot him the appropriate dirty look in response, he took a giant step backward and pretended to study something on the ceiling.

Carson cleared his throat and rocked back on his heels. "So... I guess you're not grounded anymore?"

"Grounded?" It took me a moment to realize that was the excuse I'd given him when he'd asked me out. "Oh, you mean when I was *grounded* for my grades."

Carson looked confused and Q rolled his eyes.

"Um, yeah," Carson said.

"Yeah, so..." I shrugged. "I'm not grounded anymore."

He frowned. "I kinda gathered that."

I laughed, though it was a pitch too high to sound

natural. "Right. I, uh, managed to ace a couple of tests and that got my mom off my back."

"Cool." He grinned.

I never noticed it before, but the cleft on his chin deepened when he smiled. It was kinda cute. If only my heart wasn't ground into pulp, I could have seen myself going out with someone like him.

He fidgeted with the leather cuff on his wrist. "So if you're not grounded, maybe you'd want to … I don't know … "

Oh crap. Oh crap. Oh crap. Oh. Crap. He was going to ask me out again. And my seatbelt wasn't fastened and my tray was not in an upright position. I wasn't ready! I looked to Q for help but he only winked. I was so going to kill him.

Okay, think, Rileigh! You could come up with an excuse to let Carson down easy. Maybe I could tell him I had leprosy…

" … you and me could … but you don't have to … "

Leprosy wouldn't work; I couldn't fake falling-off limbs. I could tell him my religion didn't allow dating. That I'd volunteered for a NASA trip to the moon. Or, I could put on my big-girl panties and just tell him the truth—that I'd given my heart to someone who'd used it for a punching bag. That it hurt too much to open myself up. That I'd never be able to be with anyone ever again without comparing them to the love I'd lost—the samurai I'd loved from one lifetime into the next. The very guy that was heading this way with his arm around another girl.

Son of hibachi.

Carson continued to stutter through asking me out, oblivious to the couple approaching.

But Q wasn't. I glanced over my shoulder and he'd turned a ghostly shade of white. Awesome. I'd get no help from him.

They stopped behind Carson. Sumi glared at me and tightened her hold on Kim's waist.

He didn't seem to notice. His eyes stayed locked on mine. The look was unreadable. It killed me to have his eyes on me again. If I wasn't so stubborn, I would have turned away.

Kim opened his mouth, but I wasn't about to listen to the bullcrap about to spill out.

"You know what?" I interrupted both Carson's rambling and whatever Kim was about to say. "That sounds really great, Carson. I'd love to go out with you."

Kim's mouth snapped shut and his lips pressed into a frown.

"Kim, I want to go," Sumi whined at his side before shooting me a dirty look.

Carson followed my line of sight and glanced over his shoulder. But he either didn't understand the showdown going on behind him, or he didn't care. Because when he looked back at me, he was all smiles. "Really?"

Something inside of me hesitated, but I ignored it. Some part of me knew I was being the world's biggest bitch by using Carson to get back at Kim. That part was overruled by the part of me that ached so badly I thought I might scream and pull my hair out in the crowded lobby. Instead, I held out my hand to Carson. "Give me your phone."

He fished it out of his pocket and put it in my hand.

"Kim." Sumi tugged on his arm.

Kim hesitated before finally allowing himself to be pulled from the theater.

I win, I thought as I punched my number into Carson's phone. No sooner did I have the thought than I wanted to thwack my head against the nearest wall. I won? Really? Because it sure as hell didn't feel like it. I stared at the phone in my hand. What was I doing? What kind of girl was I? Before I could delete my number and tell Carson that I'd made a mistake, he snatched the phone from my hand.

"I'll call you." Carson started walking backward toward the theater doors—almost as if he could sense I was seconds away from backing out, which was exactly what I wanted to do. Carson was too nice of a guy to be used.

Heartbreak was making me a bitch.

When he was gone, Quentin looped his arm through mine and ushered me to the door. "That was crazy! Did you see the way Kim looked at you? He looked devastated that you were going to go out with Carson."

"I can't do it."

He stopped walking. "What? Of course you can."

"No." I shook my head. "It's wrong. If I go out with Carson, I'd only be using him to make Kim jealous."

Q frowned at me. "I know you're not ready for anything serious. There's no law that says if you go out on one date with a boy you have to get married. Go out with Carson.

Have a good time. And if you don't want to go out with him again, don't. There is absolutely nothing wrong with that."

Well, when he put it like that, it didn't sound so bad. "You really think so?"

He ruffled my hair. "Of course." He started to say something else, but his words turned into a hiss and he pinched the bridge of his nose.

My hand hovered over his shoulder. He looked to be in so much pain I wasn't sure if I should touch him. "Your migraine?"

He nodded but said nothing.

I hated to see him suffer so much—especially when I could do nothing to alleviate his pain. "Should I take you to the hospital? This can't be normal."

He dropped his hand and glared at me. "I'm fine, okay? I don't need you making a big deal about his."

Whoa. So the Dr. Jekyll and Mr. Hyde act continued. I held my hands up in surrender and took a step back. "Sorry. I'm just worried. You don't need to bite my head off."

He blinked several times before his angry expression melted into one of surprise. "I'm sorry. I-I have no idea why I snapped at you. The migraines feel like a knife stabbing into my brain... but it's more than that. I can't think clearly. I'm not myself."

Understatement of the year, but I wasn't about to say that out loud. Instead, I nodded sympathetically. "Pain can do that." I held my hand with the palm down, like he was a dog who might bite. "Let's get you home, okay? I bet sleep will help."

He sucked in a breath. "That's probably a good idea." He took my hand and together we walked into the dark parking lot. When we arrived at his Mini, I rubbed my hands over my arms to ward off a chill from the crisp fall night. Or so I thought until I opened the car door and spotted a folded piece of paper on the passenger seat.

Q opened the driver's door but hesitated when I hadn't made a move to get in the car. "What's up?"

I stared at the piece of paper, positive it hadn't been there when I'd gotten out of the car. It was from a yellow legal pad— the same kind of paper left on the door of my old house with a threat. I glanced around the parking lot for anything out of place. "Q, did you lock your car doors before we went in the theater?"

He held up the remote on his keychain. "Always."

A locked door is a small obstacle for a ninja. I closed my eyes and allowed a small amount of my ki to slip through my skin and search the lot for anyone who meant me harm. After a few moments of detecting no negative energy, I pulled my ki inside of me and opened my eyes. "Someone left us a note." I grabbed the piece of paper and climbed into the car.

Q climbed in after me and eyed the note I held on my lap with wide eyes. "Who do you think left it?"

"Whitley." I knew without opening it. Legal pads weren't the obvious choice when it came to threatening notes and casual letters. Using the same type of paper he'd used at my old house let me know he wanted his identity known.

"But-but," Q stammered, "I thought he was dead."

I looked at him. "I don't have that kind of luck."

We sat in silence for a moment, me staring at the paper, not wanting to deal with the words written inside of it, and Q drumming his fingertips against the steering wheel.

"So ... " he began.

"Yeah, I'm going to do it." I opened the paper and read.

Meet me at the Grand Basin tomorrow at midnight.
Don't be seen and DON'T be followed.

So, yeah. Just an anonymous cryptic note leading me into a trap. Pretty much what I expected. I crumpled the note and leaned back against the seat. "Where the hell is the Grand Basin? What the hell *is* the Grand Basin?"

"I think it's the lake in front of the Art Museum in Forest Park." Q reached for the note in my lap and smoothed it out. After he read it, he looked at me. "Do you really think this is from Whitley?"

I nodded. "Yup. Now I just have to figure out why he wants to meet in Forest Park. There are a lot more convenient places to murder someone."

His eyes widened. "So you think it's a trap?"

"I don't know. Did you receive an invitation from Whitley for an early surprise birthday party for me?"

"Uh, no."

I shrugged. "It's a trap."

Q glanced at the paper. "Well, then I guess it's easy enough to avoid. Don't go."

"Yeaaaaaah." I stared out the window so I wouldn't have

to look at his "stern" face. "You see, that sounds all well and good. But the problem is, the ninja attacks have been escalating. And if I don't show up, Whitley knows where I live. He could attack me there. My mom would totally ground me if I had a ninja fight in the condo while she was out of town." I looked over my shoulder and gave him my most dazzling smile.

He scowled.

I stopped smiling. I really needed to work on my dazzle.

"My mom is having a Scentsy party tomorrow," he said.

"The scented-wax thingies? Random. But go on."

He laced his fingers together on his lap. "I was thinking... I know how much you love to smell things."

I nodded. I could spend hours in a candle store sticking my nose inside every jar. "True. I do love to smell."

"Well, instead of going on your suicide mission, you could just come to the party. We could go smell crazy and even sneak a few of my mom's JELL-O shots. Eh?" He poked a finger in my ribs. "Epic, right?"

I laughed at his sorry attempt to convince me not to go. "Yes, but as much as I love smelling things and hangovers— and just so you know, I really don't like the last one—the party wouldn't be that epic if a bunch of ninja showed up and stabbed everyone to death. That's kind of a buzzkill."

He made a face. "Like that would happen."

"Right. Because it wasn't like they bombed an entire dojo or anything in broad daylight."

Q opened his mouth only to snap it shut again.

I patted his leg. "They're not going to stop until I'm

dead, Q. And I promise you, I'm going to try really hard not to be dead."

He crooked a smile. "It's not like my mom doesn't throw a dozen of these parties a year. We can always go to another one if we survive tomorrow night."

I blinked at him, hoping I had heard wrong. "We?"

"Well, duh. It's not like I can let you go gallivanting off to your death alone. What kind of friend would that make me?"

"A smart one."

He rolled his eyes. "Please don't give me any crap about you not wanting me to go because you're worried I'll get hurt and blah, blah, blah. Because I'm coming with you. Who knows?" He shrugged. "Maybe I can even help."

As if I was going to let him risk his life. I folded my arms. "And if I say no?"

He smiled. "Then I'll tell Dr. Wendell what you're up to and I'm sure he'll insist on going. The way I see it, someone is going with you. It comes down to whether it's me or Dr. Wendell."

I glared at the conniving evil genius that was my best friend. I didn't doubt for a minute he'd tell Dr. Wendell if I didn't let him come. And, while Dr. Wendell had some martial arts experience, he was still ... Dr. Wendell. I was sure he would insist on running the show. Not going to happen. This was my death trap, and if I was going to die, I was going to die on my terms. If worse came to worse, I'd figure a way to get Q out of there.

"You win," I said. "Be at my house by eight."

33

I don't think he's coming." Q picked a blade of grass and proceeded to shred it into ribbons.

"Why send someone an invitation for a fight to the death and then stand them up? Talk about rude." I fidgeted on the stone bench we sat on. It stood at the top of a hill that overlooked the man-made lake known as the Grand Basin. I'd chosen the spot because it was shielded from behind by a hedge, and a large oak tree several feet down the hill hid us behind a canopy of orange and brown leaves. As far as cover, it was good a spot as any. But we'd sat here for nearly an hour and, aside from the shushing sound of the fountains in the lake, the night was quiet.

Q shrugged. "We don't know for sure that the note was inviting you to a death match."

I made a face.

"Okay, you're right." He waved his hand dismissively.

"Maybe Whitley got cold feet considering how things went the last time you fought?"

"Maybe..." But then I saw the black outline of figure rounding the side of the lake and begin to climb the hill leading up to the Art Museum. I stood. "Or maybe he was just running late. Look!"

Quentin followed my finger and jumped to his feet. "What do we do? Charge?"

I held my hand out to block his chest in case he decided to do something rash. "Easy there, tough guy. The first thing we need to do is assess the situation."

"Okay." I felt the muscles of his chest slowly unwind. "So what does that mean?"

I crept forward, keeping my back to the hedge despite the branches that pulled at my shirt. I motioned for Q to do the same. "Stick to the shadows. We're going to follow him and make sure he's alone. If the other ninja are here, I don't care what happens, you run." I stopped and looked at him. "Promise me?"

He frowned. "But—"

"No matter what," I insisted. "Promise me."

He sighed. "Fine."

"Good." We continued down the line of bushes until it ended at the street in front of the museum. The shadowy figure continued to climb the hill.

Q hovered above my shoulder. "Do you really think it's Whitley?"

I shrugged. "I guess we're about to find out."

At the top of the hill, he stopped in front of the giant

statue of St. Louis atop his horse that overlooked the lake, and glanced in our direction. It was hard to make out who it was from our hiding spot. Despite having long blond hair that hung in such a way it covered half of his face, I knew it was Whitley. The chills that pulled at the hairs along my neck were all the proof I needed.

"Is he looking at us?" Q hissed in my ear.

I raised a hand and motioned for him to be quiet.

The guy smiled and jogged across the street. But instead of running up the main entrance stairs to the museum, he veered right and disappeared around the corner.

"That was ... strange," Q said.

"It doesn't make sense," I agreed. I motioned for Q to follow me and we sprinted to the St. Louis statue and peered around the corner. I stood there for several moments and watched the corner of the museum until I saw the guy appear, look in our direction, wave us over, and disappear again.

Uh-huh. I could take a hint. "He wants us to follow him."

"Why?"

I peeled myself off the base of the statue. "Apparently the trap is that way." I pointed to the side of the museum. A funny pressure pushed against my insides, different from the telltale buzzing that indicated I was about to lose control of my ki. The feeling inside of me was warm ... and sticky. Like my blood had been replaced with honey. Not exactly unpleasant, but not that fun, either.

"Are you ready for this?" he asked.

Ready to put a stop to the ninja attacks? Totally. Ready

to engage the most powerful adversary I'd ever had in a battle? Not so much. "As ready as I can be, I guess."

Q nodded and pulled a black ski mask over his face. "Let's do this."

I blinked. "Where the heck did you get that?"

His voice came out muffled. "Last year's Aspen trip. Don't worry, I got you one too." He handed me a hot pink ski mask. "This was Carly's."

I tossed it into the nearest bush. "That's gross. There's no way I'm going to breathe in her nasty, dried-up snot."

He shrugged. "Suit yourself."

I held up my hand, motioning for Quentin to remain still as a car drove by the road. When I was sure the coast was clear and no one else was around, I motioned Q forward. We darted across the road, veering to the right of the building and tucking ourselves into the shadows of the neighboring trees. We wound ourselves around the perimeter and arrived several feet away from a side entrance that closed with a soft click as we approached.

I leaned against the wall next to the door and braced my hands on my thighs as I tried to regain some control of my galloping heart.

Quentin rubbed his hands together next to me. "Okay. Now what?"

"Whitley went inside and he obviously wants us to follow him, but ... " I pointed to a blinking security camera trained on the door. "Before we do, I have to take care of that. The last thing I need right now is to go to jail for breaking and entering."

"That does look bad on a college application," Q said. "But how are you going to deal with the cameras?"

"I'm not sure, exactly. But I'm going to try something." I kept my eyes trained on the security camera as I fell inside of myself. I followed the energy that pushed against my body until I found the source—my spirit. It pulsed in greeting, the prickly feeling spreading throughout my body immediately. I stumbled forward and placed a hand against the wall to steady myself.

Q rushed to my side. "Are you okay?"

I grunted an answer through clenched teeth. The pain was unbearable. A hundred porcupines rolled through my body, under my skin. Why did it have to hurt so much? What had happened in the last couple of months to make my ki both unpredictable and painful? "I'm going to let go," I told him. "Stand back."

He hesitated, as if unsure he should leave me. Finally, he took several steps backward. "Okay."

I nodded. The pressure ballooned under my skin until I thought I might burst into tattered shreds. I couldn't let the pain take control because if it did, there was no telling what I would do. Who I would hurt. Despite the ripping sensation tearing through my skin, I kept my focus on the security camera. I imagined it shutting off along with every other camera and alarm inside the building.

The pressure burst through my skin, rushing from my chest and fingertips, searching for its destination.

I gasped.

Q was back at my side. "What just happened?"

"Wait for it," I whispered and motioned to the camera with my eyes.

A second later, the red light above the lens pulsed once before going out. With the task completed and no other job to do, all of the energy I'd just released came flooding back inside of me. I jerked back from the force of the collision, barely able to keep my balance. Luckily, Q was able to grab my arm and keep me righted.

He stared at the camera. "That's a nifty trick. I didn't know you could do that."

I opened the door to the museum and looked at him. "Me either." I ducked inside.

He jogged to catch up to my quick strides. His eyes were wide as he gazed around the darkened corridor. "So how do you know it worked?"

We came to the end of the service hallway. I pushed against the utility doors and glanced both directions down the dark museum hallway. "I don't." I caught movement to my right—Whitley. I grabbed Q's shirtsleeve and pulled him into the hallway with me. "C'mon."

We jogged to the end of the hall and I stopped to glance around a corner. The shadow moved into a large exhibit hall.

Our sneakers made no noise as we raced across the hardwood floors. We followed the figure into another hallway with pictures of half-naked women draped across chaise lounges.

"Do you know where he's going?" Quentin hissed behind me.

I shook my head as we followed the darting figure

deeper into the museum. It didn't make sense for Whitley to lead us on such a wild-goose chase just for a fight. No. He wanted us here at the museum for a reason—and I was pretty sure I wasn't going to like what it was. Q and I sped around another corner and found ourselves at the foot of a massive staircase.

We climbed the steps two at a time. The last couple weeks of climbing twelve flights of stairs on a daily basis at the condo had been the perfect workout to get me ready for this. I had barely raised my heart rate when I'd reached the top. Q, on the other hand, was huffing behind me.

The figure left the stairs and darted into a corridor.

I waved Q on. "Just a little farther."

We trotted past an exhibit of Grecian pottery and into a room with a giant silk screen. Japanese cranes were painted on it in varying degrees of flight, illustrated in broad brush strokes.

We skidded to a halt—the room was a dead end. And other than several glass cases illuminating various Japanese treasures within, the room was empty.

Or so I thought.

A shadow peeled itself from the wall and stepped forward until the room's dim lighting revealed the half of his face not concealed by hair.

Whitley.

Even though I'd spotted him several times before, I still hadn't been ready to come face-to-face with the living ghost of the guy who'd tried to murder me. I forgot how to speak. I tried several times, but the sounds it took to form words wouldn't come—at least not coherently. I managed a strange sort of gurgling noise.

Whitley smiled. His gorgeous face the perfect disguise for the complete psycho beneath. "Hello to you too."

Anger at what Whitley had done to me, what he was still doing to me, ignited in my body and loosened my tongue. "You're supposed to be dead."

He made a face that clearly told me I'd said something stupid. "Do I look dead?"

I was hit from behind and it took me a moment to figure out it was Q trying to claw his way over me, his fingers stretched out, inches from Whitley's neck. "I'll take care of that!" Q snarled. "For what you did to Rileigh, I'll kill you myself."

A smirk spread across Whitley's face. "I'd love to see you try."

I gripped Q's arm and shook it until he looked at me. "Look, I get dibs on killing him. But first, I'd like to know why we're at the museum. This is a really weird place to have a fight."

Whitley snorted. "I'm not here to fight. I need your help."

I folded my arms. "With what? An art report? Because that really could have waited until the museum was open."

He rolled his eyes. "Very funny. I need you to help me steal this." He gestured to the case beside him and an antique Japanese hairpin labeled *kanzashi*. It looked like two silver prongs with a cluster of silver flowers at the base, each flower containing a coral bead in its center.

"What?" I started to ask him if he was crazy before I

remembered I already knew the answer to that. "I'm not going to help you steal anything."

Whitley didn't answer. He used his elbow to smash the case. After the glass lay pooled around our feet, he grabbed the kanzashi and tossed it to me. Instinctively, I caught it, just as the wail of a security alarm screeched around us.

Whitley laughed. "Looks like you just did."

34

I stared at the kanzashi in my hands and then back at Whitley. My shoulders tightened and I took a step toward him. Over the wail of the alarm I screamed, "I'm going to kill you!"

He tsked. "Is that any way to talk to someone who's trying to save your life?"

Oh, that was a new one. What kind of idiot did he take me for? "How—"

But he cut me off before I could finish. "Not here. We don't have time." He grabbed a fistful of Q's shirt and pulled him forward. "Let's go!"

I didn't have time to argue. Instead, I followed him as he ran down the staircase and around the corner into an Egyptian gallery. He started to make a sharp turn into a neighboring hallway, but skidded on his heels as a dancing flashlight beam appeared from around the corner.

Son of hibachi! We were so busted.

I jumped back as Whitley turned into me, dragging Q behind him. He pressed a finger to his lips and motioned for me to go the opposite direction with the jut of his chin.

I darted down the hall as the tumbling of multiple footsteps ascended the stairs we ran past.

"We're going to jail!" Q's panicked voice shouted behind me.

"Not if I can help it." I took another right into the room with a twisted metal sculpture made out of rusted car parts. I darted behind it and pulled Q beside me. Whitley crouched behind him. "We'll hide here until they pass," I whispered.

Whitley shook his head. "We can't just hang out here. That's only going to give the cops time to swarm the building."

I glared at him. "You know, we wouldn't even be in this mess if it wasn't for you."

He glared back. "You really are that clueless, aren't you? You have no idea what you're holding or what I'm trying to do."

I glanced down at the kanzashi clutched in my hands. Whatever the hairpin meant to Whitley, it wasn't like I could mull it over given my current circumstance. I opened my mouth to tell Whitley exactly that, when the sound of approaching footsteps killed the words on my tongue.

Invisible hands squeezed at my heart. I glanced around the room, but the only way out was the way we'd come in. I sank back on my heels. If I wanted to keep felony theft off my record, I had to come up with a plan. And fast.

Q's voice hitched in his throat. "What are we going to do?"

Whitley stood and unsheathed a katana strapped to his back. "We fight," he said simply.

"What?" I stood next to him. "You can't fight the security officers. They're just doing their jobs."

He dropped the sword to his side and sighed. "You know, I thought when I'd enlisted your help that you'd be, oh, I don't know, a little more *help*."

The footsteps were right outside the room.

"I think I have a way out of this in which nobody has to die." I jammed the kanzashi into my pocket, spread my arms, and reached for Whitley and Q's hands. "Let's just hope it works."

35

The first security officer entered the room. She was barely in her thirties. Her mouth dropped when she caught sight of us, her lips forming an O of surprise.

Quentin's fingers tightened around mine. Whitley's hand was cool and rigid. I closed my eyes, channeled my ki, and hoped to hell what I was about to do would work.

I prayed they both knew enough to keep silent.

The security guard blinked several times at us before mashing the heels of her hands against her eyes.

"Are they in here?" Another officer, a black male in his fifties, joined her side and waved his flashlight around the room.

She shook her head. "I thought—I just—" She sighed. "I need to get off the night beat. I'm seeing things."

She continued to stare at our corner.

A heavyset guard shuffled into the room, pausing in the doorway to wipe the sweat from his brow. "The rooms behind us have been searched. If the intruder is in the museum, they have to be up ahead."

The older guard nodded and readjusted his grip on the flashlight. "Let's move out. The cops should be here soon and they can help search." He jogged out of the room without a glance in our direction. The heavyset guard followed him. The woman hesitated and, instead of following them, took several cautious steps toward the spot where we huddled.

Both Whitley and Q tightened their grip on my hand as the guard studied the shadow we hid in. Quentin's grip was so tight and painful that I had to bite down on my lip to keep from crying out.

The guard narrowed her eyes and I held my breath.

After an eternity, she shook her head. "I'm going crazy," she mumbled. She gave our corner one last look before trotting out of the room.

When I was sure she was out of earshot and no other guards were on their way in, I let go of Whitley's and Q's hands.

They both released their held breath with a collective whoosh of air.

"Ri-Ri," Quentin's face had paled to an ashy gray. "Why was I invisible?" He stared at his hand, turning it over as he studied it. "Why, Ri-Ri?"

I shrugged. "Um, I'm not exactly sure."

Whitley stared at me as if I had spiders crawling out of my ears.

"What?" I snapped.

He smiled coyly. "You're more resourceful than I thought.

Too bad your little tricks will only delay your death. You really need me if you want to stay alive."

"Yeah? Because it looks more like you need me." I narrowed my eyes. "Care to tell me why?"

"I'd be happy to," he answered. "But first, we need to get out of here before the cops show up. Meet me at the Denny's on Grand. Think you can get out of here without being seen?"

"I don't like it," Q growled. "This loser drugged us, stabbed you, and set your house on fire. And now he's got us involved in some sort of museum heist. I think we should kick his ass and leave him for the police."

I fingered the hairpin in my pocket. Come to think of it, Q's plan wasn't entirely a bad one.

Whitley laughed, flashing the single dimple that wasn't hidden by the curtain of hair covering half of his face. His dimples had once sent shivers through my body. Now, they made me cringe. "Let's not do anything hasty. You may not think so, but you guys need me." He dipped his chin and his single exposed eye bore into mine. "You're in a lot of trouble, Rileigh, and I have the answers you desperately need." He held out his hand. "The hairpin, please?"

I withdrew my empty hand from my pocket. Whitley had dragged me into this museum robbery and I wasn't about to give him anything until I found out what was going on. Because, chances were, if Whitley wanted the kanzashi, it was probably powerful and dangerous. With the strange way he wore his hair, I doubted he wanted to accessorize. "I think I'll hold on to it for now."

He chuckled. "Okay, fine. Just meet me at Denny's. I'll explain things to you there."

That was it? No fight for the kanzashi? No assassination attempt on my life? I looked at Q who looked just as confused by Whitley's behavior as I was.

Did I really think that Whitley was offering to help me out of the goodness of his heart? No. But if I knew Whitley as well as I thought I did, he was after something. And he needed me to get it.

36

don't like this." Q turned off his car.

I wasn't thrilled to be at a Denny's at two in the morning to meet my arch nemesis. At least the public setting ensured enough witnesses to discourage a murder attempt... I hoped.

Q looked at me, his eyes set with worry. "You're not really going to give him that hair thingy, are you?"

"I don't know... " I stared at the kanzashi in my hand, trying to figure out where I'd seen it before. There was something about it, a memory that refused to surface.

I wasn't exactly keen on keeping a stolen artifact—there had to be some bad karma in that somewhere. But if Whitley went through all of the trouble of having us help him steal it, the reason for him wanting it couldn't be good.

Quentin gripped the steering wheel. "I don't trust that guy, Ri-Ri."

"Me either. But like the saying goes, keep your friends close—"

He rolled his eyes. "And your enemies closer. Yeah, yeah. I get it."

I carefully placed the kanzashi inside my backpack. "Whitley is the one sending the ninja after me, or he knows who is. Either way, I feel better having him close enough that I can keep my eye on him."

"Didn't you tell me he betrayed you and killed everyone you loved in your past life? He's a liar and a backstabber."

"I know. Which is exactly why I won't let my guard down for a second." I opened the car door and stepped out into the cool night air, hoisting the backpack over my shoulder.

"You won't be the only one." He fell into step next to me as I walked into the restaurant.

Inside, the smell of grease and coffee greeted us. A haggard-looking man with a dirty beard sat on a stool at the counter and a college-aged girl sipped coffee in a booth, surrounded by various textbooks. Neither of them set off my ninja alarm, so I continued to the register.

"How many?" A guy with teal-colored hair and three lip piercings leaned across the counter and scratched his scalp with the back of a pencil. His nametag read Trace.

"We're meeting someone," I told him.

Trace jutted his chin to a corner booth. "The emo convention is that way."

"Thank you?" Quentin and I exchanged glances as we left the register.

"I'm a little insulted," Q said as we walked through the dining room. "I mean, I'm wearing all black and that guy just assumes I'm some emo kid? Like the possibility I just pulled off a major museum heist never even crossed his mind?" He huffed. "Maybe I should get a tattoo. How is one supposed to be taken seriously as a criminal nowadays?"

I ignored him and kept walking until I stood next to the booth. Whitley glanced up from his menu and set it aside with a grin. I had to give Trace some credit—with Whitley's hair hiding half of his face the way it did, he really did look a little emo. But Whitley's new hairstyle was the last thing I was concerned about.

"So I came." I slid into the booth across from him. Q sat next to me.

"Obviously." Whitley folded his hands across the table. "Did you bring the kanzashi?"

I patted the bag next to me. "If you think I'm just going to hand it over to you, you're a few ninja short of a clan."

He shook his head. "No. I knew you'd make this as much of an annoyingly difficult situation for me as possible. Some things never change."

"Difficult for you?" I huffed. "What about us? Do you think we actually thought, 'Oh, it's such a beautiful night. We really should rob a museum.'"

Q grabbed my arm, motioning his head to the patrons who were now staring at me.

I inhaled sharply, trying to diffuse the anger burning through my blood. When I spoke again my words were low, almost a growl. "You stabbed me."

Whitley waved a hand in the air dismissively. "Yes, yes.

And you left me in your house to burn alive. I'd say we're even, wouldn't you?"

A choked noise escaped my throat. "Are you kidding me? I lost everything because of you. My house, my clothes, photographs, memories—they're all gone!"

Whitley leaned across the table, viper-quick. I threw an arm protectively across Quentin to block whatever attack was coming.

But Whitley didn't strike. Instead, he pushed his hair back, revealing the scars that had distorted his skin, shiny and slick. It looked like half of his face was made of melted wax.

Quentin went rigid next to me and I gasped.

"Wah! My clothes. Wah! My precious memories. Look at my face!" Whitley's right eye bulged from the socket, looking as if it were on the brink of falling out.

At that moment, all I wanted in the world was to look away. But I knew that was exactly what Whitley expected me to do. So I stared at his face without blinking. "I don't understand what your point is," I said. "Are you expecting me to feel sorry for you?" I grabbed hold of the table to keep from wavering under his horrific gaze. "Honestly, I think you got off easy."

Whitley didn't move for a few seconds. And then, very slowly, he released his hair so that it fell back over the mangled half of his face. "Yes, well, what happened to my face is nothing compared to what *she'll* do to the both of us if she gets her hands on the kanzashi."

Q laid his arms on the table and leaned forward. I'd never seen him so aggressive. "Who's *she?*"

Whitley took a long drink of his water before he answered. "*She* is the most powerful kunoichi who ever lived and *that*"—he gestured to my backpack with his glass—"was her hairpin."

I groaned. Suddenly, it all made sense. "So you wanted to steal the kanzashi so you could try to kill this poor girl and steal her power like you did with me? Whitley, I knew you were crazy, but you really must be out of your mind if you think I'd stand by and let you do that."

His eyes narrowed and a chill settled over the table. "You have no idea what you're talking about." His voice cracked as if he had trouble containing the emotion behind his words. "This *poor girl* that you speak of makes me look like a saint."

I made a face. "Yeah right. You'd say anything to get what you want."

"You think so?" He leaned over the table and lowered his voice. "You think I was responsible for your deaths in Japan, right? Well, you forget that I was merely doing what I was paid to do. The ninja attack on the village? Lord Toyotomi's death? Your death? I was carrying out orders. *Her* orders."

A jolt ran up my spine and I shivered. An old memory clicked into place. "Your benefactor," I whispered.

He nodded. "The famous kunoichi. If you want someone to blame for the slaughter in Japan, she's the one. I was merely a hired hand. If I hadn't led the attack, it would have been someone else."

I closed my eyes. Inside the darkness, I could see my Yoshido lying on the ground, his body contorted into an odd angle as his lifeless eyes stared through me. My knees trembled. "You think that matters?" I opened my eyes and glared at him. "When you were Zeami, you were still a brother samurai. You betrayed us all."

He rolled his eyes. "Get over yourself. That was a lifetime ago. Besides, it wasn't like things worked out entirely in my favor."

I glared at him. "Let me guess. Your sheets didn't have a high-enough thread count?"

He made a face to show me he was clearly not amused. "No. This." He pointed to the faint pink line that ran across the length of his neck. A line he'd shown me the night he tried to kill me. "You already know that serious and fatal injuries show up as birthmarks in a next life, right?"

I nodded. Q shook his head.

Whitley's voice dropped to a whisper. "After the attack that left you all dead, I went to kunoichi for my payment and, instead of rewarding me as she'd promised, she had me beheaded."

I leaned back in surprise. So that was how Whitley was beheaded—he was betrayed after betraying us. Score one for karma. "If you think I'm going to feel bad for you—"

"Of course not!" he cut me off. "I'm telling you this so you can see the type of woman the kunoichi is. I made one tiny mistake and she vowed to hunt me down and kill me in every lifetime."

"What did you do?" Quentin asked.

Whitley waved the question away. "Doesn't matter."

"Okay," I said. "You don't like her and she doesn't like you. Got it. How does the kanzashi factor in?"

"Because we can't let her get it!" He slammed a fist against the table, rattling his water and drawing curious glances from the two other patrons. He lowered his voice. "If she touches the kanzashi, then she'll transcend. And if she regains her power, she'll be unstoppable. We'll be as good as dead."

37

I looked skeptical. "Why would she even care? Maybe she's over it?"

Whitley laughed, a desperate sound that made my gut clench. "Several ninja attacks have led me to believe otherwise."

That got my attention. "Wait, what? I thought you were working with the ninja. I saw them follow you into that abandoned building."

Whitley sighed and shook his head. "You really do reinforce the whole blonde cliché. You know that, right?"

I scowled at him.

He smiled back. "The ninja were there to kill me. You just showed up at the wrong place at the wrong time."

I folded my arms on the table. "Then why did I find a business card for an elevator-repair service? You want to tell me you weren't involved in the elevator hijacking."

He leaned forward. "I tried to *stop* the hijacking. I've

been keeping an eye on your building for your own good. That's how I found out the ninja screwed with the elevators. I called another repair service in hopes the ninja's sabotage attempts would be discovered." He shrugged. "You're welcome."

I leaned back against the booth. Huh. Whitley was trying to *save* my life? This was getting more confusing by the minute.

Trace appeared at our table. "Can I get you something to drink?"

I blinked at the waiter. His question swirled inside my head with the hundred or so already there.

"Coffee," Q answered. "For both of us."

My stomach roared to life. "And cheese fries," I added. Stress made me crave carbs something fierce.

The waiter nodded and disappeared into the kitchen.

"So let me see if I can figure this out." I pressed my index fingers into my temples. "You botched up your mission and pissed off this kunoichi person in Japan so now she wants to kill you in this life, right?"

Whitley made a face. "Thanks for your concern. And yes, I was sent to kill all of Toyotomi's samurai, *except* Yoshido. I think she thought she could convince him to lead her army. How was I supposed to know he'd sacrifice his life for you? Needless to say, when I didn't return with Yoshido"— he drew a line across his neck with his finger— "the kunoichi was a little upset with me."

I swallowed the bile that had risen in my throat at the mention of Yoshido's death. "Okay, great. But I still don't understand why she's sending ninja after *me*. Honestly, I could care less whether you live or die."

His lips curled into a twisted smile. "If you knew what was good for you, you would."

Quentin leaned forward. "Is that a threat?"

"Not in the way you think." Whitley's eyes burned into mine. "Here's a fun little bit of trivia I learned because of recent events. You and me? We're soul mates, babe."

"What?" My laugh was loud enough to draw a startled glance from our waiter who stood behind the counter pouring coffee. "In case you forgot, we did the whole dating thing—it didn't work. As it turns out, having a guy stab you is kind of a turnoff."

Before Whitley could answer, our waiter walked over and set two steaming mugs of coffee on the edge of our table. "I'll be right back with your fries." He retreated back into the kitchen.

After he was gone, Whitley folded his hands on the table. "I don't mean we're soul mates in the way that you think. We're not going to get married and have little samurai babies or anything." He shuddered. "But you are the other half of my inyodo."

I froze in mid-sip of my coffee, and looked at Q. "Is that some perverted slang I don't know? Because if it is, I'll kick his ass."

"No." Whitley sighed. "The inyodo is Japanese yin-yang. The world runs on balance. For every yin, there is a yang. For every black, a white. For every evil, there must be a good to balance it. Balance keeps the world spinning. Without balance?" Whitley mimed an explosion with his hands.

"So what you're saying," Quentin began, "is that you're Rileigh's opposite? You're the anti-Rileigh?"

Whitley grinned. "Look at that. One of you has a brain."

I tightened my grip on my mug and debated whether or not to toss it into his lap. "Okay. So if what you're saying is true and you're my... *soul mate*"—a thought that made me throw up in my mouth a little—"that still doesn't explain why the kunoichi wants me dead."

"Doesn't it?" Whitley looked surprised. "Let me spell it out for you. The world revolves around balance. If something disrupts that balance, nature will find a way to fix it."

I still didn't understand. If I was the balance of Whitley, and something happened to me... Realization tightened my lungs and forced a gasp from my throat. "You mean if the kunoichi kills me then—"

Whitley's smile widened. "I die," he finished for me. "Which is exactly why the kunoichi sent ninja after you—if she kills you, then she kills me by default. But it works in reverse too. If she does kill me, then you die. So now you see why you and I have to work together."

"Son of hibachi," I muttered. This sucked on so many levels.

The waiter set the plate of greasy cheesy goodness in front of me, only now I was too upset to eat. Whitley, however, helped himself to a forkful of fries.

"I know this comes as a shock," Whitley said, after he finished chewing. "I was surprised when I realized it. Obviously,

I wouldn't have tried to kill you if I'd known I'd be endangering myself." He shrugged. "But we're both still alive, so no harm, no foul."

I exchanged an incredulous look with Quentin before pulling the plate of fries out of Whitley's reach. Rileigh Martin did not share cheese fries with boys who stabbed her.

Whitley, unfazed, wiped his hands off on a napkin. "I just can't believe I didn't figure it out sooner. In our last life, I died within twenty-four hours of your death. That should have been my first clue. Not to mention you're everything I can't stand." He shook his head. "I should have put it together."

"Well, this is just fantastic." I threw my hands in the air. "I'm being forced to work with my arch enemy, the person who murdered me and everyone I loved in my past life, just so I can stay alive in this one?"

Whitley looked thoughtful. "Yeah, that sums it up nicely."

I propped my elbow on the table and set my chin on my fist. "I honestly don't know how this can get any worse."

Whitley's expression darkened. "I'll take gruesome deaths for $500, Alex."

"What are you talking about?" Quentin asked.

Whitley leaned forward and lowered his voice. "If the kunoichi gets her claws on the comb, she'll regain her former power. And trust me when I say this, it would be a very, *very* bad thing. Remember the lightning I used to kill Yoshido?"

I gripped the table so hard my knuckles ached. "It would be wise of you not to bring that up," I growled.

Whitley waved my threat away. "The power I used was

a gift from the kunoichi. And it was only a fraction of what she could do."

I forced my eyes to stay open, afraid if I blinked I would see Yoshido lying dead in the darkness behind my eyelids. "How did she get so powerful?"

He shrugged. "Why can you manipulate ki? Why am I so good looking? Everyone is born with their own special talents."

I wondered how hard and how fast I would have to strike to stab my straw through Whitley's neck. But then I realized if what he said was true, I'd only be killing myself in the long run. I let my forehead fall to the table with a thunk.

My life had officially hit ten on the suck-o-meter.

"Now that you know what's going on," Whitley said, sliding his hand across the table so it rested by my face, "you can give me the kanzashi."

I didn't move, but instead stared at his outstretched hand as I pulled the backpack against my body. Whitley, if he wasn't lying to me, only wanted the hairpin to protect us. But if he was lying, there was no telling what trouble he could cause.

Whitley withdrew his hand with a sigh. "Oh, come on. After everything I told you, you're still not going to trust me?" He folded his arms across his chest. "All right. Don't give me the comb. But at least destroy it. And do it in front of me so I can be sure you did it correctly.

That didn't sound unreasonable. I sat up. "Okay. Fine."

"Good." He reached into his wallet and tossed a twenty onto the table. "Let's go. I have lighter fluid and matches in my car. I'm not leaving anything to chance."

He stood and slid out of the booth. Quentin and I followed him outside. I clutched the bag to my chest just in case he tried to pull something funny. Whitley stopped at his black BMW and opened the trunk. True to his word, he pulled out a bottle of lighter fluid and a box of matches. He offered them to me. "I'll let you do the honors."

"Uh, thanks." I took the bottle and matches from him and set them on the ground so I could unzip the bag. I couldn't help the pang of regret that ran through me as I pulled the kanzashi out. It was a beautiful piece of history. And here I was about to burn it in a Denny's parking lot.

I sighed. Oh well.

I set the comb on the ground and cringed as I doused it with lighter fluid. Such a shame. After making certain it was saturated, I took a match and lit it.

Whitley held his breath.

I paused, letting the flame burn dangerously close to my fingertips. I didn't want to destroy such a gorgeous antique, but if I wanted to live I didn't really have a choice. "Here we go," I whispered as the match fell from my grasp. But as I watched the flame tumble toward the comb, I detected movement to my right. Before I could turn and figure out what was happening, Quentin darted in front of me and snatched the comb before it could ignite.

I stared at him, trying to figure out the meaning of his actions. "Q?"

He turned to me, his eyes wide. He looked just as confused as I felt.

I took a step forward. "What are you doing?"

"Yes." The threat lining Whitley's words was unmistakable. His body tensed and his weight shifted to the balls of his feet. I knew he was seconds away from pouncing. "What *are* you doing?"

Quentin's eyes flicked between me and the comb in his hands. "I have no idea."

My ki stirred inside of me—a warning, but of what I couldn't figure out. I held my hand out. "Please give me the kanzashi, Q."

"No!" His eyes blazed with anger and he hugged the kanzashi to his chest.

I froze and the buzzing inside of me intensified. Something was seriously wrong.

Whitley stepped beside me. "Give us the comb or I'll take it from you by force."

Q looked at me, the anger on his face melting into confusion. "What's going on? I don't understand . . . " He looked at the kanzashi in his hand.

Whitley edged forward, but I stopped him by holding my arm out, thumping it against his chest. I didn't understand why Q was acting so weird, but I wasn't about to let Whitley at him. "Cool it, Whitley."

Whitley glared at me.

I turned my attention back to my best friend. "Q, are you feeling okay?"

He blinked. "Yes . . . no . . . I feel . . . I feel . . . " But instead of finishing, he hissed in pain and dropped the kanzashi to the ground. He pressed his palm into his temple and doubled over. "Oh, God. It hurts!"

"What hurts?" I was at his side in an instant, wrapping my arms around his shoulder. Panic squeezed my chest. Quentin was in pain. I had no idea why, and no idea how to fix it.

He cried out again and would have fallen to his knees if I hadn't shifted my hold to his waist. I staggered forward, trying to keep him on his feet, and shot a pleading look at Whitley. "Do something!"

Whitley stared at us, unmoving. He cupped his chin with his hand. "Interesting..."

"This is *not* interesting!" I shouted. "What is interesting are the various places you can stab a person without killing them—and I know them all! So do something!"

Whitley rolled his eyes before walking over and hooking an arm under Q's. "Easy," he muttered. Then to me, "Let's get him to the curb."

Q groaned. His head rolled around his shoulder like a flower with a snapped stem.

My breath knotted in my throat. "Do you know what's wrong with him?"

Once Q was safely seated on the curb, Whitley released him and stood back. He cocked his head in observation.

Frustration wove knots into my stomach and itched along my skin. We were getting nowhere fast. "Forget I asked you to help," I told Whitley. I pulled my cell phone from my pocket.

Whitley turned his attention on me. "Who are you calling?"

"An ambulance. Something is really wrong with him!"

I gestured to my friend groaning on the curb. "I can't sit here and do nothing."

"Don't." Whitley grabbed my wrist. "They can't help him."

I shook free from his grip and glared at him. "How do you know?"

He turned away from me and crouched in front of Q. "I'm pretty sure I know what's going on with you. And I think I can help. But I'm going to need your complete trust. Do I have it?"

Quentin looked at him, uncertainty showing in his tear-filled eyes. Finally, he nodded.

"Good." Whitley pulled a switchblade out of his back pocket.

I tensed, my heart fluttering like a frightened bird. "What are you doing?"

Whitley flicked a switch and a three-inch blade flipped out of the hilt with a click. "The kunoichi got to him." He held out his hand to Q. "Give me your arm. This will only hurt for a second."

"No! Absolutely not." I stepped in front of Q and faced Whitley. I should have known better than to think he could actually help. "What the hell do you think you're doing?"

He shrugged. "Look. You said you wanted my help, so I'm giving it. If you're going to be all snippy about it, I can just go. He gestured to Q. "Good luck dealing with it on your own. The kunoichi has infected his mind."

I glanced at Q. "What does that mean—*infected*?"

Whitley inspected the blade in his hand, turning it over.

"It means she's manipulating his mind. It's kind of her specialty."

Mind manipulation? I had no idea that was even in the realm of possibility. A shudder ripped through my body and I hugged my arms across my chest to suppress it. "But I don't understand. How did she do it?"

Whitley shrugged. "I only know what she can do. I don't know how."

Quentin blinked several times before dropping his forehead into his hand. "I don't think I can handle this."

"She's obviously using him to work against us," Whitley continued. "Haven't you noticed him acting strangely?"

Quentin looked up and we exchanged glances. He had been having a lot of mood swings lately. But I'd assumed they were the result of his migraines which, come to think of it, were pretty odd too. I crouched beside him. "Do *you* think your mind's been manipulated?"

He opened his mouth, closed it, and shook his head. Finally, he shrugged. "I don't know ... I mean, I haven't felt like myself for awhile. I've been so *angry* ... especially with *you*. And I don't know why." He made a pained sound, pinched the bridge of his nose, and looked away.

Even knowing his mind might be manipulated, his admission cut into me like a blade. My Q, my best friend in the world, couldn't stand to be around me? I stood and cracked my knuckles. This kunoichi just messed with the wrong samurai. I turned to Whitley. "What if you're wrong?"

He held the blade in front of him. "Then he's going to need a big Band-Aid."

"Why?" I stared at the knife, trying to swallow around the lump of fear that had risen in my throat. "What's the knife for, exactly?"

Whitley held the blade in front of him, a hungry look on his face. "The migraines," he answered.

"What about them?"

He dropped the knife to his side. "Really? Do I have to do *all* the thinking?" When I didn't answer, he sighed and pointed at Quentin. "The migraines tell me that your friend here is more than he appears."

Quentin and I exchanged more confused looks.

"The migraines are a sign he's fighting the kunoichi's mind manipulation."

"That a good thing, right?" Q asked.

Whitley smiled. "Well, it's a curious thing. You see, most people can't fight mind manipulation. The fact you're doing it leads me to believe you're more than *most*."

His revelation knocked the wind from my lungs. I sucked in a breath. "Wait, what?"

Quentin only stared at Whitley, his eyes bulging from their sockets.

Whitley looked at me and wagged the knife in the air. "How often does he get sick?"

I thought about that and frowned. I couldn't remember a time when Quentin had the flu, a sore throat, or even the sniffles.

"That's what I thought." Whitley stepped around me. "You see, mind manipulation is a type of infection." He grabbed Quentin's arm. "Do you know what kind of person can fight off a powerful mental infection?"

Q shook his head, his eyes never leaving the gleam of the blade in front of him.

But I knew. Whitley's words had jogged a fragment of a memory from the past. I remembered returning to the village after a particularly bloody battle. One of the twins, Yorimichi, had been struck in the thigh, right through an artery. Poor Yori had been so pale. Yoshido rode behind him in his saddle just to keep him from toppling over. I was sure he was going to die. But Lord Toyotomi had summoned a woman in a white robe, a woman who laid her hands over my dying friend.

And saved him.

I swayed slightly under the weight of my revelation. "He's a healer," I whispered.

Whitley smiled. "Very good."

I looked at Q, who still wouldn't take his eyes off the knife. "Did you know?"

"Know what?" He winced and I knew he must be experiencing another wave of pain. "I have no idea what you're talking about."

"I believe him." Whitley raised Q's arm over his head. "I don't think he knows what he is. He hasn't opened himself to his power, which is why he hasn't fully been able to heal himself of the mind manipulation." He leaned in close to Q, a smirk on his face. "But don't worry. That's where I come in."

It was at that moment I figured out Whitley's plan. And,

despite his intentions, I couldn't let him do it. I wouldn't let him risk my best friend's life.

Whitley brought the knife to Quentin's arm and I snatched it away before the blade could do more than prick his skin.

"Not Q." I flipped the knife over and handed it back to Whitley, hilt first. "Cut me instead."

Whitley's smile was too eager for my liking. "With pleasure."

"What? No! What are you doing?" Q's voice wavered.

Instead of answering, Whitley brought the knife down on my arm. And despite gritting my teeth, a small yelp managed to push past my lips. The pain was white hot, almost to the point of blinding. After I got over the shock of the initial cut, a burning sensation spread across my arm. I pressed my hand to the wound, but the blood managed to squeeze through my fingers and fall on the pavement in fat droplets. "Damn it, Whitley!" Panic fluttered through my heart, speeding up my heart rate and making the blood fall from my fingertips that much faster. I should have known better than to trust him. "You cut too deep!"

Whitley shrugged. "I'm only trying to help."

Help, my ass. I cradled my injured arm against my chest, ignoring the warm sticky blood soaking into my shirt and, more than likely, ruining my bra—which sucked even more because those things weren't cheap.

Q looked at the blood falling from my arm with terror in his eyes. "Why did you do that? I don't understand ... What is it you want me to do?"

Whitley looked offended. "I am trying to help you, you idiot! Your healing powers aren't strong enough to get rid of the kunoichi's mind manipulation. But if you would quit your sniveling and focus on Rileigh's arm, you might be able to awaken your full powers."

Might. Not exactly a comforting word when you're bleeding to death in a Denny's parking lot. I tried to ignore the tendrils of doubt wrapping around my gut. Blood saturated the front of my shirt. "This better work." Panic edged into my voice.

"Of course it will," Whitley said. "If you die, then so do I. Do you think I'd really risk my own life?" He used the corner of his shirt to wipe my blood off his knife.

No. Whitley wouldn't risk his life. Not unless he'd been lying to me about the whole soul mate thing and this was a ploy to slit my wrist. *Stupid Rileigh!*

I turned to Q. "I know this is a lot of pressure, but I have faith in you. You have to do this." I stepped toward him and wavered on my feet. The blood loss already made me dizzy. With my good hand clamped on the cut, I thrust my arm at Q. "And you have to do it fast."

He stared at my arm with a look of horror. "This is ridiculous. We have to get you to a hospital!"

Blood was everywhere, hot and sticky on my skin, soaked into my shirt, and filling my nose with its metallic scent. "There's no time." I took another wobbly step. "You can do this. I believe in you."

He swallowed. "But I ... I don't know the first thing about healing someone."

I thought back to the healer in Japan. She hadn't said anything, she just placed her hands on Yori until color warmed his face. "You'll know if you try. Place your hands on my arm, close your eyes, and the rest will come to you."

He frowned.

"Please, Q." A black cloud darkened the edges of my vision. I had only minutes until I lost consciousness and... worse. "You have to try. For me."

He bit his lip and nodded. Without speaking, he took my arm and tightened his hand on the wound. I dropped my hand and trickles of blood squeezed through the edges of Quentin's fingers. If he was grossed out, he didn't show it. His eyes met mine, his expression unreadable. "Let's do this."

38

Quentin closed his eyes.

I closed mine too.

And waited.

And waited some more.

If something was happening, *other* than me bleeding out in a dirty parking lot, I sure wasn't aware of it. I swayed and Q's grip tightened. The pain in my arm faded until I could barely feel anything at all. I remembered the same thing happening when I'd died—it was a very bad sign.

"Is it working?" Q asked.

"Keep concentrating." I hoped I didn't sound as desperate as I felt.

"Okay."

Another minute passed. A heaviness settled across my shoulders and threatened to pull me to the ground. I was so tired. My knees buckled. I wanted to prepare for impact but all my strength was focused on staying conscious. Another second and I'd kiss the pavement.

And that's when it happened.

A faint warmth spread from Q's fingers into my body. At first I thought it was the heat from his skin. But the warmth intensified into a delicious burn, like the heat from a fireplace on a snowy winter's night.

Q gasped but kept his grip on my arm.

The heat spread from my arm, into my chest, where it branched out, reaching from my fingers to my toes. My knees stopped wobbling and I felt stronger. The dizziness inside my head dissolved.

Q released me and the warmth flooding my body vanished. I opened my eyes and looked at my arm. What blood remained was tacky and flaking. But the wound itself had disappeared without so much as a scar.

"Holy sh—" Q jumped back, stumbled over a parking block, and landed on his butt. He skittered several feet away before stopping.

Whitley yawned. "You're welcome."

Q's wide eyes reflected the glare of the streetlight. "But I—that's not—I don't understand."

A-freaking-mazing. I rubbed my arm, it didn't even ache. And there was something else too. My ki, the raging wind of power constantly threatening to explode from my skin, had settled inside me. I closed my eyes and pressed my hands to my chest just to be sure.

Yep. No more spirit-energy hornets swirling around trying to beat their way out. I opened my eyes. "My ki—"

"All better, is it?" Whitley cut me off with a smug smile.

"How did you—"

He waved my question away. "Your mind had been manipulated too. I've been keeping tabs on you and, in doing so, I found out about your little ki *episodes*. My guess is that the kunoichi tried to suppress your powers but didn't quite succeed."

Anger ripped through my veins like a bottle rocket. My hands reflexively curled into fists. "So that's why my ki has been so jacked up lately? Because this kunoichi bitch did something to my *mind*?" I'd never felt so violated. It was one thing to try and kill me, but it was a whole other thing to screw with my head.

"Yes, well, it didn't work, did it?" he said. "Probably because she didn't have a whole lot to work with."

I held my hand out and channeled a small amount of ki into my hand. The difference in my control was amazing. Before Quentin healed me, manipulating ki felt like a constant struggle to harness the tornado of energy inside of me. Now, it was more like funneling a breeze. With a flick of my wrist I sent Whitley staggering back against his car door. "What was that?" I asked.

Whitley hit the door with a grunt. After he straightened himself, he looked at me, his eyes wide and his hands held up in surrender. "What I *meant* to say is she doesn't have much to work with because she doesn't have her full power, yet."

"*Uh-huh.*"

"Anyway, you should be thankful." Wincing, he rubbed his shoulder.

"And why's that?"

He stopped rubbing and dropped his hand to his side. "Because she obviously helped your powers grow. With your ki raging and you constantly struggling to keep it in check, you were able to move to a whole other level. *Helloooo?* Super-cool invisibility powers? That's totally worth a couple of death attempts."

I wondered how many death attempts I'd have to survive to turn him invisible. *Permanently.*

Whitley plucked the hairpin off of the ground. "It's been … well, not fun." He shrugged. "If it weren't for the kanzashi, it would have been a complete waste of time." He turned to his car.

"Wait!" I started after him. "What are you going to do with the kanzashi? And what about the kunoichi?"

He glanced at me over his shoulder, his eyes narrowed. "I suggest that, even though it will be an unpleasant experience for the both of us, we team up. Make no mistake. She'll kill us if we let our guard down. If we work together, we might stand a chance."

I nodded, digesting his words. "Okay. So what do we do in the meantime?"

"I'm going to destroy this." He held up the kanzashi. "And then I'm going to track down the kunoichi."

"And if you find her?"

He smiled. "*When* I find her, I'll need help. I'll be in touch."

My mind reeled as I struggled to process everything that had happened to me. I didn't like the fact that Whitley was leaving with the comb, but I had more important things to worry about at the moment. "What about Q?"

He shook his head. "Look, that's really not my problem. Just get him calmed down and get the kunoichi out of his head." He started to climb into his car.

"But how?" I asked. "What if I can't?"

Whitley hesitated, smiling. "Then you'll have to kill him. Because if you don't, he'll eventually be consumed by the hate the kunoichi's implanted in his head. And then he'll kill you. Have fun." He waved before shutting the door and driving away, leaving me alone with my mentally ambushed best friend who, by the way, was now puking in the bushes.

Awesome.

39

Q sat on my bed hugging his knees to his chest and rocking back and forth.

I lit several candles and turned off the lights. "Close your eyes," I told him. "And concentrate on breathing slowly." With any luck we could pull this off without waking Debbie or—*shudder*—Dr. Wendell.

He nodded and closed his eyes. His chest convulsed as he struggled to steady his ragged breaths. "Now what?"

I wasn't exactly sure—I knew nothing about being a healer or how their abilities worked. But I did remember Lord Toyotomi's lessons in ki manipulation. I hoped the same principles applied here. Healing had to be just another way of moving energy ... I hoped.

I sucked in my own deep breath. "Okay. First things first, you have to find your center. Breathe in through your nose and exhale through your mouth. Concentrate on your breathing and nothing else. If it helps, imagine yourself floating out of your body."

He frowned. "I don't know. This sounds kind of ridiculous."

I flicked my fingers at him, releasing just enough ki to ruffle his hair. "Was that ridiculous?"

He opened his eyes and nodded. "Yes. Yes it was."

I chuckled and sat next to him. "Fair enough. It's ridiculous that I can conjure up fireballs in chemistry, shield my body with energy, and disappear into shadows. It's also ridiculous that you can heal a deadly knife wound in seconds without leaving a scar behind." I held up my arm. "But you can. So now you have to work around your doubt. You need to understand there's more to this world, there's more to *you,* than you realize."

"Okay." He sounded skeptical.

"Close your eyes."

He obeyed.

I folded my legs underneath me and took hold of his hands. I really had no idea what I was doing. I was navigating on gut instinct. I only hoped it would be enough to save my friend. "What did it feel like when you healed my arm?"

He shrugged. "I don't know ... it's kind of hard to explain. Even though my eyes were closed, when I held your arm ... I could see this disgusting green—the color of mold—swirling in the darkness."

"And then what?"

He shrugged. "I'm not exactly sure. All of a sudden I saw a yellow light. It just appeared and grew brighter and brighter until the ugly swirling green disappeared inside of it."

Yep. That was nice and mysteriously vague. "Can you do it again?"

He frowned.

I squeezed his hand. "Don't answer that. We're just going to do it whether you think you can or not."

"That doesn't make sense."

"Doesn't matter."

"It kinda does."

"Shush!" I ordered. "No more negativity. Close your eyes and concentrate on your mind. What do you see?"

"Nothing," he said. "I really don't think—" But he bit off his words before he finished. His body went rigid, his fingers felt like stone in my hand. "No. Wait." His voice lowered to a whisper. "I can see it. It's..." He shuddered. "Horrible."

I tightened my grip on his fingers. "You can do this. Focus on creating a light and burning away the green."

Q was silent for several moments. Then he gasped, his fingers painfully grasping mine. A hiss escaped through his clenched teeth.

My heart shot like a rocket up inside my throat. "What is it? Are you okay?"

He shook his head, his face pinched with pain. "It's so deep. The infection... it's surrounding my mind... it's rooted inside of it. It won't move!"

"Yes it will!" It had to. There was no way I was going to lose him to the kunoichi. "Focus on that light, Q. Burn it away."

He groaned. "It hurts..."

My muscles tensed, readying myself for action—my

go-to response whenever I was afraid. The problem was—with the battle raging inside Quentin's mind—there wasn't a damn thing I could do to help. "I'm here." I rubbed slow circles on the top of his hands with my thumbs. "You can do this, Q. You're stronger than you think. I believe in you." I gave his hands an extra squeeze to emphasize my point.

"No." He opened his eyes and looked at me. "I'm not strong like you and the others. I'm not a samurai." He shook his head. "I don't know why you hang out with me. I'm weak. I slow you down. I can't fight so I only get in the way."

I jerked him forward so our foreheads almost bumped. "That's BS. The kunoichi's infection is making you think that." But I wasn't sure if that was true. Did Quentin really feel that, because he wasn't a samurai, he didn't deserve to be my friend? "Q, you are the bravest person I know. When that mugger attacked us last summer, you jumped in front of me without hesitating. And tonight, you were ready to fight Whitley—and he's psychotic."

A pained smile pulled at his lips. "Maybe I'm just stupid."

"No. It means you're a good friend. The best friend I have. You're the only one who hasn't abandoned me. And you were able to fight a mind assault from a powerful kunoichi. You are strong, and I'd be happy to have you fight by my side."

The smile dissolved from his face. He closed his eyes and fell silent. When he didn't move for several moments, I leaned forward, my lungs tight with worry. "Q?"

He opened his eyes, only they were no longer his eyes. Gone were the beautiful green irises, replaced instead by a milky white haze.

"Q!" Threads of fear laced across my chest. What if I'd been wrong? What if, by trying to help him, I'd only helped him root the infection deeper into his mind. What if he was ... gone? I placed a hand on his shoulder and shook him hard enough to make his head bobble on his neck. "Look at me!"

He blinked several times, and gradually the white haze faded, leaving his eyes shining with relief. He smiled. "It's gone."

I stared at him, afraid to touch him and shatter this too-good-to-be-true moment. "Are you sure?"

Q threw his arms around me and crushed me to his chest. "I'm sure." His voice hitched around a sob. "Ri-Ri, I'm so sorry. I never meant the awful things I said to you or the horrible way I treated you."

I hugged him back. "It wasn't your fault." And it wasn't. The kunoichi better hope Whitley found her before I did. Either way, I was going to make sure she paid for the hell she'd put me and Quentin through.

Q didn't answer, only continued to hug me to his chest. Locked inside his arms, I realized the knot of tension had been the only thing keeping me together. Now that it was unraveling, I felt myself coming undone. A sob escaped my throat and Q brought a hand to the back of my head. I was so tired. So tired of the ninja, my heartache, and so tired of feeling like I was in this alone.

But now I had my best friend back. And I was going to do whatever it took to make sure the kunoichi didn't mess with us again.

40

I never would have guessed after being chased through a museum by security guards, the next night I'd be doing something even less fun.

Carson and I exited the mall's movie theater and walked down the wide aisle between the clothing shops and jewelry stores. He shuffled next to me, his stride uneven as he struggled to match the pace of my short legs.

I shouldn't be here. It made me twitchy just thinking about the kunoichi and what she might have planned next. I should be with Whitley, hunting her. Not on the world's most uncomfortable date.

As we walked aimlessly, our swinging hands accidentally brushed. I flinched and Carson jammed his hands into his pockets.

This was going to be a long night.

"So, uh ... " Carson's voice broke our marathon of silence.

I looked at him expectantly. He had to realize this date

was a disaster. We hadn't said more than a couple of words since he picked me up. We barely made eye contact. I didn't know about him, but I just wasn't *feeling* it. I silently wished he would suggest we call it a night.

"Do you want to grab a bite in the food court?"

No such luck. I shrugged. "Sounds good." Even if the date was a disaster, that didn't mean I couldn't enjoy a greasy egg roll.

As I walked with Carson to the food court, I couldn't help but wonder if I'd ever find someone I'd love as much as Kim. Just thinking about him made my heart clench in pain. How long would it be until I could go out with another guy and not spend the entire time thinking about Kim? How long until the mention of his name didn't rip claws through my chest? How long until I could walk through the mall without seeing him exit a luggage store with a brand-new carry-on set in tow?

Wait. What?

I hadn't meant to stop walking, but my feet had rooted themselves to the ground and wouldn't budge. I couldn't breathe. He was really here. Close enough that I could run up to him and throw my arms around his neck.

But no. I couldn't do that. I couldn't do that ever again.

"Rileigh?"

I blinked at the flannel-shirt-wearing boy next to me and tried to remember who he was and what I was doing with him. I shook my head, forcing my eyes away from Kim. "Sorry, Carson. I-I know that guy."

Carson glanced at Kim and a pinched look crossed his

face. "The guy from the theater. I remember ... Do you want to say hi or something?"

I barely suppressed a laugh. That was the last thing I wanted to do. Actually, I wanted to punch Kim in the face. Really hard. I wanted to make him suffer, make him bleed for ripping out my heart and pretending I didn't matter.

But at the same time, I wanted to throw my arms around him and kiss him. I wanted him to admit he still loved me. That he was sorry for hurting me. I wanted him to take back all of the hurt he'd inflicted on me and promise he'd never do it again.

And then I'd hit him again. And kiss him again. And I'd keep doing both until I'd burned every ounce of torment from my body.

Yeaaaaah. That didn't sound healthy. But I'd worry about that later.

I shook my head. "I don't want to say hi. We were friends once. But now ... not so much." I thought of Yoshido and all the nights we'd spent entwined in each other's arms. I thought of his kisses and the words he whispered hot against my neck. I shivered. "Yoshido is dead."

Carson's eyes widened. "*Who's* dead?"

I laughed nervously and waved my hand dismissively. *Stupid Rileigh.* "Nothing. Let's get some food."

"Okay." He smiled and held out his hand.

I paused, staring at his open palm as another awkward moment passed between us. Finally, Carson dropped his hand and looked away, but not before I saw the hurt pass through his eyes.

God, I was making this so much worse. "No. I'm sorry." I snatched his hand and curled my fingers around his. His hand felt weird entwined with mine. His fingers didn't overlap quite right with my much smaller ones. We didn't fit. Not like Kim and me. But there was no Kim and me. There was only me, the mall, and Carson. Who was a cute boy. A nice boy. This could work. I would make this work.

Carson stared at me with an unreadable expression. "You're a hard one to figure out, Rileigh Martin."

"Yeah, I know." We continued to the food court. I resisted the itching inside of me that ached to watch Kim walk away. I couldn't help but wonder why he needed a new suitcase. But it didn't matter. Nothing Kim bought or did was any of my concern. "I'll give you the Wikipedia summary and save us some time."

Carson waited.

"Likes—skating and greasy food."

He nodded. "Both good things."

"Dislikes—getting stabbed."

His laugh was both surprised and nervous. "Yeah, I'm not a fan of getting stabbed, either."

I smiled back. We had things in common. That was good, right? Maybe I could do this dating thing, after all. Easy-peasey.

As we approached the food court, the smells of frying oil and salt greeted my noise. Ahhh, heaven.

"What would you like?" Carson asked.

I surveyed the various fast-food counters with everything from the greasy Americanized version of Chinese food to the greasy Americanized version of Mexican food and everything greasy and Americanized in between. "One of each, please."

He laughed and pulled me toward a pizza counter. "How's this?"

I opened my mouth to answer him when a prickly, cold sensation spread across my body. A feeling that could only mean one thing: Someone here wanted to hurt me, and not just in a clog-my-arteries-so-I-die-of-heart-disease kind of way, either.

Son of hibachi.

"Uh, Rileigh?"

I glanced at Carson, who was staring at my white-knuckled grip on his hand. I quickly let go. "Sorry."

He flexed his fingers as he shook his hand. "Did anyone ever tell you that you're kind of strong for a girl?"

I ignored him and surveyed the food court. It was almost eight o'clock, so there weren't many diners. Two young mothers and their toddlers sat at a table to my right. To my far left sat a man surrounded by shopping bags; the woman he was with chatted away on her cell phone. Definitely not ninjas.

But they were here. I could sense them … somewhere.

"Rileigh, are you okay?"

I shook my head as I continued surveying the passing shoppers. "I don't think so. All of a sudden my stomach feels all flip-floppy. I think it was the jalapeño nachos I ate at the movie."

"Really? You seemed fine a second ago."

"Funny how fast those things work through your system, huh?"

I grabbed his hand and pulled him away from the food court, retracing our steps toward the theater and the parking lot beyond. I had to get Carson out of here before whatever was going to happen happened.

I half-jogged, half-pulled Carson through the thinning crowds of shoppers. But the pressure under my skin continued to build until I felt like an overinflated balloon. Somewhere, somehow, the ninja were closing in.

I pulled Carson into the nearest store, hoping to lose the ninja by ducking through the racks. And then maybe I could catch a glimpse of whoever was after me.

"Um, Rileigh…" Carson fidgeted in place, his face crimson. He looked really uncomfortable.

And then I spotted the table full of bras next to him and realized why. I had pulled him inside of a Victoria's Secret. Lovely.

"Hi!" A perky blonde with a French twist and a black pantsuit approached us. "What can I help you find today?" She pulled a measuring tape off of her shoulder. "I'd be happy to measure you to make sure you're wearing the correct cup size."

Carson stared at the ceiling, his cheeks burned so red they bordered on purple.

"Um…" Sometimes I missed the simplicity of being a samurai long ago. If someone was after you, you could just cut their heads off. And if you did it in public, odds were people would even cheer. If I did that now, I was pretty sure

I'd no longer have a social life. "My cups are fine, thanks." As soon as I said it, I wanted to bash my head against the nearest wall.

Before the saleslady could argue, I pulled Carson out of the store. So much for hiding. Walking through the mall, the sensation buzzed below my skin greater than before. My skin crawled and my pulse skipped. I half-walked, half-ran toward the parking lot, lugging Carson behind me like a frightened pony. We'd just turned a corner around a cell phone kiosk when I spotted them.

A tall, dark-haired boy wearing a black T-shirt and jeans walked briskly in my direction, followed by a dark-skinned girl with mocha hair and chili pepper lips. Her smile oozed acid.

They weren't the same ninja from my street fight, but if the buzzing beneath my skin was any indicator, I had no doubt these two intended to bring the hurt.

So, I had a decision to make and fast. Of course they were here to kill me. But what did I do about it? They didn't want to throw down in the middle of the mall, did they? But of course they were ninja, so anything was possible. Either way, I couldn't let them get close to me or Carson. They'd use his inexperience against me.

If I could just make it to the parking lot, maybe I could convince Carson to leave without me. And then I could take care of the ninja on my own. But if Carson wouldn't leave, well, I doubted he had *Be killed by ninjas* penciled in on his schedule. I only hoped I could get us out of this in one piece.

41

I kept my gaze locked over my shoulder, watching the two ninja close in on us from behind. If we could pick up the pace, we'd reach the doors to the parking lot. Just a little farther...

"Rileigh." Carson jerked free from my grip. "Look out."

Before I could glimpse what he was warning me about, I collided into something hard—something that smelled like sandalwood.

Son of hibachi.

I wobbled back, dazed from my Kim impact, when Carson took my hand and pulled me against him. "Sorry about that. My girl isn't feeling so great."

My girl? I fought the urge to make a face at him. I had more important things to deal with than Carson's sudden possessiveness.

I watched the ninja, who hung back but still watched the scene with interest. At least I knew they weren't going to make their move around bystanders. This was good news. Maybe I could find a way to ditch Carson, after all.

"Are you okay?" Kim asked. His soft tone pulled at the slivers of thread keeping me together. God, I'd missed his voice.

I locked my jaw and dared to look at him. To my surprise, I didn't burst into flames of agony. But I did feel the knife of pain, still buried in my heart, twist. I would never forgive him for doing this to me. Not in this lifetime. Not in a thousand lifetimes.

Carson cleared his throat, pulling me back to the world that existed beyond me and Kim—a world with ninja who wanted to kill me.

Right. Focus, Rileigh.

"We have to go," I told Kim. I tightened my grip on Carson's hand, knowing it was the only thing keeping me rooted in place. Even now, with all my anger, I could still feel his pull, the need to stand next to him, to touch him, to—*NO!* I had to focus. "Later." I only hoped it hurt Kim to see me with someone else as much as it hurt me to see him with Sumi. Still holding Carson's hand, I brushed past Kim, not bothering to keep my shoulder from bumping against him as I walked past. I didn't have time for personal drama. I had staying alive to worry about.

"Rileigh, wait."

My feet stopped moving. Just like that. Despite the fact I'd rather be trapped in an entire room full of ninja than to be in a five-mile radius of Kim, he still had the ability to stop me in my tracks. And I hated him for it—for the hold he had over me. Anger simmered in the pit of my stomach. Anger at Kim for making me love him, and anger at myself for being unable to stop.

Carson's hand slid out of mine.

"What, Kim?" I didn't bother to hide the acid in my voice.

Next to me Carson snickered. "His name is Kim?"

Kim frowned, as if noticing him for the first time. His eyes traveled over Carson's frame and I knew Kim was sizing him up.

Awesome. Not only did I have ninja to deal with but now I had a pissing contest between two boys.

I tried to ease the tension by smoothing the anger out of my voice. "Is there something you wanted?"

Kim looked at me, but his gaze kept flicking to Carson. "Yes ... I need to talk to you."

I wanted to laugh. He had a month to talk to me. So why now, on ninja date night, was it so important? "Now's not really a good time."

"Why?"

"We're kinda on a date, dude." Carson's shoulders tightened.

I fought the urge to roll my eyes. Of course this was happening *now*. I considered waving the ninja over. I would have preferred fighting them to this.

Kim let go of his suitcase. "This is more important than your date, *dude.*"

Carson's eyes narrowed. "Get a clue. Rileigh said she doesn't want to talk to you." He took a step forward. I wasn't sure what he was going to do, but I had to stop him before he got hurt. In a way, it was cute to think he thought he was defending me. Little did he know, I could break every bone in his body using only my index finger. I placed a hand on Carson's chest and pushed him back.

"I got this," I told him.

Slowly, he backed off. But he didn't look happy about it.

Kim, on the other hand, was smiling a stupid cocky grin. So annoying.

I placed my hands on my hips. "Look, Gimhae, you want to talk to someone? Remember those three friends I made outside the art gallery downtown? Their buddies are here. Why don't you go talk to them?"

The smile melted from his face as his eyes widened in shock. He scanned the passing shoppers. "Are you sure?"

"Positive."

He stared at me a moment longer, as if trying to tell me something—but I wasn't getting the message. Finally, he gave a curt nod. "You know, maybe I should be going."

Carson folded his arms across his chest. "That's probably a good idea."

Ignoring him, Kim grabbed the handle of his suitcase and wheeled it behind him. "Where are you parked?"

I nodded to the exit down the hall. "Out there."

He smiled. "What a coincidence. That's where I'm parked, too."

Carson scoffed. It wasn't like I believed Kim, either. But if we were about to have a showdown with ninja, I definitely didn't mind the backup. Now I just had to figure out what to do with Carson.

As we started down the hall, the ninja followed. Kim watched my gaze and nodded to let me know he'd spotted them too.

Our subtle communication was second nature. It renewed the ache inside me. The hurt reminded me of the way things were and the way they were supposed to be. But I needed to pull myself free of the past. Whether I liked it or not, Kim was no longer a part of my life and it was time to kick some ninja ass and move on.

The moment we stepped outside, the energy pulsing beneath my skin accelerated. I clenched my teeth together to keep from grimacing. The attack was moments away.

I stopped walking and Carson stumbled, tightening his hand around mine. "Rileigh?"

My mind raced as my skin burned from the cold beneath it. I had to think fast. "Carson … I … uh … I don't think I can go with you." I flinched at my own words. God, being a bitch was hard.

"What?" Hurt flashed in his eyes. "Is it because of this loser?" He gestured to Kim.

"No." I had to clench my teeth together to keep from defending Kim—always my first instinct. We'd been protecting each other so long, it was habit. "This has nothing to do with Kim."

"Then why are you ditching me? Not even fifteen minutes ago you wanted to get something to eat." Angry heat flushed his face. "I don't know what's going on, but I'd like some answers."

Kim stepped forward before I could answer (which was

a good thing considering I had no idea what to say). "It's not what you think," he said. "Rileigh's not ditching you. There's something else going on."

"Like what?" Carson folded his arms.

For one terrifying moment I wondered if Kim was actually going to tell Carson we were moments away from a ninja attack. But that notion was quickly squashed when Kim took another step and struck. He moved so fast that I barely registered the impact as more than a blur of motion.

Carson blinked once before his eyes rolled back into his head and he fell to the ground.

"You knocked my date unconscious?" I ran forward and kneeled in front of Carson's unmoving body. I placed my fingers against his neck and found his pulse steady and strong. I rocked back on my heels and stood. "Don't you think that was a little dramatic?"

Kim smiled. "I just hit a pressure point. It's not like I gave him a concussion. He'll be fine."

"You're an ass." I scowled at him, even though I secretly appreciated his quick thinking. And I knew Kim had extensive knowledge of pressure point combat. Carson wouldn't be hurt when he woke, but he was going to have one hell of a headache.

Kim ignored me and surveyed the parking lot. "How long have the ninja been following you?"

"A better question would be, 'When aren't they following me?'"

He whipped his head back to me, his eyes wide.

"You didn't know?" Sarcasm dripped from my words

like venom. "Then again, how would you? You're obviously much too busy going to the movies with Sumi and taking shopping trips to the mall. How would you have the time to find the ninja you promised to take care of?"

He frowned. "It's not like that."

My emotions rolled inside me like a washing machine on spin cycle. I wanted to laugh. I wanted to cry. I wanted to hit him hard enough to break through his rib cage and pull his heart from his chest like he'd done to mine. "What sign have you given me otherwise?"

He opened his mouth, but before the words came out, someone laughed behind us.

I turned to find one of the ninja, the tall boy, walking toward us with the girl in tow. Both grinned widely. "How do you like that?" The guy motioned to Carson's motionless body on the sidewalk. "They started without us."

The girl flexed her fingers. "That makes our job that much easier."

I shook my head. I missed the days when you could fight without the clichéd banter. Nowadays, it was all, "Blah, blah, blah…you don't stand a chance…blah, blah, blah…revenge will be mine." I missed the simplicity of get in, kill, and get out.

Kim brought his hands in front of him into a defensive position. For a moment, it was all I could do to remember there were ninja who wanted to kill me. Having Kim beside me, ready to fight, was just like old times when, together, we could take on the world.

God, I missed him so much.

"Ready?" he asked me, his eyes locked on the ninja.

So ready.

The ninja smirked at each other. They reached into their pockets and withdrew small black sacks. A second later they hurtled them in the air. As the sacks tumbled toward us, their contents spilled out in an arc of twinkling powder—like fairy dust from hell.

Crushed glass. Not awesome.

"Metsubushi!" Kim cried. "Close your eyes!"

Metsubushi, or bags of crushed glass, was a really sucky weapon to come across. If you got even a little bit of the crushed glass in your eyes, it could blind you for life. And I was a big fan of looking at things. But they were ninja, so of course they played dirty. And despite all of the misery Kim had put me through, I couldn't—wouldn't—let him get hurt.

"I got this." I stepped in front of him and let go of my ki. Energy poured from my outstretched fingers, painlessly and without effort. A shimmering blue wall stretched above our heads and collected the shower of glass. I raised my other hand and, with a conscientious flick, sent the broken glass hurtling back at the ninja.

They cried out in surprise and pulled their jackets over their heads as a shield.

"Nice." Kim straightened his stance. "I see you've regained control of your ki."

No thanks to you, I thought.

After the dust settled, the ninja uncovered their faces and brushed themselves off.

Kim raised his fists. We were lucky it was late in the

evening and no people milled about. "Which one do you want?" he asked.

I turned away from him, my defensive stance mirroring his. As good as it felt to fight beside Kim, I knew it wouldn't last. I was on my own, and it was something I had to get used to. "Both of them."

Kim didn't say anything for a moment. But then I heard him move back. "I'm here if you need me."

Words. Empty, meaningless words.

I pushed thoughts of Kim from my mind and concentrated on the energy swirling within me. I had to be careful; ki was the energy of my spirit. And each time I used it, it took time to replenish. If I used too much? Well, when your entire spirit left your body, the odds of survival were pretty slim.

The two ninja charged, their eyes zeroed on me. After all, ninja were a dishonorable lot. If I was the one they were getting paid to kill, they'd avoid dirtying their hands on anyone but their target.

My ki moved from my center into my hands where it pulsed against my fingertips. I held my stance, the energy building, my fingers burning, second by second, until a groan escaped my throat.

The ninja were almost to me and Kim hadn't moved. He got a few brownie points for that. He trusted me to take care of this and I would.

When the ninja were only a few feet away, I released my ki, letting out just enough to form another shimmering wall in front of me.

The ninja didn't see what hit them. Literally.

Both of them cried out and stumbled backward. The girl doubled over, covering her nose. Blood seeped from the cracks of her fingertips.

The guy got off a little easier. Rather than hitting face-first like his friend, he lay on his back with his knee pulled against his chest. I called the ki back to me and it answered in a rush, fluttering the hair around my face in its return. Easy-peasey, now that the kunoichi was out of my head.

I lifted my fists in front of my face and licked my lips. Thanks to the kunoichi messing with my ki, it had been awhile since I had the upper hand in a fight. I missed it. "You don't have to do this," I told the ninja. "You could return the money to whoever paid you and we could all go home and watch television in our jammies. This fight? So not worth it."

The guy slowly rose to his feet. "You're pretty cocky for someone about to die."

I sighed. How anyone could choose a fight to the death over a movie night at home was beyond me.

He rushed me. Before I could move, he ducked down and grabbed my wrist, pulling it behind my back. A twinge of pain coursed along my shoulder and he twisted it farther, daring to pull it from the socket.

Kim stepped forward, but I gave him a look that stopped him in his tracks. "I got this," I said between clenched teeth.

I crouched down, jumped up, and pushed off of the ninja's thighs. I flipped over backward and landed on my feet with my arm untwisted in front of me. Locking my fingers around the ninja's wrist, I pulled him closer to me.

His mouth gaped in surprise.

I whispered, "We could be home in our jammies." With our hands still locked on each other's wrists, I used my free hand to push hard against his chest. He stumbled back, and I used his lack of balance as the moment to yank down on his arm. As he fell forward, I ducked down and balanced on one foot while kicking the other until my heel collided with his head.

He crumpled to the ground without a sound.

"Well done," Kim said.

I stood and cracked my knuckles. The fight wasn't over yet. The remaining ninja watched me warily from the ground, her blood-coated hands still cupped around her nose. I kneeled beside her. "I want this to stop."

The girl dropped her hands and smiled, her teeth stained pink from the blood streaming from her nose. "I'm sure you do. But do you think *she* will stop? Even if you kill me. Even if you kill us all. She will find more. She won't stop until you're dead." The ninja shook the blood from her hands.

I stood and brushed my hands on my jeans. "I thought you might say that. That's why you're going to give the kunoichi a message for me."

"Kunoichi?" I could hear the surprise in Kim's voice. I should have known he wouldn't have a clue about anything going on—so wrapped up in his new life with Sumi. "Rileigh, what's going on?"

I shook my head. It didn't matter if he knew or not. It didn't change things. I fought alone now. Well, unless you counted Whitley, but that was too weird to think about.

I gathered the remaining energy swirling inside of me

and pushed it into a ball inside my core—so tight my body shook. My fingers trembled from the force of harnessing so much energy into a space so small. I'd never done this particular trick before, but I needed to prove a point. It was going to work or it wasn't.

"The only message I'm going to deliver is your head." Her eyes narrowed with hate.

"Yeaaaah, no. I'm keeping my head and you're going to tell the kunoichi that her Jedi mind tricks didn't work. Not only did I unlock my powers, but they've grown."

The girl laughed. "That's impossible."

"Is it?" Viper fast, I grabbed her throat and squeezed down with enough pressure that I could feel her pulse struggle against my hand.

She gasped.

My ki exploded, swirling my hair above my head like an invisible tornado. I pushed it into her screaming mouth and down her throat until I found my target. If I closed my eyes I could feel them—her lungs and the air within.

"What are you doing?" Kim asked from beside me. Funny, I hadn't noticed him move. There was something in his voice. Fear maybe? I didn't have time to think about it. I couldn't break my concentration or my hold on her would be lost. Instead, I concentrated on drawing the oxygen from her body.

She gasped and clawed at her throat. I let go of her neck; I could keep my hold on her without touching her. It felt like invisible lines of silk connecting the spaces between us. I pulled on the invisible lines and she fell to her knees, a hissing croak escaping through her flapping lips.

I stared at her. "You will not breathe until I let you. Got that?"

She nodded, her eyes impossibly wide and lined with swollen veins, threatening to burst. She clenched a hand into a fist and beat it against the concrete, over and over until her skin split and blood coated her knuckles.

And yet, all I could do was watch, transfixed. I wanted her to suffer. Suffer for the pain she'd caused me in this life. And suffer for the pain ninja had caused me in the last life. I wanted her to hurt. I wanted her to stare into the eyes of death and see that he had no pity and played no favorites.

"You're killing her." Kim's voice was a whisper in my ear. Matter-of-fact, without a hint of condemnation. I wondered if he harbored as much hate for the ninja as I did.

But as much as I would have loved to rid the world of one more ninja parasite, I needed her. I crouched beside her, cocking my head as I watched her struggle. "And you'll deliver my message? You'll let the kunoichi know that I'm through playing games?"

She nodded her head so fast it looked like she was convulsing—maybe she was.

"Good." I let go of my hold on her.

She released a ragged gasp. Her chest shuddered and her back arched as she sucked in gulps of air. "The kunoichi's not going to like this," she said when she was finally able to speak.

"I really don't care."

"You should." The girl glared at me a moment longer, as if deciding something. Finally, she gave a curt nod and rose unsteadily to her feet. "I hope you have a plan. She's not going to stop until you and the boy are dead."

I lifted my chin. "You let me worry about that."

She nodded, spun on her feet, and trotted away, disappearing into the shadows of the parking garage.

I glanced at her abandoned partner, motionless beside Carson's unconscious body. Ninja ethics. I snorted. A samurai would never leave a fallen comrade behind.

I stepped toward Carson only to come nose to chest with Kim. I stumbled back before I collided into him. "What the—?" I had my ki, he had his annoying super-fast movement.

He crossed his arms. "You want to tell me what the hell is going on?"

I walked around him. "Nope." What good would it do? It was better that I kept him out of my problems, and out of my life.

"I can't help you if you don't tell me what's going on." He grabbed my shoulder, my muscles tightening under his fingers.

"I neither want nor need your help." I fought the urge to shake his hand off.

He let go of my shoulder and I continued walking to Carson.

"I'm leaving."

I paused. "Yeah, I kinda figured. You've been away from Sumi for what? A whole hour? You better run along before she gets herself killed by bandits." I flinched inwardly as soon as the words left my lips. It was a nasty thing to say, but that's what heartache does. It doesn't play nice, it doesn't care about feelings, it pulls the worst from you and lays it on the table.

"No," Kim said. "I'm leaving the country."

That stopped me. "What?" Turning slowly, I saw his eyes locked on the new suitcase by his side.

"I'm going back to Japan."

Something inside of me cracked and I couldn't breathe. Pain unlike any I'd experienced before ripped through my gut. "For how long?"

He shook his head. "Rileigh, I'm ... I'm not coming back."

I didn't think I'd ever feel agony worse than the moment I'd thrust my own dagger into my gut to end my life. I was wrong.

And still he wouldn't look at me. His eyes remained locked on the damned suitcase. "Sumi wants a fresh start away from ..." But even though he left his sentence unfinished, I knew exactly whom Sumi wanted to get away from.

"Me." My voice wavered. I balled my fingers into fists to keep them from trembling. But my effort was for nothing. The tremors traveled from my arms into my chest and down into my legs until my entire body shook.

"Yes." His voice choked with what sounded like regret. Or maybe that was just wishful thinking.

I didn't remember walking toward him, but there I was, within touching distance, my empty hand reaching for ... I had no idea. Realizing what I was about to do, I dropped my hand to my side. "Why?" I asked. "I still don't understand why you're doing this."

"I know!" He looked at me then, his eyes wide and full of pain. "I don't understand it entirely, myself. I just know it's the right thing to do. I feel it. I owe it to her."

I wanted to shake him, no, hit him. Anything to get him

to realize that he was making the biggest mistake of his life. "You don't owe her anything! Her death was not your fault."

He shook his head and stepped forward, but instead of stopping in front of me, he sidestepped so that he stood next to me, our shoulders touching, but each of us looking a different direction. "I miss you so much. God. It's killing me."

Surprised, I looked at him. His eyes were closed, but even so, he looked every bit as miserable as I felt.

His fingers entwined with mine and the jagged pieces of my broken heart climbed inside my throat and threatened to choke me. But I couldn't let go. As much as I wanted to, I couldn't let go.

"I'm worried," he continued. "I know danger premonitions are your thing, but I can't shake the feeling that something really bad is coming for you. That's why I told Sumi I didn't want to leave yet. That I couldn't leave until we caught whoever was after you."

"And what did she say?"

He sighed. "Honestly? I don't remember. All of our arguments seem to blur together nowadays. Something about you being able to take care of yourself." He shook his head. "I love you, Rileigh. I'll never love anyone else the way I love you."

I stared at our entwined fingers, the gesture, like everything else, was a lie. Anger rose from the shambles of my heart like a phoenix, igniting my entire body with its heat. "Sometimes, Kim, I hate you."

He nodded. "I know." He wrapped an arm around my waist, pulled me close, and kissed me.

42

I glanced at Carson who blinked at me lazily from the passenger seat of his truck as I drove home. Poor thing. He didn't deserve to be brought into my mess. And speaking of mess, I brought my fingers to my lips, daring to see if they were really on fire. They hadn't stopped burning since Kim's kiss.

Carson groaned and I dropped my hand back to the wheel. "How are you feeling?"

"My head is pounding." He blinked at me. "What happened?"

"Don't you remember? You got into a fight."

"I did?" His brow furrowed in confusion. "Was it with that Asian guy? I remembered he was bothering you. But I don't remember what happened next ... "

"You don't?" I faked surprise. "You kicked his ass. But you were a little unsteady after the fight so you let me drive." I mentally patted myself on the back for a lie well constructed. Boys were fragile creatures and, after forcing Carson to suffer through the world's worst date, the least I could do was stroke his ego a bit.

He frowned. "I kicked his ass?"

"Totally laid him out. You really don't remember?"

"No, wait. I kinda remember." I could almost see his ego inflating inside of him as his chest puffed outward. Guys were so easy. He flipped down the visor and inspected his face, tilting his chin this way and that. "I just don't understand why my head hurts so bad."

I shrugged, keeping my eyes trained on the road in case they betrayed the BS I fed Carson. "I don't know. The fight was over so fast. I think maybe he hit you in the head before you knocked him out. You don't have a bump, do you?"

He ran a hand down his skull. "No."

I reached over and patted his knee. "See? You'll be fine."

He nodded but didn't say anything else. In fact, he didn't say another word until we reached my condo's parking garage. "Do you think you'll be okay to drive home? I could follow you in my car if you like."

He shook his head. "That's okay. I'm feeling a lot better now."

"Okay." I gave him a weak smile. He didn't deserve what happened to him. His only mistake was asking out the wrong girl. I reached for the door handle, but before I was able to swing my legs out, Carson placed a hand on my shoulder.

"Rileigh?"

I looked at him, noticing the way he refused to meet my

gaze. I shut the truck door and settled back into the seat. "What's up?"

"Look, I think you're really great, you know?"

Oh jeez, here it was. Not that I could blame him. I felt bad that he'd gotten so mixed up in my world. It was my fault, of course. I shouldn't have gone out with him in the first place. I wondered how I should play it. Not too cool or he'll think I don't care—and he deserved better. I needed to be just the right amount of upset so he'd know I was devastated, but not enough to turn into a stalking psycho.

Okay. Rileigh gets broken up with. Scene one, take one. Aaaaaand *ACTION!*

Carson placed a hand on my shoulder. "I don't think this is going to work out."

"Oh." I crumpled my face and did my best to look like I was on the verge of tears.

"I'm sorry." His hand slid from my shoulder. "Between the broken nose, the coffee scalding, and now this ... It's just—dating you is proving to be hazardous to my health."

Fair enough. I pretended to sniffle. "You don't have to explain. I get it."

He nodded. "Can we still be friends?"

I offered him a weak smile and dabbed at imaginary tears. "Okay. I'd like that."

He smiled back. "Good. For what it's worth, I think you're a really sweet girl. I'll see you around, okay?"

I nodded, pretending to be too grief-stricken to answer him. I wondered how sweet he'd think I was if he'd seen me nearly choke the life out of the ninja.

I slid out of the truck and closed the door behind me. That had to be some kind of record—two guys telling me goodbye in the same night.

I touched my still-warm lips again, and this time the tears that fell down my face were very real.

43

I stood outside the door to my condo, crushing the last of my tears with my palm. Lately, Kim was nothing but a black hole of pain that I kept getting sucked into. Well, it looked like I wouldn't have to worry about that anymore. He'd soon be out of my life for good.

I wish that made me feel better instead of completely shattered.

I gave myself a moment to smooth back my hair and let my blazing cheeks cool before opening the door. Just as I expected, Dr. Wendell was on the couch while Debbie sat at the kitchen bar with her back to me, gabbing on her phone. God, did that guy ever stay at his own place anymore?

He clicked the remote and the television turned off. "I would ask you how your date went, but I see I don't need to."

Right. Because, with a glance, he could read all of my problems like an open book. I glared at him and lowered my voice so I wouldn't draw Debbie's attention. "I saw Kim."

It wasn't that I wanted to share bits of my personal life with him, but I wasn't about to let him think I was crying over a bad date. *As if.*

He opened his mouth, but before he could say anything I held up a hand to stop him. Then I gestured to my mom and motioned him to follow me. After we were both inside my room, I whirled on him. "I thought we had an understanding."

He frowned. "I'm not sure what you're trying to get at."

"I'm not stupid." I almost laughed and, at the same time, hot tears welled in my eyes. The emotional overload of every feeling battling within me was too much. My knees buckled and I grabbed onto the side of my dresser for support. "You told me you have to keep tabs on me. And you also keep tabs on Kim. You *knew* he was going to leave. And you didn't tell me. I thought we were cool."

"We were—we are cool!" But his face betrayed his guilt.

I shook my head.

He sighed. "You're right. I know he wants to leave. But I've been working very hard to convince him not to. I didn't want to tell you until I was absolutely sure Kim's decision was made. You've been under so much stress as it is."

My fingers curled against the wood. "Well, guess what? His decision is made."

His face softened and he held a hand out to me. "Rileigh, I'm … I'm just so sorry."

"Me too." I ignored his outstretched hand. "I'm sorry that I trusted you. I'm sorry I thought we were finally starting to work together."

"What?" He dropped his hand to his side. "We *are* working together. It's my job to protect you. What would be the point of telling you something unless I was certain it was true? I care about you and I don't want you to get hurt."

This time I did laugh. "Well, it's too late for that." I stormed past him and motioned him out of my room with a sweep of my hand.

"Rileigh." The tone of his voice told me he thought I was being unreasonable.

I tapped my foot impatiently. "Sorry. I don't talk to people who suck." After he'd gone, I slammed the door shut and, after the day I had, wasn't the least bit surprised to see my closet door open and Whitley stick his head out.

"Son of hibachi," I muttered. Now I would have to add burning all of my clothes to my list of things to do.

"What?" He exited the closet with a smile. "I don't even get a hello?"

I held up a finger. "Wait right here."

He shrugged.

I shut the door behind me and marched back into the living room and pointed at Dr. Wendell. "You. Come with me. Now."

Wide-eyed, he rose from the couch and followed me to my door. Before I opened it, I turned to him. "You said part of your job was to protect me, right?"

He nodded, his brow knit in lines of confusion.

"Just to prove how bad you suck at your job, look at this."

I swung open the door and Whitley waved from his perch at the end of my bed.

Dr. Wendell's mouth dropped and he took a step back. "Wait. What is—who is that?"

"That"—I gestured to the boy on my bed—"is Whitley, aka Zeami, aka the psycho who tried to kill me, steal my powers, and burnt down my house."

Whitley smiled. "Guilty as charged."

I folded my arms and glared at Dr. Wendell. "If you're supposedly *protecting* me, how could you let my past-life murderer walk right into my bedroom and hide out in my closet?"

Dr. Wendell shook his head, his skin a shade paler than it had been moments ago. "But I—I didn't—how—" He looked at Whitley. "How did you get in here?"

Whitley rolled his eyes. "Through the door. Duh."

Dr. Wendell pushed me behind him, bringing his shaking fists in front of his face. "It doesn't matter. If you want to kill Rileigh, you're going to have to get past me."

Whitley's eyebrows arched and he smiled. "That's adorable. It's kind of like having a Chihuahua as a guard dog." He looked at me. "Leash your dog, Rileigh, before he gets hurt."

"Chill." I pushed Dr. Wendell to the side. I didn't doubt for a second that Whitley would hurt him or worse.

Dr. Wendell dropped his hands. "But I—" He looked back and forth between me and Whitley. "I don't understand."

"You don't need to." Whitley stalked toward us, his movements slow and graceful, like a tiger on the prowl. When he stopped in front of us I couldn't help but notice that Dr. Wendell was shaking. So much for that black belt.

Whitley held his hand out to me. "We don't have time for

this. Are you ready to go? I got a lead on the kanzashi. The *real* kanzashi."

"Wait. What?" I folded my arms. "What about the kanzashi we stole from the St. Louis Art Museum?"

"The *what* you stole *where*?" Dr. Wendell's voice was filled with panic.

Whitley shrugged. "That was the wrong one. I could tell as soon as I destroyed it."

"How?" I asked.

He brought his hand up to his neck and ran his finger along the faded pink mark. "I can feel her power growing. It means the kanzashi, the *real* kanzashi, is still out there and she's closing in on it. I really don't feel like dying anytime soon and we're running out of time. So if you wouldn't mind?" He gestured to the door.

"No." Dr. Wendell stepped in front of me. "Absolutely not. I can't allow that."

So, my options were a night at home with my super annoying handler who wanted to control my life, or my psychotic past-life nemesis. Wow. Look at me all popular with the guys.

I sighed and pushed past Dr. Wendell. I was tired. Tonight I'd been attacked by ninjas, dumped, and discovered that my soul mate intended on moving half a world away just to get away from me. If finding the right kanzashi was the key to stopping the kunoichi, then I was all for it. Besides, if she were to regain her power after receiving my *message*... yeah, kinda didn't want to think about that. "Let's go."

Dr. Wendell grabbed onto my shoulder. "Rileigh, you can't be serious. This guy is psychotic. He tried to kill you!"

"Ritually sacrifice," Whitley corrected. "Big difference."

I glared at him. "You're not helping."

"Yeah, that's kind of my thing. I don't care." He smiled. "I'll wait for you downstairs. Meet me there when you're done"—he wiggled his fingers at Dr. Wendell—"with whatever this is." He turned to leave but paused, casting me a long glance over his shoulder. "Bring your katana."

I made a face. "Please. You think that's smart? Walking around St. Louis with a sword at my side."

The smile melted from his face. "Do you think if we encounter any ninja tonight that they won't be armed? Besides, I left you a present. It's on your bed."

I glanced to the spot he'd been laying and discovered a long white box tied with red ribbon. It was the kind of package that might hold long-stemmed roses. I narrowed my eyes. "Whitley, so help me if you've sent me another snake I'll deliver you to the kunoichi myself, despite whatever consequence that might have on our little inyodo."

He laughed and kept walking. "See you outside."

I approached the box, but Dr. Wendell sidestepped me and blocked my path. "You can't be serious. Tell me that you're not serious."

"Fine." I shrugged and moved around him. "I'm not serious."

His shoulders drooped and he sighed with relief. "Really?"

"No." I picked up the box and shook it, waiting for a rattle or a hiss, anything to alert me that a venomous reptile waited inside. Nothing moved. And since I had no premonitions of danger, I guessed it was safe to assume that whatever was inside didn't have fangs.

Dr. Wendell shook his head, looking more flustered by the minute. "Well, you can't go. As your handler, I forbid it."

I laughed and pulled the blood-red ribbon from the box, discarding it on my bed where it crumpled into a pool of silk. "*Please.*"

He was silent for a moment. "Okay. You've left me no choice. I'm going to call Kim."

I shrugged. "Fine by me." It wasn't like he'd been especially helpful lately. And now that he was leaving for Japan, I highly doubted he cared what I did. I pulled the cardboard lid off the box and peeled back the tissue paper. I didn't understand what I was looking at. From what I could tell, it was a long piece of leather with two padded nylon straps. "What on earth..." I mumbled. It wasn't until I pulled the contraption from the box that I noticed the slit on top just wide enough for a sword. I laughed at the genius of it.

Dr. Wendell was not nearly as amused. "Rileigh, be reasonable! This could be a setup. This guy cannot be trusted!"

I set the sheath down and looked at him. "I'm not stupid. Of course I don't trust Whitley. And I don't trust you or the Network you work for. The one person I thought I could trust ended up breaking my heart. I'm a samurai, not an idiot. So that means I'm a fighter, not a wait around to die-er." I scrunched my nose at the awkwardness of my own made-up word. "Anyway, this kunoichi has hurt me and my best friend. She's made my life miserable and she won't stop until I'm dead. So I'm going to take care of it. Tonight. Now, if you don't mind, I have lives to save."

He opened his mouth as if to argue with me, but closed it before any words came out. Finally, he said, "You're right. You're absolutely right. Your life has been in danger. And the Network has done little to help. And for that I apologize. You have every right to be angry. If you have a lead on the person behind the ninja attacks, then I absolutely agree that you should go ... but I'm going too."

I blinked at him. "You can't be serious."

He tilted his chin up. "Oh, I'm completely serious. Your safety is my responsibility."

I narrowed my eyes. "My safety is my *own* responsibility. Don't forget that."

He dared to take a step closer to me. "That doesn't change the fact that I care about you. And I don't want to see you get hurt. And I mean that solely as your friend, Rileigh. Not as a representative for the Network."

I didn't know what to make of that. Too many emotions juggled inside of me. Maybe Dr. Wendell was telling the truth. He had been spending a lot of time at the house and he seemed to genuinely care about my mom. And when we were having one of my better days, I didn't *exactly* hate him. But he was also a member of the Network and that meant his motives weren't always clear. But unfortunately, I couldn't sit around and argue with him all day.

I pointed to his neck. "You have a little something right there."

He angled his head back to look. "What? What is—"

Before he could finish, I hit his neck with the side of my hand in the same way Kim hit Carson earlier tonight. Dr. Wendell's eyes rolled back in his head and he fell forward. I caught him under the arms and laid him gently on the ground.

"Huh." I placed my hands on my hips and surveyed my handiwork. "That's a nifty little trick." Part of me felt bad for using a pressure point to knock Dr. Wendell out. But the other part of me knew he'd been serious when he said he wanted to go with me and, even though he was a major pain in the ass, I'd feel bad if he got himself killed by a ninja.

Ugh. I think I was starting to … kind of … almost … maybe just a little … like him. That was annoying.

But I didn't have time for the Happy Fun Time Feeling Show. I had a kanzashi to find. I snatched Whitley's gift, my sword, and an oversized shirt and walked to the bathroom. Inside, I peeled off my tank top. I swung the sheath around so it rested against my spine. From there, I fastened the nylon straps around my shoulders. Afterword, I slipped a different, bigger shirt on and studied my reflection in the mirror. The sheath was invisible. Next, I slid my katana into the spine sheath and fluffed my hair over the handle. Aside from the occasional weird bulge when I twisted at the waist, the average person wouldn't be able to tell I was armed.

I stared at my reflection. "Is that a katana strapped to your spine or are you just happy to see me?" A samurai was nothing without her sense of humor.

44

Whitley and I didn't speak as we drove to, well, wherever it was we were going. I figured I'd find out soon enough. After zipping through the various side streets and alleyways between skyscrapers, it became apparent that our destination didn't require an interstate. So, yay, another night spent downtown. *Awesome.*

"Do you like your present?" Whitley asked, pulling me from my thoughts.

I shrugged. "While I was disappointed this one lacked venom and didn't try to kill me, I guess it's alright."

He laughed and I couldn't help but smile back—which I found deeply disturbing. What the hell was going on with my life that one of my only friends was my psychotic sworn enemy? When had my life become so ... wrong?

I didn't want to tell Whitley, but I adored his gift. There was something so calming about having my sword rest against my body. I felt stronger, braver. My sword had saved my life countless times in the past. I could trust it—which was a whole lot more than I could do with the guys in my life. But who needed a boyfriend when you had razor-sharp steel?

Whitley stopped the car in an alleyway I was already familiar with. *Son of hibachi.*

"What's wrong with you?" Whitley frowned. "What's that face?"

"It's my *I can't believe this is happening* face." I rested my forehead against the cool glass of the passenger-side window. We sat parked in the same alleyway I'd been in when I was first attacked by the ninja. A chill skipped down my spine as I looked at the rusted Dumpster that had almost turned me into a splat sandwich with Kim's car. "What are we doing here?"

Whitley pulled the keys from the ignition. "The kanza-shi is here. I saw the announcement in the paper this morning for a Japanese jewelry exhibit. It was supposed to happen more than a month ago, but the shipment was delayed. Apparently it includes several kanzashi."

"How do you know the right one is here?"

He stared out the window into the dark alley. "It has to be. I know it's nearby, and I know the kunoichi knows it too. I can feel her power growing. There aren't many ancient Japanese artifacts in St. Louis. But if it means stopping the kunoichi, I'll find them all."

"That sounds ... dangerous." We had a really close call with security at the Art Museum. I wasn't exactly eager to repeat the experience.

Whitley looked at me, his eyes deadly cool. "It would be more dangerous if we didn't."

Yeah, there was *that*—the whole "if the kunoichi gets her powers back we're all going to die" thing. And, while that would suck, I really didn't want to keep stealing from museums and art galleries. It was dishonorable, something a ninja would do. I shuddered at the thought. If we didn't find the right kanzashi tonight, I vowed to find a different way to locate it that didn't involve breaking and entering.

But since we were already here, it didn't make sense to back out now. I put my hand on the door, but before I opened it a movement to my right caught my eye—something or *someone* lurked in the shadows.

I sighed. And so it began.

I opened the car door and jumped out. Reaching behind me, I grasped the hilt of my sword. "Show yourself!"

"Relax, Ri-Ri." Quentin stepped under the streetlight decked out in another one of his ridiculous cat burglar outfits.

Just Q. I exhaled, loosening the knot of anxiety inside my chest, making it easier to breathe. But then a new worry crossed my mind. "What the hell are you doing here?"

Quentin crossed his arms and spoke in a high falsetto. "Oh, Q, thank you so much for leaving your house in the middle of the night to help me. I know it's late and you were asleep, but who else am I going to be rude to in a stinky alley?"

"My voice does *not* sound like that." I turned to look at Whitley. "This was your idea?"

He gave me a look that implied I was an idiot. "Do you really want to go into battle without a healer at your side?"

"That healer is my best friend and he's not a fighter. We're going against experienced killers and he's only going to be in danger." I glanced at Q to find him scowling at me. "Uh, no offense."

His hands dropped to his side and he pushed his shoulders back. "Offense taken. Don't assume to know what I can and cannot handle. Why don't you worry about finding the kanzashi and I'll worry about taking care of myself. Who knows? Maybe I'll surprise you."

"See?" Whitley glided past me to the side door. The same door Kim and the other samurai disappeared inside of the night the ninja first attacked. "He can take care of himself."

I glared at Whitley as he removed a lock-picking kit from his pocket and began fiddling with the door. Whitley looked out for Whitley, and he only wanted Q with us to save his own ass. But if Q got hurt, I doubted Whitley would care.

But Quentin made a good point too. Maybe I was being a little overprotective. He could make his own decisions and, as long as he knew what he was signing up for, who was I to tell him no? "Alright then," I told Q. "Since you're coming with us, maybe you could stay close to me? Just as a precaution?"

He raised his chin. "Maybe you should stay close to me. Just as a precaution."

I suppressed a smile. "Fair enough."

The lock clicked and I turned to find Whitley holding the door open and gesturing us inside.

"Wait a sec." I raced up the stairs and placed my hands

on the door frame. Last time I was here, the kunoichi had used her powers to trap Kim and the others inside the building. But the metal door frame was cool against my fingers, betraying nothing from the dark magic that had possessed it only months ago.

"Well?" Whitley's voice tickled the hairs on the back of my neck. "Do you sense anything?"

"No." Whatever magic was there before wasn't now.

Whitley nodded and walked inside.

I motioned for Quentin to go ahead of me and I brought up the rear, shutting the door behind me.

Inside, a single fluorescent bulb lit the dark interior of the gallery. In the corner of the room, a small red light brought my attention to the security camera perched there.

Whitley stood next to me and followed my line of sight. "You don't have to worry about that camera," he said. "It's a dummy."

"But the light?"

He shrugged. "It's part of the illusion. I cased the place earlier today. Their security is ridiculous."

You'd think after being robbed last month they would have beefed up security. I looked at him. "If the security is so ridiculous, why do you need me? Why not just come back and take the kanzashi on your own."

He smiled, clearly amused. "Because I'm being followed. And whoever is doing it is good. Really good. I can't catch sight of them no matter how hard I try. They're always just outside the corner of my vision." He looked around the room as if he expected someone to jump out of the shadows.

Heck, maybe someone would.

"You're not the only one," I said. "I was attacked while on a date tonight."

He didn't look surprised. "I imagined their attacks would increase. Especially now that we're working together and closing in on the kanzashi. That's why I asked you here tonight. We're both being followed, but we're stronger together."

"Maybe..." I thought about the message I asked the ninja to deliver. "Or maybe the kunoichi will come for us herself."

Whitley's eyes flashed with... fear? I couldn't tell because the emotion was gone as fast as I'd seen it. "Let's hurry, okay?"

I nodded.

I followed Whitley across the large room, our shoes not making a sound on the polished hardwood floors. We stopped beside Quentin who stood in front of a glass case. He looked at us, his brow creased into lines of worry. "We have a slight problem."

"What?" But I'd answered my own question the moment I peered into the case. Inside, five Japanese kanzashi were mounted on display. And in the case next to that, another five. I counted a total of six glass cases with nothing but Japanese hairpins of various ages and design.

"What do we do?" Q asked. "There's more than thirty."

Whitley brought a gloved fist up to the first case and smashed it down, shattering the glass at our feet. "We take them all. We destroy them all."

My throat tightened. Destroy them all? These hairpins were hundreds of years old. Irreplaceable and beautiful in design. I couldn't—wouldn't do it. "No," I told him as he stuffed the kanzashi into a sack. "There has to be a better way."

Whitley sighed impatiently. "Don't be such a girl. If we have to smash the pretty things, we have to smash the pretty things. Get over it."

I narrowed my eyes and snatched his wrist before he could grab another hairpin. I shoved him back. "For once in your life, have some respect. You're stealing pieces of history. Our history. You of all people should understand the importance of that."

"Please." His sneered. "I appreciate my BMW and air conditioning. But if you long for the days of your servitude, then fine. If I have to agree to leave the kanzashi unharmed to get you to speed up? Fine. But then it's up to you to figure out which one is the one we're looking for."

I bit my lip. Yeah there was that...

Q walked to another case and peered in. "The combs are grouped together by their century of origin. Most of them are from the 18th and 19th century. What century is the one we're looking for?"

"Fifteenth," Whitley and I answered in unison.

Q wandered to another case and looked in. He shook his head and went to another, and then another, before stopping. "Here!" He tapped the glass with his finger. "This case has three combs from the 15th century."

Whitley darted over. He drew his hand up and brought it down. But instead of shattering the glass, his hand bounced off the top with a sickening thud. He cursed and cradled his hand against his chest.

Weird. I studied the case. It didn't look any different than the rest of them. "What happened?"

His eyes held the wild look of an injured animal. His lip curled in a snarl. "Magic," he hissed between clenched teeth. "That kunoichi bitch infused the glass with it."

I stared at the case, but nothing about the glass appeared out of the ordinary. "Are you sure?"

"Yes, I'm sure!" He rubbed his injured hand with his other hand. "I think my hand is broken."

"What do we do?" Q asked.

I was at a loss. If I couldn't make it bleed, my options were limited.

Whitley dropped his swollen hand to his side and cocked his head. "Do you hear something?"

I snapped my mouth shut and held my breath. And that's when I heard it. A hissing sound, just loud enough to over-power the buzz from the fluorescent bulb. "What the—"

"Gas!" Q pointed to a thin cloud of smoke seeping from a vent high on the wall.

No sooner had he spoken than smoke began filtering out of two other vents on opposite sides of the room until we were surrounded by a toxic cloud.

I took a step back only to bump into Whitley and Q.

"If you've got any good ideas," Whitley said into my ear, "now would be the time for them."

45

deas? My breath hitched in my throat. I thought it was obvious. "We need to get out of here."

"No!" Whitley placed his palms on the case. "The kanzashi is here and the kunoichi knows it. This"—he gestured to the gas filtering from the vents—"and this"—he gestured to the display case—"is her magic. This means she's on her way. If we don't take the kanzashi before she gets here, we're as good as dead."

"We'll be dead if we stay!" I watched as the tendrils of smoke uncurled and reached for us from every corner of the room.

"We're not leaving the comb," Whitley repeated. "Buy us some time."

Buy us some time? Um, *okay*. But how could I fight gas? My mind raced as fast as my beating heart. Maybe there was one thing I could try.

I reached for my sword. "It's been a long time since I've done this..."

"Less talking, more doing." Whitley took a step back until his back pressed against mine. Q backed up against our shoulders. We were surrounded by a wall of smoke. Even if we wanted to leave, we couldn't.

I closed my eyes and channeled the ki inside of me from my body to my fingertips where it bled into my sword until the steel blazed blue. When the steel held all the energy it could, I closed myself off, twisted the blade in my hands, and slammed it down into the floor. And then I muttered a quiet apology to the building owner whose floor I just cracked.

The katana pulsed once and then bled my ki into a shield that surrounded the three of us and the kanzashi case. I let go of the sword and took a tentative step back. "It won't hold forever," I told them. "We'll have to work fast."

"So what do we do?" Q asked.

I shrugged. "I'm open for suggestions."

Gas flooded the entire gallery, so much that I couldn't make out more than a couple feet beyond the shield.

Whitley studied the case. "I'm willing to bet the magic infusing the glass is location centered. If we carry the case outside, we can break it open there."

Q frowned. "But the case must weigh a ton."

"And you're forgetting something else." I tapped the shield that rippled under my fingertips. "This shield is held in place by my sword. The moment I pull it from the ground, it will disappear. And then the dying will commence."

Whitley didn't look at me. Instead, he pushed against the case, sliding it a couple inches across the floor. "So move the shield with us."

I laughed. "You're joking, right? A moving shield? Do you know how much energy that would take? It would kill me and then you by default."

Whitley stopped pushing the case and glared at me. "Yes, but you forget you have a healer with you. Draw from him."

I blinked at him. Draw energy from Q? I'd never used another person's energy to supplement mine before. "Isn't that dangerous?"

Whitley shrugged. "If you use all his energy, yes. Then we all die."

The color drained from Q's face.

"No." I shook my head. "I won't do it. I'm not about to risk my best friend's life."

"Too late for that." Whitley tapped a finger against the shield. "This isn't going to hold forever. How much air do you think we have left?"

"Um…" Typically, I only used my shield as temporary protection during an ambush. I didn't have the energy to sustain them for long periods of time and I never housed multiple people inside of them. "Maybe a minute or two?"

"Exactly." Whitley lifted the corner of the case off the pedestal and tested its weight. "So you better think fast."

It didn't look like we had any other option. But still, I was going to do something so risky without Quentin agreeing to it. "Q—"

"Let's do it." Quentin stepped beside me, his mouth pressed into a determined line.

A knot twisted inside my stomach. He trusted me. I could do this. I *had* to do this.

Q licked his lips. "How's this going to work?"

I glanced at Whitley. "Do you think you can handle that case on your own?"

He nodded. "It's heavy, but if we're fast I think I can manage."

"Okay." I took Q's hand in mine and squeezed. "On the count of three, I'm going to pull my sword out of the ground. Before I do, I'm going to push more of my ki into it to keep the shield from disappearing. Normally, that would take too much energy for me to do on my own, so I'm going to take some of your healing ki."

"Have you ever done this before?"

I shook my head. "Nope."

He swallowed but said nothing.

"Can you wrap up the pep talk?" Whitley slid his hands under the case. "The remaining air isn't going to last forever."

He was right. I could already feel a difference. I deepened my breaths, but couldn't get enough air into my lungs. Not to mention I was starting to feel light-headed. Not good.

I looked at Q. "Ready?"

"Ready."

I sucked in another unsatisfying breath and reached for my sword. With my fingers around the hilt, I pushed my remaining ki into my sword at the same moment I pulled the blade free from the floor. The sword pulsed blue and the shield wavered like a bubble on the end of a bubble wand, but it stayed intact. I wobbled on my heels. It had taken more energy than I anticipated, but I had done it. I should have felt relieved, but instead all I could concentrate on were the black dots flooding my vision.

I stumbled and would have fallen on my face if it weren't for Q's arm suddenly around my shoulder.

"Give her some energy, you idiot," Whitley snarled. "Before she passes out and then we're all as good as dead."

"Uh." I could hear the uncertainty in Q's voice. "Okay. Let me concentrate."

"Hurry!" Whitley said.

I wanted to tell Whitley to shut up, that Q was doing the best he could, but the words turned to mush on my tongue. My eyelids drooped. All I wanted to do was slide to the floor and take a nap. Just a short one. I tried to push away from Q but his grip tightened.

"Stay with me, Ri-Ri," he whispered.

Exhaustion pulled at me with velvet fingers. Why was he bothering me? Couldn't he see how tired I was? I slumped forward but something caught me around the waist. It didn't matter. I was tired enough to sleep bent over. But even as I drifted into unconsciousness, a strange warming sensation spread through my body. It got hotter and hotter until I thought my skin would burst into flames. But it didn't hurt. It felt good—no, great.

My eyes flew open and I jerked upright with a gasp. Quentin released his grip on my arms. The fire inside of me cooled, leaving my skin tingling and my muscles coiled. I shivered and tightened my grip on the katana. "What the heck was that?"

"Me … I think." Q shrugged. "But I don't know how long it will keep you strong, so we need to hurry."

"Agreed." I held up my free hand and flexed my fingers, half expecting to see electricity shooting from the tips.

Whitley grunted behind me and I turned to find him hoisting the case off the pedestal. "Let's go."

I held my sword in front of me and said a little prayer. I'd never moved a shield before and, quite frankly, wasn't sure it could be done. I raised my free hand and pushed a bit of my newly refreshed ki out of my body and thrust it against the shield. To my surprise, the shield moved an inch.

Whitley made an impatient sound. "You're going to have to do better than that."

I shot him a dirty look. "I'm sorry I'm not instantly good at something I've never done before. Now if you could shut up and let me concentrate, I can focus on getting us out of here before we suffocate and die." Before he could respond I turned back to the shield and pushed again, harder this time and with more energy. The shield moved a couple of feet. Better.

Keeping my concentration on the shield, I said, "We're going to have to hamster-ball our way out of here, so make sure you keep up." I thrust again and the shield jumped forward. I continued pushing, scooting the shield at a speed fast enough that Q and I had to jog and Whitley huffed and puffed behind us.

The gas pressing around the shield made maneuvering

through the gallery difficult. I bumped into several display cases, knocking an expensive-looking vase off a pedestal where it shattered on the floor. I flinched, muttered an apology to the artist, and kept moving. After another minute of wandering through the thickening gas, the air inside our shield had grown so sparse we were all gasping for breath. Just as I wondered if we were going to make it out in time, I spotted the red exit light through the haze, like a lighthouse beckoning through the fog.

Whitley's breathing turned ragged and Q stumbled beside me. We had to hurry.

I shuffled us forward and pushed the shield as close to the door as it would go. "On the count of three. One … "

"Three!" Whitley shoved past me, pressing himself to the front of the shield.

The shield, weak as it was, fell apart like a popped balloon. I was thankful I had held my breath as we were instantly surrounded by gas. Whitley rammed his hip against the exit door bar and the three of us stumbled outside.

Q fell to the ground, clutching his chest and gasping as I slumped to my knees beside him. Air had never tasted so sweet.

Whitley swayed on his feet, the muscles on his arms straining under his shirt as the glass case slipped from his fingers. I had only a moment to dive out of the way to avoid the shattering glass. After brushing myself off, I stood on shaky legs and started to tell Whitley to be more careful. But when I caught sight of the hairpin lying next to me, the words died on my tongue.

I picked up the kanzashi and examined it under the moonlight. It was tarnished, but I could remember a time when it gleamed. Crafted from silver, two long pins were joined by a silver basket overflowing with coral flowers. Thin pieces of silver dangled from the basket, each holding a coral bead at its base. I closed my eyes and listened to the tinkling of the chimes, knowing—but not how—that I had heard its melody before.

But how was that possible? I opened my eyes and studied the hairpin, the ring of familiarity striking a chord inside of me. When I was a samurai, I never wore anything quite so ornate—hair accessories weren't exactly practical for a warrior. So if it wasn't mine, did that mean I'd seen it on the kunoichi?

Did I know who the kunoichi was?

46

Before I could come up with an answer, the kanzashi was snatched from my hands.

Whitley barely glanced at it before he tossed it into a sack with the other hairpins. I guessed it didn't ring familiar with him. Interesting. "Alright, boys and girls, it's time to move before our ninja friends show up."

"Where do we go?" I kept my eyes locked on the bag. I had to figure out where I'd seen the hairpin before. I knew it was the answer to figuring out who the kunoichi was.

"Your place." He hoisted the bag over his shoulder. "We can destroy the kanzashi there and, afterward, both be on our merry little ways, never to cross paths again."

"I like that idea." Q reached a hand out to me and I helped him to his feet.

But I wasn't so sure. While I rejoiced at the idea of never seeing Whitley again, I didn't know if it was such a good idea to destroy the kanzashi until I figured out where I'd seen it before. But before I could voice that out loud, a burst of electricity jolted down my spine, freezing me in place. "Crap," I muttered.

Whitley pulled his keychain from his pocket and unlocked his car doors with the remote. "What now?"

I reached a hand out and grabbed Q's arm, pulling him close. "Ninja." I closed my eyes and concentrated until I felt the prickly heat of vicious intent closing in. I opened my eyes. "Five, if I'm not mistaken."

"Shit." Whitley ran a hand through his hair and looked at me. "Can you do that invisible thing with us again?"

I shook my head. "There's no way. I used up most of my ki and Q's ki just getting us out here. It would kill me."

Whitley sighed and dropped his keys in the bag with the kanzashi and tied the bag to his belt loop. When he finished, he pulled what looked like a two-foot metal jump rope from the inside of his jacket.

Q's breath hitched in his throat. "What is that?"

Whitley held one of the metal handles and let the other end dangle from his hand. "Manrikigusari. They didn't have these when I was a samurai, but I'm rather fond of them."

God, I was so sick of chains. If I made it out of this alive I was going to stop wearing necklaces for good. I reached behind me and pulled out my sword.

Q's eyes darted around the alley. "What should I do?"

"Wait in the car," Whitley and I answered together.

I stared at Whitley who smirked back. "Soul mates," he sang, swinging the chain in front of him. "Before you know it, we'll be picking out china patterns."

I snorted. "The only china I'll buy is a plane ticket to the actual country. For you. One way."

Whitely shrugged but kept smiling.

"No!" Q said.

Whitley forgotten, I turned my attention to Q and the anger in his voice.

"No," he repeated, and folded his arms across his chest. "I am *not* going to wait in the car. That's ridiculous. I can help."

"How?" Whitley stopped swinging the manrikigusari. His eyes narrowed. "You're a healer, not a fighter. The most you'll be able to do is heal yourself when you get hurt. That's not exactly *helpful*. You're more useful to me staying out of harm's way in case I get hurt and need you."

A tendon flexed in Q's jaw. "Thanks for your *obvious* concern, but I can do more than that."

Whitley laughed "Like what? Give them fashion tips?"

"Listen up, *asshole*." Q's hands curled into fists. Anger rolled off of him in hot waves I could feel prickling against my skin. "To you I may be just another gay cliché, but I know I'm more than that. And if you don't believe me, why don't you go wait in the *damn* car and I'll show you what I can do."

Both Whitley and I stood silently exchanging wide-eyed glances. As much as I loved my best friend and didn't want to risk his life, I had to admit, I was pretty damn proud of him at that moment. Every fight was a dance with death. A true warrior knew not to turn away from that dance but, instead, pick the music.

Q was a true warrior.

Whitley opened his mouth, probably to argue some more, but I held out my hand to stop him. "He stays."

Q blinked several times before a wide grin spread across his face.

Whitley scowled at me. "But—"

"He says he can help." I lifted my chin in a challenge. "And I believe him."

Whitley started to argue but appeared to think better of it and stopped. He waved a hand in the air. "Whatever. If he dies, don't say I didn't tell you so. I'm not about to risk my life to babysit." He pointed at me. "The only reason I teamed up with you is because we're connected."

Anger surged inside of me, boiling through my blood and curling my fingers into fists. I took a step toward him. "The feeling is mutual. In fact, I'd kill you right now if I could."

To my surprise, Whitley smiled, but it held no malice. It was warm and genuine. "Likewise."

I shook my head. "You are so weird."

Before he could answer, the distinct sound of footsteps on gravel echoed against the brick wall. We were no longer alone.

Five figures dressed from head to toe in black stepped into the alley. I had no way of knowing if these were ninja we'd faced before or new enemies. And if they were new ninja, where the heck was the kunoichi even finding them? It wasn't like you could call 411 and ask for a listing of ninjas-for-hire … or could you? I made a mental note to give it a try if I survived the night.

Whitley swung the chain over his shoulder and stilled the swinging end with his free hand. His muscles were tight, his eyes wide, and his lips stretched into a frown. I could tell he was afraid.

But it wasn't like I was the spokesperson for calm and collected. My ki was drained and I was exhausted. Not a good combination for a fight. In fact, between the sweat trickling down my neck and my pulse rocketing through my veins, the only product I should endorse were Depends.

I tightened my grip on my sword and held it in front of me. Q said nothing, as he shifted his weight from foot to foot.

The ninja in the middle stepped forward and extended his hand. "We've come for the kanzashi."

Whitley laughed. "So this is the smack-talk portion of the fight? We tell you 'No,' and you tell us you'll make our deaths as painless as possible?" He yawned. "Call me when you come up with some new material."

"Not quite." The middle ninja's eyes creased in such a way that I knew he was smiling under his mask. "We'll make your deaths painful. I just thought we could save some time."

Together, all five ninja pulled katanas from their sheaths. Whitley didn't waste any time. He charged for the closest ninja, swinging his manrikigusari in front of him. As they collided in combat, the manrikigusari wrapped around the ninja's sword. Whitley yanked on the chain and pulled the katana from the ninja's grip.

Before the blade clattered to the ground, two ninja confronted me with their swords drawn. As I ducked the blade, I watched Q fall to the ground only to jump back to his feet. A ribbon of fear twisted around my heart as I dodged another attack. Oh God, please don't let him get hurt. I couldn't bear it if something happened to him.

"Watch it!" Whitley stepped in front of me and blocked a hit I hadn't seen coming. "If you die, I die. And that's really going to piss me off. Get your head out of your ass." He kicked, his foot landing in a ninja's gut.

Whitley was right. If I focused on Q instead of the ninja, I was as good as dead.

Two ninja attacked me at once. I ducked below a strike aimed at my head and jumped over a sweeping kick. I dropped to the ground, placed my free hand against the pavement, and swung my legs over my head like I'd done so many times on the half-pipe. When I landed, I slammed my elbow into the ninja's knee. I heard the distinctive snap of bone before the ninja fell to the ground, groaning.

Before I could congratulate myself, Q cried out. I whirled around in time to see him clutching his side as blood bloomed across his T-shirt.

I watched, helpless, as Q fell to the ground. My stomach convulsed and I couldn't breathe.

From far away, I heard someone yell my name. I looked up in time to catch a blur of silver as a sword careened toward my face. I stumbled backward. The blade missed my face but passed close enough to rustle my hair. Surprised, I took another step, but my heel caught the edge of a crack in the pavement and I fell, landing on my shoulder.

The pain barely registered. All I could think about was getting to Q and making sure he was okay. But as I laid on the ground searching for him, I couldn't find him.

Panic kicked my heart into a gallop. Where was he? The clang of metal on metal sounded behind me and I propped myself up on my elbow. Before I could climb the rest of the way to my feet, someone kicked me from behind. I slid against the gravel, tasting blood in my mouth.

"Get up!" Whitley screamed.

I tried, but another foot landed in my gut. I collapsed on the gravel as burning fire replaced the oxygen kicked out of my lungs. I coughed, gasping for air that wouldn't come. I willed my body to move, but my muscles refused to cooperate.

Two black feet appeared before me and I lifted my watery gaze to find a ninja with his sword drawn. He spoke, his deep voice muffled by the fabric across his mouth. "The kunoichi sends her regards." He raised the katana over his head.

I closed my eyes and waited for the blow to fall.

47

Even with death only a few seconds away, I couldn't help but worry about Quentin. Where had he gone? What had happened to make him bleed so much? And how could I have let him get involved in the first place? Regret laced through my ribs and pulled tight, crushing me from the inside out. If I was about to die, maybe it was because I deserved to.

But instead of a skull-crushing blow, I heard the unmistakable thud of a body falling to the ground beside me. I opened my eyes, but what I discovered didn't make sense. The ninja who'd been seconds away from killing me was now lying on the ground unconscious. I mashed the heels of my palms into my eyes, blinked, and looked again. The scene remained unchanged.

"What the—?" I began.

"Hey." Q walked over to me and held his hand out, a wide grin spread across his face. As he helped me stand, I couldn't help but notice his torn and bloody T-shirt. If the wound underneath looked half as bad as his shirt, I wondered how he was able to stand, let alone help *me* up.

My gaze darted between his bloody shirt and the ninja on the ground. "Just—how?"

He shrugged. "I told you I could help."

"But—" Before I could finish, the ninja stirred at my feet. I swung my arm back and prepared to strike, but Q grabbed my wrist before I could.

He shook his head. "It's cool now."

"What are you talking about? They're killers!" I watched the ninja stand on wobbly legs. My biceps burned from the strain of holding back my fists. Why wouldn't Q let me fight? Had the kunoichi infected his head again? I prayed that she hadn't because I had no idea how I was supposed to fight my best friend.

The ninja blinked lazily as he brought his hand to his face. He tentatively touched the fabric covering his mouth before pulling it off of his face. The boy underneath looked to be my age, and cute—if I were into ninja. He stared at me with unfocused eyes, like someone just waking up from a nap. "Do I know you?" he asked.

Definitely weird. I chanced a glance at Q. "Why isn't he trying to kill me?"

Before Q could answer, Whitley walked over to us, swinging his manrikigusari in a lazy arc. He pointed his free hand at the still-blinking ninja. "Want me to take care of this last one?"

"No." Q stepped in front of the ninja and folded his arms. "I already did."

Whitley frowned and looked to me for an answer. I only shrugged.

"Um, excuse me." The ninja stepped out from behind Q. "Can any of you guys tell me how I got here?" He looked down. "And why I'm dressed like a ninja?"

Q turned and placed a hand on the guy's shoulder. "Me and my friends found you guys passed out in this alley. From the looks of it, you were at a costume party and had too much to drink."

Whitley and I exchanged more confused glances.

The guy frowned. "I don't remember going to a costume party...but my head *does* hurt really bad."

Q nodded. "You're probably going to have a wicked hangover in the morning. You should go home, drink a glass of orange juice, and get some sleep."

"Yeah," the guy echoed. His eyes swept over the four unmoving ninja littering the ground. "That must have been some party."

"Epic." Q agreed. "Don't worry about these guys. We'll take care of them."

The guy nodded, mumbled something about how his mom was going to kill him, and shuffled out of the alley. He turned the corner around the building and disappeared from sight.

What just happened?

Q rubbed his hands together. "Well, that takes care of that. Now to take care of the rest of these guys."

Whitley grabbed Q's arm. "You're not doing anything until you tell us what the hell just happened."

Q shrugged off Whitley's hand and stepped around him. "I healed him."

"Of what?" It was my turn to move in front of Q and halt his progression to the fallen ninja. "I mean, I always knew ninja were a nuisance, but I never considered the possibility they were a disease."

Q laughed and gently pushed me aside. He walked over to the first ninja and leaned over the body. "They're not really ninja." He pulled the scarf off the ninja's face, revealing another young guy.

I shook my head. "Q, if they look like a duck, walk like a duck, and quack like a duck, it means they're—"

"Ninja," Whitley finished for me, crossing his arms over his chest.

"Not necessarily." Q squatted next to the ninja. "These guys are just normal teens. This ... kunoichi you talk about? She's planted false memories into their heads. I can't really explain it." He put his hand on the guy's forehead. "When I touch them, I can feel the wrongness festering inside their minds—like a puss-filled blister."

Invisible spiders raced up my spine. "Wait. She can make people think they're ninja when they're not?" It was bad enough she'd messed with my ki and turned Q against me. I suppressed a shiver. So not good.

He removed his hand from the guy's head and moved to the next body. "Think of the human brain as an inflated balloon." He removed the third ninja's hood, revealing another teen guy. "The more air you blow into a balloon, the greater the strain on the balloon until—" Q mimicked an explosion with his fingers. "Bam. The false memories the kunoichi implanted does the same thing to the brain. That's why when I was infected I had migraines. The longer the kunoichi has a hold on these guys, the greater chance they'll experience brain trauma."

The horror of what she was doing made me sick to my stomach. "Like a concussion?"

"Exactly." Q nodded and placed his hands on the boy's forehead. He closed his eyes for a few seconds and opened them. "There. All better. When these guys wake up, they'll think they had a little too much fun at a party."

Whitley coiled his manrikigusari around his wrist and tucked it into his pocket. "They won't remember their time under the kunoichi's mind control?"

"Normally, they would." Q stood and walked to the remaining two ninja, who were draped on top of each other. "But I can make them forget their time as ninjas. I figure it's less traumatizing for them that way. And as a healer, isn't that what I'm supposed to do? Help people?"

I didn't know what to say to that. In fact, I didn't know what to say about any of this. Things were changing faster than I could take them in. I glanced over at Whitley to see what he thought, and the hungry look on his face made me wish I hadn't.

Whitley licked his lips. "You mean to tell me you have the power to take away someone's memory?"

Another wave of shivers raced along my spine. I didn't like where this conversation was headed. It hadn't occurred to me that my best friend's gift could be dangerous. Leave it to Whitley to figure that out first.

Q finished placing his hands on the two ninja and stood. "I guess so. I think it comes with the healing."

That made sense. But if there were other people with that power and they used it for the wrong purpose ... I shuddered. "When did you realize you could do this?"

"Just now." He looked at me and frowned. "Why? What's wrong?"

What was wrong was I didn't like the way Whitley was looking at Q—I could almost see the possibilities playing through his eyes, and none of them were good. "Nothing." I plastered on a fake smile, grabbed Q's arm, and pulled him away from Whitley. As long as Whitley fixed his beady little eyes on him, I wasn't going to let Q out of my sight. "We have the kanzashi, and sooner or later the kunoichi is bound to realize her ninja aren't coming back. We should leave before she does."

Whitley laughed, amused. "Agreed. I can drop you two off at your condo and take the kanzashi—"

"Stop right there." I turned to face him. "You're not taking the kanzashi anywhere. We'll go to my condo and the three of us will destroy the kanzashi *together*."

Whitley pressed his hands to his chest in mock insult. "I'm hurt. After everything we've been through, you still don't trust me? I've already told you, I have no other motives other than to destroy the kanzashi and keep the kunoichi from coming into her powers."

I made a face. "Right. It's not like you've never lied to me before." I pulled Q with me as I walked to Whitley's car.

Whitley's laughter behind me was his only response.

48

Tell me again why we can't take the elevator?" Quentin panted behind me as we ascended the last flight of stairs leading to the roof.

"Because they're nothing more than evil ninja robot assassins." I climbed the last couple of stairs and stood with my hand on the door, waiting for Whitley and Q. When they finally caught up, I opened the door and stepped onto the roof. The combined effects of the wind and dizzying heights nearly bowled me over.

Q stepped next to me and braced his hands on his knees as he hunched over to catch his breath. "But why couldn't we do this inside? In your room?"

"One." I held up a finger. "Debbie has this rule about not setting fires in my room." I lifted another finger. "Two. I have a hunch that Dr. Wendell may be a little pissy over the fact that I knocked him out earlier. I'd like to delay *that* lecture for as long as possible."

Whitley chuckled and tossed the bag containing the kanzashi at my feet.

I flinched. I knew we had to burn the kanzashi to keep the kunoichi from coming into her powers, but a part of me still hated to destroy such beautiful antiques.

Whitley reached into his pocket, pulled out a silver flask, and twisted off the lid. He smiled and held it out to me. "It's time to celebrate."

I waved the flask away. "No thanks. I remember what happened the last time you offered me a drink."

He shrugged and took a swig from the flask before capping it and putting it back in his pocket. "You really know how to hold on to a grudge."

"A grudge?" I snorted. "You stabbed me and set fire to my house. I don't think being upset about that qualifies me for any psycho ex-girlfriend awards."

"Pssh." Whitley rolled his good eye and waved a hand dismissively. "You left me trapped inside and half of my face burned off. You don't hear me with the constant snide comments, do you?"

I opened my mouth to tell him what I'd like to do to the other side of his face, but Q stepped forward, interrupting me. "Guys, I think we need to focus on the comb right now. Before the kunoichi sends anyone else after us."

I nodded. Q was right. Ignoring Whitley, I squatted down and emptied the contents of the velvet pouch onto the ground. Again, I was drawn to the same silver and coral kanzashi. I picked it up and stood, studying it under the moonlight. I knew I'd seen it before. The memory was like a butterfly, floating by my fingertips only to dart away just before I could catch it.

A crunching noise pulled me from my thoughts. I looked up to find Whitley grinding the broken pieces of several hairpins beneath his heel. When he finished, he pulled a bottle of lighter fluid from his jacket and doused the pieces. After saturating them, he set the bottle aside, grabbed a book of matches, and lit the pile on fire.

I watched, transfixed, as the metal blackened and the pieces of shell turned to ash.

Whitley turned to me and held out his hand. "Give it."

Instinctively, I hugged the comb to my body and took a step back. I wasn't ready to let Whitley destroy it, at least not until I remembered its secret. I couldn't put my finger on it, but it felt important to figure it out.

"Rileigh." An edge to Whitley's voice revealed the warning underlying the words.

"Just a second." I stared at the kanzashi in my hands, willing myself to remember. It didn't work. "I know I've seen this before. I'm trying to figure out—"

"It doesn't matter *what* you're trying to figure out." Whitley made a swipe for the hairpin and I jumped back, clutching the comb to my chest. His eyes narrowed. "Give it to me."

I shook my head. "What if it's important?"

"It's not." His voice was a growl. "You probably saw one of the whores in your pleasure house wearing one just like it. Besides, nothing is more important than destroying it."

Anger ignited within me. He never seemed to get tired

of reminding me where I'd come from. I tightened my fingers into fists.

"Ri-Ri." Q's eyes darted nervously between Whitley and me. "You know I hate to agree with Whitley on anything. But right now he has a point. Does it really *matter* that you might have seen the comb before? Does it change anything?"

"Exactly." Whitley thrust his hand at me. "Hand it over."

I took another step back. "But if you'd just give another minute to think. Maybe I could—"

"Get us killed?" Whitley offered. "This is stupid. The sooner we destroy it, the sooner we'll be safe. I'm sure the kunoichi has several ninja on their way right now ... if she's not on her way herself."

"I know!" I kept an eye on Whitley as I paced a circle around the burning combs. They were right. The only thing that mattered was keeping the kunoichi from regaining her powers. But still ... I shook my head. It didn't matter.

I stopped pacing and gave the kanzashi one last glance before I held it over the fire. There was no going back.

"Besides," Whitley added, "it's not like it belonged to you or anything. Yoshido wasn't exactly the type to gift girls with hair accessories."

Yoshido. The hairpin teetered on the edge of my grasp and I tightened my fingers around it before it could drop. The memory crashed into me with enough force to rock me on my heels. "That's it!" I followed my heart to the ground where I sat and stared at the kanzashi in my hands.

Whitley huffed. "You're telling me this was Yoshido's comb? Was he moonlighting as a cross-dressing geisha?"

I rolled my eyes. "Of course not. It wasn't always his. It was all he had left after ... oh my God." I braced a hand against the ground as the realization hit me in the gut. We were in a lot more trouble than we'd originally thought.

"Ri-Ri?" Q squatted next to me. "What's going on?"

My mind spun as the memories crashed into me. "It was Chiyo's."

Q frowned. "Chiyo? Wait a minute. Isn't that—"

"Sumi." Her name left a bitter taste on my tongue. "Yoshido kept it as a reminder of his so-called failure. He said it inspired him to become a better warrior. That means this kanzashi"—I lifted it toward Whitley—"can't belong to the kunoichi. Because Chiyo was dead before I became a samurai, long before the kunoichi ordered us killed."

Whitley folded his arms. "Are you certain?"

Before I could answer him, my cell phone rang. I pulled it out of my pocket to see who would be calling me so late, but the phone number wasn't one I recognized. Weird.

"Who is it?" Q asked.

I shrugged.

Whitley walked over to us and stared at the ringing phone in my hand. "I have a bad feeling. Don't answer it."

I had a bad feeling, too—which was exactly why I was going to answer it. "What if someone we know is hurt or in trouble?" I pressed the talk button. "Hello?"

"Rileigh."

It was the same whiny voice that I heard countless times begging Kim to come back to the dojo to fix one problem or another.

"Sumi?" For the life of me, I couldn't figure out why on earth she would be calling me at such a late hour. My only guess was that by mentioning her name I'd accidentally summoned her. "What do you want?"

"You have something of mine," she answered. "And I want it back."

49

Still holding the phone, I jumped to my feet. My mind reeled as I tried to make sense of her words. "The kanzashi? How did you even know about that?"

Her laugh was an angry bark. "I've been looking for it for quite some time. And when my ninja didn't return to me, I figured you must have gotten to it before me."

"*Your* ninja?" My eyes widened as I struggled to process the new development. It didn't make sense. How could Sumi be the kunoichi? Chiyo was dead long before the kunoichi rose to power... unless Sumi had lied about being Chiyo.

I felt the blood drain from my face, and my hand shook the phone against my ear. I looked at Whitley and mouthed the word *kunoichi*.

His spine went rigid and he swiped his hand across his neck, signaling me to disconnect the call. But I couldn't do that. She had Kim tricked into thinking she was Chiyo and he was ready to move to Japan for her. I had to figure out what she was after and why.

"I know you've teamed up with Whitley," Sumi continued. "And I know you've been hunting and destroying kanzashi. I would strongly suggest you leave mine unharmed."

I glanced from the small bonfire of burning combs to the kanzashi I held in my hand. If Whitley was right, the kunoichi's comb was in the fire burning while Chiyo's remained safe and sound. But with an endless supply of ninja at her disposal, I'd put *telling Sumi we'd destroyed her comb* on my list of things I was *not* going to do, right above *making out with a porcupine*. "I'm afraid that you're out of luck. You see, Whitley and I are seconds away from making s'mores and, wouldn't you know it, we ran out of sticks."

"I would advise against that," Sumi growled.

My fingers tightened painfully around the phone as I struggled to contain the anger rolling inside me. "I don't really think you're in a position to make threats."

"Aren't I?" She sounded amused. "You forget, I have something that belongs to you, too."

Kim. Sumi had Kim. I wondered if he was okay, if he'd figured out who Sumi really was. And if he had ... tremors of fear ripped through my chest. I gasped.

Sumi laughed. "I take it you've figured it out. Good. Then we've come to an understanding. You will bring me my kanzashi. Tonight. And I won't kill Kim."

Invisible hands tore inside my chest and ripped into my lungs. I'd been so angry at Kim for leaving me. But the thought of something happening to him clawd my heart into ribbons. So what choice did I have? Of course I would meet her, even though I knew she'd like nothing better than to kill me.

"Let me add," Sumi continued, "I'm not feeling particularly patient. So if you have to think this over, I suggest you do so quick before I carve—"

"No!" It didn't matter what she was about to say. I wouldn't let her hurt him. Even after everything, he was still my Kim. I loved him. "Just... don't touch him. I'll be there. I'll bring the comb."

Whitley's lips pressed into a line so thin they all but disappeared.

"Good." I could hear the smile in her voice. "There's an abandoned barn—I'll text you the directions. Meet me there in an hour."

An hour. That was all the time I had to figure out a way to find Kim and get him away from Sumi before she killed us all. But I wasn't stupid. "Fine. But just so we're clear, I know it's a trap."

She laughed. "Of course it is." The phone clicked and the call ended.

I slid my phone back into my pocket. My mind raced as I tried to formulate some kind of plan. So far I had nothing.

Whitley stalked toward me. "Tell me I didn't hear what I think I heard."

I stared at him. "Chill out, Whitley." I pointed to the fire. "We've incinerated the kunoichi's real comb. I'll bring her Chiyo's kanzashi instead, and hope she doesn't realize it's not the right one until I can escape with Kim."

"What?" The color drained from Q's face. "That's your plan?"

Whitley shook his head. "You're an idiot."

"Probably." My muscles tightened reflexively as he closed the distance between us. "But Sumi has Kim. She says she'll kill him if I don't bring her the kanzashi. What other choice do I have?"

Whitley's eyes blazed with fury. "Oh, I don't know. How about you say, 'To hell with Kim.' If you bring her the comb—especially the *wrong* comb—she'll kill you and that will in turn kill *me*. And being dead is my least favorite thing to be." He stopped in front of me, his shoulders rigid. "Besides, she'll probably kill Kim anyway, just for kicks." He positioned himself between me and the exit. "You're not leaving this roof."

Awesome. Just what I needed—another fight. As subtly as I could, I shifted my weight to the balls of my feet. "I'm going."

He lifted his chin and glared at me. "No. You're not."

I stared at him for a moment, watching the tendons flex along his jaw. I didn't have time for this. I yanked down on my shirt collar and slid the twines of the comb onto the middle of my bra. Now that my hands were free, I lifted them in front of me. "Okay, you want to fight. Fine. We'll fight. But just so you know, after I kick your ass, I'm still delivering Chiyo's kanzashi to Sumi."

Whitley's lip curled into a sneer. "I'm not going to fight you."

"Well, you're not going to kill me, either. You said so yourself. If you kill me you die."

"Right." Whitley spun and grabbed Q's arm, pulling him against his chest. He reached into his jeans pocket and pulled out a switchblade. After flipping it open, he pressed the knife point against Q's neck. "But I'll kill him."

Q's eyes widened, but he didn't move or speak.

I froze as needles of fear dug into my heart. How could I not have seen this coming? How could I be so stupid? When I spoke, my voice was strangely level, hiding the rage that burned inside me. "If you hurt him, I swear to you, Whitley, I will end you. Even if it means I die too."

Whitley pressed the blade deeper into Q's neck until a red line of blood appeared, trickling down Q's neck. Q hissed and clenched his eyes shut.

I ground my teeth together but remained still, fearful of Whitley digging the blade in farther.

"Think very carefully, Rileigh." Whitley tightened his hold on Q. "You have a choice. Your best friend or your ex-boyfriend. You can only choose one."

I opened my mouth to answer but the words weren't there. Partly because I didn't know what to say. I was supposed to choose between my best friend and a man who'd loved me enough to sacrifice his life for me in the past?

"What's it going to be, Rileigh?"

Son of hibachi. What other choice was there? Slowly, I raised my palms in surrender. "Fine. I'll stay. Now let Q go."

Q opened his eyes and stared at me. "Rileigh, I—"

I smiled at him. "It's okay. Kim's a samurai. Maybe he'll come to his senses in time to stop her?" The hope I'd put in my voice sounded fake to even me.

Q shook his head. "It's not that, though I appreciate the gesture. It's just … this." He spun in Whitley's grip and grabbed onto his shoulder.

Whitley's eyes widened. "What the—" But before he could finish, Q put his free hand on Whitley's cheek. A couple of seconds later, Whitley made a strange gurgling noise. His head snapped back a second before he fell to the ground. He looked around the roof, seemingly unable to focus.

Q stepped around him and gave me a quick hug. "You should get going."

I stood limp in his arms, too shocked to hug back and unable to tear my eyes from Whitley, whose head rolled lazily on his shoulders.

He smiled back at me with a crooked grin. "I guess you're going to leave now. Good luck and stuff. Try not to get killed because I really don't want to die." He leaned back on his arms, tilting his head to the sky, and started whistling.

I backed out of Q's grip. "What the hell did you do to him?"

He shrugged. "I altered his serotonin levels. For the next couple of hours, he shouldn't have a care in the world."

"Wow." I blinked at him. "That's a pretty neat trick."

"Did you guys ever notice that the stars kinda look like shuriken?" Whitley asked, averting our attention back to him. "It's almost like the sky is full of fighting ninja." He waved his hands in front of him shouting, "Hiya!" like a cheesy kung fu movie martial artist.

I shook my head slowly. "Wow … just wow."

"See?" Q placed his hands on his hips and smiled. "I'm not so helpless."

I looked at him. "I never thought you were helpless."

He rolled his eyes. "Maybe not helpless. But you thought I was a liability."

I wanted to argue but, the truth was, I couldn't. He was right. I'd been terrified he'd get hurt. But just now he'd taken down one of the most dangerous samurai I knew with just a touch. Shame burned hot on my cheeks.

Q waved a hand in the air. "It's okay. I understand. I didn't bring it up to make you feel bad. I just want you to know that you don't need to babysit me anymore, okay?"

I nodded.

Q smiled. "Good. So now you're going to let me come with you?"

"I wish you could." I shook my head. "I'd love nothing more than to have you fight by my side. It's not that I don't think you can handle your own. But Sumi told me to come alone. I don't want to think about what she might do to Kim if I bring backup. I can't risk it."

"I get it." He sighed and hunched his shoulders. "I just—" He sucked in a breath. "Do me a favor would you?"

I nodded. "Name it."

He hugged me again, this time crushing me against his body. His chest shuddered against my cheek. "Come back alive."

50

Japan, 1492

Senshi crouched on top of a ledge overlooking the bandits' camp below. Thin wisps of smoke from dying campfires filtered into the twilight sky.

"Where are you, Yoshido?" Her fingers grasped the boulder in front of her. He should have been back by now. Senshi shifted her position again, but it did nothing to relieve the rope of tension knotted around her ribs.

Yoshido never took longer than twenty minutes to sweep through a camp and gather information on the enemy. But it had been more than an hour and a half since he crept down the ledge and into the darkened valley below. Something must have happened.

Senshi stood and drew her sword. She was done waiting.

She eased her way down the steep hill, keeping her back to the rock and her sword to her side. The cliff shifted under her foot and she quickly shifted her weight before the rock could pull free and alert the bandits below. If she had to kill every single bandit—and she would if they'd hurt Yoshido—then it was better to have the element of surprise.

She approached the glowing embers of a dying campfire and spotted a man asleep beside it. Or so she thought until she stepped closer and noticed that his chest didn't rise or fall in breath. She crouched beside him and pushed his body over, exposing the gaping slash across the man's neck.

Senshi smiled. She'd found Yoshido's trail.

She wandered deeper into the camp, sticking to the shadow made by the tattered tents. A horse tethered to a tree caught sight of her and snorted in surprise.

"Who is there?" A man called out from within the closest tent.

Senshi froze.

Seconds later the tent flap rustled and fat little man with insect eyes stepped outside. His mouth was pressed into a scowl until he caught sight of her. After, it uncurled into a sinister grin. "Well, well." He licked his lips and staggered toward her. "Looks like my lucky day."

"Not quite." The stench of alcohol and smoke emanating from him burned Senshi's nostrils. She held her breath and plunged her sword through his chest.

His mouth moved, but the only sound he made was a gargled cough. Slowly, his eyes rolled into his head and he slumped to the ground, sliding off of her sword, leaving it coated in blood.

"Dog," she muttered. She shook her sword, smattering crimson droplets on the already filthy tent before moving on.

Twice she encountered corpses bearing clean neck wounds—the telltale signs of a quick and sure dagger. Wherever Yoshido was, she had to be closing in.

The rest of her journey was a quiet one, except for the drunken snores of bandits from within the tents she passed. But when Senshi reached the center of the camp, she heard two voices—a man's and a woman's—arguing.

Curious, Senshi crept around the corner of another weathered tent only to find a tent several times larger than the ones surrounding it. Instead of the dirty white canvas of the neighboring tents, this one was made of brilliantly woven silk in colors of red and gold. The entrance had previously been guarded by two men, who were now facedown in the blood-splattered grass.

As the voices within rose in anger, Senshi stepped around the fallen guards. She peeled back the silk curtain door and dared a peek inside. Immediately, she covered her mouth to muffle her gasp.

But it was too late, both Yoshido and the woman he was arguing with turned their attention to her.

"Senshi." Yoshido's face conveyed both sorrow and surprise.

Despite the obvious fury burning in her eyes, the woman with Yoshido was more beautiful than any Senshi had seen before. She felt her own cheeks warm as jealousy burned through her blood. Who was this woman that made Yoshido act recklessly enough to forget his stealth and his promise to return to Senshi with haste? Senshi tightened her grip on her sword.

The woman stepped beside Yoshido and folded her arms across her chest. Despite her frown, her lips had the delicate curve of a rosebud. Her long black hair trailed over the shoulders of her loose, red silk robe. "Who is that?" She glared at Senshi.

Yoshido lifted his chin. "She is none of your concern."

The woman laughed and turned to face him, her robes spinning around her feet. "Some samurai you are—making promises you never intended to keep."

"That is a lie!" The tendons along his jaw flexed. "Look at you! Look at what you have become. I only had one betrothed, and she was killed by bandits. You *are* a bandit."

He turned from her and looked at Senshi. "We are going."

Senshi nodded, still trying to make sense of their words. Even though a part of her wanted to know what promise Yoshido could have made with a bandit and what it had to do with his dead betrothed, another part of her wanted to get as far away from the camp and this woman as possible. Something about her felt hidden—like the lightning buried inside of a thunderhead. There was more to this woman than there appeared. Something dangerous.

Yoshido held out his hand and Senshi took it. His fingers tightened around hers to the point of pain. She could feel how much of her strength he needed, and the realization startled her. Until that moment, she'd thought it was her who needed him. She'd needed him to validate her worth as a samurai, she'd needed him to see her as more than a girl from the pleasure district, and she'd needed him to love her even when she felt she didn't deserve it.

But something was happening here, something she didn't understand. And Yoshido needed her to get him through it. Maybe he'd needed her all along.

As they turned to leave, the woman cried out, "Wait!" The anger was gone from her voice, replaced by desperation. "Yoshido, no!" She ran up to them and, if it wasn't for Yoshido shifting his body so it blocked her sword, Senshi couldn't be sure she wouldn't have taken the woman's head off.

"You cannot leave me." Tears spilled from her eyes as she fell to her knees at Yoshido's feet, twisting her hands into his obi. "You promised. You *owe* me."

His eyes narrowed. "My debt to you has been repaid tonight." He stepped around her but had to stop when her grip on his obi wouldn't allow him to move farther. "Release me." His voice was low and dangerous.

She shook her head. "How can you say that? You have repaid nothing."

"You are wrong. On this night, I am walking away from you and allowing you to live. If you want to keep breathing, you will leave this area and never return." He looked at Senshi and gave a slight nod.

Senshi nodded back. In one fluid movement, she severed the end of Yoshido's obi with her katana, barely missing the woman's fingers and leaving her nothing but a fistful of silk.

Together, the two of them left the tent to the screams of the woman vowing her revenge behind them.

51

I missed the turnoff. Twice.

"Dang it!" My GPS reprimanded me and I flipped it the bird. Without a single streetlight on the country road, I could barely see more than a couple of feet in front of my car. I pulled onto the shoulder and performed another illegal U-turn. I let off the gas and slowed to a crawl. That's when I saw it—the gravel road hidden within a row of trees.

I turned off and followed the winding road until it emerged from the trees and my eyes adjusted to the moonlit-bathed field sprawled before me. As far as I could see, there were no houses, and no other people, only a single wooden barn that cast an eerie glow from light filtering through its worn, wooden planks.

I stopped my car several yards away and cut the engine. "Awesome," I mumbled as I opened the door and climbed out. A cool fall breeze sent a chill down my back. Or maybe it wasn't the cold. I closed my eyes and concentrated. That's when I realized the sensation rippling over my spine and tickling the hairs on the back of my neck was a premonition of danger. I opened my eyes and sighed. "Tell me something I don't know."

I knew I was walking into a trap. The trouble was I couldn't get a read on how many people waited for me inside. Every time I closed my eyes and tried to feel the place out with my ki, the reading came back fuzzy. Oh well. I guessed it was better I didn't know. At least then I could assume I was only outnumbered instead of *horribly* outnumbered. That's me, Rileigh Martin, eternal optimist.

I surveyed the surrounding area as I walked a dirt path to the barn. Aside from a chorus of cicadas singing from the trees, no other sound could be heard. But I knew I wasn't alone. I could feel them. Waiting.

As I drew closer to the barn, the smells of decaying wood and moldy straw grew stronger. The rotted wooden door hung slightly ajar. Inside I could see a flickering fluorescent bulb illuminating a dust-coated workbench. The shadows surrounding it made it impossible to see anything else. Given the ki buzzing under my skin like an electric charge, odds were a line of shuriken waited to be thrown at my head. I sucked in another breath. I could do this. I had to.

For Kim.

I drew my sword from the sheath at my back, pushed the door open with my shoulder, and stepped inside. Instantly, the room filled with blinding white light. No longer certain of my position in the room, I whirled around with my sword raised, ready to defend myself from whatever direction the attack came from.

But it never did.

After blinking away the spots dancing in my eyes, I discovered the light came from a motion-detecting flood lamp. Now that I could see, I took in my surroundings. The barn was mostly open. A few beams lined the side wall, supporting a mostly caved-in hay loft. The dirt floor was covered sparsely with damp, moldy hay. Various rusted farm tools lined the wall and something I couldn't quite make out lay huddled in the far corner beside the workbench.

Walking slowly with my sword held out in front of me, I approached the object. As I got closer and could make out arms and legs, I realized it wasn't an object after all.

"Kim!" I gasped and dropped to the ground beside him.

My heart leapt inside my throat, threatening to choke me each time I swallowed. Time seemed to freeze in the agonizing seconds it took me to place two fingers to his neck. And that's when I felt it, a faint ripple beneath my fingers.

I had to get him out of here.

I set my sword on the ground, gripped his shoulder, and gave him a firm shake. "Kim!" He didn't move. I ran my hands down his arms and across his chest, looking for any signs of bruising or bleeding. I found none. So why didn't he respond to my attempts to wake him up? I shook him harder, which only made his head bobble on his neck. "Kim!" When that didn't work, I reared back and smacked him hard enough to leave a red imprint on his cheek.

Nothing.

Prickling waves of panic raced across my skin like the legs of a hundred spiders. What was wrong with him?

"You can keep trying, but you'll never wake him." A voice spoke from behind me.

Grabbing my sword, I spun on my knees and rocked to my feet in the same motion. Sumi stood in the doorway dressed in a red silk Japanese robe. Her black hair had been woven into intricate knots and pinned to the top of her head. Sweeping lines of eyeliner rimmed her eyelids, ending in drastic angles at her temples. She looked like a gothic geisha nightmare.

I held my katana in front of me. "You look … very weird."

She smirked.

"Is that why you're late?" I positioned myself so I stood between her and Kim. "Working the street corners must be exhausting."

Her smile faded. "If you knew who I was, you would not be so bold."

I laughed. "Who *you* were? Please. Do you have any idea how many ninja I've killed in my day? You're no different."

She arched a penciled eyebrow. "Aren't I?"

She held her hand out and Kim's spine arched at a drastic angle. His eyes remained closed but his lips curled, revealing teeth clenched in pain. He screamed, an anguished sound that twisted my insides.

"Stop!" I shouted.

To my relief, Sumi dropped her hand and Kim lay still, but his breathing remained ragged. She glared at me, her eyes narrowed into dangerous slits. "That is just a taste of what I can do." She walked to the center of the barn and extended her hand. "Now give me my kanzashi."

Son of hibachi. If I gave her Chiyo's kanzashi, how long would I have until she realized I'd given her the wrong one? What I needed was a plan. And, since I didn't have one, I'd have to stall until I did.

"He obviously means nothing to you." I pointed the tip of my blade at Kim. "So let him go. Then you and I will discuss the kanzashi." At the very least, I was grateful her *real* kanzashi sat in a pile of burning rubble. I'd never seen someone wield so much power, and to give her more would have been devastating not just to me but to anyone she came in contact with.

Her eyes widened. "You think he means nothing to me? Oh, how stupid you are. He means *everything!* He's the entire reason I'm doing this. I'm finally setting things right. He was supposed to marry me. *Me!* But then he met you and discarded me like trash."

That was news to me. "You're lying. Yoshido would never have slummed around with a ninja. The only woman he was betrothed to was Chiyo."

She sneered. "I *am* Chiyo."

This was getting more confusing by the minute. "But I thought you were the kunoichi."

She stamped her foot impatiently. "I *am* the kunoichi, you idiot."

"No." I glanced at Kim, wishing he would wake up and explain to me what the hell she was talking about. "That's impossible. Chiyo died. She was killed by bandits. Yoshido mourned for more than a year."

She shook her head, a twisted smile on her lips. "Oh, really?" She tsked. "That poor man. But forgive me if I don't properly appreciate his suffering while he *mourned* me. Maybe it's because, during the time he was *mourning* I was being beaten and raped." She lifted hear arms and balled her hands into tight fists. The rusted tools began rattling against the wall.

Oh no. I struggled to swallow past the knot that had risen inside my throat. If what she said was true, if she really was both Chiyo and the kunoichi, that meant I held the key to unleashing her full power in my pocket. With the kanzashi, she'd be unstoppable. The urge to bang my head against the nearest wall was overpowering. *Rileigh Martin, you really are an idiot!*

Sumi's eyes clouded until her irises disappeared behind a milky, white film. "After my father paid my ransom, the bandits told him I was dead. That's what bandits say when they don't want a girl's betrothed to come looking for her. They kept me as their plaything."

I felt sick. Even though Sumi was a mega bitch, she didn't deserve a fate like that. "I'm so sorry, Sumi. I didn't know."

"Maybe not." Her jaw tightened and she pointed to Kim. "But *he* did. He snuck into the camp one night looking for the leader of the bandits. And he found the leader—me. I was overjoyed at being reunited with him. But he was disgusted with who I'd become. But what other choice did I have? I seduced the leader of the bandits and slit his throat while he slept. If I hadn't become their leader, they would have eventually killed me. I did what I had to do in order to survive. But Yoshido wouldn't listen. He'd already replaced me—with *you*."

Her words hit me like an icy fist to my gut. She was the woman in the bandit camp who had begged Yoshido not to leave. Yoshido knew she was Chiyo and he still walked away. Kim knew Sumi and the kunoichi were one and the same. Which meant Sumi had manipulated Kim's mind just like she did to Q and the ninjas. Kim hadn't wanted to break up with me after all! A strange combination of relief and rage burned my blood to a boil. I had to force myself to keep still and not charge her with my blade extended. "So you paid Zeami to lead a band of ninja to kill us all out of revenge."

She smiled. "You're half right. I wanted *you* dead. But that idiot Zeami was supposed to capture Yoshido and take him to me—alive. But he killed him instead." Her smiled withered. "Careless. That's why I beheaded him when he returned to me without Yoshido. And that's why I've vowed to kill him in every life. He will pay for all eternity for killing the man I love."

Wow. So there was crazy, and then there was the hot mess standing in front of me who took it to a whole other level. "Okay. But if Zeami hadn't killed Yoshido, do you really think he would have forgiven you for killing everyone he cared about? Did you really think you two would have lived happily ever after? If you do, then you didn't know Yoshido at all."

"Honey." Sumi placed her hands on her hips. "With the power I had, it would have been nothing for me to erase his memory. One second you're the love of his life"—she snapped her fingers—"and the next, he doesn't even know your name."

My fingers tightened on my blade. I'd make her pay for screwing with Kim's mind and putting us both through hell. But then another thought niggled in the corner of my mind. She had the ability to alter memory and manipulate minds just as Q used his ability to erase the boy's memory of being a ninja. I connected the dots. "You're a healer!"

"Finally figured it out, did you? Yes, this is what a healer can do when they choose not to . . . *heal*." She spoke the word as if it disgusted her. "Instead of taking pain away, I bring it. I can alter the body just as much as I can alter the mind."

I shook my head, stunned that someone would twist such a great gift into something so evil. "Your powers were meant to help people."

"They do. They help me. Or at least they would if I had my full powers back." She extended her fingers. "The kanzashi. Now."

I was out of time and no closer to a plan. Odds were I was going to have to fight. But how could I fight someone who could inflict pain with a flick of their wrist? Retreat was my best option. But how could I get both Kim and myself out of here before she stopped me? Sumi stood between me and the door. I would need another way out. I did a quick survey of my surroundings, looking for possible escape options. Maybe if I stalled a little bit longer . . . "I don't understand why you need the kanzashi. You seem to be doing just fine without it."

She waved a hand in the air. "Apparently not. Everyone

keeps fighting off my control. You. Your annoying friend. Kim."

"What a minute." Despite the danger, I took a step toward her. My body hummed with the threat of violence. "Kim fought off your mind control?"

"Not for long," she mused. "But he's stronger than most. I have to cloud his mind every night to keep him in line. This evening he broke free long enough to tell me he was too in love with you to go to Japan with me." She snorted. "Luckily, once I have my kanzashi and transcend, I'll be able to wipe you from his mind completely."

The horror of what she wanted to do twisted barbed wire around my stomach. I couldn't let her do it. I touched the outside of my pocket where the kanzashi lay. It had been a mistake to bring it. Somehow, I had to keep it away from her.

As if reading my thoughts, Sumi rolled her eyes. "I'm bored." She raised her hand in the air and snapped her fingers.

A chill rippled my skin and I knew that whatever came next, it wasn't going to be good.

I caught movement from the far corners of the barn. The shadows seemed to fall from the walls and bleed onto the floor only to rise up into the shapes of three ninja wielding swords.

Sumi backed away with a smirk as the ninja made their approach. I wondered what poor kids she'd manipulated, but as they drew closer, I noticed something different about these three ninja. As they drew closer, I saw they weren't wearing masks. And then I noticed another important difference.

These ninja were my friends.

"*Man*," I whined to myself. As much as having friends who thought they were ninja sucked, it did make sense. If Sumi manipulated their minds, it explained why they'd been blowing me off. And, unfortunately, it also explained why they walked toward me with swinging katanas and menace in their eyes.

"So what?" I asked Sumi. "You couldn't get your own friends so you had to brainwash mine?"

She laughed. "I thought it would be fun to isolate you from the people you cared about, just like I was isolated from my friends and family when the bandits took me."

Fair enough.

Michelle, Braden, and Drew encircled me just like they had the first night I'd met them in Kim's dojo. Only instead of testing me and my powers, this time they *actually* wanted to kill me. But it wasn't their fault. The kunoichi had made them prisoners inside their own heads. I couldn't let them kill me, but the question was, could I fight them off without hurting them?

Drew struck first and I met his blade with mine, our steel hissing as we pushed against each other. I shoved forward and he stumbled back but quickly regained his footing. This gave Braden and Michelle time to split and come at me from both sides. I spun out of reach of Michelle's blade, only to have to drop and roll to avoid a hacking strike from Drew. I climbed to my feet, my mind racing. It wasn't like I could lash out at them as I would other attackers. But if all I did was deflect their blows, eventually they'd wear me down.

I opened up my ki, pushed it into my sword, and slammed the blade into the dirt floor. A blue light pulsed once before a blue transparent bubble shimmered around me. Not a permanent fix, but it would buy me some time.

My three friends approached my shield and hacked at it with their swords. The shield shimmered and swayed, but held strong. I braced my hands on my knees and fought to catch my breath. My friends were wearing me down and, without being able to fight back, I was a goner. Obviously, this was exactly what Sumi had in mind.

Michelle held her sword over her head and I crawled as close to her as the shield allowed. She swung the sword down where it bounced off the shield only inches from my face. I didn't flinch. "Michelle, can you hear me? You have to fight this."

Her unblinking eyes seemed to look through me. "Kill Rileigh."

Sumi laughed. "Do you still think my powers are weak?"

I raised my middle finger in response.

She smirked. "You can't stay in there forever."

No duh. I crouched on my heels and watched as my friends continued to hack away at my shield. A tiny hole appeared at the top and grew larger with each strike from Drew's blade. Great. I was out of time and left with two options:

Kill my friends or let them kill me.

52

Braden spun and kicked his heel against my shield. His foot caught the edge of the hole and tore it wide enough for a person to squeeze through. My three possessed friends grinned.

So much for that. I pulled my sword from the ground and withdrew what remained of my ki. I didn't have enough energy left to do any good. My only option left was to fight. I raised my sword in front of me.

Sumi leaned against one of the barn's support beams and made an impatient sound. "You'd be saving us a lot of time if you'd just hand over the kanzashi."

"And put an end to all this fun?" I grunted and met Michelle's blade with mine. I shoved hard and she fell on her butt, only to scramble back to her feet. She hadn't slowed down one bit since the fight began. None of them had. If Sumi's mind control made it so they didn't feel fatigued, there was no way I could continue to fight them off without having to hurt or possibly kill them. And that was a choice I couldn't live with.

Drew swung and I raised my katana before his blade swept across my neck. But he was stronger. He lifted his elbow so it paralleled his shoulder and pressed forward. My aching arm wobbled as my own blade was pushed dangerously close to my face.

Lines of sweat trickled down my temples. Of all the ways to die, I'd never guessed it would be at the hands of one of my friends.

"Hey, Rileigh! Over here!"

I chanced a glance at the door just in time to see Q and Whitley rush inside. I'd never been so happy to see my best friend and psychotic arch-nemesis in my life.

Sumi pushed off the beam, her arms falling to her side. "What the hell are you doing here?"

"We're here to rescue Rileigh." Whitley wore the same stupid grin that let me know he was still under the effects of Q's mood enhancement.

If I wasn't balancing razor-sharp steel mere inches from my face, I would have laughed out loud. "Then rescue me, dammit!"

Q's eyes widened as he took in the scene. "Right."

Whitley nodded and walked forward.

"Not you!" My sword continued its slow advance toward my face. "You take care of Sumi." If Whitley tried to stop Drew or the others, I couldn't trust him enough not to kill them.

"You got it." He gave me a thumbs-up, pivoted on his

heels, and charged. Sumi reared back, holding her hands in front of her with her fingers pointed down. Praying mantis kung fu, I realized. Definitely not a martial arts style taught at Kim's dojo. I wondered what else she'd learned from her time with the bandits.

My muscles burned as I fought to keep Drew from driving my blade into my face. As it was, it was close enough to kiss. "Hurry, Q!"

"On it!" He darted from the door and wove around Michelle and Braden, who didn't bother a glance his way. He placed his hand on Drew's temple and a flash of light glowed from under his fingers.

Drew's eyelids fluttered and he dropped the sword. He groaned, swaying on his feet before finally crumpling to the ground.

I let out a sigh of relief. "Thanks."

He smiled. "I told you I could help."

"It looks like you might get another chance." I pushed him to the side and spun the opposite direction just in time to miss Braden's spinning kick.

Q blinked from his back on the ground.

"Are you okay?" I swung my sword, driving Braden back. He nodded.

"Good." I swung again, purposely going wide so I wouldn't hit Braden, but he still had to step back. "Hold your hands out," I told Q.

He did and I hooked my leg around Braden's knee. He tumbled backward into Q's waiting arms. Before Braden could push his way up, Q placed a hand on his temple. Again light flashed from under his fingers and Braden's body went limp in his arms. Q lowered him to the ground and stood.

"Rileigh?" From across the room Whitley ducked and dodged a series of viper-fast kicks from Sumi. "I don't like this. I'm ready to go home now."

"Just a little bit longer." I answered him. If he could keep her busy for a few more minutes, Q and I could take care of Michelle. And maybe then we could figure out a way to get everyone out of here—alive.

Michelle moved forward with her blade held above her head. I tightened my grip on my katana's hilt and braced for impact.

But Q was faster. He snaked an arm around her neck and touched her face. Her eyes widened before they rolled back into her head. She fell to the ground with a thud.

I dropped my sword. "Man, I wish I could do that." But even as I said the words, I caught movement in the corner of my eye. "What the—" I jumped back, but not in time to avoid Whitley as he careened into me, knocking us both to the ground.

"Get off of me." I pushed him to the side and scrambled to my feet.

Whitley lifted his head and looked at me, squinting through his good—now swollen and purple—eye. A line of blood trailed from the corner of his mouth. "I don't know what I'm doing here, but I can assure you I'm not happy about it."

"Really? Because I'm having the time of my life. In fact, I'm going to suggest *Ninja Death Match* as the theme of this year's prom." I offered him a hand, but he ignored it and climbed slowly to his feet.

I turned my attention to Sumi and braced myself for her next move. But she appeared frozen. Her leg was halted in mid-kick, but her eyes were trained on a spot on the ground a couple feet away from me. I followed her gaze and almost choked when I realized what she was staring at—the kanzashi. When Whitley crashed into me, he must have knocked it loose from my pocket.

"Son of hibachi," I squeaked.

Sumi and I dove for it at the same time. We collided, her fingers scratched at my face and ripped my hair. I grabbed her wrists and tried to push her away, but she only dug in deeper. We rolled across the floor, a tangle of nails and teeth.

"What are you doing?" Whitley called. "Get up! You're fighting like a couple of girls."

I agreed with him, even as I raked my nails down Sumi's face. I knew I should have been embarrassed. This was not an honorable way to fight. But when you hated someone, there was something so satisfying about digging your fingers into their skin and feeling their blood pool beneath your nails.

And Whitley could mock all he wanted. It was more than obvious as he hung back against the wall, he wasn't going anywhere near Sumi.

Sumi reared back and shook a wad of my freshly ripped hair from her fingers. I reached for her throat. We tumbled and clawed until we came to a stop beside the kanzashi.

The world seemed frozen in the seconds we blinked at each other, our hands clenched around each other's necks.

Then we pounced.

I reached the comb first, but as I grabbed it, Sumi jammed her fingers into my eyes. Pain exploded in a display of white fireworks behind my eyelids. Tears sprung from my eyes and trailed down my cheeks. I blinked rapidly, but it did nothing to clear the blurriness. Reaching blindly, I made a grab for her but managed to only snag the end of her robe.

Sumi kicked out and the heel of her shoe connected with my nose. Another explosion of pain crashed into me hard enough to make me sway on my knees. Something warm trickled down my chin. I licked my lip and tasted the coppery tang of blood. I had a brief girly moment where I wondered if she'd broken my nose, but that moment disappeared when I heard Sumi's triumphant laugh. Then I realized my problems were so much worse than a busted nose.

I ground the heels of my palms into my eyes and blinked several times. Once my vision cleared, I saw I was too late.

Sumi held the comb.

Before I could react, her head snapped back and her mouth peeled into a scream, though no sound came out. I knew what was happening as I'd experienced the same thing several months ago.

She was transcending.

53

Sumi closed her eyes. Her skirt swirled and her hair tangled in a wind that didn't touch anything else. Sparks jumped from her fingertips, and the hairs rose along my arms as the barn filled with an electric charge.

Invisible claws of fear dug into my heart. How was I going to get everyone out of here? I chanced a glance at Whitley, who stared back in wide-eyed terror. Q's face paled to the same colorless hue as his bleached hair. Kim and the other samurai still lay motionless on the floor.

There wasn't enough time.

Sumi opened her eyes. Her pupils dilated and a lazy smile curled on her lips. She looked drunk—and maybe she was from the onslaught of power.

I was so dead.

We all were.

"You." Her head tipped forward and she glared at me with a look of pure hate. She lifted her hand. Blue lines of electricity danced between her fingers. "Now you die."

My muscles tightened as I looked around for opportunity to escape. But I was backed against a wall with nowhere to go. I could only watch as the lightning left her fingers and arced straight for me.

Q dove forward.

My breath caught in my throat as I realized what he was trying to do. "No!" I screamed. But he didn't stop. I dug my heels into the ground, hoping to stand firm, but Q had too much momentum. He slammed into me, knocking me against the wall while he took the full force of the lightning.

My head cracked against a wooden plank, but I ignored the pain. "Q!" I pushed off of the wall and fell to my knees beside him. A thin line of smoke curled from the singed fabric of his shirt. He didn't move.

"Oh my God, no." A sob clawed its way up my throat and lodged itself on the back on my tongue. I held my hand above his chest. The heat from his smoldering clothes prickled my skin. "No." This couldn't be happening. Q was my best friend. He was going to be the world's greatest psychologist. He wanted to help people. He tried to help me.

And this was what he got for it. Sumi dusted her hands on her skirt. "God, he was annoying."

Something hard lodged inside my chest—jagged and fire hot. The warmth of it spread across my body, growing hotter until I thought my skin would ignite. I stood, turning away from Q, fueled by a rage I'd only known once before.

Sumi was going to die.

I didn't know where my sword was, I'd lost it during our tussle—but it didn't matter. When I killed her, I wanted to do it with my bare hands. I wanted to feel the moment her heart stopped beating. I gave a battle cry and launched myself at her.

She smiled and lifted her hand.

Before I'd realized what hit me, a cold shock twisted through my body and drove me to my knees. I didn't hesitate a second before I stood back up. I wasn't going down that easily.

Sumi's eyes narrowed. "That was just a taste."

I stood and squared my shoulders, trying my best to contain the spasms that wracked my body.

Electricity crackled from her curled fingers. "How I've waited for this moment—to rid you from Kim's life the way you pushed me from Yoshido's." She lifted her hand and extended her fingers. "Finally." It was more a sigh of relief than an actual word.

I didn't have my sword and I didn't have enough ki left to make a shield. But I had a samurai's spirit. I would win this fight. Or I would die. And if I died right now, at least I could be at peace with the fact that I did so with honor.

"I pity you." I spit the words through clenched teeth. "You have to brainwash people to get them to love you. If I die now, I know I'll die with Kim's heart. That's something you'll never have."

She snarled. The light crackling against her fingertips grew brighter, to a level that would shock the life from my body.

I took a deep breath and closed my eyes. This was it. The moment every samurai trained for. Death—the unbeatable opponent. I wasn't scared to die. But a pang of sorrow wound through my heart as I realized that, this time, I'd have to navigate the afterlife alone.

Or maybe not. Maybe this time, instead of Yoshido, Q would be waiting with an offered hand. The thought made me smile.

I was ready. I took another deep breath—maybe even my last. Because Rileigh Martin, teenage samurai, had come to the end of another life. And she'd done so by filling her existence with friends, family, and love. It was enough.

54

One thing I'd learned through all my close calls, is that death is a woman. I know this because she's a total diva. She likes to maintain a mysterious rock star image. So when you least expect it, she storms in with the attitude that she owns the place. And when you're waiting for her, she's almost always fashionably late.

So there I was, waiting to die and, of course, it wasn't happening.

I opened my eyes to see the reason for the holdup. I'd expected to see Sumi with her hand extended, wearing a sinister grin, and having one of those clichéd villain moments where she wanted to savor my death.

Instead something, moving fast enough to blur, crashed into Sumi and knocked her to the floor. She screamed and struggled against the person wrestling her to the ground, but he pinned her arms behind her back. Once she was safely secured, her captor's eyes met mine.

Kim.

He hauled Sumi to her feet. She kicked and thrashed but remained firmly in his grasp.

I started for him.

He frowned. "Don't."

I stopped, even though his words drove a spike into my heart.

His gaze softened. "She's dangerous. She's transcended. She'll *always* be dangerous."

I nodded. That didn't leave us with a whole lot of options. "How is she not hurting us now?"

"Her power is in her hands." Kim inclined his head, motioning to Sumi's wrists ensnared by his hands. "If I let her go, it will be all over for us."

Sumi stopped struggling and smiled. "That's right. And you can't hold on to me forever. So you might as well let me go."

"No." Kim must have tightened his grip because she flinched. "I was a fool to let you live in the last life. I'm not going to make the same mistake in this one. You've caused enough damage."

"You think I've done *damage*?" She unleashed a high-pitched hysterical laugh. "I've done nothing but put things right. How things should have been before *she*"—Sumi spit the word like venom—"came between us. We can be together now as we were meant to be."

"No." Still holding her wrists, he spun her in his arms so she came face-to-face with him. "I don't love you. I never loved you. I felt an obligation to you as I was bound by honor. But that obligation ended the moment you became *this*. I could never be with someone so full of selfish hate. Someone who manipulates the minds of others so she can control them. You disgust me."

She flinched, her eyes widening in horror. "I—I don't believe you. This is her doing." She twisted in his arms to glare at me. "She confused you. She made you forget. When she's gone, we can go back to our lives. It can be like it was."

"You don't get it," Kim said. "I love Rileigh. I will always love Rileigh. From this life into the next." He met my eyes, sending small shivers racing along my skin. How could I have been such an idiot to believe he'd ever choose to leave me for her?

Sumi's face flushed and her eyes brimmed with tears. "So what are you going to do?" Static danced along her fingertips. "You can't hold me forever."

"You're right." He looked at me with a sadness in his eyes I couldn't decipher. "Rileigh, I need you to get your sword."

A chill rippled down my spine as I nodded. I walked to the spot where my sword lay abandoned on the floor and picked it up. As a samurai, it was my duty to rid the world from someone so dangerous. But as I walked back to where Kim stood holding Sumi, I couldn't help but notice an uneasy quiver that brushed along my skin. Something about this didn't feel right.

As I drew closer, Sumi flailed in Kim's arms. Despite the uneasy feeling, a part of me wanted her to suffer. I wanted her to hurt like she'd hurt me. I shook my head and struggled to push those feelings down into the pit of my stomach. I needed to be calm and emotionless for what I had to do next.

I stopped and raised my blade.

Sumi shrieked and thrashed. "Don't you dare! What Kim's not telling you is that if you kill me, you'll inadvertently kill him. We're soul mates."

I froze. My breath lodged in my throat. There it was— the reason for the uneasiness twisting my insides into knots. I lowered my blade and looked at Kim. "How could you leave out that little detail?"

"Doesn't matter." He shook his head. "You have to end her. It's the only way to make sure she won't harm anyone again."

I blinked at him. Was he insane? How could I kill her knowing that Kim would die shortly after?

"Rileigh, please," he said. "Look at me."

I looked up and fell into his dark brown eyes.

"You have to do this. For me. It's because I love you. Because I always will. Death won't change that."

His words unraveled me. Desperation filled his eyes. I couldn't imagine the physical toll Sumi's manipulation took on him. Or how hard it was for him to fight her off. He couldn't have much energy left, which meant I didn't have much time to decide.

But the fact remained, I loved him so much. And I wasn't sure how I was supposed to live a life without him. He had to know that if I killed him, I'd be killing a piece of myself as well. "Kim, I don't—"

"Yes, you can." A faint smile appeared on his face. "You are a samurai. The strongest of us all."

I choked back a sob. "I know," I answered, quoting the words he spoke to me more than 500 years ago.

He laughed and the sound shattered what remained of my heart.

I raised my katana. It felt heavier than I remembered it being. For the first time since I began my training, it didn't feel like an extension of my body. It felt foreign and awkward in my grip. Two times it almost slid from my fingers before I tightened my hold.

Sumi shrieked and began thrashing all over again.

Kim twisted her to the side so he could look at me directly. "I'm so sorry you have to do this. But you're the only one who can." His eyes bore into mine with a ferocity I'd only seen on the battlefield. "I promise, I'll find you again."

Hot tears burned down my cheeks and my sword wavered in my hands. I hiccupped and tried to gain some composure but quickly gave up the attempt. Though it had never been stated, I was willing to bet even samurais were allowed to cry when they had to kill someone they loved.

It wasn't fair. We'd been through so much, and overcome the impossible, only to be torn apart again. And the reason why was struggling in Kim's grip. I glared at her, hating her in that moment more than I'd hated anyone else before—in this life and the last. I welcomed the feeling, allowing it to course inside my blood and burn my sorrow away until I was numb from the inside out.

I stepped forward.

Sumi's lip quivered and her eyes never left my advancing blade.

I averted my gaze to Kim. "How long will you have until—" I left the sentence dangling in the air, unable to voice the words out loud.

He shook his head. "I don't know. Maybe an hour or two … maybe only a minute."

I nodded and raised my katana over my head. "I love you."

55

Wait!"

I froze, my blade hovering an inch above Sumi's nose.

Sumi cracked an eye open. "No. It can't be."

I lowered my sword and whirled around to find Q staggering to his feet. He grimaced as he stood upright, pushing his shoulders back with a hiss of pain.

I didn't move, didn't breathe out of fear I would somehow awaken from the dream I'd stumbled into. I saw him take the bolt of lightning and crumple to the ground. I thought he was dead—he looked dead. "Please tell me you're real," I whispered.

He smiled. "No generics here."

An earsplitting squeal erupted from my mouth but I didn't care. I ran to him, but he stopped me with an outstretched hand before I could hug him.

"I'm a little tender."

"I can imagine." I couldn't stop bouncing.

"How?" Sumi called out from the spot Kim still held her. When I looked at her I noticed her face was paler than normal. "No one has ever survived my electrocution."

Q walked over to her. "I'm a healer. When you have this gift and use it in the way it was intended, the power grows into something amazing. But you wouldn't know that, would you?"

She tried to shrink back, but Kim's body kept her locked in place. "You're not stronger than me. That's impossible."

Q shrugged. "Not impossible. In fact, it would be my pleasure to give you a demonstration." He unbuttoned his sleeves and began rolling them up.

"What are you going to do?" Sumi pushed against Kim's hold. "Don't you come near me! Don't you touch me!"

Kim looked at me, his brow pinched in confusion. "What's going on?"

"It's okay," I told him. "Q's got this."

He frowned. "A lot has happened while I've been out of it."

I nodded. I didn't dare tell him about Whitley. Speaking of… I looked around the barn. Drew, Braden, and Michelle rested peacefully, but Whitley was nowhere to be seen. I shook my head. I don't know why I was surprised. The coward probably made a break for it the first opportunity he had.

"Don't you dare mess with my mind!" Sumi shrieked, tossing her head back and forth. "I'll hunt you down in every life. I'll kill you in a thousand different ways. I'll torture your loved ones. I'll—"

"Do absolutely nothing." Q smiled. "Want to know why?"

Sumi shook her head. Her lip quivered.

"You'll do nothing because I'm going to make it so you won't remember any of this. Now or ever again."

Kim's eyebrows shot up. "You can do that?"

"Yes he can!" I grinned. It was the perfect solution. Now no one had to die.

Q nodded. "The abuse Sumi encountered in her last life scarred her. Her hatred is a disease. I'm going to take away her memories of Japan. I'm going to take away all the hurt and anger she's been carrying around." He looked directly into Sumi's eyes. "I'm going to give you the chance to live a normal, happy life."

Even after Sumi had almost killed him, all Q wanted to do was help her. I couldn't help but thank my lucky stars I got to be best friends with someone so amazing.

Q rubbed his palms together until a white light glowed from his fingertips. He reached for Sumi.

"No!" She shrieked, kicking her feet.

Kim adjusted his grip, the muscles in his arms straining to hold onto her thrashing body.

Q hesitated. "Maybe you should let go."

"I can't." He spoke through clenched teeth. "If I let go she'll unleash her power and you'll be dead."

Q's hands were glowing so bright I had to squint through the light. I wanted this over with so we could get back to our lives. I couldn't wait for the moment when I'd finally be able to fall into Kim's arms.

The glow from Q's hands reflected bright orbs into Sumi's wide eyes. "We'll do this," Q said. "Just don't move. We wouldn't want any accidents." He bit his lip and stretched out his hand.

I held my breath and leaned forward on my toes. In just a couple of seconds this would all be over. And then Kim and I could be together and we could pretend this whole thing was just a nightmare.

But just as Q was about to touch Sumi's face, she planted her feet and threw herself at Q. I watched Kim's eyes widen in surprise. He managed to keep her in his grasp, but her movement caught him off balance. Together, they tumbled forward. As they fell, Sumi turned to look at me. The fear on her face only moments ago had been replaced with a look of triumph.

"No." My cry was barely a whisper. I watched, helpless, as Q tried to get out of the way. But there hadn't been enough time. Both Sumi and Kim collided into Q's outstretched hands. The moment they touched, light filled the room so brightly I was forced to shield my eyes with my arm. This wasn't happening. It *couldn't* be happening. I had to believe when I opened my eyes everything would be fine. Kim would be fine. I couldn't consider the alternative.

A few seconds later the light died. I dropped my hand and opened my eyes. Q sat on the ground with a hand pressed against his temple. His eyes met mine. "Rileigh, I-I'm so sorry. I couldn't get out of the way. There was nothing I could do."

I shook my head. "It's okay." My voice wavered. Kim and Sumi laid on the ground, unmoving. I rushed over to Kim, dropped to my knees, and propped his head in my lap. My fingers trembled across his skin as I stroked his cheek. "He's going to be fine. I bet you missed him."

Q's eyes dropped to the ground. He didn't answer me. He didn't have to. His silence said everything.

Kim's lashes fluttered and I snatched my hand away.

Panic squeezed my heart in a too-tight embrace. I held my breath. He just had to be okay.

And when he smiled at me, I knew he was. "Oh, thank God." Waves of relief washed over me and the tension knotting my muscles unwound. "You're okay."

"Of course I am." He propped himself up on his elbows and looked around the room. The smile melted from his lips and lines of confusion pinched his forehead. "But I do have to ask…" He looked into my eyes and said the words that ripped me half.

"Do I know you?"

56

Someone knocked on my bedroom door.

I cracked open an eye. With my concentration broken, my legs wavered over my head. I locked my elbows to keep from toppling over. The rush of blood pooling into my head set fire to my cheeks. "What?"

Dr. Wendell opened my door and stepped inside. If he was surprised to find me hanging out in a handstand, he didn't act it. Instead, he gave a little sigh and crossed the room until his argyle-covered ankles were inches from my face. "You got another postcard."

Oh, goody. After my fight with the kunoichi, I thought I'd never hear from Whitley again, but he seemed to get a kick out of sending me *Wish You Were Here* postcards from around the world. "Where's this one from?"

"Egypt. Don't you think it's weird he sends you those things?"

Weird? Definitely. But personally, I slept a lot better

at night knowing he's on the opposite side of the globe. I pushed off my arms and landed on my feet where I took the postcard from Dr. Wendell's outstretched hand. As usual, it was signed, "Your soul mate, Whitley."

Ugh. I tossed it beside the growing stack on my desk and turned my attention to Dr. Wendell. "Is that all you wanted?" I dusted my hands on my yoga pants. "Or is another historic bad guy on the verge of getting their memory back?"

He shook his head. "No. You've done such a good job, things are pretty quiet."

That sucked. I was hoping for some action. Even though I swore I never would, after Kim lost his memory, I started working missions for Dr. Wendell and the Network. Turns out I'd been right all along about them. The missions did occupy most of my free time. But now that I had no social life to cut into, that was just the way I liked it. It had been more than six months since Kim's memory was wiped, and anything I could do to avoid thinking about him was just peachy.

The problem was, it'd been three days since my last mission and I was growing increasingly aware of the ache gnawing at my heart. I needed a distraction, and fast. "Okay. If there are no bad guys to fight, are there any artifacts I can look for?"

"Not at the moment."

I huffed. "Some papers that need filing? I can go to the office supply store. You can never have too many paperclips."

"We don't need paperclips." He looked away and shifted uncomfortably. "But there is *something* you can do."

Uh-oh. I knew that look and I knew what it meant. "No. Absolutely not."

He swept a hand through his hair and met my eyes. "You know I wouldn't ask you unless we were in a bind."

I shook my head so hard I could feel my brain jostle in my skull. "Uh-uh. No way. Why can't Drew check on him? They're neighbors."

Dr. Wendell nodded. "Yes, but Drew's out of town. He wanted to go to some comic convention and I told him to do it. This thing with Kim has been hard on him, too. He lost his brother, you know."

Guilt twisted my stomach and I bit my lip. Sometimes I forgot I wasn't the only one affected by Kim's memory loss. "What about Michelle? Or Braden?"

He made a face. "It's prom and they wanted to go. I didn't think it was fair of me to ask them to cut their night short. Especially when you've made it abundantly clear you didn't want to go to the dance. And without a mission, you've got no plans for the night."

Prom. I'd forgotten all about it. It felt like a million years ago since I sat in my algebra class daydreaming about what dress I might wear and how I'd style my hair. I shook my head as if to dislodge the memory from my brain. It didn't matter now. The only person who I could imagine dancing with had no idea who I was.

I folded my arms. "I may not have plans, but you don't look like you're doing anything important right now, either. Why can't you do it?"

Dr. Wendell sighed. "Rileigh, I would if I could. But I've got a meeting with a few Network officials in New York and my flight leaves in a couple of hours. I still have to pack."

I turned away from him and flopped onto my bed. "Is this really necessary? Kim's a big boy. Don't you think he'll be okay if he goes an entire day without someone checking in on him?"

Dr. Wendell sat next to me. "We don't know enough about Quentin's powers and their effect on the human mind. Who's to say Kim won't recover some or all of his memories? This is why it's imperative he be watched on a daily basis just as Sumi is under constant surveillance."

I buried my face in my pillow and groaned. I hadn't seen Kim since the night he'd lost his memory. And for someone who lost the love of her life, I thought I'd been holding up remarkably well. I was eating, getting dressed, and fighting the occasional reincarnated warlord. But if I had to see Kim and that blank look in his eyes when he looked at me, I was convinced it would undo all the work I'd done trying to keep it together. "Do I have to?"

"Please, Rileigh?" Dr. Wendell stood. "You won't even have to talk to him. While the new dojo is being built, he's teaching classes at the YMCA. He'll be there or at his apartment. Just drive by if you must. Make sure everything looks on the up and up and head home. If you do this for me, I promise I won't ask you again."

I sighed. If I was the only one available, what choice did I have? I opened my mouth to tell him exactly that when my mom appeared in my doorway. Her arms were folded across her chest and her lips pinched in a frown. Awesome. More good news.

"You're in some trouble, young lady." She dropped her

arms to the side and marched into my room shaking her head as she walked. "Why didn't you tell me your prom was tonight?"

Because Debbie would never believe I didn't want to go. She'd assume I was pouting because I didn't have a date and before I could say *Calvin Klein,* she'd be on the phone with one of her clients and I'd be escorted into a crepe-paper-covered gymnasium on the arm of an underwear model. Mortifying. "Mom, please. It's not a big deal. I didn't tell you because I'm not going. They're short volunteers at the hospital and Dr. Wendell asked if I could go."

He nodded dumbly in agreement.

She frowned at him. Yay! I wasn't the only one in trouble. "You're going to have to find someone else. Rileigh is going to prom."

I folded my arms. "No, I'm not."

Debbie directed her narrowed-eyed stare at me. "Then why is Q here to pick you up? He's waiting in the living room." She wagged a finger at me. "It's a good thing I picked up that vintage Versace last time I was in LA. Otherwise, you'd have nothing to wear. Honestly." She shook her head. "I'll get the dress. Hurry up and do something with your hair, okay?" With that, she spun on her heels and strode from my room leaving me blinking in her wake.

What the hell was going on? I jumped to my feet. "Q!"

Dr. Wendell flinched and wiggled his pinky inside of his ear as if I deafened him. I didn't care. I'd told Q a thousand times I wasn't going to prom. And if he thought he could just show up and convince me, he had another thing coming. I charged from my room and found the guilty party smiling sheepishly on my couch.

Q stood, the tails of his black tuxedo extended past his knees. He held up a pleated-gloved hand and took a step back. "Just calm down a second, Ri-Ri. Let me explain."

I placed my hands on my hips. "You don't need to explain. You thought you'd waltz in here wearing a tuxedo and think that, even though I already told you a thousand times I wasn't going, you could guilt me to go to prom with you?"

"Yes and no." He licked his lips. "I didn't want you to go with *me*, exactly."

"What the hell does that mean?"

He offered a weak smile. "It means that, no matter what happens, I need you to remember that I'm your best friend and everything I do, I do because I care about you and want you to be happy."

"And what the hell does *that* mean?"

His eyes darted nervously toward the door. "It means I did something you're not going to like so please, *please,* don't kill me."

Oh God. My hands dropped to my sides. "What did you do?" I followed his eyes to the door. My muscles tightened reflexively as though a hundred ninja might burst through at any minute.

"I'm going to go help your mom pick out your dress." Before I could stop him, Q ran down the hall to Debbie's bedroom calling her name.

"Coward!" I shouted after him. I had half a mind to follow him when a knock at the door froze me in place. I turned slowly around. A tremor tickled down the length of my spine. I was afraid, though for the life of me, I couldn't figure out why I should be.

The knocking grew louder, more urgent.

I had to clear my throat before I could answer. "Coming."

I walked to the door, my pulse thundering inside my head with each step closer. When I reached the knob, I hesitated. It could be anyone. What if Quentin had somehow talked Carson into a pity date for the sake of prom? I shook my head. If that was the case, I'd send Carson right on home. I didn't need pity or a date to prom. I survived the ninjapocalypse Sumi'd rained down on me. I'd survive this too … I hoped.

I took a deep breath, steadied myself to send Carson packing, and threw open the door. The only problem was, Carson wasn't on the other side.

But a very pissed-off looking Gimhae Kim in a tuxedo was.

I tried to form words, but the shock to my system choked the breath right out of me. It didn't matter, though. Kim didn't wait for an invitation. He pushed his way past me and spun a circle around the living room.

"Where is he?" he growled.

I blinked rapidly, trying to make sense of his words. "He?" What the hell was going on? "He who?"

"The guy with the pointy hair." He didn't look at me but proceeded to walk into the kitchen and glance behind the counter. Anger rolled off of him in hot waves. "He has them!"

Oh, Q. What did you do? I had to jump out of the way as Kim charged past me back into the living room and threw open the coat closet. I edged back into the living room, never taking my eyes off of him. "I'm sorry, what does he have exactly?"

Q peeked his head out of Debbie's room, but when he caught site of Kim sifting through the coats in the closet, he jerked back inside and shut the door. *He was so dead.*

Kim slammed the closet door and jammed a hand through his hair in frustration. It was such a familiar move it made my heart ache to see it. "My clothes." Kim turned and looked at me.

Seeing him again, being this close to him, it scrambled my mind like eggs in a skillet. My pulse raced as my thoughts jumbled together. This was exactly the reason I'd been avoiding him for so long. "But you're, um, wearing clothes." I gestured to his tux.

Kim looked down and met my eyes. An emotion I couldn't quite decipher crossed his face, unraveling the angry lines from his brow. "These aren't my clothes." The edge was gone from his voice. "*My* clothes were stolen off a locker room bench while I showered. This"—he motioned to the suit—"was left behind along with a ransom note. It was either put on the tux, or leave the gym in a towel."

I could feel my cheeks flush as the not-so-unwelcome mental image played through my mind. I faked a cough. "I'm almost afraid to ask. What did the note say?"

"The note?" He shook his head. "It said to come to this address if I wanted to get my clothes back."

I couldn't help but laugh. Only Q could conjure up such a wild scheme. "And you listened to the note? Why not just go home a tuxedo richer? Those must have been some pretty special gym clothes if you decided to go through all this trouble."

Kim looked at me a long moment before a smile broke through the angry lines on his face. I felt the crack inside my heart widening. Damn. And I'd been doing so well up until now. God, I *so* did not need this.

"It is ridiculous, isn't it?" He shrugged and laughed softly. "But when someone steals your smelly gym clothes, replaces them with a tuxedo, and leaves you a ransom note, there is a level of curiosity that compels you forward." He took a step toward me.

I choked on the last of my laughter. *Warning. Warning.* Alarm sirens blared inside my head. He was too close. My muscles twitched, threatening to betray me by throwing myself in his arms. I couldn't let that happen so I took a step back.

"So." He took another step forward. I took another step back until the back of my knees met the arm of the couch. *Son of hibachi.* "Now that I'm here, what do I have to do to get my clothes back?"

"Wha—*do*?" A high-pitched giggled bubbled from my throat before I could clamp my hands over my mouth. *Get it together, Rileigh!* When I was sure I'd gotten myself under control, I dropped my hands and cleared my throat. "I wish I could help you, but I don't have your clothes. I'm sorry."

Kim didn't respond. He just kept staring at me with that damned smirk on his face.

"And … " I nodded to the door. "I guess you'll be going now?"

Before he could respond, the door to Debbie's room opened and Q stuck his head out. "I have your clothes. The only way you'll get them back is if you take this girl here to her senior prom. It starts in an hour. And I must warn you, she won't want to go, so use of excessive force is permitted." He smiled wickedly at me before ducking back inside the room.

Ohmigod, I was *so* going to kill him! That was one of the perks of having a best friend who was a healer. I could keep doing it over and over again. My cheeks burned flame hot. "You don't—it's not—you don't have to. I can force him to give you your clothes back now."

"Prom?" Kim's folded his arms across his chest and smiled. "This has been the weirdest clothes-napping experience of my life."

I looked at him. "And you've a lot of experience with clothes-napping?"

His smile wavered. "I don't—I—maybe?" He shrugged. "I teach martial arts. Several months ago I took a pretty bad blow to the head. I have some pretty big holes in my memory." He frowned. "It's frustrating to say the least."

I swallowed, my throat suddenly dry. "But maybe that's a good thing? For example, I could do without the memory of what's happening to me right now. What if some of the memories you're missing are bad or painful? Not having them could give you a chance to start fresh."

"I disagree." He stared at me without blinking and I

fought the urge to shrink from under the weight of his gaze. "That would never be better. The past shapes who you are. Without my memory, I don't know who I really am. I feel empty. Something is missing..." He looked away and I curled my fingers into my yoga pants to keep from reaching for him. I remembered how traumatized I'd felt when Kim had tried to tell me about my past life. I couldn't—wouldn't do it to him. And even if I did, who was to say he'd believe me?

"It's funny." He lifted his eyes to mine. "But I have this feeling that I know you—that you're important to me."

My legs trembled and I leaned against the arm of the couch to keep from falling over. Could it be possible he would eventually remember me? Remember us? It was almost too much to hope for and I dared not wish for it out of fear of being crushed under the weight of disappointment if it didn't happen.

"But that's probably a long talk and we don't have a lot of time." Kim glanced at his watch. "We should probably get going, right?"

As much as I hadn't wanted to go to prom, there was a greater part of me that wasn't ready to let Kim walk out my door. Especially not when he'd sparked a hope inside me that maybe he wasn't as lost to me as I'd assumed. I glanced at my yoga pants and T-shirt. "I'm not dressed yet."

Kim blinked before his eyes glanced over my outfit. He laughed. "You're so stunning, I didn't even notice."

I fought off the smile that pulled at my lips. "You so did not just give me some cheesy pickup line."

"It's not cheesy when it's true." He opened his mouth to

say more, but stopped. Confused lines pinched the bridge of his nose. He folded his arms across his chest and cocked his head to the side. "I had the strangest feeling of déjà vu just now."

A lump wedged inside my throat. "Yeah?"

He nodded. "You remind me of someone . . ."

I was too scared to move, too scared to breathe out of fear of breaking whatever spell had taken over the moment. "Who?"

He shook his head before a wide grin took over his face. "I have no idea. Isn't that crazy?" Before I could answer he continued, "I guess that doesn't really matter does it? We're late, I'm rambling, and you need to get ready."

Did I? Would I ever be ready? But I nodded because there were no words to say. I started to walk to my bedroom when he called out to me.

"I feel kind of silly asking you this—as we're about to go to prom and all—but can I get your name?"

Now that was a loaded question. But there was no sense confusing the poor boy. I'd make things simple. I glanced over my shoulder. "Rileigh."

"Rileigh," he repeated. Something broke inside of me. I never thought I'd hear him say my name ever again. "That's really pretty. My name's—"

"Gimhae Kim," I answered for him before I could stop myself. "But you prefer to be called Kim."

"Right." He didn't flinch or seem surprised at all that I knew his name. Instead, he smiled. "Go get dressed."

I nodded, but hesitated. I was afraid that if I lost sight

of him for even a moment, he might disappear never to return.

"Don't worry," he said, as if sensing my hesitation. "I promise that even if I got a whole truck full of smelly gym clothes, I'd stay right here, waiting, until you got back."

I smiled and continued to my bedroom.

"Oh, and Rileigh?"

I froze without turning. "Yes?"

"I hope I remember you first."

Photo by Kyle Weber

About the Author

When Cole Gibsen isn't writing she can be found shaking her booty in a zumba class, picking off her nail polish, or drinking straight from the jug (when no one is looking). Cole currently resides in the Greater St. Louis area with her husband, daughter, and one very cranky border collie.